A STATE OF SIN

AMSTERDAM OCCULT SERIES

BOOK TWO

A STATE OF SIN

AMSTERDAM OCCULT SERIES

BOOK TWO

By Mark Hobson

Copyright © 2021 Mark Hobson.
All rights reserved.
The moral right of the author has been asserted.
ISBN: 9798724812566

Published by Harcourt Publishers.
Except where actual historical events and characters are being used for the storyline of this novel, all situations in this publication are fictitious and any resemblance to living persons is purely coincidental.

Book cover design by Ken Dawson at Creative Covers.

To Sophie, Emily, Jacob and Leo

PART 1

ABDUCTION

Chapter 1
The Afrikaner

Following the narrow hiking trail, Johan Roost slowly wound his way down from the high mountain pass. The steep, switch-back course zig-zagged back and forth, its descent marked by huge slabs of rock. To his left a waterfall fell in narrow ribbons, throwing up a fine white mist, and he paused momentarily to enjoy the cool water droplets.

Shrugging off his small backpack, Johan found a spot on the nearest boulder and sat down with a sigh, taking the weight off his tired legs. Today's hike had been a long one, about fifteen miles, much of it over rough terrain and through the high mountain pass at a height of over 3000 metres, and even though he had lived in this region of South Africa for most of his life, those kind of altitudes were starting to take their toll on him these days. After all, he was in his late fifties now, and although still physically very fit and well-toned, the thinner air was bound to have an effect.

Reaching into his backpack, he took out his water bottle and took a long swig, and then chewed on the last of his biltong, turning to look up at the mountain range behind him.

The Drakensberg Mountains. In Zulu, they were known as *uKhahlamba*, or Barrier of Spears, and the name was apt. The range stretched from horizon to horizon, an immense grey wall that separated KwaZulu-Natal from Lesotho, and they dominated the region for hundreds of miles around. The view never failed to bring a lump to his throat even though he saw it every single day from his lodge on the outskirts of the tiny community of Elandskop. And in the midday sun in early December, the height of summer, they looked especially magical.

Johan turned his gaze downwards, past the fast-moving stream, towards the smaller hills below, their smooth shapes stretching away eastwards in a series of green waves. He could just make out his home where the land flattened, the lodge perched above the cultivated pastures of his farm.

His family had owned land here for the best part of two hundred years, ever since the Great Trek of 1836-38 when his Dutch ancestors, the Boers, had descended through these very mountain passes in their search for new land away from British rule. It was hard to picture their journey, travelling as they did in small covered carts and wagons pulled by teams of oxen and mules, their passage blighted by disease and injury, by thunderstorms, flood and drought, travelling through a hostile land. Their journey, and the subsequent struggle they had endured ever since, was what had shaped the Afrikaner mentality over the centuries. And although the modern world was changing, the Dutch descendants of those original trekkers were still a hardy bunch to this day, with a few diehards – like himself – still refusing to drop their old values and ways. The political landscape may have changed in South Africa, but here, far from the big cities of Pretoria and Johannesburg, the old Boer dominance, like the geography, was constant and untouched by the twenty-first century.

Johan remained sitting on his rock for another five minutes, romanticizing about the past, and then packed up his few things and readied himself for the final leg of his hike. It was all downhill from here and another hour, or two at the most, should see him back home.

Just as he was about to push on a faint noise came to him. His keen ears filtered it out from the natural sounds, and he turned his head, trying to pinpoint its source. It came to him as a faint pulse, almost a thrumming of the air, which gradually grew in volume and pitch, becoming deeper the louder it became. Then it echoed down from the mountains behind, bouncing in a concussive wave, and Johan spun in time to see what had caused it.

The helicopter flew directly overhead, its rotor blades slapping at the air, and although it passed a good fifty or so feet above him, he involuntarily ducked and cringed. He watched as it flew on, the pilot probably unaware of him just below, now dipping lower and hugging the hills, sometimes seeming to skim the tall grass at head height.

Johan followed its course, the engine noise becoming a faint high-pitched tone that gradually faded away, and he soon lost sight of it in the summer haze.

He scowled heavily and kicked at the ground, a dejected feeling weighing him down.

Johan headed home.

It was mid-afternoon with the sun past its blazing peak by the time he reached his lodge. Walking along the dusty track that led around the side of the main building, Johan stopped dead when he saw the chopper parked in the empty paddock beyond the fence. The pilot was still seated inside, ear mufflers clamped over his head and wearing aviation sunglasses, looking smart in his freshly-ironed white shirt. He turned to look at Johan briefly, before turning back to his instrument panel, so Johan marched around the corner and stomped across his front lawn.

Dalton, his head gardener, made a beeline for him, shuffling along at his side but with his eyes cast down. "Mister Roost, you have a visitor," he informed him somewhat needlessly.

"Yes, so I see."

Johan glanced up at his veranda, seeing the figure of a person seated in one of the wicker chairs, their features indistinct under the shaded roof. Not that he needed to see them clearly to know who his visitor was.

"Fetch me a beer will you, Dalton?" he instructed, before clomping his way up the wooden steps.

At the top, he paused and looked directly towards his surprise guest.

The beautiful young lady looked straight back, holding his gaze with her steady, brown eyes. She smiled, and said, "Hello Uncle Johan."

Johan Roost simply grunted and continued to stand there unmoving.

The lady flicked her blonde fringe out of her eyes and crossed her legs, her summer dress showing off her immaculate figure. A twinkle glittered in her eyes, all mischievous and playful, and he couldn't help but feel himself relax a little. His niece always had this effect on him, no matter how hard he tried not to let it. He had a soft spot for her, there was no doubt about that.

Removing his backpack, Johan lowered himself into another one of the chairs, and slowly shook his head. "You still like to make a grand entrance don't you, Charlotte?" he told her.

Charlotte Janssen tilted her head. "Of course. You know me."

"Nothing like keeping a low profile eh? Surprising, after all of the trouble you've been causing. I thought you'd have wanted to avoid attracting attention."

"You've heard then? About my spot of bother during the spring?"

"I think the whole world heard all about it."

"Oh," she breathed, swatting at the air, "it was all so exaggerated by the media. Blown out of all proportion. But someone like me can only lie low for so long before I get bored - and restless."

"So you thought you'd pay me a visit? A little trip to see the family? Out here in the middle of nowhere?"

"You're the only family I have left, Uncle. I'm guessing you know about mum and Bart?"

Johan was silent for a few moments, and then he glanced away, looking out across the lawn. During the lull, Dalton arrived with his glass of beer, which he placed on a side table, before making his way back to the garden. He took a sip, savouring the cool liquid as it glided down his throat, then he turned back to Charlotte.

"Yes. Famke, your mum, she was a bitch when we were little, so I can't say I'm sorry. But Bart, now that was a shame. He was a good lad at heart, just troubled, that's all. People led him astray, corrupted his mind because they knew he was weak and easy to manipulate. People used him for their own ends, and he was too stupid to see that. Your silly little scheme cost him his life Lotte, and for what? What did you gain? What did you achieve, except to make you the most hunted woman in the whole of Europe? Ahh, silly girl!"

Lotte said nothing, just shrugged her thin shoulders demurely.

"And now here you are. Paying me a surprise visit. The first time I've clapped eyes on you in years."

Johan put his glass to one side and leaned forward in his chair, his strong and muscular forearms resting across his knees. He looked at her with hard eyes, ignoring the pleasant smile, now getting directly to the point.

"What is it you want? Because if you're looking for somewhere to hide, somewhere to keep your head down, then you can get straight back on that helicopter and fly right back to where you came from. The last thing I want is the police, or fucking Interpol or whoever, coming sniffing around here. You know the set-up I have going, and I don't want you messing it up for me."

"Don't worry Uncle, I have no intention of staying. It's too hot, the place smells, and there are too many flies. I'm a city girl, I like my creature comforts."

"Then what are you here for."

This time it was Lotte's turn to lean forward. Whispering, she said: "I have a job for you."

"I must be fucking mad," Johan had replied, after she'd told him exactly what this 'job' entailed.

As the afternoon wore on and the shadows lengthened across the lawn, they had retired to his inner office at the back of his lodge.

Johan was seated in his leather swivel chair behind his large mahogany desk. The desk surface was strewn with papers and notepads, a pair of synched laptops, pens, pencils, a telephone, a small printer/scanner, as well as a number of hunting trophies. One of the laptops was on and currently downloading a long movie file – Lotte saw it was called **Monks Cowl to Spitsberg # 12**. One of Uncle Johan's hunting videos, no doubt.

Behind the desk the blinds covering the room's only window were pulled down and closed, blocking out the evening sunshine and stopping prying eyes, and the door was locked from the inside.

Covering the walls were several framed photos and certificates. Lotte strolled around, looking at them, seeing most were of groups of people, mostly men, holding high-powered rifles with telescopic sights. On each one, at their feet, lay a dead animal shot through the forehead; sometimes an elephant, perhaps a springbok or a kudu or a Mountain Reedbuck, even a giraffe on one. She moved from picture to picture, her face impassive and her thoughts private.

Sitting in his chair, Johan watched her silently. Not for the first time, he asked himself how she had become the person she now was? Although he had had very little to do with her and her brother's upbringing, from what he knew they had led a relatively normal – if privileged – childhood. They had spent several summers here with him in South Africa, their mother, his sister, Famke accompanying them, probably to escape the freezing winters they had in Amsterdam. They had seemed carefree as teenagers, Bart the oldest at about eighteen being a young man, and his sister Lotte six or seven years younger. Yet even back then, it had been apparent to Johan how much Lotte had dominated her big brother, how she had him wrapped around her little finger, the lad already overweight and soft from eating too much junk food. Johan had tried to instil a bit of masculinity in him, giving him jobs around the farm, taking him hunting – what a disaster that turned out to be – and hoping to draw him out of his shell, out from his sister's shadow, but it had been to no avail. The young man was too weedy, big and strong, yes, but totally lacking in fibre or initiative. Always traipsing around after his sister, doing anything she asked. Was he gay? Johan had wondered, or retarded? Certainly that was a possibility, especially considering who his grandparents had been and the lunatic DNA he must have had slopping around in his genes. Which also, now that he thought about it as he sat in his chair watching Lotte, might explain the way she had developed in her adult years. He shook his head, too weary to think about it too deeply.

And now here she was, with her crazy offer to him – with its crazy financial reward!

His reverie was interrupted just then, when she glanced back over her shoulder.

"How's the hunting these days?" she asked.

"Lucrative."

"I should imagine it is. These people in the photos are seriously rich, I'm sure I recognize one or two from TV."

She'd paused in front of one particular framed image. He knew the one. It showed a guy holding a rifle, the stock resting on his thigh and the barrel pointing skyward, his foot resting on the young buck he had killed. A young homeless man from the township.

"Isn't he that American politician? A Senator, right? Jeez, how much did he pay for that?"

Johan cleared his throat. "Half a million dollars." Half of what she had just offered him, he thought to himself.

Lotte whistled between her teeth, shaking her head. "You certainly do have a good thing going here, Uncle. You must be building yourself quite a reputation amongst the rich and famous who go in for this kind of thing?"

"A reputation built on discretion," he corrected her, "and trust."

"For you and your clients surely? Considering what it is you and they are doing? By its very nature, it guarantees their silence."

She reached up and touched the photo, running her fingers over the image of the dead man.

"How did you persuade them to let you photograph them?"

"It's part of the contract. My insurance, you could say."

Lotte giggled, her back still to him.

Johan sighed and pushed himself back from his desk, his patience growing thin.

"Listen, this job - one million you said, paid in bitcoins, right?"

His niece turned and sashayed across, and sat in the chair opposite. She nodded. "The transfer could be in your account by this evening."

"And where is it?"

"Amsterdam of course."

"Shit, it'll be freezing there at this time of the year," he grumbled.

Lotte shrugged, her small white teeth showing as she grinned impishly. "Amsterdam is pretty at Christmas time. You'll enjoy it."

Johan rose, now his turn to stroll back and forth, thinking hard. Which was a bit pointless he knew, for his decision was already made. He was simply trying to convince himself he'd made the right choice. He glanced across at his niece, seeing her waiting quietly, watching him go through this pretence. For some reason, this annoyed him even more.

"And you'll get everything prepared? The whole thing set up?"

"Yes, events are already in motion, as they say. The whole thing should take just a few days. Before you know it, you'll be on a plane flying back home."

"And the target? This man? You can guarantee that he'll be exactly where you say he'll be? I don't like last-minute hitches, especially when I'm working in a foreign country."

"Don't worry Uncle. I have it all worked out. Everything will run as smoothly as clockwork."

Johan gave a short, humourless laugh.

"I've learned from my past mistakes," Lotte added, an edge now in her voice and a small frown of irritation on her brow, which made him feel uncomfortable for some reason, and so he averted his gaze.

He paused in his nervous walking and lifted a part of the window blind to peer outside. Across in the paddock, the pilot was now having a snooze, his head leaning against the glass cockpit of the helicopter.

"The other stuff, all of that weird shit you do, I want nothing to do with that crap you understand? I had enough of that nonsense from your mother when we were growing up."

"I'll take care of that," she replied, her tone now softer again. "You just do what you specialize in, and I will do likewise."

Johan Roost turned back from the window and looked her square in the face.

"In that case, you have a deal."

Chapter 2
A foggy night in Amsterdam

He drove the specially-converted black delivery van slowly along Vondelstraat, the engine humming quietly and the headlights penetrating the swirling December fog. At just after 7pm at this time of the year, this quiet and exclusive suburban street was all but deserted, the residents of the large, gated townhouses safely inside their homes, perhaps sitting down to enjoy their evening meals or watching the TV news.

Over to the left was the large park, empty now and filled with shadows. On the right, the ornate stone building housing the Hollandsche Manege, the historic riding school and stables.

Following the road around the large red-bricked church, the driver slowed down even further, his eyes roving left and right, looking for the correct building, and when he saw the huge gates he turned the wheel and drew to a halt before the entranceway. Pulling down the peak of the baseball hat that he wore, hiding his face from prying eyes or cameras, he sat in his seat and studied the large house before him.

Having thoroughly prepared and rehearsed for tonight, the building was already very familiar. Plans of the inside and outside were ingrained in his memory: the grey stone exterior, large windows on the lower floor and smaller square windows above - the flat roof with twin gables. The new carport on the left, the gravel drive, the gates with their intercom system. The layout of the rooms, with the large and modern kitchen, the dining room and living room with their connecting arched doorway, the wood staircase twisting up to the bedrooms and bathrooms on the upper floor. The smaller dormer rooms right at the top, in one of which the daughter slept. The alarm and security cameras which hopefully he would not need to worry about. All very plush and modern, perfect for a young and beautiful family. A millionaire's home.

Despite all the money spent on keeping the place secure from intruders, getting inside would be simple. Rich people tended by nature to be quite naïve and not very streetwise. Therefore his plan was simple. Drive up in his van, dressed in the smart uniform and hat of a well-known delivery company, here to deliver some packages to the homeowner. On the passenger seat beside him were several cardboard boxes, each one addressed to Dr Christiaan Bakker. He even had a barcode scanner, purchased off the internet several months ago. He had a fake ID badge clipped to his breast pocket. Attached to his waist belt was a small black object that looked like a mobile phone but was in fact a fully charged Taser, and on the inside of his jacket were three hypodermic syringes, each filled with a light yellow liquid. 2mg of Midazolam, a strong sedative that also had an amnesiac effect and was very fast-acting. One for the father, one for the mother, and one for the daughter. Using these would be easy, all he had to do was just reach into his jacket, pull one out and jab it down hard into a large muscle mass anywhere on the body, the back or upper arm for instance. The drug did sometimes have a few side effects and could cause violent reactions or even respiratory arrest if delivered in too high a dose, but he was willing to take the risks. He had practiced by injecting the sedative into random strangers on the metro late at night to watch the effect, to time the speed that people reacted and to test his technique, and that had been good fun, watching these involuntary guinea pigs stagger and twitch, their legs buckling and collapsing, sending them crashing to the floor in a heap. But that was just for practice, a giggle yes, but only a dress rehearsal. Tonight was the real thing.

Lowering his window, he reached out and pressed the intercom button on one of the gateposts, seeing the small camera on the high wall. Keeping his face tilted downwards, he waited for a reply, and when the female voice came through he replied in a gruff tone.

"Parcel delivery for a Doctor Christiaan Bakker. To be signed for."

A slight pause, and then, "please come in."

"Thank you."

There was a loud click and with a gentle buzz the large double gates swung inwards, and he drove carefully though.

Turning about on the gravel driveway he slowly backed up to the carport and switched off the engine. Before grabbing the cardboard boxes and jumping out, the driver twisted and glanced over his shoulder into the back of the van. He'd mostly cleared everything out over the weekend, before converting it for tonight's purpose. On the bed of the van was an oblong-shaped metal storage box, about five or six feet long, welded to the floor. The lid was open and the inside of the box was lined with blankets and a sleeping bag. Attached to the side was a small magnetic LED lamp, all switched on and ready. Next to it was a large plastic container. Satisfied that all was in order he climbed out.

Approaching the large side door underneath the carport, he rang the doorbell and waited, parcels clutched in his arms, a ready smile on his face. He heard the clip-clop of footsteps, high-heels on the tiled floor, and then the door opened and an elegant lady with brown hair was standing before him.

He recognized her as the mother, Elise, thirty-something. She didn't recognize him, even without the baseball hat on she wouldn't know him from any other delivery guy, because she'd never met him before.

She was waiting with an irritated look on her face.

"Hello," he said merrily.

"It's a little late for deliveries isn't it?" she inquired in her cultured voice. "We are just about to have dinner."

"I'm sorry about that ma'am."

"Very well. Where do I sign?"

"I'm afraid Doctor Bakker has to sign for them himself. They are medical files, so they require his ID number as well."

Mrs Bakker sighed loudly, shook her head in exasperation. "Well in that case you'd better bring them in, they look heavy."

She moved to one side and he squeezed past, and then she turned and led him down the short hallway. Indicating a small occasional table at the foot of the ornate staircase, she instructed him to place the parcels there. "I'll get my husband, just one moment." She turned to go.

"Actually, there's no need," he replied as he popped them down. Quickly reaching for his belt, the driver zapped her with the Taser on the back of the neck, and her whole body stiffened before going straight over like a felled tree, catching her temple on the balustrade.

Mark Hobson

He watched as she lay sprawled across the bottom step, completely still, and for a moment he thought that she'd knocked herself out cold. But then she stirred slightly, and a loud gurgling moan escaped her lips, followed by a peculiar wheezing. Christ, he thought in a sudden panic, the whole house will hear her.

Quickly slipping his hand inside his jacket he grabbed hold of one of the syringes and popped the cap off with his thumb. Leaning forward, he tugged at the neckline of her evening dress and yanked it down, and then jabbed the needle hard into the soft flesh at the back of her neck, pushing in the plunger to inject her with the full 2mg of sedative.

Breathing heavily, the driver stood back and watched as the drug immediately started to take effect, first causing an involuntary squirming, and then the brief and violent kicking of the legs as her body tried to fight the strong anaesthetic coursing through her system, with one of her legs catching the table and sending a vase of flowers crashing to the floor. Then a slowing down of her movements and a quiet mumbling, before she was fully unconscious.

The racket caused by the shattering vase could not have failed to alert everybody within earshot, and sure enough a male voice, coming from the living room next door, called out earnestly, "Honey, is everything alright?"

The driver turned just as the sliding wooden door was pulled aside, to reveal a short but squat man with a grey beard standing there and taking in the scene, no doubt wondering who this stranger in the baseball hat was. Then the gentleman glanced across to see his wife lying on the floor, before his eyes flicked back to the driver, mouth hanging open in alarm.

"Who are you?" he managed to splutter ridiculously, before the driver flung himself forward with another syringe clasped in his hand. Swinging his arm down he stabbed the needle straight through the man's white shirt and into his chest, bringing a cry of alarm.

The driver watched as his victim stumbled backwards into the living room with the syringe still sticking out of his chest. He crashed into a wooden cabinet but remained upright, and then slithered along a wall, heading towards the arched entrance to the dining room. Yelling loudly in terror, he turned and stumbled away on his short legs, and the driver followed, expecting the sedative to start working. Yet to his alarm nothing seemed to be happening, the man was not losing his strength, and a few seconds later he slipped through the far doorway.

Snarling in anger, the driver chased after him, pulling out the third syringe.

Rushing through the door, he found himself in the dining room. The other man was incredibly still on his feet, and now moving quickly across the floor and making for the telephone on the wall, sending chairs crashing.

There must have been something wrong with the second dose of Midazolam, a faulty batch perhaps, either that or the doctor had an iron constitution. Whichever was the case, he had to stop him before he reached the telephone, and so once again he charged after the portly little man.

He barely made it in time. Bakker was just reaching out for the cordless phone when the driver grabbed a hold of his shoulder and yanked him back, and the two of them fell to the floor with a thud. The full weight of Bakker pressed down into him, knocking the wind from his lungs, but somehow he was able to slip his own arm around the other man's body and stabbed down into his fat stomach, jabbing the needle into him over and over and squeezing every last drop of sedative out of the syringe.

With a violent twitch and a spasm, the drug at last hit him. The driver could hear him gasping loudly, his body arching and turning this way and that, crushing down onto him even further, before eventually he felt him sag. All of the strength seemed to go out of the man, and finally all movement ceased.

The driver pushed the body away and squirmed out from beneath it, and scrambled to his feet, struggling to get his breath back. Standing there, he looked down at the unconscious man.

It had taken 4mgs to subdue him - way too high a dose, and which would more than likely trigger a heart attack. Not that it mattered too much, not ultimately. But what it did mean was that he'd used up all three syringes, and there was still the daughter to deal with.

Everything was still alright, he told himself. His carefully worked out plan had gone out of the window, but he still had the Taser. All he had to do was find the girl.

She must still be in the house, he concluded. Probably upstairs in her room, hiding or hopefully blissfully unaware of the commotion downstairs. Well then - time to get down to business and finish this.

Sure enough, he found her cowering in her bedroom, curled up into a foetal position and wedged into the far corner, with her eyes squeezed shut in terror. She had a tight hold onto an iPhone, and no doubt she had dialled 112 to plead for help. No matter. It was inevitable that someone would eventually call the emergency services, all this meant was that he had to move that little bit faster.

Quickly he hit the girl with a short burst from the Taser, worried that too big a jolt might seriously harm the twelve year old. Then, whilst she was convulsing on the carpeted floor, he blindfolded her with a black scarf he pulled from his pocket and then hurriedly tied her hands and feet with the cords from a pair of dressing gowns, before shoving one of her own socks into her mouth to gag her and stifle the screaming. Then, hefting her onto his shoulder in a fireman's lift, he carried her down the two flights of stairs, stepped over the unconscious body of the lady, and went straight out of the open front door.

Unlocking the back of his van, the driver carefully laid the young girl into the metal storage box and banged the lid closed and snapped the padlock shut. He paused momentarily, to slow his heart rate and steady his nerves, and then grabbed the plastic container, which was heavy as it was filled with petrol, and after locking up the van doors, he returned to the entrance hall of the big house.

Working quickly, the driver splashed the liquid all around the floor and over the walls and curtains, doing the same inside the living room. Dumping the container, he remembered to scoop up the cardboard boxes and barcode scanner, and then backed outside. Taking out a cigarette lighter he flicked it with his thumb, watched the small flame for a couple of seconds, and then tossed it inside.

With a blast of hot air and orange flame, the flammable liquid caught light. The driver turned away, climbed back into the driver's side of the van, and dumped the boxes back onto the passenger seat. Backing out through the gates onto Vondelstraat, he smiled over his shoulder.

"Let's go home," he told the girl.

Pulling the baseball hat even further down over his face, he slowly drove away into the foggy night.

Chapter 3
Aftermath

As was usually the case, the nightmare crept up on him. In it, he was strolling along a wide and empty beach. The sky overhead was a vast expanse of dark, broiling clouds, and a strong offshore breeze buffeted against his thin frame. The sea, a leaden and grey threatening presence, was whipped up into white-topped waves. It seemed to breathe, swelling up and down, and he was convinced it would swallow him whole.

Veering away, he headed towards the sand dunes, and it was as he approached them that he first saw her. Far off in the distance, nothing more than a small silhouette standing atop one of the sandy hillocks. But he knew it was her. It was always her.

In the dream he hesitated, but somehow he still drew near, as though something was dragging him forward, and when he glanced down he saw with mild curiosity that his feet floated above the sand.

Looking back up, he was just in time to see the person atop the sand dune shimmer and then disappear, and he looked about in a sudden panic. Moving into the dunes, he caught sight of her again, walking just ahead and disappearing around the next bend, and whenever he was close to catching up, she would fade away once more, only to reappear tantalizingly close but always out of reach.

Until finally he found himself on another open stretch of beach, but in this one the sand was black and the sky was red, like the most stunning sunset he had ever seen, and she was standing here as though waiting for him.

He knew exactly who she was even though she was wearing that same goat-skull over her head, the white bone and large horns exactly as he remembered them, every detail the same including the pentangle painted with blood on the skull's forehead and the long flowing gown emblazoned with those weird symbols that she was wearing.

Her long blonde hair was whipped up behind her by the strong, gusty wind. Lifting her arms out she welcomed him forward to embrace her, and against his will, he was gliding closer, when suddenly she burst into flames. Her gown was afire and so too her arms and legs, and flames shot out from the top of her head making the goat's eye sockets glow ruby red. The fireball flared out and he closed his eyes against its searing heat.

A gentle tapping on the car window woke Inspector Pieter Van Dijk.

The call about the fire on Vondelstraat had come through to his mobile just before 8pm, as he was setting off back home from Police HQ on Elandsgracht. Normally it would have been transferred over to one of the detectives just starting the night shift, but apparently someone had called in sick with gallstone problems, and as it was only a five-minute drive away they forwarded it to him. Strange, he would think later, how fortuitous events could come out of such small twists of fate.

When he arrived the building had been well and truly alight. The whole of the ground floor was ablaze, and flames were shooting out of the upper windows and part of the roof where it had caved in. The street was by then clogged with fire trucks and bystanders, and the surface of the road was a jumble of thick and twisting hosepipes, and so to keep out of the way Pieter had parked his car on the corner of Anna Van Den from where he had a good view of events. There was a nursing home right on the side street, and the elderly residents had their faces pressed up against the windows, enjoying the show no doubt.

He had stayed in his car watching as the firefighters tackled the huge blaze, slowly but surely bringing it under control, but at some stage he must have nodded off for when he snatched a look at his watch he saw it was now coming up to eleven o'clock.

Outside a female firefighter was knocking on the glass again, her small and mean mouth saying something. He wound the window down and asked her to repeat herself.

"I said it's ok for you to come and take a look now."

Pieter glanced past her and saw that the fire had been extinguished. The building looked to be a blackened shell, and water was still being hosed onto it to cool and dampen the smouldering ruin, but for now, the drama seemed to be over. He climbed out of his car.

The firefighter shoved a yellow hard-hat into his hands, told him to put it on, and once he'd done so, instructed him to follow her down the street.

The smoke from the fire seemed to have made the fog even denser and the strong acrid smell scratched at the back of his throat as they threaded their way through the emergency vehicles towards the ruins of the large house. As they approached Pieter saw that the whole of the ground floor was a burnt-out empty shell, and most of the side wall had collapsed, spilling bricks and timber onto the driveway. This, along with other sections, had been taped off as still too dangerous to approach, but the front entrance beneath the carport was accessible. A young policewoman was standing beside the door, fiddling with her mobile, but when she saw Pieter approach she quickly put it away and became more alert.

The firefighter stepped through the wrought-iron gates and then turned back towards him.

"Don't go poking around too much, especially in the places marked by tape. Not unless you want the whole place to come crashing down on your head."

"Understood."

She slipped away, and he stepped towards the front door.

The uniformed officer came forward to meet him. She too had a hard hat on, and her dark hair hung down in loose strands, giving her a slightly dishevelled appearance. Aware of how she must look, she grinned sheepishly. "Inspector Van Dijk?"

Pieter nodded. He thought he recognized her as one of the new intakes down at HQ.

"Kaatje Groot isn't it?" Her eyebrows went up, pleasantly surprised. "I've seen you around, working with Floris in the files section," he explained.

She beamed back at him.

"Is this a temporary assignment?"

"Not sure really Inspector. I think they sent me over because there was nobody else available from the night-shift."

"Same here actually."

"But I'm hoping it might be permanent," she added quickly.

"Paperwork not your thing?"

She shrugged and pulled a face.

"Ok, let's see how tonight goes then."

He tilted the nib of his helmet back and looked up at the scorched doorway and carport.

"So tell me, why have we been summoned to a house fire?"

"A number of reasons sir. First of all, the firefighters think it might be arson. They say an accelerant – probably petrol from the smell of it – was used to start the fire, just in the hallway here. Also, we have at least two bodies inside. It's hard to tell for sure, but they look like an adult male and an adult female. And thirdly, the family who lived here, two parents and their daughter, have recently received several death threats. Which they had reported to the police."

"Two bodies you say? What about the daughter? How old is she?"

Officer Groot studied her notebook. "Twelve years old sir."

"Do they know her whereabouts?"

"Not at the moment, although the general opinion is that they will probably find her body soon, maybe upstairs."

Pieter nodded. From the ferocity of the blaze it seemed very unlikely anyone could survive, especially if they had fled upstairs away from the flames and smoke, as children were wont to do. "Who exactly were the occupants? This street is for the mega-rich, almost as posh as Hooftstraat."

"The homeowner was a Doctor Christiaan Bakker, and his wife Elise and their daughter Nina."

"A doctor? I presume not your average quack then, unless the wife was a woman of means?"

"No, he had a private clinic. He specialized in eye surgery. Had quite a few famous clients in fact, politicians, footballers, that kind of people. Quite well known in exclusive social circles, he and his wife liked to mix with movie stars. They were very well respected."

"Not by everybody, apparently."

With Pieter leading the way they both stepped over the threshold and into the hallway.

Inside, the atmosphere was still hot even though the fire had been extinguished. It was like opening an oven door and Pieter immediately felt a claustrophobic-like heat pushing down on him and sapping his strength. The air was thick with charcoal dust, which not only clogged up his throat but instantly set his eyes off itching, and he rubbed at them vigorously. He saw beside him officer Groot similarly affected, and her eyes were already red-rimmed. She coughed loudly.

"Let's make this quick eh?" he croaked, and she nodded emphatically.

In the hallway, two separate teams were already at work. As with all arson cases, the procedure was the same, and Pieter knew the basics. If it were suspected that a fire had been started deliberately, then the fire officer in charge of the incident would put out a call to the Fire, Police and Forensic Science Service, who would send out teams of specially trained fire investigation personnel. One would be made up of fire officers, and their job was to locate the seat of the blaze as well as ascertain how the fire had spread, and also to determine whether it had been started by an incendiary device or an accelerant. The second team, this one containing police officers, would gather evidence and take samples similar to a normal crime scene investigation, and send this off to the NFI forensic lab in The Hague.

The next phase was to decide the reason for the act of arson. There are two main categories of arson fires: arson without a motive, and arson with a motive.

The vast majority of fires that are started deliberately without any obvious motive are generally the result of vandalism. This might be kids burning down their school, yobs setting fire to cars, or a pyromaniac setting fires for the thrill of it.

Where a fire has been started deliberately then there may be a motive. This might be financial in the form of an insurance claim, emotional where the arsonist has a grudge or a grievance against the owner of the property, or to cover-up another serious crime that has been committed.

Of course the presence of two, and probably three, bodies in this case did not necessarily mean that the culprit intended for the occupants of the house to die in the blaze. He – and most arsonists were male – may have thought the house was empty at the time, or that the young family living here would have time to escape. Perhaps they had only intended to scare them and the fire had quickly got out of control and become a deadly inferno. He may be in a state of shock at what he'd done. He may also be injured and in need of medical attention, so an alert would need to be put out to all of the hospitals across Amsterdam. Whatever the case, the arsonist might be looking at a manslaughter charge, rather than murder. Only time would tell, dependent on the results of the twin investigations now taking place, and the results of the autopsies.

Not wishing to interfere too much in the work of the fire and police forensic teams, Pieter nevertheless felt it was necessary to see the bodies in situ for himself.

The first one lay on the hall floor just ahead, at the foot of the staircase. Three or four people, clad in their white forensic get-up, were clustered around the burnt husk of a human body, and Pieter and officer Groot carefully stepped over the debris towards the small knot of figures.

They were just rolling the corpse over onto its back, not easy as the body and clothes had partially melted into the floor, and parts of the flesh and hair came away. Pieter cringed inside, but Kaatje seemed totally unfazed.

The corpse's face was mostly unburnt and it was easy to recognize the features were that of a female of the right kind of age as Elise Bakker. Formal ID would still be required, as standard.

Standing there and looking down at the victim Pieter had a sudden flashback to his dream, of a figure on a beach engulfed in flames, and he metaphorically batted the image away.

Stepping back, he glanced down at Kaatje, who was hungrily taking in all of the details.

She was certainly keen, just as he had been when he'd first switched to the murder squad, but he wondered how long before she became jaded and then disillusioned, her nights beset with bad dreams.

"Where is the other one?" he asked her.

His voice drew her concentration away from the corpse, and she pointed behind them. "Through there," she responded.

Pieter stepped across to the doorway she'd indicated. Beyond was what looked to be a living room, filled with the charcoal remnants of furniture and tables and a cabinet by the door. Kaatje came up alongside him and nodded towards an arched opening in the opposite wall. She had one hand up over her mouth, and when she spoke, there was a slight wheeze to her voice, sounding like an accordion that was going down. "He's just behind the corner through there. That's the dining room. He's lying on the floor near the telephone. I took a quick look sir, and noticed something a little strange."

"Oh yeah?"

She coughed. "Yes. He had something sticking out of his chest. It was all burnt and everything, but it looked like a small knife, from what I could tell."

Well, well, Pieter considered. That changed things.

"Come on, let's get back outside," he said, deciding it wasn't necessary to see the second body, under the circumstances; if they lingered here any longer they'd both soon be in the back of an ambulance, suffering from smoke inhalation.

They turned to go, but just then his foot caught something, and Pieter glanced down. Amidst all of the wreckage on the floor, his eye caught sight of a tiny yellow object, because it stood out so much from all of the blackened pieces of wood. Strange that it hadn't been burnt like everything else. One of the oddities that occurred in house fires occasionally, he assumed.

Bending down for a closer look he immediately recognized it for what it was. The plastic cap off a syringe.

Back outside, they breathed in deeply, trying to rid themselves of the fumes and smell from the fire. His head throbbed madly.

Kaatje was looking at him with an earnest expression on her face, no doubt itching to help him crack the case. Sadly, he had to disappoint her. As a rookie, her main job was to guard the premises and to keep an eye on who was coming and going. Besides, he was actually heading home. There was nothing to be achieved in him staying here as there would be no results or conclusions to draw until forensics came back with their initial findings. Plus, the firefighters still had to find and recover the body of the child, and that could take a while. He didn't want to feel like he was in their way, certainly not after the brusque way the mealy-mouthed firefighter had been earlier.

"Well, I'd best get on," he told her, and he turned away from her crestfallen expression.

Walking down the driveway, stepping over hosepipes, Pieter paused and looked back.

"Perhaps I'll see you at the station tomorrow?"

She grinned and nodded enthusiastically.

He went through the gates and was about to head back down the street to his parked car when a loud voice drew him to a halt.

"Van Dijk!"

"Fuck," he whispered to himself when he saw who was bellowing.

Parked right in the middle of the busy road and drawing annoyed looks from the fire crews was a large black car with blacked-out windows. One of the windows at the back was wound down, and a big, fat face was scowling out at him. His boss, Huijbers.

Huijbers liked to be driven around town in his brand new American SUV, with a small security detail and his very own driver. He also liked to wear a silly baseball hat and a Kevlar vest, because he wanted to look important.

Now he was calling Pieter over and from the look on his face it wasn't for a friendly catch-up.

Pieter reluctantly dragged himself over and stood waiting.

"Van Dijk, whoever gave you this case must need a fucking lobotomy," he snarled. "It's a travesty that you are still on the murder team, never mind having a big one like this falling into your lap."

Pieter thought about mentioning how he was here purely by chance, not by choice, but he was too deadbeat to explain. He just wanted to get home, have a shower and hit the sack.

"You fucked up royally with the Werewolf murders."

"I did?" he asked.

"Too many people died last time, Van Dijk," Huijbers continued with barely a pause, "the fucking scandal will tarnish our reputation for years, and the person responsible is still on the run, in case you'd forgotten. Your girlfriend wasn't she? Living right under your nose."

"She wasn't my girlfriend."

"Shut the fuck up!" He wagged his chubby finger at Pieter, like he was admonishing a naughty child. "Make sure you don't screw this one up as well, you hear? These people, the Bakkers, they were a very highly respected family. Dr Bakker even treated members of The Royal Family."

He leaned even further out of the car window, the hat looking ridiculous on his big, sweaty head.

"Now listen carefully. I want this case cleared up quickly, with no loose ends. Do your job and find the fucker who did this and put him away - fucking understood?"

With that, he slapped the side of the car to signal to his driver that it was time to go, and the car pulled away.

Pieter gave a jaunty little salute as the red tail-lights disappeared down the street.

* * *

While driving back to his home on Singel Canal Pieter considered his reflection in the car's rearview mirror.

The face of the man looking back at him had changed almost beyond recognition over the past six months. With its sallow complexion and dark rings around the eyes, and sharp cheekbones and three-day stubble, it was the face of someone who suffered frequent sleepless nights or night-terrors; a person haunted by the recent past, which had affected both his physical health as well as his mental well-being. His hair was greying at the temples and a permanent frown marred his brow, and he'd picked up the paranoid habit of looking over his shoulder whenever he heard footsteps approaching, especially at night.

His psychiatrist had told him straight; he was suffering from burn-out and needed a complete break, from work and the city. Take a holiday, go somewhere to relax, perhaps a few weeks on the coast. Well, Pieter reflected ruefully as he drove through the quiet streets, that hadn't exactly worked out had it? Not when Lotte – Charlotte Janssen, as he now knew her as – had somehow tracked him down and popped up right in the small guesthouse where he was staying. Somehow evading the massive international manhunt and paying him a brief visit, to remind him that she was still around.

He shuddered at the memory of that fleeting glimpse of her standing on the pavement below his window, smiling and mocking him. Then, in the next instant, gone. And since that day neither he nor anybody else had laid eyes on her. She had melted away, vanished, dropping completely off the radar, leaving him convinced that she was still out there somewhere, possibly still right in this city.

That was one of the reasons why Pieter had not moved house. It seemed pretty pointless as she'd no doubt still be able to find him. Amsterdam was a small city, she knew where he worked, so discovering his whereabouts would be easy for someone of her means. Besides, somewhere in the back of his mind was this vague hope that she would make a move, maybe come for him again. At the present it was probably their best hope of catching her.

Pulling down his street Pieter opened his automatic garage doors using the fob on his keyring, and after parking his car and setting the house alarm, went upstairs to the living quarters. Taking out the leftover remains of yesterday's pizza, he popped it in the oven – a new addition to his bachelor pad – and went to take a shower whilst it heated up.

Dumping his clothes in the laundry bag, he stepped into the cubicle and turned the hot water up as high as he could stand it.

It was well after midnight by the time he'd eaten supper and drank a beer. He felt shattered. Hopefully tonight would be one of those rare occasions when he actually slept through.

But first, there was one more thing he had to do.

Bending down, he retrieved a small glass jar from underneath his bed. Unscrewing the lid, he proceeded to pour the contents onto the bare, wooden floorboards, something he did every single night without fail.

Working carefully, he completely surrounded the bed with an uninterrupted circle of salt, as protection through to sunrise.

Chapter 4
Nina

Twelve year old Nina Bakker felt rough hands pull the blindfold away from her eyes and she lay on the bed, her eyes blinking rapidly in time with her racing heart. Her blurred vision slowly came back into focus and she gasped at what she saw.

Standing over her was the figure of a short and squat man. He may not have been particularly tall, but she could see straight away that he was powerfully built, with thick biceps and a barrel chest and huge hands. He was wearing a brown boiler suit and heavy work boots, but when her gaze shifted upwards to look at his face, she gave a little gasp.

His features were hidden behind an old leather hood. At the front, where the eyes should be, was a small horizontal glass visor set in a rusty iron frame. The hood came down to his shoulders so that the whole of his head and face was hidden from view.

It was the type of hood that welders wore, Nina realized. Her grandfather used to have a similar one, for when he was repairing his vintage motorbikes in the garage. But this one was old, more like the sort that men who worked in the old docks used to wear in the past. The sight of it petrified her, especially the dark visor. The thought of those hidden eyes watching and staring at her was enough to make Nina cringe back onto the mattress, and she squirmed, her hands and feet still bound together.

"Calm down," came the muffled voice from behind the hood.

These words had the opposite effect, and she felt herself breathing in quick and shallow gasps, and her eyes welled up with tears.

The figure reached forward with one of his huge hands, and although she shrunk away from him, he grasped a hold of one of her narrow shoulders and actually squeezed it gently.

"Take it easy now girl. Get your breath, and try to stay calm." As if to try to reassure her further he added, "I'm not going to hurt you."

During the terrifying journey in the back of the van, locked inside the oblong metal box with its small LED light showing through her blindfold, feeling the sleeping bag beneath her, Nina was convinced she was going to die. She was only twelve years old, but she was much more streetwise than people gave her credit for, and she knew how the world worked. She was well aware that there were lots of bad people out there, men who abducted children in order to do all kinds of horrible things to them, before later killing them and dumping their bodies in a ditch somewhere. The TV was full of documentaries and movies of such things, real-life abductions of kids or young women taken off the street or snatched from their bedrooms, never to be seen alive again. And so Nina was sure this was going to be her fate. Taken from her home, from her parents, who would spend the rest of their lives wondering what had happened to their daughter.

Her parents! Lying squashed into the metal box, she'd felt the fear swell up inside her, her concern for herself momentarily superseded by the worry she now felt for her mother and father. Had something bad happened to them? Surely it had, she had heard the screaming and commotion downstairs, the violent fighting that had sent her scurrying to her bedroom in terror. Her parents would never allow her to be just taken like this. They would both do everything in their power to stop this man from snatching her and driving away. They must have been hurt... or worse.

Nina had peed, unable to prevent herself, and she had cried quietly as the van rocked her back and forth, the sound of the engine reverberating around inside the confined space of her tiny prison.

After what seemed like an age, the van had slowed down. She could tell from the volume of the engine, but also with the motion and juddering, and then they had turned slowly about, the wheels bumping over something in the road, before coming to a halt. The engine gave one final splutter and then fell quiet.

She had waited, her whole body quivering, and she had tried to stifle her sobs, thinking crazily that if she remained quiet the driver might somehow forget about her, which was stupid and childish she knew, but Nina was desperately afraid and panic was seizing her, making wild thoughts flit through her imagination.

She heard the driver's door slam shut, then the crunching of footsteps on gravel, followed by the loud scrape of the van's rear door being yanked open. Laboured breathing, then the snap of what must be a padlock right beside her ear, hinges squeaking loudly. Finally, strong hands grabbing her, shoving the gag further into her mouth to silence her scream, and before she could think straight she was being manhandled out of the box and carried away. Freezing cold air brushed against her face and she caught the faint whiff of something familiar, which she was sure was the smell of the sea. Yes, she could hear waves breaking on a shore close by, could recognize the salty tang blowing in the air.

Then they must have been inside somewhere, the man carrying her huffing and puffing as he lugged her along, the chill making her bare arms go all goosebumpy. Nina had felt herself lowered to the floor, and the simple command of: "Stand."

A key turning in a lock and the recognizable noise of a heavy door opening, then she was scooped off her feet again, the door banging shut. Down some steps and finally she was placed gently onto a soft mattress and the gag removed from her mouth, the blindfold from her eyes.

Now the man telling her he wasn't going to harm or hurt her.

"That's not why you are here," his gruff voice coming from behind the leather hood. "I'm not like that."

Nina turned her gaze away from him and surveyed her surroundings.

She was in a large room, laying on a small bed pushed into the corner, which had clean sheets and blankets. There was a wardrobe and a set of drawers which also acted as a nightstand, with a lamp on top. On the wall above the bed were a couple of posters showing pop stars, although they were quite old with the corners curling inwards and she didn't recognize who they were. Beyond this small sleeping area, the rest of the room opened out into a large space containing a couch and a small TV, a tiny square table with two wooden chairs, a rug on the bare stone floor. A bookcase contained a mixture of books and magazines, plus what looked like a selection of DVDs. Over in the far wall was another open doorway, and through there Nina glimpsed a shower cubicle together with a sink and toilet. In the corner of the main room was a wooden staircase that led up to a big, rusty door. It was slightly ajar, and through the gap was the bluish glow of a flickering fluorescent light.

Nina stared hard at the opening, a feeling of desperate hope temporarily flashing through her mind, but when her eyes moved on, a tiny shudder passed through her, for what she saw next crushed that fleetingly brief notion of escape. For beneath the staircase was a tiny metal cage. Just a few feet square, with a small door in the front, and inside a rolled-up blanket. She looked at the cage, and again tears welled up in her eyes, and she shook her head. She was determined not to cry.

The man in the hood must have noticed her reaction for he turned to follow her gaze, and then swivelled his head back in her direction.

A silence stretched out, and after a minute Nina was finally able to speak, her small voice trembling.

"Who are you?"

"You can call me Tobias, if you like," came the muffled reply.

"Where are we?" Her eyes darted about the room again, noticing for the first time that there were no windows at all.

"That does not matter for now. But you are safe here."

"Where are my parents?" Nina dreaded hearing the answer. "I want my mum and dad."

The man gave the tiniest shake of his head. "I'm afraid that won't be possible. I'm afraid that you won't be able to see them again. Not for a long time."

He stepped a little closer, and she could hear his laboured breathing again.

"This is your new home now. You will be staying here. Is that clear?"

Nina did not respond. A horrible empty feeling in her stomach made her suddenly nauseous, and she was afraid she might vomit.

"I have made a lot of effort making it look nice for you. It is clean and warm, there is heating which you can turn on or off, and you have your own bathroom for your privacy. There is hot water, and a kettle for you to make drinks, with a choice of coffee, hot chocolate, plus snacks. I will bring you food for breakfast and in the evening, or sometimes if I am away I will leave you sandwiches. The TV works and you have lighting, plus books and even some jigsaws. In the wardrobe are new clothes, which I hope will fit you."

Nina listened as he went on.

"The rules are simple. If you behave and do not cause me trouble then I will treat you kindly. I will not harm you or touch you, I will not do anything inappropriate. Do you understand what that means?"

Nina nodded.

"Good. But if you break the rules, if you give me problems or are unruly, then there will be punishments. Do I need to spell those out for you?"

Again Nina looked over towards the cage in the corner, and she meekly shook her head.

"Very well. I am going to untie you now. Do not scream, do not fight, or bite, or spit. Understand?"

"Yes," Nina managed a strained whisper.

Reaching forward, the man unfastened first her feet and then her hands, and he quickly stepped back. Nina curled up into a foetal position and pressed her back into the wall behind her.

"Now try to sleep. I will bring you food in the morning."

With that, he turned and walked away.

Nina watched him climb up the staircase and pull the heavy door shut behind him with a resounding thud, the narrow strip of light from the room above disappearing, taking all hope with it. A key was turned in the lock, bolts were snapped shut - then silence.

Chapter 5
112 Emergency

Telephone call logged as commencing at 7:12pm

Operator: Emergency call-centre 112. Who do you want to talk to?

(inaudible)

Operator: Hello, which service do you require please?

Nina: (whispers) Help, please.

Operator: How may I help you?

Nina: There's someone in the house.

Operator: Who is in your house?

Nina: A man I think. He's downstairs and (inaudible)

Operator: There's a man downstairs? Is he inside your house? Can you see him?

Nina: I'm upstairs, but he's with mum and dad. They are shouting.

Operator: Your mum and dad are shouting? Are they arguing? How old are you dear?

Nina: Twelve.

A State of Sin

Operator: And what's your name? Are your mum and dad having a row?

Nina: My name's Nina. There's a man, and he's shouting.

Operator: Is it your daddy shouting dear?

Nina: No, the other man. I think they are fighting. I heard them fighting and there was screaming.

Operator: A man is in your house and he is shouting and fighting with your parents? Is that what you mean?

Nina: Yes, he rang the buzzer and then they were fighting and my dad was screaming.

Operator: Ok dear, please give me your address. Do you know your house address?

Nina Bakker provides her home address.

Operator: I'm going to send the police to your house. Is the man still in the house dear?

Nina: Yes, he's downstairs and I can hear things breaking.

Operator: And whereabouts in the house are you Nina?

Nina: Upstairs, in my bedroom.

Operator: Very good. Please stay where you are Nina. Don't go downstairs alright?

Nina: But I think he's hurting my mum and dad. I can't hear my mum anymore, but my dad keeps shouting and screaming.

Operator: I understand dear, but it's very important that you stay in your bedroom.

Nina: (whispers and crying) OK.

Operator: Do you know who this man is Nina? Do you recognize him?

Nina: I don't think so. I didn't see him, I just heard his voice and then they started shouting.

Operator: Has this man broken into your house? Is that what you think has happened?

Nina: I think so. (long pause) It's gone quiet now. They've stopped fighting.

Operator: The police are on their way Nina. They should be there very soon.

Nina: Should I go downstairs? Can I go and find my mum and dad?

Operator: No Nina, you need to stay where you are. Wait until the police arrive. Do you understand?

Nina: Yes.

Operator: Good.

Nina: I think (inaudible)

Operator: I didn't hear you Nina. Can you say that again?

Nina: (whispers) I think someone's coming upstairs (crying)

Operator: Nina? Do not leave your room. Unless it is your mum or dad, or the police, do not leave your bedroom.

Nina: It's him. I can hear him coming upstairs. (inaudible) scared.

Operator: I know, dear. Please try and hide somewhere, the police are coming as fast as they can.

(inaudible) (crying)

Operator: Can you hear me Nina?

A State of Sin

Nina: He's outside my room. Please, oh please come quickly.

Operator: Nina, try and stay calm and tell me –

Call ends at 7:16pm

Police Radio message logged as commencing at 7.20pm

Arrest and Support Unit car number 166-D: It was Vondelstraat wasn't it? Confirm please.

Dispatch Operator: Yes, Vondelstraat 175.

Car number 166-D: Can't see a fucking thing in this fog. I think we came in at the wrong end, it must be down past the church.

Dispatch Operator: Confirm address is Vondelstraat 175, resident's name Christiaan Bakker, plus spouse and one female child.

Car number 166-D: She was the caller right? The kid?

Dispatch Operator: Just checking. Yes, she gave her name as Nina.

Car number 166-D: She definitely gave the correct address didn't she? Because we can't – wait on – fuck me, there's smoke everywhere. Hold on.

Dispatch Operator: Are you at the scene 166?

(inaudible shouting)

(muffled sound of car doors slamming and running footsteps)

(long pause -30 seconds)

Car number 166-D: There's a fucking fire! The whole place is burning! The whole damn building! Send back-up now!

Dispatch Operator: Can you repeat your last?

Car number 166-D: The house is on fire, damn it! The front entrance is like a fucking furnace!

Dispatch Operator: Vondelstraat 175?

Car number 166-D: Yes, yes, send help, send everything you have! We can't get near!

Dispatch Operator: Acknowledged.

Radio message ends at 7.23pm

    The main Amsterdam Police Headquarters building on Elandsgracht was an ugly red-bricked modern office block, its roof bristling with numerous radio antennae and satellite dishes. The inside was not much better, with every room filled to capacity with untidy desks and chairs and PC monitors, the tired and harassed police officers and civilian admin staff working their fingers to the bone.

    Inspector Pieter Van Dijk had managed to acquire for himself one of the few corner offices, up on the top floor. It was small and cramped, with one tiny window looking out onto the busy squad-room, and another overlooking Marnixstraat and the canal outside. To add a bit of festive cheer he had stuck a tiny piece of tinsel on the top of his PC monitor with blue tack, and on the table in the corner was an old plastic Christmas tree covered in coloured lights, which he'd found in a cardboard box in the storeroom. The cheap lights flickered occasionally from a loose bulb, but Pieter hardly noticed.

    He was too busy re-reading the transcripts from last night's emergency 112 call, and the subsequent police radio message from the cops first on the scene. They made for grim reading, particularly the call from twelve year old Nina, Mr and Mrs Bakker's young daughter. The terror in that call was clear, the girl's pleading for help and the operator's futile attempts to keep her calm. Even though it was a printed transcript set out verbatim and therefore cold and soulless, the fear of that brief conversation still came through, and Pieter shivered at the emotional impact it had on him.

    At lunchtime, a little over an hour ago now, he had received a brief update from the scene of the fire. The police and fire service forensic teams, working in tandem, were still in the process of picking their way through the debris, but several things had already been established. First was that arson was definitely confirmed to be the cause of the fire. Traces of a flammable liquid, in this case petrol, had been discovered in the downstairs hallway, with the heaviest concentrations around the front doorway and over the floor. This was the seat of the fire, the exact spot where the damage was worst and therefore where the inferno had been started. It was also the location of the first body, initially only presumed to be the corpse of Elise Bakker (Pieter could still see her face when one of the techs had rolled her over). This had now just been confirmed by STRs and mtDNA sequence results rushed through the NFI lab in The Hague. They had also verified the identity of the second body, recovered in the dining room; this was indeed the husband, Dr Christiaan Bakker.

So far, so good. Nothing unusual up to that point. They were still searching through the upper floors of the large house for the body of the child, and Pieter expected any time now to hear that her remains had also been recovered. But in the meantime, an odd bit of news had reached him; a piece of info gleaned from the early search of the crime scene. Which connected nicely to something that officer Kaatje Groot had told him last night.

The object that she had observed sticking out of the chest of the male corpse, and which she thought was a small knife, was in fact a hypodermic syringe. This in turn led his memory back to the small plastic cap that he had accidentally caught with his shoe on their way outside.

Pieter hadn't thought anything of it at the time. He just assumed that it was for someone's medical requirements. Perhaps a member of the family was diabetic or needed regular injections for another ailment, or maybe it was connected to Christiaan Bakker's occupation.

But this unusual development regarding the syringe sticking out of the doctor's chest certainly changed that, and now Pieter was wishing that he'd bagged and tagged the yellow plastic cap.

He hadn't however, and the chances of ever finding the cap again were slim to non-existent, he reckoned. Not with the number of people passing to and fro through the building, and with the firefighters still damping down the place, and dragging debris out to check for more bodies and to ensure the place was safe and stable.

Of course, he could be barking up the wrong tree. The presence of the syringe might mean absolutely nothing. They would have to wait for any blood and toxicology test results to come back from the lab to see if Dr Bakker had been injected with anything that may have contributed to his demise, instead of this being a case of death resulting from an arson attack.

Yet there was the phone call. The 112 emergency plea for help, and the young girl's description of an intruder, and a violent struggle involving her parents.

And finally, there were the death threats.

A number of different warnings had apparently been received by the Bakkers, some by telephone and some by hand-written notes. Initially, these threats were only made to Dr Bakker, and in order to shield his family from them, he had decided not to tell them, hoping the threats would either stop or that perhaps he could deal with the situation without alarming his wife and daughter. But later, these messages had been directed at his wife, Elise. And they had grown increasingly menacing, to such an extent that Dr Bakker had decided to report them to the police.

Sitting in his office Pieter read through the file. There wasn't much there. The threats had been logged into the system, but no action had been taken, mostly because as quickly as the messages had begun they had stopped, at the exact time that the Bakker's contacted the police. It may have just been coincidence, but more likely the perpetrator of the messages had got wind that the police were involved, and panicking, he or she had decided to quit rather than risk arrest. The last threat was over three months ago, and since then, nothing.

So, thinking the problem had gone away, Mr and Mrs Bakker, and their daughter Nina, had got on with their lives.

Until last night, that is.

Pieter scrolled back to the previous page on the file and made a note of the evidence bag docket number of this last threat, which had been in the form of a handwritten message. Standing up, he went across to the window looking out onto the squad-room office.

Kaatje Groot, the young rookie officer from last night, was at her desk. She had been hanging around all morning, he'd noticed. Technically, she should have been downstairs with Floris De Kok helping him in the files section, but somehow she had managed to find some task that kept her up here in the main squad-room instead. Her desk was also suspiciously close enough to Pieter's office so that she could keep one eye on his door, and she had angled her chair and laptop so that she was facing in his direction.

Pieter gave a little shake of his head and smiled to himself.

He tapped on the glass to get her attention, and her head snapped up. Beckoning her over, Pieter reached for the yellow Post-it note he'd written on, and in the three seconds this took, she was there in the doorway, looking at him with her wide brown eyes.

"Hello sir."

"Officer Groot. What time did you finish last night?"

"Oh, about 5am this morning"

"Shouldn't you be off duty until later? Getting some shut-eye?"

Kaatje Groot shrugged her shoulders. "I'm not a very good sleeper sir. I don't see the sense in mooching about back home when I could be here, working and, you know, helping out."

"I admire your commitment. Long may it last."

He handed her the Post-it note where he'd scribbled the evidence bag number.

"Pop down to Floris will you, and ask him to find me this? He has his own crazy system for filing evidence and paperwork that I haven't mastered yet."

Kaatje took the note. "Will do sir."

As she hurried away Pieter could hear her happily humming Christmas tunes to herself.

Five minutes later she was back.

Placing the small clear plastic evidence bag on his desk she loitered in his office, looking over his shoulder.

Pieter glanced around.

"That will be all for now officer."

"Oh, of course. I'll be just outside if you need anything else sir. That's my desk," she pointed, "just there."

When Kaatje was gone Pieter turned back and picked up the slim bag and peered at the contents.

Pay your debt, or get what's coming.

The message was hand-written on a small scrap of lined notepaper. The letters were written in a very basic form as though purposely over-simplified, no doubt to fool any handwriting experts. But that in itself could be revealing as to the sort of personality and characteristics of the person responsible.

As to the actual contents of the message? Well, it was short and to the point, and it certainly carried a direct threat, but what that threat and the wording alluded to was harder to conclude. What *debt* was it referencing? Also, if this *debt* wasn't forthcoming, what was waiting just around the corner for Mr and Mrs Bakker and their daughter?

The motive to most murder cases could nearly always be found by looking into the victim's personal life or financial circumstances, and that was always the first step. Getting forensic evidence to back up any theories came second, as often any results from the lab could take days or weeks, and sometimes months, to come back down the line.

Get someone to check the family's background and their associates, and find out if they had any enemies. And whilst the police were doing that, hope that the boffins at NFI would ferret out any forensics.

Pieter read a couple of notations in the file. The handwriting and notepaper hadn't yet been tested. Presumably once the threats stopped any urgency to do so ceased to be a priority.

So he filled out requests for EED and Electro-static Detection Apparatus tests to be done on the paper, as well as to run the handwriting sample through the database.

Just then his phone buzzed and vibrated on his desk, and he picked it up to see he had a text message. He checked the sender – Fleur van den Heuvel, the Chief Fire Officer on the scene. He remembered the sour-faced female firefighter from last night, and his lip involuntarily turned up.

REMAINS OF TWO ADULTS RECOVERED.
NO THIRD BODY. FULL CHECK OF THE PREMISES COMPLETED.

He thought about texting back, perhaps adding a love heart, but the compulsion soon left him.

So, there was no sign of the daughter, which begged the question: where was Nina Bakker?

Chapter 6
Arrival

While Pieter was at work slowly reaching the conclusion that they were now dealing with a murder and kidnapping/abduction case, Johan Roost's flight from Johannesburg was just coming in to land at Schiphol airport. The long twelve-hour overnight flight had been the usual never-ending nightmare of uncomfortable seats, combined with tasteless food, ridiculously bad movies to watch on the entertainment system and stale recycled air. So, even though he hated crowded and hectic airport lounges, he was glad when it was time to get off the plane and stretch his legs as he strolled through Arrivals.

His niece, the beautiful and hypnotic Lotte, had made it quite clear that he should under no circumstances draw attention to himself, or that they should be seen in public together. And although she could easily have arranged for a driver to meet him at the airport, he actually preferred to travel incognito, and with minimal fuss. So he followed the signs for the NS station beneath the airport terminal, to travel by train to Amsterdam's Centraal Station.

He had just one medium-sized suitcase with him. His other kit, containing the AX338 Sniper Rifle as well as specialized surveillance gear, had been re-routed from South Africa to The Netherlands via Russia, and thanks to some old contacts he had there from the Soviet era, had been repackaged in crates stamped with a diplomatic seal and the necessary customs forms filled out, all to ensure they arrived untampered with. They should all be in place waiting for him.

So he walked through the airport, mingling with the crowds, looking like any other tourist here to enjoy a few days in the Dutch capital.

When he was down on the train platform he took out one of three cheap burner phones he carried and switched over to the national mobile network. He sent a quick text to a memorized number – **LET'S HIT THE TOWN BUDDY?** – and then deleted the message. Moving casually down towards the end of the platform Johan removed the SIM card and dropped it into a litter bin, and then, ensuring nobody was watching, he dropped the phone itself onto the rail tracks near the tunnel entrance.

Onboard the train he stood near the door and watched the scenery through the windows, the white and frosty fields soon giving way to the city's outer suburbs. It was sleeting, and the sky was a dismal grey colour, the light already leaking from the sky even though it was only mid-afternoon. He was freezing cold. He longed for the warmth and open spaces of home, yet an undeniable thrill passed through him.

The familiar and electrifying buzz that he always felt when carrying out a hit.

* * *

After a short rest, Johan had hired a car using a cloned credit card and driven through the confusing network of roads across Amsterdam's Old Centre, weaving his way around trams and bicycles, and then found a place to park near the canal on Elandsgracht. Just over the road was the main Police Headquarters building.

From where he sat he had a clear view of the area reserved for staff parking, just at the side of the red-bricked office block. He could also keep watch on the main entrance, and could see people coming and going.

He waited for nearly two hours. Outside, it grew dark, and he sat with the car's heating turned up to full, feeling the cold seeping through the thick fur-lined jacket he wore.

Eventually, a little after seven o'clock, he spotted his target emerge from the building and stroll along the pavement before turning down the side street. Johan watched him climb into his car, turn on the headlights, and then slip out into the flow of traffic.

Turning the ignition, he waited until the other vehicle was about fifty yards ahead, before he pulled out and followed on behind.

It was only a short journey to the policeman's house. Johan already knew the address and he could have just waited for him there, but whenever he was on a job he liked to learn a bit about the target, his route to and from work, his daily routines, whether he diverted to visit friends or family, if he might call for a drink or a bite to eat and where his regular haunts were and what kind of car he drove, his habits, the gait of his walk even. Every tiny detail could prove to be important when the time came, and careful reconnaissance work like this could prove the difference between success and failure, and how to deal with any unexpected hitches that might crop up. The more he knew and learnt, the more groundwork he carried out, the better.

They drove down Prinsengracht, Johan noting all the lights everywhere, with all the bridges over the canals lit up in fancy displays of colour. He remembered Lotte mentioning some special annual event, The Festival Of Light or some such shit, which he admitted to himself did look pretty, with all the nice reflections rippling on the water in a thousand different patterns. Part of the Christmas celebrations he presumed. Yes, certainly the city did look nice at this time of the year, just as his niece had said. If only it weren't so fucking cold.

On the far side of the canal loomed the tall spire of Westerkerk, and shortly after, the car up ahead turned right. Johan followed, and they drove over four different bridges before turning left onto Singel Canal. Here, he slowed down in order to hang back, and he watched the other car slowly crawl down the cobbled road. It came to a brief halt, an electronic garage door opened below one of the houses, and the other car was steered inside. The door came back down.

With his own car engine idling quietly further up the road, Johan watched and waited. A couple of minutes later, and the upstairs lights went on in the tall canal house.

Johan eased his car forward and parked up just opposite the closed garage doors, and he turned the engine off.

A State of Sin

Twisting sideways, he reached behind him and retrieved a slender aluminium case from the backseat. Placing it on his lap he tapped in a six-digit number into the small touchscreen keypad and popped open the lid.

Inside were a small laptop and an integrated 8-Antenna handheld 4G IMSI – catcher. The mobile-phone interceptor was an EU/UK P8-LG version, with a 30-metre radius, and would be perfect for the job.

An IMSI device acted like a fake mobile phone mast to intercept calls and texts. It could be used to listen in to phone conversations or to record them and play them back later from any targeted mobile phone. Incoming and outgoing calls could be tagged, likewise with text messages. A handy gadget, completely illegal, but easily purchased online.

Johan booted up the laptop and phone-catcher and ran the software to automatically scan the surrounding area within a 30 metre radius of where he was sitting, which easily included the tall canal house over the road. Five different phone numbers in the locale appeared on-screen. He typed in the target phone's long IMSI number, and a few seconds later the words **TARGET CAPTURED** popped up and began to flash.

Satisfied that all was in order Johan sat back in his seat. Now all he had to do was wait.

Pieter made a stir-fry for dinner, and afterwards tried to watch a bit of TV, but he could find nothing interesting in the schedules and he wasn't in the mood to watch anything on-demand, so after a half-hour, he switched it off. For a while he pottered about. Yet his mind kept returning to the case, unable to stop going over events and running through various scenarios. Eventually he decided to go up to the attic and switch on the old PC, to check his emails and any updates from work.

As he suspected, there was nothing yet from forensics or the post mortems, plus it was still too early to know what was in the syringe sticking out of Christiaan Bakker's chest. Waiting on any results from the lab could be the worst part of the job, particularly when dealing with a murder case. If they were also looking at an abduction then time was of the essence, and considering that the missing person was a twelve year old girl gave things an added level of concern. The clock, therefore, was ticking.

Mark Hobson

Tomorrow afternoon a press conference had been scheduled to update everyone on the current state of affairs. His boss, Commissaris Dirk Huijbers, had decided to helm the media circus, and Pieter was grateful for small mercies. If Huijbers wanted all the limelight then that was fine by him. However, Pieter had received instructions to bring the Commissaris up to speed on where the investigation was, and their face-to-face meeting was scheduled for one hour before the press briefing was due to kick off, and this early in the case he had very little to report. Huijbers no doubt knew this. He was just happy to make Pieter squirm, especially after the fiasco of the Werewolf case. But whether he liked the idea of getting another rollicking or not was neither here nor there. He had to have something to give to Huijbers, some small scrap of progress, if only to see the smirk disappear off his face, so hence the reason for tonight's bit of out-of-hours prepping.

Pieter once again considered the possible motives for a double murder and abduction. The latter part was self-explanatory: whenever a young child, especially a girl, was taken then the sexual element was always at the forefront of the list of reasons as to why a child was taken.

Most abductions tended to fall into two categories. Either the victim was known to the perpetrator, and he or she had held unhealthy thoughts about the victim for quite some time – perhaps a relative or close friend of the family. Or it was a stranger who, unable to control his desires any longer, grabbed the first opportunity to abduct a child to quickly satisfy his perverted desires. Yet with the second category – a stranger snatching a child – the vast majority of times these were unplanned, a quick grab and snatch of a child walking home from school for instance, and last night's abduction didn't feel like that. It was early days of course, but Pieter had the sense it had been carefully planned and prepared. In which case it most likely fell into the first category of child abductions - that the person who took Nina had actually known her.

However, once again that didn't feel right. Why take the huge risk of taking her from home? Why not arrange to take her from a safer location? So much could have gone wrong last night for the kidnapper, there were so many unknowns. Also, committing a double-murder was a huge step-up from some sick paedophile with a liking for young girls.

So, was child abduction the real motive here, Pieter wondered? Was Nina even the real target? Taking her to hold for ransom seemed unlikely given the fact that her parents, who were both wealthy, had been murdered. If that were the motive – taking the child for financial gain – then why murder the parents?

Which brought him back to Christiaan and Elise Bakker.

The motive to most murder cases could nearly always be found by looking into the victim's personal life or financial circumstances. His own thought from earlier came back to him, and tonight, sitting at the wooden desk up in the cramped attic room of his canal house, Pieter considered this.

Yes, first thing tomorrow he was determined to open a new element to the investigation.

Perhaps murder was the main motive, and the taking of the child was secondary.

Looking into the parents' private lives might be the key. Did they have marital problems, or issues at work, or money worries? The latter seemed unlikely given their apparent wealth, but of course appearances could be deceptive. Perhaps Christiaan Bakker had run up debts (the threats referred to such a possibility) and he was keeping this from his wife, a very common thing where male pride was concerned. Had this resulted in his making enemies?

Pieter got up from his chair and strolled around the attic room, thinking fast.

They would have to look into the Bakkers banking arrangements. Plus get access to their mobile records, their email correspondence, and their browser history. The fire damage would delay this, but remote access to the necessary details wouldn't be too difficult, but it would take several days.

In the meantime, there was something he could be doing.

Pieter picked up his mobile from the desk and scrolled through the list of contacts from work. He found Kaatje Groot's number, and after a moment's hesitation, he messaged her.

HEY, YOU FANCY TAKING A TRIP IN THE MORNING?

He tucked the phone into his rear pocket and strolled over to the small dormer window. The earlier sleety weather had cleared, leaving a cloudless night sky sprinkled with stars. It would be cold tonight, with a heavy frost in the morning. Maybe the canals might freeze over this winter, which would be nice.

His phone buzzed with a reply, which read:

YES PLEASE ☺ WHERE ARE WE GOING BOSS?

He tapped out a response:

IT'S A SURPRISE. I'LL PICK YOU UP AT YOUR PLACE. 8am SHARP

Pieter hovered his finger over the mobile's keypad and decided to add a smiley of his own at the end. He tapped SEND.

A couple of minutes later and Kaatje replied with her home address.

Sitting in his car across the street, Johan Roost followed the exchange of messages.

Chapter 7
The Basement

On the second morning, Nina Bakker was woken by the sound of the metal door scraping open, followed by the *clomp-clomp* of heavy work boots coming down the stairs.

She stirred, reluctant to open her eyes and come to full consciousness. She had been dreaming about her parents, a memory of the time last year when they had gone to Kinderdijk to see the windmills there, and Nina clung to the dream in desperation. But the images broke up in her mind, dissolving like the spring dew on the grass, and she rolled over on the bed. Sitting up, she looked across the basement room, rubbing the sleep from her eyes.

The man in the welder's hood and boiler suit was back. He was standing by the small dining table, holding a tray of cereal and orange juice and toast, which smelled nice. He placed it on the wooden surface and then turned to her, his body posture non-threatening but still guarded, hanging back as though not quite sure what to do next.

Through the narrow visor his eyes, which during his visits yesterday she'd seen were a clear blue colour and soft, so soft, appraised her calmly, and despite the horrible situation she was in Nina no longer felt quite so scared.

Yesterday had been her first full day here, and sitting on the edge of the bed now, and looking back at him, she thought back, her mind going over the previous day's events.

Like today he had brought her breakfast. She'd no idea of the time but presumed it must be quite early. Through the leather hood, he had mumbled a quick hello, and then left, locking the door behind him.

Sliding off her bed and still wearing the same clothes that she'd been wearing the night before when she had been snatched from her home and her parents, Nina had cautiously approached the dining table. He'd brought her hot pancakes with syrup, a glass of fruit juice and a bowl of yoghurt and apple slices. Looking at it, with her tummy rumbling, she'd realized just how famished she was, and so she'd sat in one of the chairs and ate ravenously, keeping one eye on the door at the top of the stairs.

Finishing her breakfast, Nina stayed seated and cast her eyes around the room again, once more taking in the basement area. She thought about taking a shower as she felt grubby and smelly, but was too nervous to place herself in a potentially vulnerable position like that. At least not yet, not until she knew she could trust him. He'd made it quite clear last night that he didn't intend to do anything weird but until she felt more at ease, washing and showering could wait for now. But what she could do was quickly change her clothes.

Stacking up her breakfast things and leaving them on the table – presumably he would return and collect them at some point – Nina stepped back into the sleeping section of the basement, her bedroom she guessed she should call it, and opened the wardrobe and chest of drawers.

Inside she saw freshly laundered and folded t-shirts and pyjamas, socks and undergarments, jumpers and tops, and hanging up on coat hangers were a variety of jeans and leggings and a dressing gown, thicker fleeces and cardigans. At the bottom there were several pairs of footwear such as deck shoes, plimsolls, and some pink fluffy slippers. There were other items such as clean sheets and spare blankets for the bed, a hot water bottle, sanitary products and soaps and shampoos, even a cuddly teddy bear tucked up on a shelf.

In one of the drawers was a paper laundry bag. She quickly changed, putting on fresh clothes and hoping he wasn't spying on her – strangely, she sensed he wasn't – and dumped her old clothes into the bag, but she kept back her running shoes and tucked them under her bed. Then she dropped the dirty laundry by the table.

Next Nina decided to explore her new surroundings.

First of all, she went over to the couch and sat staring at the TV. Reaching for the remote, she pressed the power button and the screen came to life. She'd intended to go straight to the news channels RTL.NL or BVN TV, hoping to see something about herself or her parents on the breakfast news shows. But as soon as the screen lit up her heart sank. The television set was pre-tuned to channel AV1. There was no HDMI1 or HDMI2 channels, and no way to change it either, plus there was no smart TV fire stick plugged into the side. Which meant there was no way to watch any of the regular stations or shows. All she would be able to watch were DVDs. There was no way she could follow the news or find out anything about the outside world.

Sighing in frustration, she turned it off.

She wandered over to the bookshelf and browsed through the contents. A few magazines mostly either about fashion or celeb gossip, a few old National Geographic brochures, some puzzle books, plus some paperback fiction novels aimed mostly at the young-adult market. There was a good choice of DVDs including comedy movies, chick-flicks, boxed-sets of TV series, a few sci-fi movies, James Bond, the Jason Bourne series and so on. Finally there were half a dozen jigsaws, mostly of castles or medieval village scenes. She picked one at random – it had a snowy Neuschwanstein Castle surrounded by forests on the front, 1000 pieces long, which she decided would at least give her something to do. Taking it over to the table, Nina sat in the chair from where she could see the door, opened the box up and tipped out the pieces.

As she was sorting them out a little and finding a few of the edge pieces, her eyes flicked over to the cage below the wooden staircase, and immediately she averted her gaze. That was the one part of her new surroundings she didn't want to think about just yet.

She spent a couple of hours working on the jigsaw. It was more difficult than she thought and was quite slow going, but she managed to get most of the surrounding frame completed with just a few final pieces to link it up which she hadn't found yet. She started to grow a little bit bored with it and so decided to find something to read.

Picking up one of the puzzle books, she flicked through it and thought it might be worth a try, but then she realized she needed a pen or pencil which she didn't have, and so she put it back. Silly of him to leave it if she couldn't do the puzzles.

Next, she pulled out one of the paperbacks. Some slim book apparently written for the teenage reader, something about dragon-eggs and a curse, which kinda sounded ok, if a little babyish even though technically she wasn't even a teenager yet, and she lay down on the bed and started to read.

After a half-hour she nodded off and awoke with a start, looking quickly around the basement. Her heart was racing away, and it took her a few seconds for her mind to get up to speed, and only when she was sure she was still alone did her nerves settle again.

Getting to her feet she placed the book down on her pillow for later and was just deciding whether or not to watch a movie to pass the time when she heard footsteps overhead and she tensed up all over again.

Once more the door opened and the man with the hood stomped his way down the stairs. Silently he placed her evening meal on the table, careful not to mess-up the jigsaw – it looked like sandwiches and a can of cola – before gathering up the breakfast tray and laundry bag, and, without a word, went back up the staircase and locked the door. There were more footsteps overhead, followed by the faint bump of another door closing somewhere.

Alone again, Nina ate the food.

Later – early evening she assumed – she watched a couple of movies, but she was distracted and found it hard to concentrate on the plots, which were fairly silly anyway. So she decided to use the bathroom, keeping the door open while she did her business, and then thought she might as well try to sleep. Quickly undressing and putting on a clean set of pyjamas, Nina slipped into bed.

Within five minutes, and much to her surprise, she felt herself start to drift off and wondered vaguely if the man in the hood had maybe crushed up a sleeping pill and mixed it into her sandwich. But before she could ponder this any further, she was asleep.

…to awake on her second morning in the basement room to the *clomp-clomp* of those footsteps.

Looking at the young girl sitting on her bed, the man felt an overwhelming sense of shame wash over him. He felt terrible for what he was putting her through – she was the total innocent in all of this. But he didn't regret doing what he'd done, especially to her parents who had both had it coming. Killing them had not pricked his conscience in the slightest, just the opposite in fact. He felt elated at that. But the girl, oh why did he have to put her through this? The poor wretch must be terrified, and she must hate him so much.

But perhaps, over time, that might change.

Once he explained the reasons for having taken her. Surely she would understand, and forgive him for that? Perhaps even agree that it was right and just?

However long that took, he would wait. He could be very patient like that.

He turned to go, before his sense of guilt became too much.

"Please take your mask off."

Her words jolted him and he froze on the spot.

After a moment he turned back and saw through his visor that she was looking straight back, seemingly no longer fearful of him, which confused him. He could hear his own breath rasping in his ears and a slight dizziness passed through his body.

"I want to see your face Tobias," she whispered.

Why was she doing this? he asked himself. He was the maniac who had murdered her parents and took her away. She should despise him. She shouldn't be talking like this, calmly and almost like a friend.

Was she trying to trick him? To make him lower his guard by befriending him, in the way that other abducted people tried? He wasn't stupid, yet he couldn't keep his identity hidden forever, not if she were going to be living with him from now on.

His head was spinning as these confusing thoughts crashed around inside his brain, and then he watched as the girl rose from the bed and slowly came towards him, her footsteps faltering but determined.

Nina, oh Nina, he thought as she stopped before him, her face just inches from his own, their eyes locked together through the glass visor.

He saw her hands come up, felt them grip the sides of the leather hood, and then lift it clear. He blinked away tears as she smiled and said:

"Hello Tobias, I'm Nina."

They sat and ate breakfast together. She passed him the toast, saying she would like him to have it, and so he nibbled at it. His eyes remained downcast throughout most of their strange little encounter, even though Nina tried to make eye contact, but on the one occasion when his blue eyes flickered up, she smiled and he gave the tiniest of nervous smiles back.

They only spoke a little. There was nothing really to say, under the bizarre circumstances they were in, but she did ask him if it were sunny out, to which he replied quietly:

"Yes, and very cold."

"Is it frosty?" she asked. "Are the canals frozen over?"

"Yes. A beautiful winter's day."

"Oh, I like the winter. I like to go skating on the canals. I would love to see them." But she realized that was a stupid request, and he didn't reply.

They ate some more in silence, and Nina appraised him, deep in thought.

He had a friendly face. His cheeks were very red, and his nose covered in burst blood vessels, and she guessed he must spend a lot of time outdoors perhaps for his job. He had a pleasant smile and tiny white teeth, and a greying goatee beard which was trimmed neatly, and his blond hair was just showing the first signs of thinness on the crown. His eyes were of the clearest blue, and sparkled even more without the glass visor, with smile lines at their edges. But they shifted around nervously, skittering across the table surface or off to the side, and she sensed that something saddened him enormously.

Nina finished eating and then drank the rest of the fruit juice, then asked him in all innocence: "Is your name really Tobias?"

But the question triggered something in him, for she saw his body suddenly go tense, and she held her breath and felt something flutter in her chest.

He stood up quickly, causing his chair to scrape back over the floor. Without saying a word or looking at her, the man quickly gathered up the plates and the leather hood and then headed for the stairs in a hurry. Reaching the top he paused briefly to look back over his shoulder, and she saw fresh tears and a pained expression, before he slipped through the door and locked it once more.

Confused and now scared again, Nina slumped in her seat.

Upstairs, a darkness descended upon Tobias, a familiar feeling of claustrophobia and fury that he'd suffered from throughout most of his life. Hatred gripped him and in seconds he was in a whirling and spitting and violent turmoil, tearing around the house and screaming himself hoarse, smashing the furniture and punching at the walls with his thick-gloved hands.

The anger was directed at himself, at the weak fool he was. He was a spineless and pathetic excuse for a man, and what made it worse was he could not vent his fury on anybody, because he'd foolishly already killed the parents, and Nina, his beautiful Nina, was so precious and perfect. So he spun and shouted and lashed out at the very air, until eventually he collapsed onto the floor from sheer exhaustion.

Curling himself up into a tight ball he cried and rocked backwards and forwards.

Later, a thought popped into his head.

Snivelling and wiping his nose, it occurred to Tobias that actually, there was somebody he could punish for this whole mess.

Chapter 8
The Clinic

The Vrije Geer Optiek Klineik in Osdorp had only been open for about two years, but already the new state-of-the-art facility had gained a reputation for being one of the best eye surgery centres in The Netherlands.

It had cost 25 million euros to build. Inside, the equipment was the best in the world, from the brand new LEN-XR Laser System and three Refractive Diagnostic Points, a 3D Visualization System and the Galaxy Wavelight Suite. The consultation rooms and theatres and reception area were high-end conceptual designs, and the aftercare wards were as plush as anything found at a 5-star hotel. Even the car park outside had been designed by one of the world's leading architects, aimed at creating a relaxing and calm environment before visitors or patients even entered through the sliding doors.

Sitting in the car's passenger seat as they crawled through the morning traffic, Pieter scrolled through the clinic's website on an iPad, looking at the photos and reading, occasionally tutting to himself and shaking his head, or sighing heavily and drawing the odd glance from Kaatje.

"This must cost a bomb," he mumbled.

"Too posh for us, Boss?"

"Yep. Only for the rich and famous, or those with very good medical insurance."

He'd picked Kaatje Groot up from her home at a little before eight. Climbing out of his car, he'd pressed the bell for her apartment, and leaned against the car's door while he waited for her to come down from the third floor. A few minutes later she'd appeared, dressed in her civvies, looking all flustered and out of breath, and he'd dangled the car keys in front of her, smiling.

"Want to drive?"

Smiling back, Kaatje had grabbed the keys, and they got in.

"So, does this make me your official driver now?" she'd asked.

"I guess so."

Osdorp was a suburb on the outskirts of Amsterdam, almost in the countryside in fact, and the drive had taken them over an hour. Overnight a heavy frost had settled and most of the narrower canals had frozen over for the first time in three years, and everywhere was covered with a white dusting of ice. Kaatje thought it looked pretty, and she kept pointing out different things as she drove, but after a while Pieter became distracted, and so to kill the time decided to go online and check out the clinic.

It certainly was posh, he thought to himself. Their clients, according to the website, included celebrities and sports stars (particularly boxers needing treatment for retinal detachment) politicians and millionaire business executives, as well as members of the Dutch Royal Family. People from overseas flew in for treatment, often staying overnight in the luxury accommodation wing. But the price tag wasn't cheap. A list of costs for what he regarded as basic surgery such as cornea reshaping or cataract extraction was eye-wateringly huge.

Christiaan Bakker was their senior Ophthalmologist, with over ten years of experience under his belt and a long list of fancy qualifications. According to his LinkedIn profile, he also enjoyed canoeing and playing tennis in his spare time, and a photo showed him holding aloft a trophy he'd won in a mixed-double amateur match last year. The guy sounded phenomenal according to various testimonials; too good to be true, in Pieter's opinion.

Just then, Kaatje slowed down and turned off the main road, and drove down a short driveway that curved beyond a stand of poplars. Pieter closed down the iPad and looked through the windscreen at the building up ahead.

The clinic was built over two storeys, the buildings spread along the edge of a wide and frosty lawn. Much of their lower floors consisted of large windows and connecting glass corridors, presumably designed to let in lots of light and to give the place a relaxed and welcoming appearance. The upper floors were covered in white-coloured cladding, the walls with curved edges, the roof of the main building topped with what looked like a viewing terrace.

At the far end of the lawn, which was intersected with several paths, the ground sloped down to a narrow boating lake which was frozen over solid with thick ice. Beyond this was the large and open expanse of the Vrije Geer Nature Park.

It certainly was a beautiful setting, Pieter admitted to himself, on the edge of open countryside but handily close to the city centre. However, after they'd parked up in the large car park in front of the lawn and climbed out, the peaceful scene was marred by a low and deep rumble, and they both glanced up to see a passenger jet fly low overhead. Of course, Schiphol airport was just two or three kilometres to the south. So, the place wasn't in as relaxing a location as the website claimed, thought Pieter, which for some reason made him feel smug.

They walked down the central path over the lawn and approached the large plate-glass entrance, and the automatic doors parted. Inside the foyer, they made for the high reception desk, where a female receptionist smiled a plastic smile and bid them hello.

"We're here to see your boss," Pieter informed her, and flashed his police ID

The smile stayed in place but Pieter saw the edges of her eyes crinkle minutely.

"I'm afraid the Director is at a conference in France at the moment. She won't be back until tomorrow. Can I help you?"

"Ok, well her immediate subordinate, your supervisor, or someone else. It doesn't really matter. Tell them we want to talk about Christiaan Bakker."

Mention of the name brought the receptionist up sharp, and her bottom lip gave a slight tremble. "Oh, yes. What a horrible thing, we still can't believe what has happened."

Pieter gave her a moment to compose herself, and his tone softened a bit.

"We are a little pushed for time, and it's important that we speak to someone as soon as can be."

"Do you have an appointment sir?"

"No." He glanced around and spied the seating area over to his left. "We'll wait over here."

Walking away – he could feel the receptionist's eyes burning into his back – Pieter led Kaatje across the foyer, their feet squeaking on the highly-polished floor.

The seating area consisted of cream-coloured couches with lime-green cushions and lots of plastic potted plants. Pieter chose one and sat down with a sigh. On the wall was a large flat-screen HD television showing the breakfast news.

He and Kaatje chatted for a couple of minutes, explaining how he had to be back in time for the press conference. So far, news that this was now also a kidnapping case as well as a double murder, had not yet been made public. Pieter hoped to use that knowledge to his advantage this morning.

Just then, a middle-aged man dressed in a white doctor's coat appeared from a doorway and strode straight towards them, his hand extended in apparent greeting. The scowl on his pale face suggested otherwise.

"Good morning, I'm Julian Visser," he said brusquely.

Pieter shook the proffered hand but did not rise. He noticed he didn't offer to greet Kaatje, in fact, he barely acknowledged her presence.

"Inspector Van Dijk."

"I understand you are here regarding Doctor Bakker? Oh, terrible, terrible business. I am – sorry, I was – Christiaan's assistant, and I'm still in a complete state of shock and disbelief over the whole sorry tragedy." He shook his head and took a seat opposite, leaning forward earnestly.

"Yes, the receptionist was saying. What we are here for Mr Visser – "

"Oh please, call me Julian. We prefer first names around here, staff and patients alike."

"Well, *Julian,* perhaps you can help us. We are just trying to get an accurate picture of the kind of person your boss, *Christiaan,* was. What was he like to work for? His professional life, his personal life, that kind of thing? As I'm sure you are aware, the manner of the murders would suggest he and his family were specifically targeted rather than the random victims of some madman."

"Well if you are asking about his private life, I really wouldn't know too much I'm afraid. But as regarding his work here at the clinic, I have nothing but praise for him. He was an outstanding surgeon and very professional. Held in the highest regard, by his patients as well as everybody who works here, a fine fellow."

"Indeed. Yet it seems somebody didn't think quite so highly of him."

"Well yes, obviously. But I can only speak insofar as his duties here were concerned. Whether he, or his wife, had issues in their personal lives that I was not privy to is a moot point. We never socialized or saw each other away from the clinic, but they did have a wide circle of friends. Perhaps your time would be better spent talking to them." A thin smile appeared, and he looked ready to get to his feet and depart.

"His wife, Elise. Did you know her?"

"No. Why would I? I only ever met her once, about a year ago, at some dinner party held at the A'DAM Lookout. They were just leaving as I was arriving. Apparently, she had had a little too much to drink and they were leaving early. We chatted for about two minutes." He shrugged. "Sorry, but no I didn't know her. Still, for this to happen to her and her husband... Such a lovely couple."

Pieter and Kaatje exchanged a brief glance.

"And their daughter?"

"Little Nina? She's a sweet thing."

"Have you ever met her?"

Visser stared straight at Pieter, his eyes flicking back and forth, a frown crossing his features.

"How do you mean Pieter?" he asked after a moment.

"It's a simple question."

"Yes, a few times. Sometimes her father brings her here, to show her around. She likes to see where he works, what he does for a job, I guess."

"She was always with her dad when you saw her? Let's think, she's twelve years old now right? And you've known the Bakkers for how long?"

Visser fidgeted on his chair, and for the first time he looked over at Kaatje, and gave a little nervous laugh.

"Well, let's think. I first met Christiaan around about five years ago, when plans were underway to open our clinic. The Director here, she actually headhunted the two of us, and brought us both in at the same time. But I only really got to know him when we started working here two years ago. As to your first question regarding his daughter, of course I only ever see her when she accompanies her father to work."

"How many times is that?" Kaatje asked.

"I don't recall."

"Are you recently separated from your partner?" she asked, and Pieter wondered where she was going with this.

"I beg your pardon? What on earth do you mean?"

"It's just that I can see on your ring finger that you no longer wear your wedding ring, but I can still see the mark it left, the imprint on your skin."

Pieter's eyes dropped down – he hadn't noticed – then they shot back up.

"Which suggests that you have only recently stopped wearing it after many years."

Visser shook his head. He tried to look annoyed, but to Pieter his behaviour came across more like he was flustered.

"Or, young lady, it might be that I simply remove my wedding ring because of my profession. Look, I'm not sure I like the tone of your questions, and all these queries about Doctor Bakker's daughter."

"We're just doing our job," Pieter told him mildly. "Ruling out all possibilities."

Visser came to his feet. "Well, you can certainly cross that off your list, if you are implying what I think you are implying. I wish you good-day." With that he spun away and disappeared back through the doorway.

They watched him depart and Pieter sat back on the couch.

"Strange that," Kaatje commented.

"How?"

"The way he talked about Bakker and his wife in the past tense but kept referring to Nina in the present tense. As far as the public are concerned, all three perished in the fire. News of the kidnapping isn't due to be released until this afternoon."

"I noticed that too, but it could have just been a slip of the tongue. People sometimes do that soon after somebody has died. The thing that I'm finding annoying is the way everyone seems determined to set the narrative of just how wonderful a person Christiaan Bakker was. Stressing at every opportunity to tell us what an upstanding, perfect and all-round Mr Nice Guy he was. Like they are trying too hard."

Pieter pushed himself to his feet, and Kaatje joined him.

"Are we leaving?"

"No, not just yet."

He glanced over to where the receptionist was, catching her watching them before she quickly looked away again.

"I want you to go and have a chat with our friend over there. See if you can find out anything. She might be more inclined to open up to you, even if it's just a bit of office gossip."

"But what about you? What will you be doing?"

Pieter gave her a mischievous grin.

"I'm going for a poke around."

Sitting, waiting on the couch earlier, Pieter had noticed a second set of automatic glass doors leading off from the foyer, and while Kaatje was busy distracting the girl on reception, he strode towards them and they opened with a quiet *shssh* sound.

On the other side, he found himself in a wide corridor. Beneath where he was standing was a series of three different coloured lines painted onto the floor and leading away down the passage, a blue one, a yellow one, and in the middle, a red one. With no real plan in mind, he decided to follow them and see where they led.

He walked quietly along. The corridor was deserted, and there were no doors or openings along its length, and the only sounds were his light footsteps and the gentle background hum of machinery.

After a minute or so, it turned slightly to the left and now became a glass corridor as he passed briefly through an outside segment of the clinic. He could see the car park over to his left, while on the right was an inner courtyard with frosted-over grass and bushes and several empty benches. The corridor connected to a separate building block, and once back inside the first of the coloured lines, the yellow one, turned sharply to the right and disappeared beneath a closed door. Overhead was a sign: **CONSULTATION ROOM No 1**. Pieter stepped across and peered through the glass in the upper half of the door.

On the other side was a small room. He saw an L-shaped desk with computer monitors and a swivel chair, and a black examination couch, with what he presumed to be various eye-testing equipment, portable microscopes, diagnostic displays and halogen lamps clustered around it. There was nobody about, and he shrugged, seeing nothing out of the ordinary.

He carried on walking.

Further along, and the blue line branched away down a short side-passage, towards a set of wide swing doors. The sign above read: **THE JACQUES DAVIEL WING.** This would be the recovery ward, the plush overnight accommodation for the rich clientele, and so he turned away and went on.

Now there was just the single red line on the floor, straight as an arrow, and Pieter followed it deeper and deeper into the facility.

So far he had not passed a single person, and he was beginning to wonder where all of the staff and patients were.

Glancing at his watch he saw he'd been exploring for nearly ten minutes. Surely by now the receptionist would have noticed his absence and would be checking her monitors, but as this thought passed through his mind, he realized that he hadn't seen a single security camera anywhere, which was more than a little odd.

Thinking he was probably about to run out of luck, Pieter was on the verge of giving up and heading back – after all, what had he been expecting to find? – when suddenly the red line swung down a cross-hallway and came to a halt before another doorway.

On the wall above was written: **OPHTHALMIC THEATRE 1B + 2AB.**

To either side of the closed door was a pair of huge and burly security guards.

They both jerked in surprise at his sudden appearance, and then came instantly alert, scowling at him.

Pieter had to crane his neck back to see their faces way above him, so tall were they, and their heavy brows and hard faces were more than a little disconcerting.

One of the men, who had a heavy black beard and his hair in a ponytail, said with a strong East European accent: "This area is out of bounds, mister. Go away."

Recovering his equilibrium, Pieter fished inside his coat pocket and flashed his ID

"I'm a senior police officer investigating a serious crime. Can you let me pass please?"

"I don't give a fuck if you're Elvis Presley himself, now piss off."

Pieter wondered if he should just walk straight past them and push through the door, just to see what happened, but after a second appraisal of the two men, he wisely deduced that that wouldn't be the best course of action.

The second guard – this one sported a tiny tattoo of a black ace-of-spades on his neck – pointed to a sign beside the door, and Pieter saw a familiar symbol warning of radiation from x-rays.

"It is a restricted section of the clinic. It has to remain completely sterile." He looked Pieter up and down, and added: "No dirt allowed beyond this point."

In unison, they both took a single step forward, and Pieter backed up and raised his hands.

"Okay, I get the message."

"Do you need escorting back to reception?" asked the one with the ponytail.

"No, I'm a big boy, I think I can find my own way back, but thanks all the same."

Pieter took one more look at the door, curious about what was on the other side.

"Nice meeting you guys."

He turned about and headed back the way he had come, stepping around the corner.

Behind him, he heard someone say: *"Oink oink,"* followed by quiet laughter.

Back out in the car park, Kaatje asked: "What do you think it means Boss?"

When he'd made it back to the foyer area she had been waiting for him in the seating area, with a worried frown on her face. The receptionist looked at him with barely concealed contempt, all pretence of friendliness gone. Another security guard stood by the entrance doors in a not very subtle hint that it was time for them to leave; apparently, the other two goons had reported back about him skulking about and making a nuisance of himself.

Stepping outside, he briefly told her what he'd found as they walked back to their car and climbed in. He mentioned the two men guarding the entrance to the restricted part of the clinic, and the strange quiet, the lack of staff or patients anywhere.

"I'm not sure," he told her, "and it's probably nothing, but something just felt a bit off, you know? They certainly didn't want me seeing what was on the other side of that door."

"It seems like a lot of security for a private clinic. The kind of people who come here aren't like your typical patients, and they are definitely not like all the junkies who hang around normal hospitals."

"Well, we can run Visser through the system, see if anything pops up on him, we have nothing to lose. How did you get on?"

"Just a few tidbits really, nothing special from what I could tell. She couldn't stop gushing about Christiaan Bakker. How nice he was, very generous with his staff, more of the same as before, blah blah. I get the feeling that she had a bit of a crush on him, but probably not reciprocated from reading between the lines. Oh, she did tell me something about Nina. She recently became a member of that exclusive riding school on Vondelstraat, you know the one, where they have the indoor stables and they do fancy dressage? It might be worth following up. Especially if the Bakkers did have any financial issues, because that place must cost an arm and a leg."

Pieter nodded. It was worth a try.

"But then the receptionist broke off to take a call," Kaatje continued, "and after that she completely clammed up, didn't utter a word or even glance at me. I guessed you'd been causing trouble or something."

"Who me? Would never enter my head."

He took one final look at the buildings opposite. Something made a shiver pass down his spine and he didn't think it was just because of the frosty morning.

"Come on, let's head back. I have to update Huijbers before he makes his big announcement."

Chapter 9
Commissaris Dirk Huijbers

When they arrived back at Amsterdam Central Police Headquarters just after midday, preparations were already underway for the press conference. The media suite on the second floor was starting to fill up with reporters and TV camera operators, and at the far end of the room, a long table was set out from where Commissaris Huijbers, flanked by two senior police district commanders, would shortly deliver his briefing to the press. A buzz of anticipation hummed through the air as rumours were already swirling around concerning just what was going to be revealed. It was probably only a matter of time before the news of Nina Bakker's abduction broke, and Huijbers seemed jumpy and twitchy, no doubt concerned that someone might steal his thunder before he made the official announcement.

Climbing the stairs with Kaatje, Pieter caught sight of his superior standing in a side room, baseball hat on his head and talking animatedly with his media liaison officer. Hoping to sneak by without being spotted, Pieter slid quietly past the door. A loud shout however brought him up short.

Giving Kaatje a look, he popped his head around the doorframe.

Huijbers was scowling at him, and he made a show of looking at his watch.

"Get in here. And bring her with you."

He and Kaatje walked through the doorway and the liaison officer made a hasty departure, no doubt glad to have an excuse to leave.

"What the hell took you so long?" Huijbers demanded. "I told you to be back in plenty of time to update me."

"The traffic was a nightmare, you know what it's like."

"Well, it's too damn late now. I'm due to give my briefing in five minutes to the world's media, I can't just change my script at short notice." He waved a sheaf of papers in the air. "How the heck will it look if I'm behind the curve with the latest information on the case, and the media get wind of any breakthroughs before me?"

Pieter and Kaatje just shook their heads and acted dumb.

"Well, I'll tell you. It will make me look like an incompetent fool, someone who can't keep up with events. The job of a police commissaris is to portray an air of calmness and control, to allay people's fears, to make them feel safe in their beds at night. Instead, I could go out there and end up looking like a complete idiot." He pulled the baseball hat down tighter.

"Well there's nothing much to report, and if there were, I doubt the media will find out."

"Oh, you think so, do you? Let me tell you something Van Dijk. While you and your partner here have been driving around cosying up to each other-"

Kaatje opened her mouth to protest at this, but Huijbers held up one finger to still her words while he continued to tear into Pieter.

"-I received a telephone call from a very disgruntled citizen of our good city, complaining about your behaviour. A Mr Julian Visser, one of the eye specialists out at that new clinic. Have you heard of him? Well I can tell you, he was not very happy, he gave me a real earful telling me all about your little visit this morning. And about your spurious and possibly slanderous allegations concerning matters of a very private nature. Particularly your accusation that Mr Visser might have a predilection for little girls."

"That's ridiculous, I was only questioning him-"

"Shut up! What on earth possesses you to come out with something like that to a member of the public, who tells me he was just doing his level best to help us with our inquiries? He could file a complaint, or even litigate and sue for damages. You've blackened his name, he claims, and left him shaking and very emotional."

Pieter just about managed to roll his eyes before Huijbers continued.

"What if he went to the press? While I'm in the middle of the fucking press conference? What a bloody mess you've dropped into my lap, Van

Dijk. Mind you, I shouldn't be surprised, you made a total balls up in the spring, so I guess I should be used to it by now."

He threw up his arms in dismay, the full repertoire of his amateur dramatic skills coming to the fore.

"Ah! I don't have time for this! I'm meant to be out there announcing that we have a child abduction case on our hands instead of wasting my time with you. But don't you worry, you haven't heard the end of this. You can update me later, and in the meantime, I will try and calm Mr Visser down."

Huijbers finally turned his gaze onto Kaatje, and then looked back at Pieter.

"And pray do tell me, what is officer Groot doing with you? She's meant to be working with De Kok on the files section."

Pieter stared back. "I thought the experience might be good for her."

"She's a rookie! Rookie officers aren't meant to be working on high-profile cases. Her job is to be De Kok's assistant, not your little helper." He flashed a furious look at Kaatje. "You, get back to your job!"

With that he stormed out of the room and bulldozed his way through the swing doors to the media suite, saying in his good-natured voice: "Hello everybody, thank you for coming."

Back out on the stairs Pieter and Kaatje hesitated, feeling uncomfortable and awkward. After a moment he caught her gaze and was sure he saw a slight tear in her eye, but she quickly turned her face away.

"I'd best get back," she mumbled and scurried away down the steps.

"Kaatje," he called out, but she was already gone, and now he felt even worse.

Pieter went through the doors to the media suite and took a seat at the back, his mouth working silently and his hard flinty eyes glowering at Huijbers.

Standing on the pavement in the cold winter sunshine, Kaatje Groot shook away the hot tears, angry with herself, annoyed at Pieter for not saying more in her defence, but mostly furious with that cretin Commissaris Huijbers.

She set off walking fast, hoping the brisk pace would shake off her temper.

Ten minutes later found her at Café Zoku on the corner of Marnixstraat and Lauriergracht Canal. This was her favourite lunchtime spot, overlooking the iced-over water and the arched bridges and tree-lined canal, their branches all frosty and white and skeletal. It was a quiet and peaceful corner of the busy city, and just far enough away from HQ to discourage any of her work colleagues from walking here on their break: they mostly preferred the burger place or the Brown Café pub just opposite.

Going up to the second floor she found a window seat and ordered a latte and a panini. The TV above the counter was tuned to one of the 24hr news channels, which was currently showing the live police press conference. A couple of patrons and the waitress were watching, but Kaatje turned away, not interested in what Huijbers had to say.

For thirty minutes she sat and ate lunch, warming her cold fingers on the hot cup, and planning her next move.

If Huijbers thought he could intimidate her into dropping this, then he was wrong. This was her big chance to impress, and maybe gain a permanent position in the homicide division. Besides, she quite liked Pieter Van Dijk.

Tobias had spent the morning buying Christmas presents.

In the Netherlands the traditional time when Sinterklass – St Nicolas – left presents for the children was on December 5th, but of course Nina hadn't come to live with him until after then. Nevertheless, he was determined that this year would be the best ever Christmas for them both, the first time they had spent it together, and so he had wandered the stores around Dam Square looking for gifts.

The huge tree at the centre of Dam looked especially beautiful this year, he thought, and he wondered about bringing Nina along one evening to see it. The idea lifted his spirits after his earlier tears. Yes, perhaps he would risk it. They could even go to Tinkerbell's toy store, she would like it there.

He decided to wander over to the flower market, which at this time of the year was transformed into a long, sprawling Christmas Market along the frozen canals. He strolled around the stalls, mingling with the crowds, looking just like any other shopper enjoying the festive season. He bought some Appelbeignets – some sweet apple fritters – as well as a tin barrel of Kerstikransjes biscuits to hang on the tree. This reminded him that he needed to pop over to the nurseries in Westerpark to buy a real fir tree. In fact yes, they could choose one together, and then take it home and spend one evening decorating it.

For the first time in a long time, Tobias smiled, feeling a warm glow pass through his heart and putting a spring in his step.

He doubled back down the wide thoroughfare of Rokin, making for Scheltema book shop, and as he rode up in the glass elevator to the children's section, he felt his mobile vibrate in his coat pocket. He looked at the caller ID as he stepped out, and Tobias felt his world shift again.

The darkness came back, all the joys and fun of Christmas were shoved violently to one side in an instant, and his hand shook in sudden debilitating fear.

Finding a quiet corner amidst the bookshelves, he brought the phone to his ear and quietly said "Hello."

The female voice at the other end simply replied: "Have you been following the news?"

"No," he croaked, his voice suddenly dry. "Why?"

"The police have just announced that the girl is missing, presumed abducted."

There was a long pause while the news sank in. Somewhere close by, a pair of footsteps went past, and Tobias waited until whoever it was had strolled away. "Right," was all he could think of to say.

"Which was only a matter of time. So nothing changes," the woman told him in a calm and smooth voice. "But their investigation will be stepped up. Is the girl somewhere safe?"

"Yes, I told you where I was keeping her. Everything is secure."

"Good. Where are you now?"

"I'm at work," he lied, and then added quickly: "But there's nothing to worry about. There's absolutely no way she can get out. And even if she did, where could she go?"

Again there was another long pause, and Tobias felt a trickle of sweat go down the back of his neck beneath his scarf.

"Don't get too friendly with her, you hear? When the time comes I will be in touch again, and you know what you have to do."

"I... uh..." Tobias stammered, "I'm not sure... if I can... do-"

"Tobias, we've discussed this before. Everything has been arranged. You agreed to this, so don't let me down."

"It's just that, well you know... Nina-"

"Who?"

"Sorry, I mean the girl... well, she's actually quite-"

"Listen to me carefully Tobias," the voice cut in, "because I am only going to tell you this once. Our mutual acquaintance Mr Roost, you remember him don't you? Yes, of course you do, you're hardly likely to forget your meeting with him, are you? Well, Mr Roost here, he is getting quite anxious to move forward with this, but he is worried about your commitment to the plan. Do I need to send him over, to pay you another visit? To remind you of your responsibilities? Tobias, do I need to do that?"

"No, no... absolutely no. I'm sorry. Everything is fine now," he promised, his insides feeling like they had turned to liquid.

"Very good. You just wait for my call, and when it comes you do what needs to be done."

Then the line went dead.

Tobias grabbed hold of the bookshelf to stop himself from collapsing to the floor.

Lotte ended the call and stood staring out of the window, at the frosted grass of the old courtyard, and the statue of The Virgin Mary, and the 15th Century wooden house just opposite her new apartment, and she sighed in annoyance.

Sitting at the table behind her, her Uncle Johan asked: "Problems?"

Turning away from the window, she looked across the room at him.

"Possibly; now we'll need to keep a watch on him as well."

Chapter 10
Man in a Van

After making the shock announcement and revealing to the waiting press that Nina Bakker, (daughter to an eminent eye surgeon and his glamourous wife, who he confirmed were both dead, found murdered in the burnt-out remains of their luxury home) was missing and the police were now treating this as a kidnapping case, Commissaris Huijbers conducted a question and answer session. Pieter stayed for the first few questions, which were fairly standard fare from the reporters, and then quietly slipped away.

He was still fuming from the earlier confrontation, and the dressing down that Huijbers had delivered. Pieter was fully aware that the Police Chief was simply using this as an opportunity to push his own agenda, to try and undermine and antagonize him publicly because of the recent history between the two of them. It was pathetic office politics from Huijbers, nothing more than silly point-scoring, and Pieter was determined not to rise to it or react. It was just unfortunate that Kaatje had found herself caught in the crossfire, and now she had disappeared, and Pieter felt dejected as he went up to the top floor and closed his office door behind him.

Booting up his computer, he checked his email messages and saw that he had one marked priority. The sender was the National Centrum Surveillance Command building next to the shopping complex at Bos en Lommerplein, the newly built nerve-centre where security camera footage for the whole of the Netherlands was gathered and analysed. Unlike some European countries such as the United Kingdom, Holland, and especially Amsterdam itself, had relatively few police surveillance cameras. In the city there were just over 200, a ridiculously small number for a place regarded as the murder capital of Europe. To counteract this deficiency, a law was passed back in 2014 that enabled the Amsterdam police to access the thousands of private security cameras throughout the city. Anybody who fitted cameras of their own, whether it was in a shop, a bar or restaurant, a museum or outside their own home (but not inside private residences: they were thankfully still off-limits), at a cashpoint, in a privately-run car park, or anywhere else, they then had to register them in the central database at NCSC. The police could at any point log into their live feeds, or see recorded footage, without having to ask for prior permission or to get a warrant. At the flick of a couple of switches they could tune in to any security camera anywhere in Amsterdam and the rest of The Netherlands to see what they revealed.

The email waiting in his inbox contained a short AVCHD encrypted video file from NCSC labelled **VONDELSTRAAT – 7:08PM** and dated the night of the abduction. The recording lasted approximately two minutes. There was an additional note informing him that the footage was from a street surveillance camera, but the small camera fixed to the Bakkers' gatepost had not been working at the time. Which was a damn shame, thought Pieter! The email also stated that after a thorough trawl, this was the *only* footage of a possible suspect to the abduction yet discovered.

Pieter clicked on the file and eagerly waited for it to download. It was better than nothing, he supposed.

It turned out to be disappointing.

Leaning close to the computer monitor, the first thing Pieter noticed was just how dense the fog had been that night. The whole of the frame was filled with thick, swirling clouds, with just a faint glow from a couple of street lamps showing through the impenetrable grey mass. Then he saw a twin set of faint headlights come into view, moving through the fog like a pair of sickly yellow eyes, and a darkish vehicle – a van, he thought – glided slowly past. He watched as the headlights halted for a few seconds, before turning left. Now he was looking at red tail-lights and nothing else, for the fog was just too dense. Another few seconds ticked by, and as he watched Pieter worked out what he was seeing. The van, and he was certain it would have been a van, was in the Bakkers' driveway in front of the huge gates, presumably waiting for them to open. Yes, now the tail-lights were moving forward once more and were quickly swallowed up by the swirling grey clouds.

There was a brief fuzz of interference on the screen and the logged time jumped forward to 7:18PM and the footage resumed, this time showing the yellow headlights reappear and the vehicle turning back onto Vondelstraat and disappear in the opposite direction, away from the camera. A few seconds later and an orange glow flickered into view from just off frame and grew brighter by the second - the fire.

The video file came to a stop, and Pieter sat back in his chair, pondering things over.

On his desk were the print-outs of the two emergency calls from the night of the abduction. Reaching across for them, Pieter again noted the times, seeing that everything matched up. The van on the security camera appeared four minutes before Nina's 112 call timed at 7:12PM and then left the Bakkers' house barely two minutes before the police patrol car arrived at 7:20PM - two minutes. They had missed the abductor by barely two minutes. Even more disheartening: the police patrol car had entered Vondelstraat from the opposite end from which the van driver, with Nina probably bound and gagged in the back of his van, had left the scene. Thus the two vehicles had not passed one another, and the van would not have been caught on the police car's dashcam.

Pieter rubbed at his temples and got to his feet. In the corner, the coloured lights on the small Christmas tree were still flickering intermittently, so he strolled over and started tightening the tiny bulbs one by one, checking for a loose connection. As he worked his mind mulled over what the footage meant.

It didn't show much, but it was nonetheless quite revealing.

What it suggested was that whoever the man in the van was, he must know the Bakkers, confirming his earlier theory. The van had temporarily halted before the entrance gates, as though waiting for someone to open them. There was an intercom system on the gatepost, so the obvious scenario was that the driver had buzzed through to announce his arrival, and on confirming his identity, somebody inside had opened the electronic gates for him. Either that or the driver was pretending to be somebody else as a ruse to gain entry.

It was just a damn shame that the camera footage showed nothing they could follow up on. No images of the driver and no clear shots of a number plate meant they were at a dead end with this thread.

Unless?

Pieter stopped what he was doing.

On the night of the fire, before he even knew they were dealing with a double murder and an abduction, Pieter had waited in his car while the firefighters doused the flames. He'd parked alongside the nursing home at that end of the street, and he remembered seeing the elderly residents eagerly watching the drama unfold through the windows.

It was a long shot. Because of the impenetrable fog they would probably not have seen anything of note, just like the camera hadn't.

But it was worth a try.

Ernie Clegg was an ex-British paratrooper now confined to a wheelchair, not as a result of too many jumps, but because of an age-related deterioration in his pelvic bone. He looked resplendent in his dark blue blazer and his beret, his chest puffed up to show off his line of military decorations. He was waiting on the top landing of the nursing home on Anna Van Den, in his usual spot by the huge corner window. The carers told Pieter that he sat here most days and nights, watching the world go by, enjoying the view across Vondel Park and along the quiet suburban street.

When Pieter found him, he had a pair of binoculars pressed to his eyes.

"They have parakeets you know, in the park - in Amsterdam? Wouldn't believe it if I hadn't seen them myself, but there they are, near the statue. You see?"

He handed them over, and Pieter took a look, but it was coming up to four o'clock in the afternoon in mid-December and he couldn't see anything in the gloom. "Oh yeah," he told Ernie, "sheesh." He handed them back.

He pulled up a chair and made himself comfy.

"You the copper? They told me you were coming. Can I see your credentials? I'm saying nothing until I see some proof, Mister. For all I know you might be here to steal all my dead wife's jewellery." He turned to look at Pieter. Ernie had a big, bulbous, purple nose, with a hair growing out of the end, and sparkly blue eyes that still, even after all these years, had the thousand-yard-stare.

Pieter dipped his hand into his coat pocket, but paused when Ernie snickered.

"I'm pulling your leg, you daft bugger."

He twiddled with the joystick on the armrest, and his electric wheelchair pirouetted on the spot to turn and face his visitor.

"What can I do you for then? I presume it's about the fire the other night?"

Pieter looked through the window. From here they had a good view along Vondelstraat, towards the burnt-out shell of the large house, which was surrounded by blue police tape. Down below was the spot on the side street where he'd parked his car on the night of the fire, and where his car was now.

"You like to sit here a lot, I understand?"

"Aye lad, nothing much else to do in this place. All the others are down in the common room right now, sitting in a circle and passing around a big rubber ball. What the hell for I don't know. And later we have some young kid coming along, to plonk away on her tiny keyboard and sing us songs. She's as flat as a fart, I tell you. If I hear Roll Me Over In The Clover one more time, then I think I'll take a swan dive through that window like Professor Hawkins. It's all the old biddies sing here in Holland."

"So I presume you had a good view of everything then? Of the fire?"

"Yes, apart from the bloody fog, which spoilt things. But once it flared up good and proper, the flames got rid of that. I could feel the heat right through the glass. And before you ask, no I didn't start it to relieve the boredom, I have witnesses to back me up. I was in bed at the time. Not my bed," he added with a wink.

Pieter indulged him with a nod of understanding, one man to another.

"On the night itself Ernie, did you see anything suspicious? Or anybody acting weird?"

"Well, when the fire started, as I say, I was otherwise engaged. But someone else started hollering at the top of their voice, causing a right ruckus. They were speaking the lingo, which I don't understand too much I'm afraid, but thankfully everybody speaks perfect English and when I heard the word 'fire', well I tell you I've never moved so fast for decades. I thought this place was on fire, and I came down this corridor," he indicated the passage behind them, "well I moved so fast they might want to sign me up for the next Paralympics! It was only when I reached the window here that I realized the fire was down there." He nodded at the blackened shell across the road. "It was a grand sight I tell you. But as to your question – did I see anything or anyone acting suspiciously? I'm afraid not. The fire engines were just arriving, and with the fog and the flames and the smoke it was hard to make much out."

Pieter felt the frustration make his body sag. It had been worth a try all right, but to no avail.

"However," Ernie went on, "there was something, a couple of nights earlier."

Pieter's head swivelled around.

"There was a man, in a van. Cruising around for hours. Up and down the street and slowing down every time he went past the house there, the one where the murders happened. He would come right along here and turn along this side street, do a three-point-turn, and go back. Then, five minutes later he would be back, doing the same thing, over and over, for a good few hours."

"Did you get a look at him? What time would it have been?"

"Oh, very late. Past seven o'clock."

"So it would have been too dark to see him clearly?"

"True. If he'd stayed inside his van, that is, but he didn't. He got out at one point. Parked up exactly where you have down there – that's a nice motor by the way, Mister – and walked along the street. Went right along the pavement on one side, crossed over, and then came back along the pavement on the opposite side. All the time looking over at the house there. Thinking about it now, it gives me the wobblies, knowing what he had planned." He shivered extravagantly. "If it were your man, of course."

"And what did he look like?" He tried to keep his voice calm, but inside he felt his excitement levels rising.

"Ah well, he was shortish. Stocky, like he worked out or something, or maybe had a manual job. He had arms like Popeye."

"And his face?"

Ernie sucked in between his teeth and grimaced, then shook his head, the beret going all lopsided.

"Well that's the problem. He had a hat on. One of those baseball caps. It was pulled down tight, and he had his collar turned up, so I couldn't really make out his features, but he was wearing overalls, brownish ones, and he had huge working boots on. I could hear his footsteps quite clearly from up here."

"Was this just the one night or have you seen him around here on other occasions? Was he a local resident?"

"I only clapped eyes on him that one time, and I'm sure he doesn't live around here. This is quite an exclusive street, with well-off people walking their Shih Tzus or hosting dinner parties. That's why he stood out so much, because of what he was wearing."

Behind them, an elderly lady came up the stairs and walked by, and Pieter caught the look that passed between her and Ernie. He watched as she went down the passage and disappeared into one of the bedrooms. A moment later and she popped her head around the doorframe, looking their way.

Ernie shuffled about in his wheelchair. "Sorry I can't be of much help. Now I have to dash, I have a date."

Pieter felt his eyebrows shoot up.

Ernie had a big grin on his face. "I just tell them that I fought at Arnhem in 1944," he laughed and swivelled his wheelchair about.

"Really?" Pieter said, doing the maths in his head.

"Yes, it works every time!"

And with that, he whizzed off down the hallway towards the open door.

While they had been chatting, the Chief Pathologist Prisha Kapoor had sent him a text message. The initial results from the toxicology tests had come in, and of the findings from the lab, one in particular had caught her eye.

Both bodies of the deceased couple contained a foreign substance in their bloodstreams. They had both been injected with the strong sedative Midazolam, an anaesthetic only available in hospitals or private medical facilities, and under strict licence. Certainly not something that you could purchase from your local pharmacy.

With Dr Bakker's profession, it was feasible that he may have stored some at home, for whatever purpose, but would he have had cause to inject both himself and his wife with it?

A State of Sin

Pieter couldn't think of a plausible reason.

Chapter 11
Journeys Through the Night

When Tobias left the bookshop he could hardly think straight, and although he tried walking along Damrak as casually as possible, it felt like his head was all wobbly and lopsided, and the world appeared all askew.

The streets and people and traffic all around seemed different somehow, like he had suddenly awoken in a strange city inhabited by peculiar and unfamiliar beings. He felt lost and completely alone, a sensation that he recognized from his adolescence: as a young teenager, Tobias had developed a whole range of complexes, some of them so debilitating that even after years of counselling they still affected him now in his middle-age. Predominant amongst these was the crippling self-consciousness that had made having a normal day-to-day existence impossible, the feeling that whenever he left the house, everybody was watching him. On the bus or tram, at school and later at work, in the supermarket, or even when having a stroll along a quiet beach or through the park, he was convinced he was under constant scrutiny and observation. Thousands of pairs of eyes following his every move, every step of his leg or swing of his arm, people laughing and sniggering behind his back.

One of the results of this was the conviction that he was somehow different. Perhaps he was a robot made to look like a human? Or a guinea pig in some huge global experiment? Or perhaps he was dead, a ghost moving amidst the living.

As he had grown older these issues had lessened and faded. He learnt certain techniques to make them go away, or to push them to a part of his mind where they could be forgotten, some dusty shelf hidden away deep inside his psyche.

Yet every once in a while, when he was under extreme stress, these problems would return with a vengeance. They would come down on him like a dead-weight, making him sag both mentally and physically, and all of the bad thoughts would return with them. Thoughts of hatred. The blackness.

Moving along the street, with the hustling and bustling crowds bumping their way by him, and the cyclists and traffic criss-crossing his path, Tobias kept his eyes straight ahead, trying to ignore the grey and unfamiliar faces staring at him, the pointing fingers and the laughing teenagers calling out in derision. Walking as quickly as he could, he made his way towards Centraal Station, and, fighting his way against the tide of commuters exiting the train station, he cut left across Stationsplein and ducked into the underpass.

The tunnel below the busy station concourse was quieter with just a few homeless guys sitting in their sleeping bags, and Tobias felt his heart rate gradually begin to return to normal as he hurried along. Moving back into the open air, he went past the back entrance to the station and headed towards the free ferries that took foot passengers across the River IJ.

It was after 6pm by now, and fully dark. One of the small, blue boats was just arriving on the shore on this side, and he and a few other commuters waited while the ramp lowered to the quayside, and then he dashed forward to the front of the ferry and found a spot beside the gunwale, grabbing a hold of the handrail and sagging against the side, his eyes brimming with tears of fear and anger.

The journey over the river to North Amsterdam only took five minutes. A cold wind blew hard into his face, making his teeth throb and his cheeks go numb. As he stood there watching the lights of the city centre fade into the night Tobias finally felt himself relax and get himself back under control.

The phone call from Lotte had shaken him, not just the implied threat but the mere sound of her voice, and also the realization of just how deeply involved in her scheme he was. No matter how he felt about taking Nina, it really was too late to back out now. And this in turn filled him with dread at what was to come.

The bitch! She had taken advantage of his messed-up life, she had manipulated him and promised him all kinds of things, used him. And once he was hooked and passed the point of no return, there was no way out for him.

Tobias angrily wiped away the tears that rolled down his frozen face, and the blackness at the centre of his heart suddenly blossomed like a dead flower unfurling. It coursed through his veins, and he grimaced, and his head buzzed painfully.

By the time the ferry reached the far shore a lethal quiet had descended on him like a death shroud.

To avoid the traffic snarl-ups in the city centre Tobias had parked his black van in the large car park next to the old Tolhuis building in Amsterdam Noord, close to the river. He was soon driving through the suburban sprawl of this part of the city, and within ten minutes he was crossing the ring road. Here Amsterdam came to a sudden halt and beyond the countryside stretched away into the night, flat and featureless and devoid of all character, bisected by numerous ditches and watercourses.

There was very little traffic out here. The strong and freezing wind which whipped unobstructed across the fields, together with the emptiness between villages, deterred anybody from making anything but essential journeys, especially in the middle of winter. Very soon, Tobias found himself completely alone, the van's headlights cutting twin white beams through the cloudless night.

Just after seven o'clock he passed through the small community of Ransdorp, and beyond this the terrain became even more barren. If he continued heading north through Holysloot he would be able to pick up the N247 through Edam, and then make quicker progress home. However, he did not intend to head straight back home. The buzzing in his head had gradually worsened and was now more like a high-pitched whine that made his brain pulse just behind his eyes, and a cold fury squeezed his chest tight, and he knew he could not return to Nina like this, all pent-up and shaking. The sight of his pale face and bloodshot eyes would terrify the young girl. There was only one thing that would soothe the dark thoughts in his head. So he drove slowly along the unlit country roads, the tyres of the van gliding along the icy surface, his eyes roving back and forth. Looking and searching.

He spotted the lone cyclist just up ahead. Just what the heck he was doing all the way out here in the middle of nowhere, all by himself, pedalling sedately along without a care in the world, Tobias did not know. Perhaps he was on his way home to some shack in the countryside, having had a few drinks somewhere. He certainly seemed a bit wobbly, but that could just as easily been the strong wind buffeting him. Whatever the reason, Tobias didn't really care. All he was bothered about was that here was a perfect opportunity presented to him.

Pulling out into the middle of the road, he drove carefully by the cyclist, whose scarf trailed along behind him. Driving on, Tobias glanced in his rearview, seeing the man give him a friendly wave. Tobias laughed quietly to himself.

A little further ahead the road widened to allow oncoming traffic to squeeze past each other, and Tobias steered into the side and then swung the van around in a tight turn until he was facing back the way he had just come. A few hundred yards ahead, the guy on the bike came pedalling along, as merry as can be.

Tobias waited for a few seconds. In his mind, he could already see the outcome of what he was about to do, and everything he saw was painted and splashed with the colour red.

Taking a deep breath, he gently pressed his foot down on the accelerator pedal and the van slowly moved forward, and then he gunned the engine and stamped down harder, and as the van roared and raced straight towards the cyclist, Tobias was hunched over the steering wheel, and his mind screamed in triumph.

* * *

Sitting in Lotte's cosy little study overlooking the old courtyard, Johan Roost read the text message sent by the Chief Pathologist to the cop.

After spending several hours the previous night outside Van Dijk's house, shivering from the cold, he had decided instead to leave the hire car parked across the road from the narrow canal house with the IMSI – catcher running, while he listened in to any phone calls or intercepted any text messages from the comfort and warmth of Lotte's apartment.

He read the message again. There was nothing alarming about it. The cops had pretty much worked out exactly how the abduction had taken place, but this knowledge should not provide them with any significant leads. And even if they worked out where Tobias had obtained the sedative from, it would not reveal Nina's whereabouts.

Happy that all was in order for now, Johan leaned back in his chair and twisted his head from side to side to ease the ache in his neck muscles. Getting to his feet he wandered over to the small window, taking his steaming mug of coffee with him, and standing there and sipping the drink, he looked through the window pane at the frosty scene outside.

Lotte was sitting on the low wall that ran around the edge of the lawn, the statue of the Virgin Mary behind her seeming to glow in the moonlight.

She'd been there for nearly one hour now. Perfectly still, having not moved one inch, seemingly unaffected by the cold. Just sitting and staring straight ahead, with her eyes rolled up into the back of her head so that they looked like white marble. Twin spots of pale luminescence.

Johan shook his head. Christ, what was she doing?

Best if he didn't know.

Whatever she was up to, it gave him the creeps.

Lotte was immersed in a deep and meditative trance.

It was a form of self-hypnosis, a technique that she had learnt from a fellow practitioner of the dark arts in Paris several years ago, and which she had since refined and perfected through controlled breathing and mental visualization skills. But even though she had done this many times before, inducing a trance state still did not come easy, and it always carried inherent risks.

Slowing her heart rate was the first stage. This in turn dulled her five basic senses: touch, sight, hearing, smell and taste, so that all outside influences and distractions faded into the background, a little like turning down the volume on a radio. This left a vacuum in her mind. In this inner space she started to mentally construct her secondary body, her Body Of Light she called it.

Once she pictured her secondary body, which hovered just outside her physical form like a pale aura, she next transferred her consciousness across. Through a simple act of will she was able to visualize the detachment of her psyche from her person, and, with a slight vibration that passed through her bones like a tiny electric current, Lotte's astral form slipped free.

Rising up from her discarded physical body, which remained seated on the wall, still alive but temporarily surplus to requirements, Lotte soared up and out of the old courtyard, higher than the surrounding rooftops, and headed out over the city.

Below her lay the streets and buildings and canals and traffic and people of Amsterdam, spread out like a map. The experience of travelling on the astral plane always thrilled her, and she revelled in the sensation of moving free from her body, to soar high or to swoop low above the rooftops, to move wherever she desired, unseen, unheard. Feeling euphoric, she moved over the city, aiming northwards over the river and within moments she was flying over the outer suburbs, and then the open countryside.

Earlier she had felt something was wrong. An alarm bell had been triggered in her sub-consciousness, something concerning Tobias, and although she could not fully understand what the nature of the problem was, she felt it was necessary to travel quickly to the source and see for herself. Thus she found herself drawn along like this, seeking him out like a bloodhound drawn towards the scent of blood.

There was no sense of time when travelling in astral form. She may have soared through the night for several hours, or for no longer than a few minutes. Additionally, the cold did not affect her: she could feel neither the temperature nor the strong wind blowing across the flat landscape. As for her physical body back in the courtyard: she could maintain her trance state for several hours, and her slow heartbeat would protect her from becoming hypothermic.

Below her a long and straight road stretched across the bleak countryside, visible as a pale grey strip to her hyper-sensitive vision. Further ahead she caught sight of a vehicle's headlights and she swooped lower, and knew she was in the right place. Yes, now she could see Tobias, hunched over and pulling something along the roadway. Hovering above him silently, she watched.

He was dragging a body towards the grass verge, huffing and gasping with the effort and looking nervously around to make sure the way was clear, completely oblivious to the invisible observer floating overhead.

Lotte saw him roll the corpse into a waterlogged ditch at the roadside – she had no idea of the circumstances as to why he happened to be doing this, and she watched curiously and unalarmed. There was a quiet splash as the corpse disappeared below the surface of the water.

A few moments later and he threw in a crushed and misshapen bicycle, which also sank out of sight. With any luck the water in the ditch should freeze over overnight, sealing the corpse in and hiding all evidence, hopefully for a number of days. Which would be long enough. At least he was staying calm and not panicking, Lotte thought to herself. Then Tobias was straightening and wiping his hands on his trousers and getting into his van.

Minutes later, having turned around, he drove quietly away into the night.

Lotte snapped back into full consciousness, finding herself safely back in her physical form at the old courtyard.

She went inside to see how her Uncle Johan was getting along.

Chapter 12
Kaatje

Madame Benoit was the Centre Manager at Hollandsche Manege, the prestigious riding school on Vondelstraat. She was short and very gaunt, and Kaatje guessed she was in her mid-fifties. She sported a colourful scarf around her neck to hide the first signs of aging, and she walked with a prominent limp and used a cane walking stick, perhaps as a result of some injury that had cut short her horse-riding dreams. They stood side by side on a balcony on the second floor overlooking the large riding hall below, where several horses and their riders, led by instructors, were trotting in slow, lazy circles. Behind them was a fancy tearoom. At 10am it was already getting busy, and soft chatter drifted through the open door.

It was a Saturday and was Kaatje's day off. Still frustrated at yesterday's unnecessary censure from Huijbers, she had resolved to do a little bit of her own private snooping regarding the Nina case, but only when off-duty to keep things low-key. Not that Madame Benoit needed to know that she was off-duty.

During their visit to the eye clinic yesterday, while Pieter had been poking about and causing trouble she had chatted with the receptionist. From their brief discussion Kaatje had learnt about Nina Bakker's recent enrolment at Hollandche Manege, and so had decided this was as good a place as any to start with her little clandestine investigation.

Driving over from home, she had turned off Vondelstraat and down the short side street to the large and ornate entrance to the riding school.

Climbing out, Kaatje could see the large spire of the church just around the corner: The Bakker's house was a handy five-minute walk from here.

Parking up, she had walked through the arched entrance and along the red carpeted passage leading to the main riding hall, the strong smell of manure making her nose tickle. Catching a member of staff and flashing her police badge, she'd asked to see whoever was in charge, and five minutes later was escorted up a wrought-iron spiral staircase to the balcony, feeling like a member of the common rabble allowed an audience with royalty.

They talked in English, as Kaatje's little bit of French was too rusty and Madame Benoit had shamefully not learnt to speak Dutch despite having lived in Amsterdam for twelve years.

"Ah yes, Miss Bakker, our sweet little Nina," she was now saying. "What a lovely girl. Yes, I knew her, and her parents." She pouted and gave a little shake of her head, her thoughts staying private.

"So she was a member of the equestrian school then?"

"Oh yes, but only at an intermediary level. She enrolled about a year ago now."

"How often did she attend?"

"Two or three evenings a week initially, less so during the colder weather. We take the horses across into the park, and the younger riders aren't so enthusiastic when the conditions outside are inclement."

"What was she like?"

"Nina? She showed a lot of promise as a rider, she had a lot of natural ability. And she was always very polite. But very shy, unusually so for a twelve year old. Some of our girls can be very precocious and bossy, and they like to gossip, especially about each other. But Nina tended to keep to herself most of the time. I think she felt a little overwhelmed at times. And of course the other girls noticed this, the way girls do."

Kaatje nodded. "Was she picked on at all? By the others?"

"Oh no, nothing like that. I would not allow any bullying whatsoever. No, they just mostly left her alone. Although she did befriend one of our girls."

Madame Benoit broke off for a moment and went over to the balcony's stone balustrade.

"Tenez votre dos bien droit!" she shouted down into the hall, banging her walking stick hard onto the floor. Tutting to herself, she came back over.

"Who?" Kaatje asked.

"Sorry?"

"Who did Nina make friends with?"

"Oh yes. It was one of our stable hands, a young lady called Elena."

"Were they very close?"

"Yes, quite so. Elena was two or three years older than Nina, which I think was part of the attraction. Elena was very sophisticated, you know, quite mature in her outlook, and Nina seemed drawn to that. Perhaps she liked having an older friend."

In the tearoom, some kind of gathering was taking place, a party by the sounds of it, and there was a burst of loud laughter and applause.

"Could I speak to her, this girl Elena? It would only be an informal chat, nothing more, with her being a minor?"

Madame Benoit's eyebrows drew together in a pained expression. "I only wish that was possible. But after what happened last year, the whole tragedy, oh dear…"

Again she broke away. "Trop vite, contrôle le cheval!" She threw up her hand in despair.

"Tragedy?" Kaatje prompted.

"Yes, the accident. In the stables. One of our horses, a temperamental young thing, it kicked out at Elena while she was cleaning the hay. Its hoof caught her right in the eye." She winced at the memory, and shook her head.

"Was she hurt badly?"

"Not really, but it damaged her eye. A detached retina, or something, I'm not too sure what exactly. But it required surgery. Her father, he was not a wealthy man but he must have provided his family with very good health insurance, something to do with his job I think. Anyway, it was enough to pay for her treatment. But something went wrong during the operation, some silly medical negligence that could have been avoided."

"What happened exactly?" Kaatje could feel a small flutter in her stomach.

"Well, she lost the sight in her eye, the injured one, and the vision in the other eye was severely impaired. How that happened I do not know, as they did not even operate on that one, just the one where the horse kicked her. It should have been a routine operation, but apparently something unforeseen occurred. It was so sad. And afterwards she just changed completely. She could no longer work here of course, and I do not know all of the details, but rumours spread quickly here and it seems that she was so, so deeply affected that she suffered badly from depression. Her whole future, all of her plans, everything changed. And she struggled to cope. Then, shortly afterwards..."

Kaatje felt a lump form in her throat.

"Shortly afterwards, Elena took her own life."

Madame Benoit hobbled over to the balustrade and leaned back against the stonework, gazing at Kaatje intently.

"A tragedy," she repeated in a sad little whisper. "It caused a lot of upset with the staff and the pupils naturally, but especially with Nina Bakker. She had lost her best friend, her only friend here. Plus she felt guilty of course." Madame Benoit shrugged her narrow, bony shoulders.

Kaatje shook her head, a little confused.

"Guilty? How so?"

"For two reasons. Firstly she had been riding the horse just before the accident. It was a feisty young thing as I told you. Strong-willed. Too much for Nina to handle, with her inexperience at the time, but her parents insisted that she continue riding her."

"You said she felt guilty for two reasons. What was the second one?"

"Her father, Christiaan Bakker, he was the surgeon who carried out the operation. At the new eye clinic he runs out in Osdorp."

Johan Roost watched through the windscreen of his car as the young policewoman came striding out through the arched entrance to the riding school. He'd hired a second vehicle as the first car was still parked up outside Van Dijk's house, scanning for mobile intercepts, and he followed her from her home this morning, curious as to what she was playing at: a young rookie officer conducting important police investigation work on a major case, alone and when off-duty.

Johan tutted to himself and shook his head in admonishment. Silly young thing, he thought, a small smile playing across his lips.

When she pulled away from her parking spot Johan followed her through the busy weekend traffic.

Kaatje arrived back at the Vrije Geer Eye Clinic in Osdorp a little before midday, and after smoking a quick cigarette in the car park, she soon found herself in the reception area, talking to Julian Visser once more.

"Look, I have nothing more to say to you, ok?" he said harshly, yesterday's polite charm completely gone now, replaced by undisguised anger. "Your visit yesterday caused me a lot of upset, the nature of the questions you and your colleague were asking were, quite frankly, vile to say the least."

He looked over her shoulder towards the sliding doors behind her.

"Where is Inspector Van Dijk anyway?"

"He's busy. He sent me to continue with our inquiries."

"Really?" Visser said haughtily. "Because when I spoke to your superior yesterday by telephone, he assured me that this line of inquiry was most definitely at an end. He was very apologetic. Yet here you are again, asking me more questions of a personal nature. It vexes me."

"All I asked was if you could give me details of the operation carried out on Elena at this clinic. What the procedure was exactly, and what went wrong?"

"And as I told you a moment ago, I cannot answer your question. For two reasons. Firstly because of patient confidentiality, and secondly because I wasn't present at the time. Doctor Bakker carried out the surgery."

"But you could check the files. Give me a broad outline. Or if you are busy, perhaps your lovely receptionist could do it?"

Kaatje glanced over to the girl sitting behind the counter in the foyer, who glared back at her.

"Only if you have a court order requesting the release of the paperwork."

"You told us yesterday that the Director of the clinic was due back from her conference today. Could I see her?"

"Not unless you have an appointment. She is very busy. Now could you kindly leave?" He indicated the exit. "Or do I have to call security?"

Kaatje looked at him hard, and gave a slow, lazy blink. "No, that won't be necessary."

She turned to go, and then with an afterthought turned back.

"Could I use your toilets, please? It's a long drive back through the traffic."

Sighing dramatically, Visser pointed his finger towards a door near the seating area marked **Ladies** and then stomped off. Returning the receptionist's glacial smile, Kaatje pushed through the doorway.

The toilets were spotlessly clean and very modern, and there was piped music coming from somewhere. Kaatje quickly checked that all of the stalls were unoccupied, and then slipped inside one of the cubicles and shut the door. Closing the toilet lid she sat down and took out her mobile, and for about thirty seconds considered whether to call Pieter and tell him where she was.

After pondering the pros and cons, she shook her head. She wasn't sure how Pieter would react – he might go ballistic – and anyway, if anything came of today's endeavour, a small part of her was hoping he'd be suitably impressed at her initiative.

Before she could change her mind Kaatje exited the cubicle and went over to the row of sinks. Quickly grabbing a handful of paper towels from the dispenser on the wall, she scrunched them up into a tight bundle and put them into the sink, and then dug around in her shoulder bag for her cigarette lighter. Casting one last look towards the exit, she flicked the lighter with her thumb and held the small flame to the edge of the ball of paper, her hand shaking, and then stepped back. A little fire burst to life, and she asked herself again: what the hell was she doing? But she couldn't help the little smile that appeared on her face.

Satisfied that there was no serious danger of the tiny fire spreading, Kaatje quietly slipped back through the exit to the seating area in the foyer, found a hiding place behind one of the large potted plants, and waited for her little bit of handiwork to take effect.

Sure enough, after about sixty seconds it did.

The quiet calmness of the clinic was suddenly shattered by a loud high-pitched alarm that pierced the air, and red lights started to blink in the ceiling and corridors.

The receptionist dashed out from behind her counter and stood there looking left and right, her face a picture of panic and dismay. Unsure how to handle this sudden turn of events, eventually she decided that self-preservation was the best course of action and she hurried through the sliding doors to the car park outside.

From her hiding spot behind the plant Kaatje watched as, over the next few minutes, more and more people joined her, appearing from other buildings and annexes. From the corridor leading into the clinic, a number of people poured into the main foyer, doctors and medics and porters and a couple of angry-looking security guards, and these too joined the crowd outside, everybody standing around and looking alarmed and unsure of where to go or what to do.

Overhead the piercing alarm continued to beep loudly.

Kaatje waited a couple of minutes further, just to make sure that nobody else would appear, and when she was sure the coast was clear she moved out from behind the plant and nipped into the corridor, the doors sliding shut behind her.

She did not hang about, aware that someone would soon rumble her bit of subterfuge, and so she hurried along. On the floor she noticed the three coloured lines, and thinking back to what Pieter had told her yesterday, remembered him saying that the red line was the important one, the one which led to the secret part of the clinic, and so she followed it with a new steely determination flowing through her, her whole being now shaking with excitement.

She passed through a glass corridor and inner courtyard. Soon after, the yellow line branched off to one of the consultation rooms, exactly as Pieter had described. A minute or so later and the blue line veered off down a short passage to the accommodation wing. Ignoring this route, Kaatje pushed on.

Just then the alarm stopped, and the sudden silence that fell throughout the complex seemed full of silent echoes. Kaatje hesitated, now suddenly quite scared.

Should she give up and go back? Or find another exit and get out fast?

Damn it! She thought. She hadn't come this far to bottle it now. This was real police work she was doing, the exact kind of thing she had signed on for. Besides, what would Pieter say?

Moving forward once more, she continued to follow the red line.

A few minutes later she found herself at her destination, the door signed **OPHTHALMIC THEATRE 1B + 2AB**. What's more, the area was deserted, with no sign of the security guards that Pieter had run into: exactly as she had hoped.

Feeling her confidence bolstered once again, Kaatje stepped forward and pushed the heavy swing-door open.

On the other side was a small, square anteroom. There was a deserted nurse's station, a row of drug cabinets on the wall and a black oxygen cylinder propped up in the corner. On the left and right two doors faced each other, marked 1B and 2AB. Directly opposite where Kaatje was standing was a third entrance, a sliding door with a switch on the wall.

Above the door, in simple black lettering was a sign which read:

UNIT 1 – RED ZONE

NO ADMITTANCE BEYOND THIS POINT EXCEPT FOR RED CLEARANCE PASS-HOLDERS

Taking a deep breath Kaatje strode over and hit the button, then passed through.

She paused just beyond the threshold, her eyes scanning the long room she found herself in, a little confused at first at just what she was seeing, but as her mind absorbed the implications she felt her mouth drop open and her eyes widen.

Before she could think any further she felt something soft press against her mouth, a piece of cloth or something, held there by a strong hand. It had a slight ether-like smell, which she knew instantly was chloroform.

After this, her world faded to nothing...

...She awoke feeling drowsy and nauseous and with her head pounding.

She was lying down, but the angle of her posture was all weird, with her legs higher than the top half of her body, which made the blood rush to her head, exacerbating the pain in her temples. Kaatje moved to reach up and massage her brow, but something stopped her from doing so, and it took a moment for the fog to clear from her mind enough for her to realize why: her arm was restrained by something wrapped tightly around her forearm, holding it in place. Then she realized that actually both of her arms and both of her legs were tied down. Also, when she tried to blink, her eyelids wouldn't shut. They couldn't because something was fixed to her eyes, something sharp and painful holding them wide open.

It took a few moments for things to slowly come back to her. The journey through the city to the clinic at Osdorp – setting off the smoke alarm and following the red line down the corridor – entering the restricted part of the facility. After that point, she could remember nothing, until she'd awoken just moments ago.

Twisting her head from side to side, her eyes pinned open, Kaatje looked around.

She was in a small room, the walls painted a pale green colour. She lay upon a grey leather examination couch, her arms and legs strapped in place. Overhead was some kind of box with a small circle in the centre, like a single eye staring down at her. To her right was a large diagnostic display covered in dials and buttons. Sitting in a chair was the figure of a man: she couldn't twist her head far enough to see who it was, just that he had on a white coat.

Kaatje could feel fear course through her veins. She had no idea what was going on, but instinct told her it was something bad. Just then, a familiar voice started to speak in quiet and calming tones.

"Ah, you're awake I see."

Julian Visser moved into her line of sight, his face peering down at her.

"You're just in time. I'm just about to start."

Kaatje's heart was pounding in her chest, and again she strained against her restraints.

"What the hell's going on?" she demanded, her voice weak and trembling. "Let me get up."

"I'm afraid I can't do that. It's for your own good. If you move around too much, it might make the procedure go wrong."

"Procedure? What are you talking about?"

"Of course, if you hadn't been so nosey, looking around without permission and entering parts of the clinic that you are not cleared to see, then none of this would be necessary. So you could say that you've brought this upon yourself. No pun intended, but hindsight is a wonderful thing." Visser sniggered quietly to himself.

She saw him reach forward to either side of her head and she felt something slide against her temples. Some kind of brace, to lock her head into position.

"Shall we begin?"

He turned away and flicked a few switches on his control panel, and with an electronic hum, the box-shaped piece of equipment above her head slowly lowered itself into position, stopping mere inches from her face and with the single glass eye looking straight down.

"This is called a Lasik LEN-XR Laser System," Visser explained. "We normally use it to carry out simple and straight-forward procedures such as repairing detached retinas, cornea reshaping, that kind of thing. But today I'll be using it for another purpose."

"Look, this has gone far enough." Kaatje heard herself starting to babble incoherently.

Visser went on as if she had never spoken.

"I would normally administer a mild anaesthetic in the form of eye droplets. On this occasion, however, that won't actually be very helpful for you, so we shall skip that part. I will also adjust the setting on the laser to suit today's procedure."

She heard him tapping away on a keyboard.

"The normal range for the focusing beam is 4.5 to 7, with a maximum of 7.5. I think 15 shall do. And a pulse strength measuring 193nm is standard. Let's push that up to 300nm's shall we? That will ensure maximum depth and should result in permanent effectiveness. Very good, we are all set."

Visser leaned forward in his seat and gazed into the magnifying eyepiece attached to his diagnostic display.

"You will experience a series of rapid pulses of light, first in your left eye and then your right eye. There will also be a burning sensation as the cornea peels away under the focussing beam and XR Laser, followed by the lens becoming permanently displaced. After this, the light pulses will penetrate through the vitreous body of the eye to the optic nerve. The damage will be unrepairable."

"Please Visser, stop this. I'm a police officer! For Christ's sake don't do this!"

Visser made no comment, now too intent on his work.

Kaatje lay there helplessly, her breathing coming in quick and short gasps, hoping, praying that he was just bluffing, but when she heard a high-frequency whine come from the machinery and then saw the lens of the laser above her suddenly dilate and turn white, her fear made her heart leap up into her mouth.

A series of rapid white pulses made her vision blur, and a split-second later the excruciating pain hit her, and she screamed like she had never screamed before. It felt like someone had pushed a red-hot piece of wire straight into her eye, going deeper and deeper, and the burning agony ratcheted up so high that her brain flared red.

Kaatje bucked and twisted on the couch.

The laser seemed to melt right through her skull.

The pain went up and up.

It continued to soar.

* * *

Pieter reached his home just as it was growing dark.

He'd decided to pop in to work for a couple of hours on the Saturday afternoon, still frustrated at the lack of progress in the case, pessimistic at the potential of any major breakthrough.

Yesterday's chat with Ernie Clegg had been disappointing but at least the old soldier had given him a description of their as-of-yet only suspect, and so Pieter had entered the details into the national crime-linkage database, ViCASnl (Violent Crime Analysis System Netherlands) to see if any links with other offences or known criminals triggered a hit. Yet he didn't hold out much hope. The description – a well-built white male wearing brown overalls and work boots and a baseball cap, driving a dark van – was so vague that it probably encompassed half of the crimes committed on a daily basis throughout the country.

Next, he had popped down to see Floris de Kok (aka Adolf) down in his basement filing section to ask him to pull a list of all known paedophiles on the city's sex-offenders list and to run checks on their whereabouts and alibis for the approximate time of the fire and abduction. He also requested information on their current occupations.

He'd set off home, calling off at the minimarket on Raadhuisstraat to buy a few essentials for the weekend. Ten minutes later he pulled to a halt outside the tall canal house where he lived on the Singel canal, noticing vaguely the hire car parked by the pavement, and used the key fob to open his garage doors. Then he was climbing the stairs up to the third floor – the living area of his house – and started to unpack his shopping. Outside, it was just starting to snow.

His phone vibrated and it took him a moment to fish it out of his jacket, which was hanging on the back of the kitchen door.

"Hello," he answered without bothering to check the caller ID.

After a moment's pause a voice responded. Just two simple words, but they were enough to freeze him to the spot, and his heart skipped and twitched tightly in his chest.

"Hello Pieter," said a silky, and instantly familiar voice.

He dropped the box of eggs that he had been holding, barely registering the splat that they made as they hit the floor. A wave of dizziness nearly overwhelmed him and he quickly grasped the back of a chair.

"You?" he breathed, his throat all scratchy and constricted.

"I've missed you," Lotte told him, and, shit, she actually sounded like she meant it!

Pieter could think of no response. A whole range of thoughts and emotions whirled through his head as he tried to comprehend this unexpected turn of events. That Lotte was still around and on the run was no surprise: after all, he had seen her very briefly during his period of convalescence on the coast during the summer, and the international manhunt for her was still as active and intense as ever. But until now there had been no leads or sightings of her anywhere, no clues as to her whereabouts. Yet here she was, popping up like some horrible memory, resurfacing, leaving him feeling like he'd been kicked in the gut.

"I'm afraid that I can't see you in person. Not on this occasion anyway. Maybe next time, and we can catch-up. But I do have someone here who wants to talk to you."

There was another long pause, then a different voice, this one almost incomprehensible and talking slowly, sounding like a drunk, the words all slurred.

"Pieter… I… please, they have done something to my…"

"Kaatje? Kaatje, is that you?" A coldness went through him like his veins were suddenly filled with ice instead of blood.

"I'm sorry…" she managed to say, her voice quiet and shaky.

Then Lotte came back on the line.

"Look outside your window Pieter."

The phone went silent.

For several seconds he didn't react. He just stood there looking at the mobile phone in his hand. When the words eventually registered he dashed headlong through the kitchen door, along the short landing, and through to the lounge. He yanked the curtains aside and stared down at the street below, a sense of deja-vu flickering in his memory.

The streetlight there showed him that the lane was empty apart from the parked hire car: he could see no figures or traffic, nothing out of the ordinary, only falling snow flakes. Then, from the silence came the sound of a car's engine, suddenly increasing in volume and in seconds becoming a loud roar. It came into view and screeched to a halt just opposite, and the rear passenger door was flung open and something dark fell out into the roadway, and in an instant, the car was pulling away again, the door slamming shut as the vehicle raced out of sight.

Pieter stared hard at the object lying motionless on the cobbled road. He knew very well what it was. Who it was.

He raced down the stairs, tearing headlong from the third floor all the way to the entrance hallway at street level, and he quickly flung open the heavy front door and leaped down the stone steps into the cobbled street.

He approached the body lying in the road on legs that had suddenly turned to jelly, fearing the worst, but as he reached Kaatje he caught the slightest of movements from her, and relief washed over him as he grabbed her by the shoulder and rolled her over.

Pieter recoiled in horror.

Her face was deathly pale and her lips had turned blue, and she was quivering, her whole body now starting to convulse violently. But the worst thing, something that he knew would stay with him forever, were her eyes.

Twin bloody holes where the eyes should have been stared sightlessly back at him, as though they had been torn or ripped out, or something had bored deeply through them.

Pieter looked down at Kaatje, a deep well of pity bringing tears to his own eyes, and he held her tightly, shouting for help, for somebody to call an ambulance.

He saw her mouth move. She was trying to tell him something. He leaned his ear close to her lips, catching her whispered words.

"Visser. Visser did this."

Then she slipped into unconsciousness.

Snow continued to fall, wrapping them in a white cocoon.

Chapter 13
Unit 1 – Red Zone

He stayed with Kaatje until the paramedics arrived. They spent over thirty minutes trying to stabilize her before setting off to the hospital, and Pieter spent the whole time holding her hand as she lay in the back of the ambulance. At one point she had regained consciousness and started to talk incoherently, becoming more and more agitated, and he had tried to reassure her with words of comfort, even though there was little he could say to allay her fears: he was no expert, but it seemed obvious to him that, although her life may not have been in danger, the damage to her eyes would be permanent. She would never regain her sight.

The horror of what she'd endured sickened him. He could not fathom the pure evil involved. But as soon as she had mentioned the name Visser the motive became clear. This was an act of revenge as well as a warning, in response to their visit to the clinic yesterday. Kaatje must have returned there on her own, or been taken against her will, and it was all tied up somehow in the Nina Bakker abduction case and the murder of her parents.

Pieter had climbed back out of the ambulance and stood there in the falling snow as the vehicle pulled away, its blue lights flashing and lighting up the wintry scene. Then he had gone back inside, up the staircase to his bedroom, and retrieved his firearm from its metal locker at the back of his wardrobe. It was strictly against regulations to keep the gun at home, and he could find himself under a mandatory referral to the Dutch Police Federation Sanctions Board if anybody found out, but ever since the spring he felt the need to make sure he was prepared for if – or when – Lotte had made a reappearance. And after tonight's incidents, he now felt fully justified in doing so.

Putting on the shoulder holster, he slipped in the gun and put his leather jacket on over the top and then grabbed his car keys off the kitchen table.

A few minutes later and he was driving away.

Just what precisely Lotte's role was in all of this he did not know. That could come later. For now there was only one thing on his mind.

He raced through the evening traffic with the emergency light on the dashboard flashing a warning to the other cars and bicycles to make way, and each time he reached a junction he ignored the red lights and manoeuvred his way carefully and speedily through the cross-traffic, hoping the other drivers would slow and allow him safe passage.

Approaching the eye clinic in Osdorp he cut the siren and quietly turned off the main road, noting how few cars were parked in the car park. The area reserved for members of staff was completely deserted. There was just one single car in the far corner near where the grassy slope led down to the small lake.

Pulling up in the shadows, Pieter climbed out. It had stopped snowing again and the ground was covered in just a thin dusting of white. Overhead, a crescent moon dominated the sky. The frozen lake seemed to glow a milky-white as he crunched his way over to the main entrance.

The building was mostly in darkness. The security lights on the outside walls were switched off, and the windows of the complex were dark and impenetrable. The place had a deserted air about it, which rather than making him feel more relaxed and at ease, actually triggered an internal alarm inside him, and his nerves kicked in, making him ultra alert. The more so when he saw the sliding doors of the front entrance were wide open.

He slid out his firearm and held it with the barrel pointed down at the ground. From his coat pocket he removed a flashlight. Playing the strong beam in through the entrance, he quickly scanned the interior, and once he was sure the way was clear, Pieter carefully stepped into the foyer.

It was eerily quiet. Everything was powered down; the ceiling lights, the computer monitors on the receptionist's desk, the large HD television in the seating area. He noticed a cup of coffee on the counter in front of him, and, moving over, he reached out the hand holding the flashlight and touched it with his fingertips. Stone cold.

Pieter shook his head. During yesterday's visit with Kaatje, the place had given him the creeps, there'd been something about the clinic that got under his skin. But now, standing in the dark and empty and silent foyer, he felt himself shiver as though something had passed over his grave, and he looked back over his shoulder towards the passage leading inside the facility. He had the damndest notion that he was being watched.

Something caught his eye then. A thin sliver of light showing underneath a door, and he remembered this was Julian Visser's office.

Pieter trod silently over and pressed his ear to the door. He could hear nothing on the other side.

Switching off the flashlight and returning it to his coat pocket, he gently took a hold of the door handle and twisted it as quietly as possible, and eased the door open, the hand holding the firearm ready to come up.

The office was empty and he breathed a sigh of relief.

Passing through the doorway and leaving the door slightly ajar, he stood there and looked around Visser's cramped little office.

The place was a mess. The desk, which had three computer monitors arranged in a U-shape facing the swivel chair, was strewn with papers and pens and brown cardboard folders. A glass of water had overturned and rolled onto the carpet, leaving a damp patch on the floor near a filing cabinet. Stacks of paperwork had been piled up in untidy columns on a side-table, and some of these had toppled over, making it impossible not to step on sheets of paper as he walked over to the desk.

A potted plant on top of the filing cabinet had turned brown, its leaves all curled up and dying, and a half-eaten sandwich lay discarded in a waste-paper bin. It looked to have been there for days. A dusty smell lingered in the air, adding to the sense that Visser had not been one for maintaining a clean and well-organized workspace.

Pieter put his firearm back into his shoulder holster and choosing a brown folder at random he picked it up off the desk.

On the front, handwritten in capitals, it said: **PATIENT 27 – U1 RZ. PROCEDURE: 3 - date 22nd JANUARY**

He flipped it open. Inside was a photo of a young child, a boy of around five or six, paper-clipped to a sheaf of medical notes. The boy's eyes were all bloodshot and watery, but whether the picture was pre-op or post-op Pieter didn't know.

He scanned his gaze over the paperwork which all seemed fairly standard stuff. The child's date of birth, address, general health. There was mention of a pre-existing condition: **AMBLYOPIA,** which Pieter knew was the correct medical term for a lazy eye. But no name. Just **PATIENT 27.**

Below was a handwritten note:

***Following complications the patient was recommended for* SPECIAL PROCEDURE** *in Unit One.*

It was signed by both Dr Christiaan Bakker and his assistant Julian Visser.

Pieter dropped the file back onto the desk and picked up another.

This one was for **PATIENT 41 – U1 RZ. PROCEDURE: 3 – date 28**[th] **MARCH**, and inside was a photo of an Asian woman, who according to her notes was aged fifty-nine and requiring lens replacement treatment.

Again the same recommendation for the **SPECIAL PROCEDURE** *in Unit One.*

Another folder: **PATIENT 46 – U1 RZ. PROCEDURE: 3 – date 2**[nd] **APRIL**. A thirty-six year old male needing retinal detachment repair work, and being put forward once again for the **SPECIAL PROCEDURE**

He tossed the file onto the cluttered desktop and stood there thinking things over.

Unit One RZ? he pondered. SPECIAL PROCEDURE? Where was Unit One, and what exactly did this SPECIAL PROCEDURE entail?

Determined to find out, and wanting to ask a few serious questions about what had happened to Kaatje, Pieter left the office, his gun back in his hand. Most of all he wanted to privately confront Visser, before he called in police back-up and let the wheels of justice take over.

He moved over to the internal corridor. The automatic doors here were locked in the open position just as the main entrance was, and once again he found himself following the coloured lines on the polished floor, using the flashlight to light his way.

The place was strangely deserted. Everywhere there was a hushed and empty feel, as though the entire clinic had been abandoned, evacuated even, in a rush. Just ahead was a wheelchair left askew across the passage, and further along a patient's gown lay discarded on the floor – not that he had seen any signs of actual patients yesterday. And as he entered the glass-covered passageway he felt something crunch beneath his feet, so he pointed the beam of the flashlight down, and saw thousands of tiny red and white capsules and tablets spilled across the floor.

Stepping through them he entered the separate building block of the facility. A few metres ahead and the yellow line swung to the right and disappeared beneath a door – **CONSULTATION ROOM No 1** he remembered. He headed across.

Before he pushed through the door he noticed a bank of light switches on the wall and he reached out and flicked both rows down. To his surprise, the lights in this section still worked, and everywhere the bright ceiling lights flickered to life. Switching off the flashlight and ramming it into his coat pocket, Pieter entered, using the barrel of his gun to push open the door.

The room was familiar, and once more there was nobody here. Yesterday, during his walk around the place, he'd peered through the glass and given the place a cursory glance, and everything was how he recalled. Now he decided to have a better look around.

The first thing he noticed was that it was much tidier than Visser's office. The L-shaped desk was reasonably well organized and the chair was pushed neatly under it. On the surface, as well as the monitors and a large, square leather blotter with pen and several blank envelopes, there was a small stack of kidney-shaped stainless steel medical dishes, as well as a chunky pair of magnifying eyeglasses with small LED lights attached to both sides. He spotted nothing unusual. Putting his gun away, he tried the desk drawers, but they were all locked and there was no key.

Behind the desk was the examination couch surrounded by a bank of equipment and lights and a keratometer. On the wall opposite was a standard eye chart of the sort found in every opticians.

Tucked into the far corner there was a tall freezer with a glass door. On the shelves inside were four or five trays filled with test tube samples.

A small window overlooked the inner courtyard.

He wondered briefly if this was where they had held Kaatje and lasered her eyes away, but he concluded that was unlikely. They would do that in one of the operating theatres.

Shrugging to himself, content that there was nothing here worth lingering over, Pieter returned to the main corridor outside. Feeling more and more relaxed, sure that the place was deserted, he continued onwards without removing his gun.

Two minutes later and he followed the blue line where it branched away down a short side-passage to his left, and he pushed through a pair of swing doors into the overnight accommodation ward, named **THE JACQUES DAVIEL WING.**

It was how he remembered it from the photos on the website, which he'd scrolled through on his iPad on their drive over yesterday morning. The large ward was shaped like a huge letter U, with a curving row of large and luxurious-looking beds arranged around a series of couches and coffee tables in the centre. There was also a coffee machine, some games to play and today's copies of the daily newspapers, including The New York Times and Bild, plus a row of three laptops. At both ends of the U was a matching pair of large tv screens, visible to all of the patients recovering from their operations, but currently turned off. All very plush, spotlessly clean, and empty of patients or staff.

He wandered up and down, taking note of random things:

The neatly made beds.

The lifeless diagnostic equipment.

The half-completed game of snakes and ladders.

A jug of orange juice on a coffee table, with a pair of plastic beakers.

A mobile phone, left behind by someone. Pieter picked this up and saw that it was still turned on but pin-encrypted.

It was bizarre. It was creepy and disturbing. Everything left exactly as it would be if the place had been filled with patients and medical personnel; the only thing missing was the people themselves.

Just like the legendary ship *The Mary Celeste.*

Done with looking around and realizing he was getting nowhere with his musings, Pieter stepped back through the swing doors and continued, this time following the red line.

Shortly afterwards he reached the point where it disappeared down the cross-hallway and he cautiously peered around the corner, his hand poised to grab the butt of his gun. To his relief, the two security guards were nowhere to be seen. They had apparently upped and left along with everybody else, determined to be as far away as possible before the police descended. Pieter walked down the short hall and paused outside the wide door.

Beyond here were the two operating theatres, and although he was certain they would also be deserted, something made him hesitate. But only briefly. He pushed the door open.

Pieter found himself in a small and enclosed space, and his eyes did a quick scan around, seeing a nurses station covered in slim cardboard packages and a row of disposable urine bottles, each one full, plus some medicine cabinets and a discarded oxygen tank.

A pair of doors signed **1B** and **2AB** led off from the anteroom.

He was thinking once more about Kaatje, and what they had done to her inside one of the theatres, and he realized he had no real desire to go and take a look because the very idea made him feel queasy. Besides, opposite him was another set of doors, and the sign above drew his attention.

UNIT 1 – RED ZONE

The most restricted part of the clinic he surmised, from reading the notice declaring no admittance without top-level clearance. The place where patients were sent for the **SPECIAL PROCEDURE** according to the files on Visser's desk.

This time, before he hit the button that opened the sliding door, Pieter withdrew his gun and flicked off the safety. Then he went through.

He was standing in a dimly lit room that stretched away before him. Down the centre of the ceiling was a single strip light, turned right down so that the place was filled with shadows and blind spots. Nevertheless, the bright light from the anteroom behind him cast enough illumination over his shoulders for him to see by.

Down each side was a double row of hospital beds. He could see that these were quite basic compared to those in the expensive-looking aftercare ward he had just left. There was no comfy seating area either, just a drab and dirty floor down the middle leading to a blank wall at the far end, and there were no bedside tables or visitors chairs either. No windows, and no heating. A very dingy and uninviting hospital ward then, he thought, with absolutely no frills. So much for the high fees and world-class care that the website liked to boast about. Perhaps this area was reserved for the poorer residents, those who claimed off their medical insurance, rather than the well-off clientele who paid with their gold credit cards.

Also, that wasn't the only thing different about this ward.

For this one wasn't empty.

Each bed was occupied by a sleeping figure, lying flat on their backs in matching sets of pale blue pyjamas, their faces in shadow.

Pieter stood stock still, a tremor of dread rippling through his body. Which was stupid, he knew. They were just hospital patients, nothing more than that, left behind by the medical staff in their blind panic to flee. They were probably frightened and confused as to what was going on.

With an effort, he turned and moved slowly over to the nearest bed.

It contained a man's sleeping form. He was lying underneath the sheets, but his arms were on the outside and flat down at his sides, and what he could see of his face in the dimness revealed thin and very pale features. Pieter leaned down for a closer look.

He flinched suddenly and snapped his head away, and his left hand came up to his mouth as bile rushed up into his throat, making him gag and retch, and he just about stopped himself from vomiting in revulsion.

The man had no eyes.

They had not been burned away like Kaatje's, or even surgically removed. He simply had no eyes. In their place was an area of soft and perfectly smoothed-over flesh. Like he had never had any eyes, as though they had never formed during his life, and in their place was this shallow, empty area beneath his heavy brows.

Pieter staggered back on his heels and nearly toppled over. Quickly regaining his senses, he moved on to the next bed.

Here lay another man, older than the first, and once again with that empty gaze staring sightlessly up at the ceiling. In fact, it was impossible to know if he was asleep or wide awake.

Spinning away, Pieter stumbled across the centre aisle to the opposite row of beds, and this time found himself looking down at a young woman, perhaps in her mid-twenties, with long, golden hair. Beautiful under normal circumstances, until his gaze fell upon the centre of her face at the blank space below her eyebrows.

Further along he spotted a smaller figure lying in a bed, this one a child, and Pieter dashed down, wondering if this was…

Yes. He could recognize the face, even with the missing bloodshot eyes. The five or six year old boy from the photo in the file – **PATIENT 27.**

Pieter felt a sense of pity, even shame, grip him, and he was about to avert his gaze when he saw the boy lying before him stir.

He watched as the child's face slowly turned in his direction. Like he was looking straight at Pieter, which just wasn't possible. And the tiny hand came up and reached out beseechingly. The lips of the small mouth parted, and a quiet and pitiful keening sound came out.

Behind him, Pieter heard a general movement, a rustling of bedclothes, and he twisted around, the gun coming up automatically.

All of the patients were sitting upright in their beds. The boy too, he saw.

And in perfect unison they turned their sightless gaze upon him.

The boy started to make that same high-pitched mewling sound again, as though he couldn't talk properly, and when Pieter glanced back at him he saw for the first time the large white plaster across the front of his throat, just about where the voice box would be.

Suddenly, and again as though at the command of some hidden signal, all of the others joined in, the keening noise sounding like a quiet hum, or like a swarm of angry bees, growing in pitch. It was the weirdest sound he had ever heard and it made his skin crawl.

Pieter instinctively moved away from the boy's bedside until he was in the centre aisle. Behind him was the blank wall at the bottom end of the room. The entrance, the only way in and out of the ward, was about thirty paces away. Something about the peculiar noise the patients were making, the way it was increasing in volume, seemed to warn him that something was about to happen, something bad, and so he sensed it was best to slowly edge in that direction. Even so, when the attack came it still took him by surprise.

He was concentrating on those patients sitting in their beds to his left and right, wondering whether he should just walk calmly past them towards the door, not thinking about anything else. So when he heard the sudden patter of tiny feet on the floor coming from an unexpected quarter, from behind him, he had no time to react.

He felt something land on his back, and heard a loud hissing close to his ear, and realized in an instant that it was the boy. The next thing he knew there was an excruciating pain in his right shoulder, a sharp agony like something pricking deep into the flesh. Jesus! he thought in shock. The boy was biting him! His sharp teeth were biting down hard, the tiny jaws locked solid onto him.

Pieter cried out, and then reached awkwardly behind, striking out with the hand holding the gun to try and dislodge the boy, who had thrown himself onto his back. But the child had a firm purchase and now his tiny hands were grabbing for Pieter's face and clawing at his eyes.

He could have fired the gun. It would have been simple just to jab the barrel into the boy's body or head and pull the trigger. But something made him hold back, a natural revulsion at shooting a child.

Instead Pieter propelled himself backwards fast and crashed hard into the wall behind him, and the boy's back hit the hard surface painfully, dislodging his mouth from Pieter's shoulder and bringing a gasp from his lips followed by a slackening of his grip. Then Pieter flung his head backwards, the back of his skull connecting with the boy's nose. There was a double crack of the boy's nose breaking followed half a second later by his head striking the wall, and then the hands lost their hold and the child slithered to the floor, dazed and listless.

Pieter flung himself away and looked around.

To his dismay the young face was covered in blood, and he instinctively reached for him, but then the child hissed in fury, spittle flying from his mouth, and so Pieter drew back.

He turned again towards the room full of patients and cried out in shock.

In the few seconds he had been distracted while dealing with the boy, the others had climbed out of their beds and were now crowding together and moving on him down the centre aisle, blocking his escape route. Their eyeless faces terrified him, the way they scowled and snarled, some still making that dreadful keening sound, others shaking their heads and snapping at the air with their mouths, like rabid animals.

Pieter raised the gun and pointed it towards the crowd, swinging the barrel from face to face. "Get back!" he shouted. "Get back now!"

It had no effect whatsoever. They continued creeping forward. It was as though they could see him, and they encroached nearer and nearer with each second. At his feet, the boy crawled away to re-join his fellow patients, and Pieter found himself backed up against the wall with nowhere else to go.

A sudden fury came over him and he struck out with his gun at the nearest face, that of the old man. The painful blow stunned him and the man staggered away with a whimper, clutching his face, but in an instant someone else took his place. Pieter lashed out again twice, striking two more people, and then he kicked a third in the stomach. The woman with the blonde hair doubled over, coughing and retching from the blow, but she continued to face Pieter, her lips drawn back in hatred, and a second later she stood upright and leaped towards him.

Without thinking twice Pieter fired at point-blank range straight into her face, the roar of the gun deafening as it bounced off the walls. The woman's face exploded in a cloud of blood and bone fragments, and she toppled backwards, dragging down two more people with her, and creating a small gap in the crowd.

The shocking violence stunned the other patients into immobility, and they stood rooted to the spot, creating a chilling tableau that jolted Pieter's heart. He saw his chance, and he jumped through the gap, trampling over the pile of fallen figures lying on the floor, and in the next moment, he was sprinting headlong towards the door at the far end of the room.

Behind him the patients snapped out of their brief paralysis and they turned and charged after him, a baying and screaming and hissing mob, intent, Pieter was sure, of tearing him limb from limb.

He punched the button that opened the door and raced through. He made for the exit just opposite, which would take him back out into the hallway beyond, but on the way he grabbed at anything he could find to impede the crowd. He flung a chair in his wake, the table, a bunch of the urine bottles, boxes of supplies, and then just as he was passing through the next door he scooped up the heavy oxygen cylinder propped up in the corner.

Pieter used his shoulder to barge through the swing door and he quickly spun and pushed it shut again, catching a quick glimpse through the crack as he did so, seeing the seething and spitting crowd sprinting towards him.

Wedging the door shut with his foot, he slid the oxygen cylinder through the large door handle and pushed it all the way in, sliding it past the door frame so that it bridged the gap between the edge of the door and the door jam. It was not a moment too soon, for a second later and the crowd hit the other side of the door, and it shuddered and bulged outwards at the impact.

Pieter stepped away, expecting it to cave in as they pushed and shoved and threw themselves bodily at the door, thumping the wood and shouting in anger, but it held, the cylinder acting as a huge bolt and holding it shut fast.

He was shaking and hardly able to get his breath, and his shoulder stung where the boy had bitten him and he could feel blood trickling down the back of his shirt, and he couldn't think straight.

What the hell? his muddled mind asked. *This was crazy beyond words. Who were these people, and what had they had done to them?*

The hand holding the gun started to tremble as the shock began to course through his system, and he grabbed his wrist with the other hand to steady it.

He moved back from the door. He needed to get a grip, otherwise he would soon be crawling around on his hands and knees like a quivering wreck.

He needed to think fast.

Suddenly, the banging and gargled shouting on the other side of the door ceased, and a terrible silence stretched the atmosphere so taut that Pieter held his breath.

Then there was a loud shattering of glass somewhere to his left, followed by a tearing of metal, and moments later the rush of many feet heading his way.

Damn. They must have found another way out of the anteroom, perhaps through one of the theatres.

He didn't stop to think about it any further, but turned and fled. He raced around the corner, back into the main hallway the way he had come, and down the long passage. He risked the briefest of glances back over his shoulder and instantly wished that he hadn't. Behind him came maybe a dozen of the patients, their pyjamas flapping and their bare feet slapping hard on the floor, faces contorted with hatred. With their empty eye sockets somehow 'seeing' him.

A shaky cry of fear involuntarily escaped from between his lips, adding to the general discord of strangled and incoherent voices coming from his pursuers.

Pieter sprinted by the doors leading to the aftercare ward – no escape that way.

The others were gaining on him. He didn't need to look to see that. They were so fast, inhumanly quick.

A few moments later and the door to the consultation room flashed past, and then he plunged headlong into the gloomy front-half of the clinic, and felt the crunch of the spilled tablets under his shoes as he entered the curved glass-covered passageway.

Pieter made a snap decision then. He had to slow them, otherwise they would be on him in seconds. So he spun around at the end of the glass corridor, and aimed the gun at the nearest running figures, and holding it in both hands he squeezed the trigger twice.

Both shots found their targets, and two men flew back from the impact of the rounds hitting their bodies. One bounced off the floor, causing those behind to stumble and fall, but the other was sent crashing through the glass wall, bringing half of the passageway cascading down in a shower of tiny glass shards. They glittered and fell on the mob, cutting and lacerating their bare arms and feet and bringing howls of pain from them.

Pieter, being at the end of the glass passageway, was mostly protected from the falling daggers, but he still flung up an arm to protect his eyes from any flying splinters. When he looked again he saw with no small amount of satisfaction that the gunshots, together with the falling bodies and shattered passage, had brought the pursuing mob to a halt as they stumbled around. It had brought him a few seconds grace, and so he turned and fled for his life.

On he went, running hell for leather, skirting around the abandoned wheelchair, his breathing coming in loud and harsh rasps.

More shouting echoed down the hallway as they once again picked up the chase, but now Pieter was bursting out into the foyer area, going by the comfy seats and then the deserted reception desk, praying that the front doors hadn't slid shut and locked themselves.

To his relief, he saw they were still wide open, and the cold air wafting in gave him an extra burst of energy, and he charged through and out into the car park.

His car was parked in the shadow of one of the trees edging the large car park and now he regretted having parked so far from the entrance, for it meant a long run across the open space. There was nothing he could do about that now, and so he raced along the path leading over the frosted lawn, slipping and sliding through the thin covering of snow. Behind him, the patients flowed out of the clinic like a raging river.

Some movement in his peripheral vision made Pieter look over to his left, and with a feeling of horror he saw a second stream of people pouring around the corner of the building where it jutted out towards the frozen boating lake. He could see them quite clearly in the moonlight, dashing over the edge of the water, their feet crunching through the thin ice near the shore. They must have found another way out on that side.

As he ran, he watched the running figures switch direction and come charging up the grass embankment. They were trying to cut him off, to reach the car park before he had a chance to get to his car, and at the speed they were moving they would win the race. Again he was amazed and baffled at their speed, their uncanny ability to know where he was.

Pieter raised his gun again, aiming in the general direction of this second group, and fired three rapid shots. All three missed their targets because of his unsteady arm, but it was enough to make them duck and cringe back for a few seconds, which was all he needed. Then Pieter was at his car, yanking open the door and diving into the driver's seat, and then slamming it shut.

Not a moment too soon. The two groups of patients reached his car together and threw themselves at the doors and windows, banging with their fists against the bodywork and glass. One man even jumped on the front of the car and pressed his pale face against the windscreen, gazing in with his eyeless face, his mouth stretched open wide.

Pieter turned the ignition and gunned the engine, then throwing it into gear, he stamped down on the accelerator and the car screeched away, fish-tailing through the slippery snow.

Most of those crowding around his car pulled clear or were pushed away by the car itself. All except the man on the bonnet, who clung stubbornly on even as Pieter skidded across the car park. Pieter looked at him through the glass and he could hear somebody shouting at the top of their voice, before he realized it was his own voice he could hear, yelling and babbling. He was on the point of losing all reasoning, had never felt such perfect fear in his life, and he wondered if the nightmare would ever end.

The terror fuelled his anger and he snapped the steering wheel hard towards the exit leading on to the main road. The sudden jolt made the man outside lose his grip, and then he was sliding away over the front of the bonnet.

Pieter had one last glimpse of his face as he disappeared from view. There was a double bump as the front and rear tyres ran right over the man.

Then he was clear, the car shooting out of the car park, wheels spinning to gain a purchase on the snow.

Pieter was still shouting, and tears were coursing down his face, and he was thumping the steering wheel in triumph.

Chapter 14
Mr Trinh

"You shouldn't have come here," Lotte told Julian Visser.

He stood shivering in the hallway to her apartment, with small heaps of snow on the hood and shoulders of his overcoat, a puddle of water already forming around his feet. Through the open doorway behind him, thick white flakes came tumbling out of the black sky, covering the courtyard.

"I had nowhere else to go," Visser replied apologetically. "We had no choice but to abandon the clinic after the girl started poking around. The place will be swarming with police by now, the same with my home."

Lotte stared at him for a moment, letting him shiver in the cold blast of air blowing in.

"But you were supposed to get out of the city after dumping the girl. Get on a flight out of Schiphol, any flight. That was the arrangement."

"The airport is shut because of the weather," Visser mumbled weakly, shrugging and looking all wet and pathetic.

Lotte sighed. "Very well. You're here now, so you'd better come in." She stood to one side and he went through into the passage, shrugging off his coat and hanging it on a rack as he went. She closed the front door with a thud.

"Thank you. I'm sorry about this, but things happened so quickly that I didn't know what to do for the best."

Lotte smiled warmly and shook her head.

"Don't worry about it. Look, why don't you run yourself a hot bath while I find you a change of clothes and fix you a drink."

Visser smiled back, the tenseness visibly leaving him. His beady little eyes ran back and forth over her face, and then dipped quickly to the top of her shirt where it was unbuttoned. When he looked back up, her smile had gone, replaced by a blank expression and a straight little mouth.

"Ah right, yes, of course." Visser disappeared down the hallway.

Once he had gone Lotte turned and went back into her study, where she had been talking with her uncle before the knock on the door had interrupted them.

Johan Roost looked up as she entered. He was sitting at the table. He'd spread out some old newspapers and was cleaning the AX338 Sniper Rifle, rubbing the barrel with an oily rag.

He saw from Lotte's expression that something was wrong and he paused briefly with his task.

"The idiot!" Lotte said harshly. "What the hell is he thinking coming here?"

Johan grunted, and went back to his task.

"What's that supposed to mean?"

"Nothing. Just that I did warn you he was the weak link. That if things became difficult, then it wouldn't take much for him to crack."

"But nothing bad has happened. Everything is going exactly as I anticipated... well mostly. And anyway, wasn't it Tobias who you had concerns about?"

She was venting her frustration on her Uncle, which was unfair she knew, but she did it nonetheless.

"Him as well. The more people who are involved, the more chances there are for something to go wrong."

"A bit of gratitude from him wouldn't go amiss. I provided him with the money for the clinic, and supplied him with his volunteers for his crazy experiments. All he had to do in return was give us Nina Bakker."

Johan raised one eyebrow, thinking to himself that his understanding of the word 'volunteer' must be different from hers. But he didn't say this to her. Instead he asked: "Do you want me to tidy this mess up?"

Lotte looked at him. "What? No, it's too risky. If anybody linked you with Visser." She didn't finish the sentence.

Somewhere, they heard the sound of a tap running, then splashing water.

"I'll deal with it," she told him.

She moved across the room and picked her mobile up off the coffee table. Quickly tapping in a number, she waited while the line rang at the other end. Somebody answered.
"Mr Trinh? It's me. I'm in need of your services."

Mr Trinh arrived thirty minutes later, looking all dapper as usual in his long, grey trench coat and black trilby hat, glasses perched on the end of his nose.
Mr Trinh never spoke much. He wasn't one for pleasantries or small talk. His line of work didn't call for friendly chats over a coffee. He didn't even like to use first names. If possible, he preferred to arrive, complete the required task, and leave with the merchandise as quickly as can be, uttering as few words as he could.
Knowing how discreet Mr Trinh was, Lotte put up with his small oddities.
She let him in and pointed to the bathroom door at the end of the long passageway.
"He's been taking a bath. He's just getting dressed"
"Still alive?" Mr Trinh enquired, the tiniest of inflections in his voice giving away his surprise.
"Yes. I didn't want to get my hands messy."
With a curt nod, he went down the passage. Lotte watched him pause briefly outside the bathroom and remove a tiny scalpel from his coat pocket, and then she went back into the study, shutting the door.
A few minutes later, she and Johan heard the front door close.
Mr Trinh and Julian Visser were gone.

Amsterdam's small Chinatown district was centred on Zeedijk, the narrow and busy road that followed the course of the old 16th century sea dyke. Originally part of the Nautical Quarter and lined with notorious taverns and brothels, during the 1960's it became the hangout for junkies and dealers, a district riddled with crime and a no-go area for locals and tourists alike. However during the '90's the city council made efforts to 'trendify' the place, pushing the lowlife back into the red light district to the west, and offering tax breaks to any individuals willing to set up legitimate businesses there. The result was a flourishing area crammed with Chinese, Indonesian and Vietnamese shops and restaurants. The place cleaned up its act and the tourists flocked back in.

Yet like all such places, it could not quite escape its dark past.

Just behind the Toko Dun Yong supermarket was a long and shadowy street snaking off Zeedijk. It led to a tiny little doorway with peeling green paint. Set in the wall at the side of the door was a discoloured sign: Loon Fung Meat Processing Plant.

Mr Trinh reversed his small white van up the side-street until the rear door was almost flush with the green door, leaving just enough room for him to squeeze by but blocking off the view from any prying eyes. Taking a bunch of keys from the glove compartment he climbed out and unlocked the green door. Just inside was a wheeled sack cart. Taking it outside, he pushed up the rolling door at the rear of his van. Lying on the bed of the van, trussed up with cable ties, was the body of Julian Visser, with the gaping wound in its neck grinning at him like a second mouth.

Manhandling the corpse out of the back of the van and onto the sack cart, he turned and wheeled it back inside the meat processing plant, and after locking the door behind him and flicking a light switch on the wall, pushed it down the short hallway and through the heavy plastic curtain at the end.

On the other side was a square and windowless room. The floor was of bare concrete with several drainage gullies set in the centre, while over to the left was a large wooden cutting table normally used for butchering animal carcasses. A row of metal hooks hung from the ceiling on a racking system. Opposite the table were a pair of large stainless-steel machines with wide chutes on the top: one was for processing raw meat, the other was a bone grinder. In the corner was a door with a small wheel handle on the front – this was a walk-in refrigerator.

Mr Trinh removed his hat and coat and hung them on a hook just beside the plastic curtain. Then he slipped off his expensive shoes. He reached for a heavy-duty butcher's apron and a pair of plastic wellington boots and gloves and put them on, followed by a plastic face-screen. Thus attired, he wheeled the corpse over to the cutting table and dragged it up onto the wooden top. Then he removed Visser's clothes, folding them neatly and placing them on a counter.

Hanging on the wall within easy reach were a set of butcher's tools, saws, bone cutters, meat cleavers, knives and so on, and he studied them for a moment, deciding which to use. Choosing one of the bigger cleavers he set to work, first removing the corpse's hands and feet with single cuts. These he plopped into the meat processor.

Next, he carefully sawed through the top of the head to remove a semi-circular section of the skull. Using a long knife from the set of tools he cut through the brain stem – an awkward task that required reaching deep into the skull and twisting the soft and squishy organ until it came free. He carried the brain over to the processor – lots of nourishment here, he thought in a rare moment of light-relief, as he dropped it into the chute.

Back at the chopping block, he applied the same knife to slice through Visser's chest. Using an electric sternal saw to cut through the sternum, and a pair of long-handled bone shears to cut through the ribs, he worked diligently until the torso was fully opened up, which allowed him access to the internal organs. These he removed one by one, applying his basic anatomical knowledge gained through practice. These too went into the meat processor.

Going back to the corpse, which now had a fully-scooped out cavity in the torso, he methodically commenced to cut away the bones, snapping through the ribs and vertebrae with the shears, and moving on to the legs and arms and doing likewise, carefully dissecting the skeleton one piece at a time. The bones went into the second machine, the bone grinder, to be powdered up and turned into fertilizer for people's gardens and allotments. The skull went in last.

When he was done Mr Trinh switched on the machines. There was a loud hum, followed by the ratcheting sound of gears cutting and crunching through the meat and bones, the stainless-steel machinery shaking and grinding as they worked away, to reduce the butchered remains into tiny pieces of processed meat and ground-up bone meal.

At the base of each machine a narrow rubber funnel fed the contents into a pair of steel tubs, and Mr Trinh watched them steadily fill to the brim. The machines kicked off automatically, and two lids were stamped and sealed into place over the tubs, and labels glued on the top with the barcodes marking the contents. One was labelled garden fertilizer, the other as pet food.

Lifting them one at a time, he carried them over to the walk-in refrigerator, pushed them to the back amidst identical stacks of tubs, and shut the heavy door. They would eventually be repackaged and distributed throughout the city to end up on store shelves.

All there was left to do was to steam clean the bench and floor and tools, wash down the apron and rubber gloves and boots, clean the visor with cleaning spray, and rinse out the machinery with water and filtered industrial-strength detergent.

On his way out he gathered up the neatly folded clothes.

Once laundered they would be as good as new. He would add them to his growing collection.

Mr Trinh locked up and laughed gently to himself.

"Hehehehehe."

* * *

It was late evening by the time Pieter reached the hospital. He asked to be directed to where Officer Groot was being kept, and was told she was on the second floor on the assessment ward and under observation, but the male admitting clerk pointed out in strong terms that visiting was not permitted this late. Pieter ignored him, and headed for the bank of elevators.

Kaatje was in her own private room with a police guard outside. She lay in the bed, her eyes heavily bandaged, but still awake. She turned her head as he pushed through the door, and he saw her flinch and tense.

"It's me," he whispered gently, and she relaxed back into her pillow.

After his hair-raising escape from the clinic, he had immediately called in some back-up, and within minutes a police ERT team had arrived on the scene, sealing off the car park and throwing up roadblocks to divert traffic away from the area. Shortly after, a well-armed assault squad had made a forced entry into the building. Led by the reassuring figure of squad leader Dyatlov – who had worked with Pieter on the Werewolf case back in the spring – they searched the place room-by-room and corridor-by-corridor, scouring every inch of the clinic for any sign of the patients or staff. But apart from the bodies of those that Pieter had shot during his escape, there had been no sign of anyone. They had all melted away into the night, either into the streets or across the frozen pond towards the nature park. It was a bitterly cold night, with temperatures set to plummet well below freezing, and everybody mostly agreed that they would not last long, dressed as they were in flimsy pyjamas.

Pieter wasn't convinced. With Lotte involved, he knew this would not be a normal investigation. There would be aspects of this case that many of his colleagues would find so unusual, so out of their comfort zone, that many would dismiss as ridiculous, maybe the ramblings of a fraught and stressed out cop fresh back from mandatory sick leave, someone who was still so badly affected and traumatized that he probably should never have been allowed back at all. That's what they would say, and Pieter could hardly blame them.

Yet equally he sensed a realization from them, during the few moments he had spoken to them and explained the situation, that they had been presented with an opportunity to get Charlotte Janssen once and for all, to settle scores after the nightmare that had gripped Amsterdam during the spring. They were determined that this time she would not get away.

Yet they must not forget about Nina Bakker, Pieter told himself.

They could not afford to be distracted and focused only on finding Lotte, not when there was a frightened twelve year old girl still being held captive somewhere.

Putting these concerns to one side for the moment Pieter turned his attention to Kaatje.

Her face was turned towards him still. She was on very strong pain relief, and an operation was planned to see if anything could be done to save her eyesight, but he knew the prognosis was poor. He'd seen for himself the damage done to her eyes, and the shock and distress and worry must be eating away at her, and so he reached out and took her hand in his, giving her fingers a reassuring squeeze.

"I'm sorry," she said quietly, her chin trembling with barely-controlled emotion.

"No, *I'm* sorry. I shouldn't have hung you out to dry yesterday, after Huijber's threw you off the case. I should have spoken up for you more."

Kaatje gave a little shake of her head. "It wouldn't have made any difference. I'd have still done the same thing. It's stupid I know, but I was excited to be involved, to be helping with the case. I wanted to impress everyone. The rookie cop making the big breakthrough on a big profile case. Ah, what was I thinking? Call me an idiot if you like."

"Idiot."

They both laughed quietly.

"I also wanted to impress you," she mumbled, sounding like she was talking to herself.

She pulled her hand free, and turned her bandaged face away in embarrassment.

Sitting at the bedside, Pieter felt an odd sensation pass through him, and he found himself temporarily floundering for a response. His eyes suddenly felt all hot and prickly and he quickly rubbed at them, glad that Kaatje couldn't see, which made him feel even worse.

Who's the idiot now? he thought to himself. He shook his head, but the peculiar feeling remained.

He rubbed her bare forearm gently. "You certainly made a big impression," and his voice was all wobbly.

Suddenly Kaatje turned back and threw herself into his arms, taking him by surprise, but he instinctively hugged her tight as she shook and trembled, and Pieter bent low and kissed her bandaged eyes ever so gently, whispering quiet words of comfort, and feeling tears on his face but not caring anymore.

After a few minutes they drew apart, both of them perhaps feeling better for the release of pent-up emotion. Kaatje held onto his hand. He sensed the act represented more than mere physical contact for her.

"Tell me. About everything. About what led you back there."

Carefully, and leaving nothing out, Kaatje went over what had happened. She told him about her visit to the riding school off Vondelstraat, her talk with Madame Benoit and what she had discovered about Nina's friend, the tragic accident involving the horse. The link with the clinic, where Elena had been treated, the surgery carried out by Doctor Bakker, and then Elena's subsequent suicide. And finally of her return trip to Osdorp and the horror she had endured there.

"Did you find Visser?" she asked nervously when she was done.

Pieter thought it wise not to tell her about what he had discovered there, the files in Visser's office, the ward full of patients with no eyes. She had been through enough already.

"We're still looking for him," he replied. "There's a police officer right outside your room. No way will he come here."

She nodded, and her nails dug into his hand.

"Elena's the link, Pieter. Find the link and you'll find Nina."

Back out in the corridor, Pieter was surprised to find Commissaris Huijbers waiting for him at this hour on a Saturday night. Even more surprising, his superior was sitting in a chair and leaning forward with his forearms over his knees, staring at the floor and looking very subdued.

Further along the corridor, a uniformed officer stood with his back to the wall, his eyes fixed straight ahead, not quite sure what to make of the scene.

On spotting Pieter, Huijbers came wearily to his feet. His face was etched with lines, and he looked at Pieter searchingly.

"How's she doing?" he asked quietly.

Pieter wanted to punch him in the face.

But he felt tired to the bone. His mind was still jumpy from the fight at the clinic, he couldn't stop himself from seeing Kaatje lying in the snow outside his house with her eyes burned away, and the thought of Lotte being behind all of this sickened him. So he slumped against the wall and leaned his head back, looking up at the overhead lights. He blew out between his cheeks.

"She's a strong one, that Groot," Huijbers was saying, like he knew anything about her. "But we'll be there for her every step of the way during her recovery. We'll take care of her financially going forward, her medical bills will be paid even though technically she was off duty when it happened. I'm even thinking of recommending her for some kind of bravery award. Yes, she's a fine example of Dutch Law Enforcement, someone for others to emulate. Perhaps, when she's back on her feet, we could find a role for her in helping to recruit young volunteers, especially in the schools. Get the kids interested in joining up, that kind of thing."

"We wouldn't want to miss an opportunity like this would we?" Pieter mumbled.

Huijbers' face went bright red, and he looked visibly uncomfortable.

"Of course that's way into the future," he stressed. "The immediate priority is to offer her as much support as we can."

Huijbers took off his hat and dropped it onto his chair.

"Look Van Dijk," he continued, "I know I can be a bastard at times. It comes with the job. I'm not here to be popular or anything, to chew the fat with the lads and lasses in the ranks, have a beer with them in a Brown Café. As the Police Chief, I have to build a wall between myself and you guys. I was a rookie once myself, just like she is, and I know how it works. The big chief has to act differently because he is different, and that's how it's always been. But…" and he softened his voice here… "this has come as a complete shock to us all. I'm not a heartless man, I have a daughter myself around about the same age as Officer Groot –"

"She's called Kaatje."

"What? Yes, Kaatje. Look, what I'm saying is that I want to catch these guys just as much as you. Especially that lunatic Visser and that crazy woman, Janssen. This is the opportunity we've been waiting for, to bring her in. Now that she has reared her ugly head we can't let this chance go to waste. If only for Kaatje's sake."

Pieter pushed himself off the wall and rubbed his face, the skin on his hand scraping against his three-day stubble. Huijber's words were like an annoying bee buzzing around, his voice going in one ear and out of the other.

"Has anything been seen of Visser yet? he asked. "He wasn't at the clinic, just those loonies who attacked me. He must have gone somewhere after he left Kaatje outside my house."

"Nothing yet. He's gone to ground somewhere. But he'll turn up, and the patients who he was carrying out his crazy fucking experiments on, which makes no sense to me. People with no eyes! I wouldn't have believed it if I hadn't seen those dead ones for myself. Yes, it's only a matter of time until we find him. We've flooded the whole area with officers so he won't get far."

Huijbers paused just then, and Pieter glanced over. He was looking at the door to Kaatje's room, his mouth working away silently, and when he turned to face Pieter again, a steely determination had hardened his eyes.

"We'll get them, Pieter," he whispered with real meaning. "We'll get the fuckers who did that to her."

On his way down in the elevator Pieter found a number for Madame Benoit, the Centre Manager at the Hollandsche Manege Riding School, and despite the late hour, he rang her.

He told her he wanted as much information as possible about the stable girl Elena.

Chapter 15
The Smell of the Sea

Elena Vinke.

That was the name Madame Benoit had given him. Pieter ran it through the system at work the following morning, even though it was a Sunday.

Elena was just two months short of her sixteenth birthday and working as one of the stable hands on the weekends and during the school holidays when the accident happened. Her parents were now separated and waiting for a divorce, the tragedy having driven an irreparable wedge between them. There wasn't much on the father, but her mother was still living in the family home with her new boyfriend, and so Pieter had phoned to arrange a visit for later that morning.

Saskia Vinke was a very tall woman in her mid-thirties, with a blonde bob and ice-blue eyes, her glamorous features marred by a down-turned little mouth and worry lines radiating from her temples. She greeted Pieter pleasantly enough, but he could feel the grief was there just below the surface, a year after the death of her daughter.

She and her new man lived just around the corner from the Albert Cuyp Street Market in the De Pijp district of Amsterdam. She led him into the small kitchen and poured him a very strong coffee, telling him her boyfriend had popped out to allow them to talk freely. She sat opposite him across the narrow kitchen bar, holding her mug with both hands to warm them. It was cold, with the heating turned down, and there was a pile of dirty dishes in the sink, and from somewhere in the basement came the sound of a spin-dryer vibrating at full speed.

"You've caught me at a bad time, so please excuse the mess. Sundays are always a day for catching up on the housework."

Pieter brushed away her concerns with a casual flick of his hand. He sipped at his coffee, his eyes glancing through the door to the living room and seeing the framed pictures on the wall of a young teenage girl, smiling and laughing and surrounded by autumnal trees.

"Do you mind if I smoke? I normally only do so outside, but your phone call this morning took me unawares, and I find it easier to talk if I can smoke. It settles my nerves."

Pieter smiled and nodded and watched as she lit a cigarette, her hands visibly shaking.

Saskia blew smoke up at the ceiling and gave an exaggerated shudder of her shoulders. "That's better," she laughed nervously.

Crossing her legs, she put her elbow on the counter, holding the cigarette upright.

"I'm assuming you're here because of Elena?"

"Yes."

"You're one of the few people to have come around since it happened. We don't get many visitors and those who do bother calling tend to want to talk about other things, anything other than about Elena. It's understandable I suppose. It probably makes them feel uncomfortable, wondering if I'm going to break down and fling myself on the floor. But it is nice of you to come, even if it's only for official reasons."

Pieter looked at her and she cast her gaze away, and she drew hard on the cigarette.

"What is it you want to know?"

"Tell me about your daughter, about the accident."

"Where do I begin? It was a day just like any other, a sunny morning just over a year ago. A sunny Saturday morning, cold and crisp and clear. The riders had taken the horses across to the park to ride along the track that they have there, they do that whenever the weather is good. It's something they've done a hundred times before. Elena, with the other stable hands, waited back at the riding school as normal.

Sometimes the horses can be very frisky and excited when they come back from the park. That's nothing out of the ordinary, and so it was that day. The girls came back, with Nina Bakker amongst them, and went into the stables, and Elena was helping to remove the saddle and so on when, out of the blue, the horse Nina had been riding suddenly kicked out with its hind leg. Elena just happened to be bending over at the time and the hoof caught her right in the eye, just here."

Saskia tapped at her brow just above her right eye with the hand holding the cigarette.

"Pop, right into the socket apparently. There was a lot of blood, and the girls were screaming they say, the staff running around in a complete panic, and somebody called for an ambulance and then they called me. I was working at the time – I work part-time in a café on Waterlooplein – but I dashed straight over to the hospital and Tobias was just arriving at the same time-"

"Tobias?"

"My ex-husband. Anyway, we went in to see Elena and, thank-the-Lord, it didn't seem too bad at first. She was sitting up in bed quite enjoying all of the attention, with her eye all bloodshot and her socket all swollen up, but the damage seemed fairly superficial. She had a detached retina and mild concussion, but considering how bad it first appeared, she seemed to have got off quite lightly. They kept her in for a few days and decided she should have a minor operation, a routine procedure. They suggested we have it done out at the new eye clinic in Osdorp, you know the one?"

Pieter nodded. "Yes, I've heard of it."

Saskia went on.

"Anyway, they booked her in and they did the op later the following week. Doctor Bakker carried out the procedure and it should have been a very straightforward thing, no more than an hour and she'd be able to come home the next day. But they experienced some unexpected complications, and one hour became two or three, and me and Tobias were waiting in the reception area and the girl behind the desk would come over and give us updates from time to time. Five hours went by, and God knows what was going on, but finally Doctor Bakker himself appeared some eight hours after the operation began, and we knew straight away from the look on his face that something was wrong. He was very pale and he couldn't stop wringing his hands.

'How's my Elena?' I asked. 'Is she alright, can we see her?' I was a bit panicky because he looked so grave, but he quickly informed us that Elena was doing alright, she was just coming around from the anaesthetic, which

I can tell you came as a huge relief. But then... well, then he explained that sadly they had not achieved the results they had hoped for.

He told us quite straightforwardly that Elena had permanently lost the sight in her right eye, the one which the horse had kicked, but in addition the sight in her left eye would be severely impaired as well, perhaps down to just twenty percent of normal vision. The damage, he told us, and he was quite distraught himself, the damage would be permanent."

Saskia rose from her stool and went to lean against the door-jam leading to the living room, her gaze fixed on the photos of her daughter.

"We couldn't understand it. What had gone wrong? She only had a detached retina, but she came back out virtually blind and with a life-long disability. We brought her straight home, but Tobias was furious. He stewed on it for weeks, brewing and getting himself all worked up, threatening lawsuits even though we had signed a consent form. He blamed Doctor Bakker, threatened to have his medical licence revoked, calling him at all hours and saying he had destroyed Elena's life, all of our lives, which he had. It all became too much, all I wanted was to help Elena, but instead Tobias wouldn't let it go."

Pieter said nothing, thinking about the death threats the Bakkers had received, the handwritten message, which had suddenly ceased around about three months ago.

"I was sure he would eventually, over time, just come to accept it. But when Tobias gets worked up over something it's hard to get through to him. Normally he is the sweetest person in the world, he was a kind husband and he loved Elena with every fibre in his body; a gentle soul. But he has had a few issues during his life, stemming from his childhood. Nothing major, but just sometimes he can have fits of temper, and he can fly off in one of his rages. I think he was very sad as a little boy, and he never really dealt with that."

"Did he ever seek help? Both before Elena's operation, and afterwards to help deal with it?"

"Tobias? God no! He was old-fashioned I'm afraid, he always thought people should sort out their problems themselves, keep things private."

"Was he ever violent? When he lost his temper?"

Saskia emphatically shook her head. "Never. No, he could rant and rage and turn the air blue, but he never ever raised his hand to me or to Elena. As I say, he may have had a few issues, but he most definitely wasn't a violent man. But his behaviour over Doctor Bakker – and, by the way, I think Doctor Bakker was genuinely remorseful, devastated over what happened to our Elena, and so too was Elena's friend, Nina Bakker, she was inconsolable by all accounts – anyway, the way Tobias was over the whole thing started to have a serious effect on Elena. She was already at the lowest point in her life and having to deal with her new disability, but her father's behaviour made her much much worse. She was at such a low ebb that she was prescribed anti-depressants. But none of us for one minute knew what was to happen next."

Saskia slipped into a drawn-out silence, the cigarette in her hand going unsmoked. Pieter watched ash fall silently onto the floor.

"Pardon me for asking, Mrs Vinke, but the eye clinic out at Osdorp is quite an exclusive place. Certainly not cheap. I'm just wondering..."

"How we could have afforded it?" She smiled sadly.

Pieter waited.

"Tobias liked to tell everybody that he had really good medical insurance. Which was ridiculous. We weren't exactly a well-off family, not from my part-time job and his intermittent work. But Tobias is a proud man, and so that's what he told people. The truth is that we have Nina Bakker to thank – wrong word, probably – we have little Nina to thank for getting Elena into the clinic."

"How so?"

"She felt so bad over the accident, she unfairly blamed herself for what had happened with the horse, that to make amends she persuaded her father Doctor Bakker to perform the surgery free of charge. And considering how that turned out, it left Nina shouldering even more guilt."

"You say your ex-husband blamed Bakker for what happened? Did he ever blame Nina as well?"

Saskia swivelled her head and looked at him in surprise, as though the thought had never occurred to her before. She considered the possibility briefly, and then just shrugged her shoulders.

"I know what you're thinking Inspector," she told him quietly. "As soon as I heard about what happened to Doctor Bakker and his wife, and the announcement about Nina's abduction, it crossed my mind too. Would Tobias do something like that? I asked myself. Is he capable, the man I was married to for all of those years?"

Again, after a pause, she just shrugged.

Walking back over to the counter, she dropped the cigarette into her coffee mug. Pieter heard it sizzle.

"I'll take you upstairs, to Elena's bedroom. That's where she killed herself."

They were standing in the small bedroom, which had been cleared of all furniture and was spotlessly clean. No signs of the daughter remained anywhere up here.

Saskia had closed the door behind them, and she pointed up at a clothes hook on the back.

"That's where we found her, two days after her sixteenth birthday," she told him in a flat voice. "She'd hung herself with the cord from her dressing gown."

Pieter felt his mouth go dry, and he stared at the hook because he didn't know where else to look.

"It was just before breakfast. I came upstairs to help her as usual, and I came in, and there she was. She'd been dead for several hours so the assumption was that she took her own life shortly after we all went to bed the night before. The weird thing was that during the previous evening Elena had been feeling more positive, the best she'd been since the operation. She actually spent some time sitting with us downstairs, cuddled up on the couch with me and Tobias watching the TV. Which is stupid, as she could barely see anything, never mind the television – silly, right?"

Saskia went back outside and waited for him on the landing.

Pieter re-joined her.

"Me and Tobias separated a month or so later, just after the New Year."

"Do you know if he continued to have any contact with Doctor Bakker? After you split up?"

"I've no idea. We hardly speak. I guess it's possible."

"What does he do for a living? You said downstairs that he worked intermittently."

"He's a ship breaker. He works for NV Damen, a small business in the Western Islands. When they have enough work for him that is."

Pieter knew the place. It was just to the west of Centraal Station. He and his dad used to take walks there sometimes, when the weather was nice and his dad was sober.

"Do you have an address for him? Where is he living these days?"

He tried to sound casual, but inside he could feel his excitement starting to build.

"He moved out in January. To a small place in Warder. It's on the coast, just north of Edam. A tiny community full of fishing boats and seagulls. He was brought up in that part of Holland. Tobias has always liked the smell of the sea."

* * *

Tobias had been in another of his rages for nearly two days now.

Down in the basement, Nina heard him stomping back and forth across the room just over her head, banging doors and talking loudly but inaudibly to himself, and occasionally screaming obscenities.

She'd heard him arrive back home the night before last (on a Friday evening she thought, although she was already losing track of the days) and all that night she had lain in her bed listening to him tearing the place apart, smashing things, thumping and kicking the walls, or overturning the furniture by the sounds of it, yelling and making a terrifying ruckus, and Nina had shut her eyes and tried to block out the noise. It had been impossible. The sheer violence of his anger petrified her, making her cringe and duck at each new bang, at every guttural and muffled roar. It was only towards the early hours that things had finally gone quiet; perhaps sheer exhaustion had eventually overcome Tobias.

What was wrong? Nina wondered.

Was it something to do with what had happened that morning at breakfast, the way he had reacted after she'd asked him, in all innocence, if Tobias truly was his name? The way he had quietly left as though the question had unsettled him somehow? Thinking back, she remembered hearing him talking loudly to himself soon after followed by what she thought was the sound of crying, and then a short while later by the slamming of a door. He'd been gone all that day, returning later and launching into this never-ending rage.

The following morning she had awoken to relative quiet. A short time after, and she could make out the muffled sound of a TV or a radio. During the afternoon there was the occasional banging and scraping, a little more shouting, and then more hush. But as the day wore on the shouting became worse again, and by early evening the commotion and discord grew into a continuous uproar.

Luckily, he had not been down to see her or to bring her food, and although she was grateful for that considering his obvious anger, this also concerned her. And as Saturday night stretched into Sunday morning with no let-up in the sounds from above, and after two days of being left alone down here, Nina had come to the conclusion that she needed to get out of here. She needed to try and escape.

That Tobias – if that were even his real name – was totally and dangerously deranged was now obvious to Nina. Her attempts to talk to him, to befriend him, had failed. It had seemingly made her situation much worse, to the extent that if she didn't try and do something about her predicament, then there was only one way this was headed.

Sitting at the small table, Nina looked around at her now-familiar surroundings, wondering what she could possibly do. The door at the top of the steps was always kept locked apart from when Tobias had come and gone, so she doubted if she could somehow break out that way. There were no windows down here, nor any ventilation shafts to crawl through. The bathroom likewise was completely sealed in. Tobias had obviously taken some time to prepare the place and to make it seemingly escape-proof.

Could she distract him somehow, perhaps cause a diversion or something to get him to come down here, and then attempt to overpower him? Standing, she wandered around the basement, looking for something she could use as a weapon. The knives and forks were all of the cheap plastic types found in motorway cafes, and useless to use for stabbing or slashing someone. There were wire coat hangers in the wardrobe, but these were fixed to the rail. The small lamp on her bedside table had a short flex which if she unplugged it might be used to strangle or tie someone up, but Tobias was a strong man and she had no delusions of how successful that would be. There were the two chairs which she might be able to throw at him, along with plenty of small items like books and DVDs, as well as the cushions from the couch, even the bookshelf, but again he would probably just brush those aside with his big, powerful arms. And if she failed, if he fought her off, what then? Would his wrath and terrible temper get even more out of control? Whatever she decided to try she would have just one opportunity, and if the door were locked anyway, it would all be for nothing.

Nina slumped down onto the edge of her bed.

Her chin trembled, and she started to cry.

Overhead, Tobias had gone quiet again.

They were in position by midday.

Pieter raised the binoculars to his eyes for what must have been the ninth or tenth time in the last five minutes.

He was lying on top of the sea dyke, and he was bitterly cold even with the thick fleece he wore and the woolly hood pulled up. The ground beneath him was frozen solid and as hard as concrete, and at his back was the huge expanse of the Markermeer lake, which was really part of the North Sea but for the 30km long dam separating the two huge bodies of water. A cold wind blew over the white-crested waves straight towards where Pieter had taken up position, and he wondered again why he had chosen this spot, but knew that for all of its discomforts, this really was the best place from which to watch the house.

Overhead a seagull hovered in the stiff wind, and he hoped it didn't give away his location. There was a strong salty smell in the air.

Running along the top of the embankment was a footpath which was popular with dog walkers, and just below and running parallel with it was a narrow road. On the far side ran a shallow ditch, solid with ice, and with small footbridges crossing over every hundred yards or so. Beyond this was the bungalow.

It was a ramshackle place Pieter thought, giving it another scan. The old pebble-dash walls and doors looked on the verge of falling down, and there were clumps of weeds growing out of the guttering. One window had a taped-over crack in the corner. The kind of dwelling hurriedly constructed after World War 2 by the thousands all over Holland, and allowed to run into disrepair by their owners.

High hedges surrounded the yard out front but through their twiggy branches he could see a propane tank and a green-painted corrugated iron shed, and an empty field beyond.

It was the kind of non-descript run-down home out in the middle of nowhere that most people wouldn't have glanced twice at. The perfect location you could say. Parked in the yard was a black van.

Just then a movement caught his eye and Pieter spun the binoculars a little to the left, and he saw coming towards him a man walking a dog, crossing over the narrow footbridge next to the bungalow's driveway. Hurriedly, Pieter rolled over onto his side, ducking down out of sight below the level of the dyke, and he felt his nerves jangle.

Footsteps were coming up the other side of the grassy slope, someone muttering to themselves, and a dog's panting breath.

Then someone was slipping into position beside him, and the dog was licking his cold fingers which felt good, and a familiar face peered at him from beneath a red woolly hat.

One of Dyatlov's men, a member of the assault team.

"Well?" Pieter asked him.

"Quiet as a graveyard. Nobody stirring at all, not even a little mouse with fucking clogs on. Looks like he's having a Sunday morning lie in."

Pieter looked once again at the house and their surroundings. From here he could see the various members of the assault squad in position, ready to launch the raid from different points. They had assembled in double-quick time and rushed out from Amsterdam to the small coastal community of Warder, approximately 35km to the north, and once here they had hurriedly formulated an assault plan. Go in hard and fast but with no fanfare and with as little disturbance to the locals as possible, as the element of surprise was essential if they were to rescue Nina alive and well. Now they were all ready and just waiting on Pieter to give them the green light.

"It's your call," Dyatlov's man reminded him unnecessarily.

After a couple more beats of his racing heart, Pieter gave the tiniest of nods.

"It's a go, repeat, it's a go," the other man whispered into his walkie-talkie, and then he slipped away, taking the dog – who may have a role to play in the assault – with him.

Within sixty seconds the various teams were on the move. Working in pairs, with one man armed with an SBR Full-Auto assault rifle and his buddy carrying a Kevlar shield tall and wide enough to protect both men, they moved silently towards the target. One team trotted silently down the roadway and through the main gates, gliding towards the bungalow. A second team came from the field and slid along the side of the green shed, hugging the walls. A third team appeared through the hedge at the rear of the premises. Further along the road, an armoured police vehicle appeared and slew sideways to block access to any traffic: this was the command vehicle, from where the squad leader Dyatlov would choreograph the raid. In the village itself there were two ambulances on standby should they be needed.

From his perch atop the frozen dyke, Pieter gritted his teeth anxiously and watched the men move in.

As it happened, the opportunity for Nina to get away came about by chance.

During the lull in Tobias' shouting and raging, she had risen from the bed to make a coffee, hoping the hot drink would feel comforting.

As she stood waiting for the electric kettle to boil she noticed the sudden hush that had descended, wondering what he was doing up there. Was he sleeping, having worn himself out? Or had he left on another of his errands? Whatever the reason, she hoped and prayed that his violent episode was at an end.

Yet even as she thought this, and just as she was pouring the hot water into her mug, she heard quick and hurried footsteps overhead, and then the sound of bolts being drawn back and the key turning in the lock, and as she glanced up in sudden fear, the door at the top of the steps opened and Tobias appeared.

She saw him standing there, bare-chested and wearing just jeans and boots, his upper body sheathed in sweat despite the freezing weather outside. His face and his blue eyes were expressionless, and he looked down at her blankly as though wondering who she was and what she was doing here, and then a flicker of recognition suddenly animated his face and he came quickly down the steps, leaving the door open and smiling broadly as he moved across the room towards her.

"Elena," he said breathlessly, "I knew you'd come back."

Nina hesitated for perhaps half a second. Then she threw the scalding liquid at him. It splashed into his face, his eyes and over his chest, burning him. Tobias screamed loudly and flung his hands up and dug his fingers into his eyes, the hot coffee temporarily blinding him, and he staggered sideways and went crashing over into the television.

Nina flung herself past, jumping over his legs as he rolled around on the floor, and raced straight for the steps. She reached the bottom and grabbed a hold of the wooden pommel of the handrail and spun herself around, hearing a huge roar of anger from behind as Tobias came to his feet.

Then she was climbing, with her eyes fixed on the opening above and her mind on one thing: to get through the doorway and run, run as fast as she had ever run before, just to keep on going, and her heart leaped up into her mouth as she heard the crashing of heavy footsteps as Tobias gave chase, right on her heels.

They gained entry through the front and back in perfect sync, using hand-held battering rams to cave the doors in with one blow, the old wood providing little resistance. The team by the green shed covered them.

As was their training, once they were inside the idea was to create as much noise and confusion as possible in order to frighten and overwhelm any occupants, and so the squad members screamed and shouted and smashed their way through the building room by room, kicking in doors and clearing the bungalow with maximum force behind a wall of noise. So much so that they could not hear themselves think.

Beyond the front entrance there was a short hallway lined with wooden panels, with a right-hand turn at the end. The pair of armed men rushed down, all pretence of subterfuge gone, and they found themselves in a kitchen. There was a table and chairs, the units and shelves all covered in dust and cobwebs, and on the far side a partially-opened door leading to the basement.

Skirting the room, sticking to each other shoulder-to-shoulder, gun and shield held forwards, they approached the door.

Nina made it with inches to spare, just as she felt Tobias snatch for her ankle with his huge hands, his fingers very nearly getting a hold. She kicked out and felt her foot hit him square in the face, and he yelped and staggered back.

It gained her perhaps two or three seconds. Nina burst from the basement, through the doorway.

The kitchen was a wreck, with smashed furniture and broken crockery everywhere, the units and sink ripped apart, the shelves flung onto the floor. Above her, the fluorescent light was flickering wildly. Nina charged through the mess, her eyes darting around until she saw another door leading off from the kitchen, and she made straight for it, hoping to God that it wasn't locked.

She flung it wide and found herself in another room, a parlour by the looks of it with old-fashioned furniture and lace curtains over the windows and an ancient record player in the corner. This room was undamaged, but with motes of dust floating in the sunbeams coming through the glass, and it smelled musty and unused.

Nina gave it no further consideration because behind her she could hear Tobias coming after her, pushing through the wreckage in the kitchen to clear himself a path. Nina crossed the parlour in a flash, towards another door which surely must lead to the outside.

"Elena!" she heard Tobias roaring. "Come back!"

Twisting the door handle she pulled, and so suddenly that she couldn't quite believe it was happening, she found herself outside and running over a gravel yard, the strong smell of brine and the sea calling to her.

She stood there for a few seconds to get her bearings. She'd had no real plan on what to do if she ever reached outside, she had never really thought that far ahead and the whole thing had happened so quickly that she was dazed. Perhaps in her mind she had this idea that there would be people around and that she could fling herself into the nearest pair of arms crying for help. But the reality was different.

The place was deserted and desolate, and it was exposed to the elements with a freezing wind buffeting over a huge expanse of water, and snow was driving hard into her face. She was dressed in leggings and a hoodie and her running shoes, and after a few seconds Nina was shivering from the cold.

Behind her there came more shouting and she glanced back in time to see Tobias emerge from the building, which she now saw was nothing but a dilapidated shack with wooden walls and a tin roof with a tiny chimney pot on the top, with a lean-to on the side and a yard full of rubbish and a long greenhouse with most of its windows smashed and brown dead plants inside.

Tobias saw her and came tottering towards her, his arms flapping and tears streaming down his face.

Nina turned and fled.

The yard sloped down to a three-barred gate and she quickly climbed over and found herself on a dirt track, which was frozen hard and difficult to run on. It branched in two directions. The left went past a junkyard full of old rusty cars and boat keels, with a large crane boom towering above. The right path followed a rocky shoreline towards an empty concrete jetty and then further along it curved back to the left in a square shape, like some kind of small inner harbour. From somewhere behind her, she could hear the sound of cars whizzing by at high speed – a motorway by the sound of it. But to go that way would mean running back into the yard, back towards the house.

Then she spotted about fifty yards in front of her a small motor-launch tied up to a wooden pile on a narrow pebble beach. It was little more than a fisherman's rowing boat with an outboard motor, but it might be her salvation if she could get there in time.

Nina sprinted forward, her arms pumping hard. Onto the pebbles, which slipped and slid under her feet, slowing her progress.

"No!" she heard Tobias shouting. "NO!!"

She heard the fury in his voice, and it terrified her. If he caught her... She refused to think anymore and put all of her efforts into reaching the boat. If she considered the outcome of Tobias catching her, then she would just collapse in defeat.

Already he was gaining. She could hear him breathing hard through his nostrils, was sure she could feel his hot breath on the back of her neck.

With just a few yards to go her foot became entangled in a twisty length of seaweed and it seemed to snake around her ankle, and her foot was caught fast and down she went, hitting the beach so hard that she was winded.

Nina stretched out her hand and touched the wooden boat with her fingertips, a cry of dismay escaping her lips. Then Tobias was on her, kneeling on her back and bearing down with his full weight to pin her flat to the ground.

"Bitch," he whispered, with his mouth close to her ear.

Scooping her up in his arms and flinging her over his shoulder he carried her back up the beach, over the track and through the gate, then back across the yard, into the house.

Nina screamed and screamed.

Pieter felt his mobile phone vibrate in his breast pocket. He fished it out with his cold fingers and saw that it was Dyatlov calling from the command vehicle.

Swiping the screen he said: "Yes? Do we have her?"

Dyatlov's strong Russian voice came over the line. "Sorry boss. The place is empty. No sign of Nina Bakker or the creep who took her. It's the wrong place."

Pieter felt his head sag down onto the cold earth of the dyke, all the strength going out of him.

"I'll meet you by the entrance," Dyatlov added, and signed off.

They crossed over the narrow wooden footbridge and went towards where a vehicle track swept through the entrance gates into the gravel yard, close to the propane tank. Dyatlov led him over to the smashed-in front door, which had come off its hinges. The men of the assault team were loitering about, smoking cigarettes and joking as they came down from the adrenaline high, and Pieter avoided eye contact with them.

He'd been so sure. So sure that they would find Nina.

Inside, the place was quiet and calm. A hush had descended, and it was cold, as though the bungalow had not been heated for some time.

They stepped into the kitchen. There was a large table in the centre, with places set for three people: plates, knives and forks, glasses filled with curdled, smelly milk, chairs tucked under the table. Everything was neat and tidy but covered with a thin coating of dust. There were cobwebs strung around the lampshade. It looked like nobody had been here for quite a while.

"We found this on the table."

Dyatlov thrust a newspaper into his hands.

It was dated from May of that year, and the headline on the front read: **MASSACRE AT WEEPING TOWER.**

There was a large photo of the spring atrocity emblazoned over the cover.

In the bottom corner, a second image, this one a tiny grainy picture of himself at the crime scene, snapped by a member of the press.

Someone had drawn a ring around it in black felt-tip.

Tobias roughly manhandled her back down into the basement, his heavy boots stomping down the steps, and when she realized where he was taking her, Nina screamed and kicked and fought even more, her terror peaking.

Reaching down with his spare arm, he pulled open the hinged door of the tiny cage in the space below the stairs and pushed her inside, forcing her through the small opening.

Nina thought she was about to hyperventilate but she managed to crawl to the far end and cowered there, hiding her face behind her hands as he slammed the door and snapped the padlock shut.

Through the gaps between her fingers, she saw his contorted face scowling at her through the wire-mesh. Then he turned and walked away.

Several minutes went by.

She heard a metallic scraping noise from the room above, and then his footsteps on the stairs again, and when he stepped back into view Nina saw he was wearing the brown boiler suit and the welder's hood. He was dragging a long and heavy welder's gas tank across the floor, and she watched in terror as, without speaking, he lit the nozzle.

Shaking and gasping, she pressed herself as far back as she could to avoid the shower of white-hot sparks as he set to work.

Tobias sealed the cage door shut, welding her into her tiny prison.

Chapter 16
The Hit

During the Golden Age Holland dominated the maritime trade. Money flowed into the country, helping to pay for the huge expansion of Amsterdam's canal network from the inner canal ring within the protective arms of the rivers Singel and Amstel, to the marshy lands to the east and west, pushing out the city beyond the original sea dikes and city gates. As more land was drained and reclaimed from the sea, new districts grew. Plantage and Oost, Marken and the swampy Vondel, the Jewish quarter in The Jordaan and the majestic sweep of the Keizersgracht and Prinsengracht canals.

To deal with the increase in trade new wharves and warehouses were constructed, and the Damrak, a broad and deep inlet from the river IJ, which allowed boats to sail right into the heart of the city and disgorge their contents onto Dam Square itself, was filled in. This meant ships sailed a mile or so further west and emptied their holds just beyond the outer suburbs. Here the cargoes were weighed and taxes were paid before the goods were transported through the new city gates to the markets on the Dam and Nieuwmarkt.

This area of docks and quaysides later became known as the Western Islands, a somewhat fancy name for a series of jetties held upright by thousands of wooden piles driven deep into the soggy ground. For a hundred years or so the area flourished. But with further expansion of Amsterdam, mostly to the east along the banks of the IJ and where newer and even bigger docks sprung up, the Western Islands slowly went into a steady decline. The wharves and warehouses emptied and the once busy streets and canals fell quiet. People moved out and the place was left to rot, forgotten and neglected.

This remained the case until well into the twentieth century, and only during the 1990's did the area receive a huge cash injection, and with it a new lease of life and a new identity. The old warehouses became fancy bistros or art galleries, the canals were cleaned up and lined with parks and expensive apartments. Young people with lots of money moved in and the Western Islands were transformed. And all within a ten-minute walk of Centraal Station. It was now a much-sought-after neighbourhood.

Mostly.

There is always one exception.

Today Bickersgracht is still a narrow and cobbled lane lined with old and disused gas lampposts, running north to south on the centre of the three islands. The southern stretch of the lane is reasonably pleasant: between the road and the parallel canal, there is a children's play area, a small urban petting farm with pigs and goats and rabbits, and next door an ice-cream parlour. But as the lane pushes north it becomes seedier. Large trees overshadow the cobbled snicket, and here there are several abandoned allotments, which have been allowed to grow wild with thick brambles and nets covered in dead runner beans, there are vandalized huts, and the ground is covered in drug paraphernalia and used condoms and empty beer bottles. Even during the daytime in the middle of summer, it is dark and creepy, not the kind of place mentioned by the tourist board. In the middle of winter, with leaden skies overhead and a blizzard blowing, it is miserable and cold and damp and ugly.

The NV Damen Boat Yard fronted onto this wild and overgrown stretch of canal bank. Like the allotments themselves, it was an eyesore, full of rusty hulls with holes in their keels, the water covered in scum and oil leaks, the concrete quay piled high with wooden crates, empty gas canisters and huge pieces of iron cut into segments by the ship breakers who worked here. There were rats running around, and an old mangy-looking guard dog that spent most of the time asleep in its kennel. Its owner, and the boss of the boatyard, had a portacabin with a nice heater turned up to full, and he very seldom came out to lend a hand.

Not that there was much to do. His business, a small-fry affair clinging on to the past in an industry mostly gone from modern-day Amsterdam, only employed three other people, and all on a part-time basis. They would come in a few days a week whenever there was enough work, to earn a meagre living doing hard, manual labour, and get paid cash-in-hand at the end of each shift.

One of those who worked here was Tobias Vinke.

With his short and stocky frame, he was well suited to the job. He was strong, could work all day long with barely a break, he hardly spoke a word to the others or tried to make friends, and never complained.

His boss preferred it that way. Even if he secretly thought Tobias was a bit of an oddball, a retard and a loner with no girlfriend.

Not that he ever said this to his face of course.

On the Monday morning Tobias turned up for work as normal. As usual, he'd left his van on the north side of the IJ and caught the foot-passenger ferry across the broad river, and then slogged the ten-minute walk to NV Damen through the heavy snow, doing everything as he always did to avoid drawing any suspicion. Changing his routine would only arouse unwanted attention.

He'd left the house early that morning.

After dragging the girl back down into the basement and throwing her into the cage as punishment for trying to leave him, Tobias had spent the rest of the previous day upstairs. And likewise this morning, he had not been down to see her. She could go today without any food, he decided. To teach her a proper lesson, he concluded.

His face still hurt like hell from the scalding hot coffee she had thrown at him, and he had slathered a load of antiseptic cream onto the patchy, red skin, drawing strange looks from the other passengers on the ferry.

Walking down the overgrown path that cut through the allotments, he passed through the gate, mumbling a hello to the dog on his way, and turned towards the dry dock and the large freight barge that he was in the process of working on, his boiler suit and hood in a large canvas bag slung over his shoulder.

Just then a voice called out, causing him to pause mid-stride.

"Hey, Tobias, what you done to your face? You been whacking off again?"

Tobias glanced back over his shoulder.

His boss was standing in the doorway of his portacabin, guffawing at his own joke.

Glowering hard for a few seconds, Tobias turned away and walked on.

Hiding in the brambles and undergrowth of the allotments, Pieter watched the short face-off between the two men, holding his breath as he waited to see what happened. Luckily Vinke didn't rise to the bait, and Pieter relaxed once more, sinking back down onto his knees.

After yesterday's shambles and the raid on the empty bungalow – their investigations were still trying to establish whether or not it may have once belonged to Tobias Vinke – Pieter had concluded the best lead they had was the suspect's place of work. Given the go-ahead from Huijbers, he had arranged a stakeout, to watch and wait for Vinke to put in an appearance.

To be absolutely sure there would be no more cock-ups Pieter had four other men in position. One was hiding nearby in the allotments, another was at the south entrance to Bickersgracht, standing in a doorway and smoking a cigarette, and the other two members of the team were across on the far side of the canal, should their target use the short bridge leading over there.

Their instructions were clear. They were not to apprehend their man under any circumstances unless there was a clear threat to the public's safety. They weren't here to arrest him. They were here to trail him. To follow him in the hope that he would lead them to wherever he was holding Nina - back to his lair.

Until Vinke had turned up just now, Pieter was worried that this would end up being yet another pointless exercise. But much to his relief, this part of the information provided to him by Saskia Vinke had turned out to be accurate, and seeing him come slugging through the snow just now left Pieter with a mixed feeling of satisfaction and unease. For the first time, he looked at the person he was now convinced was the twisted killer and kidnapper they were hunting.

Pieter settled in to wait. They could be in for a long and cold day.

* * *

Lotte watched as her Uncle broke the sniper's rifle down into its component parts and stored each piece into its allotted pockets in the specially designed gun carryall. He zipped it up and then placed a Walter P5 handgun into one of the side pockets. This was his personal sidearm for self-defence should the operation go wrong, which he seemed confident would not happen.

Nevertheless, Lotte was nervous, which was unusual for her.

She'd waited a long time for this. The prospect of revenge, to seek retribution, was making her jumpy and skittish.

Johan glanced across the study at her, a faint smile playing on his lips.

"What's wrong?" he asked, seeming to pick up on her anxiety.

"Nothing," she responded, a little too quickly.

Her Uncle gave a tiny shake of his head, but said nothing back.

Glancing at the time, she told him: "You'd best get going, while I make the call. You know what to do?"

He looked at her, his expression saying *seriously?*

"Sorry," she apologized.

She waited as he quietly slipped outside, closing the door after himself. Her eyes followed him through the leaded window as he trudged through the snow covering the ancient courtyard, where the Virgin Mary more and more resembled a snowman. When he passed from sight she pulled her phone from her jeans and opened her contacts list, tapping one of the names.

A little after noon and Tobias felt his phone buzzing. It was in the front pocket of his boiler suit, and to answer it he had to first switch off his blowtorch, remove his hood and pull off one of his thick gloves with his teeth.

He stared long and hard at the screen, the name of the caller once again making him feel queasy.

He'd been expecting this call for several days now, he knew exactly what it was about, the instructions he was about to receive. Tobias felt himself stumble and he quickly walked around the stern of the barge so that he was out of sight of the portacabin, and he leaned his forehead against the steel hull, his body breaking out in a cold sweat.

The phone rang and rang.

He didn't answer, and after a minute the call stopped.

A few seconds later and it started up again, seeming to buzz louder with each ring.

Tobias walked over to the edge of the canal, brought his arm back, and threw the mobile phone with all of his strength out into the middle of the channel, where it made a loud splash.

He stood there in silence, looking out across the city, but not really seeing the buildings and warehouses and trees. In his mind's eye all he could see was the girl, alone in the basement and imprisoned in the cage.

Oh God, what had he been thinking? he thought to himself. *Why had he done that to her? His beautiful daughter?*

He quickly made a decision. He must get back to her.

They must leave, and find a new home far, far away. Where nobody knew them. Where Lotte could not find them - just the two of them.

Tobias hurriedly packed up his gear, removing the boiler suit and ramming it and the welder's hood back into his bag. Then he dashed through the boatyard, ignoring the shouts from his boss, and out of the gates.

Head tucked into the falling snow, he set off back.

Pieter had seen the strange little episode unfold, watching as Vinke threw the phone into the canal, and he made a mental note to have the water dragged; it was imperative that they retrieve that phone.

Then Vinke was heading in his direction, the path he was taking through the allotments passing just a few metres from his hiding spot, and he kept as still as possible and prayed that he wouldn't spot him lurking in the undergrowth.

Pieter breathed a quiet sigh of relief as the hulking form swept by and out onto the cobbled lane.

Reaching into the deep pocket of his coat, he brought out a walkie-talkie and lifted it to his lips.

"Target is on the move. K Team, four-man track, two by two. Maintain visual contact but do not, repeat do not apprehend. Out."

Waiting for thirty seconds to give Vinke a head start, Pieter slowly came to his feet and stepped out of the allotments and turned right onto

Bickersgracht. Vinke was already halfway along the lane and Pieter shuffled along in his wake, his head pointing down but his eyes raised to keep watch on their quarry from under the brim of his beanie hat.

Further along, the familiar figure of one of his colleagues appeared, and likewise turned and followed Vinke, the two undercover police officers seemingly not together, but maintaining their own distance from each other, looking all the world like two regular blokes walking home through the heavy snow.

Elsewhere, Pieter knew the two other members of K Team across the canal would be hurriedly getting into their beat-up old car and hightailing it onto busy Lange Eilandsgracht to join the pursuit on the far side of the railway tracks that dissected this area from the rest of Amsterdam, and which Vinke would soon be crossing.

Sure enough, at the south end of Bickersgracht, Vinke swung over to the underpass that took him below the raised railway tracks, then turned left to follow the line of viaducts all the way down to the bridge over the water inlet that fed into Prinsengracht canal, before picking up the riverside path there. In the distance, Pieter saw the tall Ibis Hotel and the grand Centraal Station building.

The road that ran parallel to the path was quieter here as most traffic heading towards the station came from the opposite direction. There were a few buses parked up near the long River Cruise boats moored here, and just an old green Cortina gliding along, belching smoke and playing loud music – inside, the two men from K Team.

They drove past Vinke and turned right. As was standard procedure while trailing a suspect, they would park up and get out, and head down a side street to merge casually back into the game of cat and mouse, with Vinke all the while being unaware he was under surveillance.

Was he making for the train station? Pieter wondered. From there he could be heading to anywhere in the country, even beyond Holland's borders. What's more the packed-out concourse would be thronging with thousands of commuters, which worried him. Should Vinke latch on to the fact that he was being followed, and if things turned violent, it would potentially put the lives of members of the public at great risk.

Just then his walkie-talkie clicked and a grating voice came over the frequency.

"Target is turning left, away from the station. Making for the ferry terminal."

He was heading north over the river.

Johan Roost decided the best vantage point to carry out the hit was up on the roof of Centraal Station. From there he would have a clear view of the surrounding area, even as far as the north bank of the river.

Getting up there was a piece of piss.

The Ibis Hotel was positioned right up alongside the train station. There was even a glass walkway over the railway lines. All he'd had to do was book a room a few days ago and turn up like any other guest, and use his door key card to operate the elevator. Walking out through the sliding doors on the fourth floor, he lingered by the glass wall, ostensibly admiring the stunning views over the city until the coast was clear.

Then he hurried across the walkway and paused where there was an emergency exit leading out onto the metal fire-escape, removed a pair of rubber-handled pliers from his breast pocket, and cut the wire that would trigger the door alarm. Pushing the horizontal bar the door popped open, and he passed outside onto the metal gantry, closed the door behind him, and then started to climb up the stairs of the fire-escape.

It took him all of ten seconds.

At the top he squeezed his frame through the gate, by-passed the door leading to the upper-level muster station, and instead he went up the short ladder leading onto the roof itself.

As he stepped out onto the series of slanting roofs the wind hit him smack in the face, and the bone-chilling cold blast temporarily took his breath away. Pulling up the hood of his grey coat and pulling the toggles to draw it tight around his face, he strode forward into the buffeting wind, following the narrow maintenance gangway around the edge of the roof, with just a single handrail separating him from a drop several hundred feet to the ground below. The heavy carryall slung over his shoulder was awkward, threatening to further unbalance him.

He chose a spot on the north side overlooking the grey river. Lowering the bag, he unzipped it and commenced to take out the various parts of the AX338 Sniper's Rifle, the most accurate rifle in the world, and piece by piece he fitted them together.

Lying down and shuffling closer to the edge he altered the legs of the adjustable front tripod, fitted the silencer to the end of the barrel, folded out the stock and cheek rest, and then snapped on the magazine containing 10 rounds of magnum cartridges.

Johan tucked himself down so that the stock of the gun fitted snuggly into his armpit and peered through the eyepiece of the telescopic sight.

All he could see was the blurry snow coming down, but with a few adjustments to the lenses, the river itself jumped sharply into focus. He would have to take the strong cross-wind into consideration, but it was mostly negligible: from pulling the trigger the round would find its target in less than half a second.

Johan snapped the bolt-action forward to feed a round into the chamber.

Finally he plugged an earpiece into his ear and turned on the radio frequency interceptor in his inside pocket. He listened to the voices of the police talking on their walkie-talkies.

Pieter watched as Vinke strode across to the ferry terminal, which was little more than a gate leading up onto the rear ramp of the little blue boats that ferried pedestrians and cyclists back and forth to Amsterdam Noord.

He boarded the one marked Buiksloterweg, which would take him on the short five-minute hop over the river to the Film Museum and the A'Dam Lookout tower, and pushed himself towards the bow with the other passengers. Pieter quickly looked around but could see no sign of the other members of K Team, and feeling suddenly nervous, he hurried forward and onto the ferry just as the ramp was going up. He was the last one onboard.

Shit! he thought to himself as the engines rumbled and the boat slowly slid away from the riverbank. He alone, out of the four-man stakeout team, was now with their target.

He just had time to whisper their destination into his walkie-talkie, and then he switched it off lest it suddenly squawk into life and give him away.

Pieter cast his eyes around to search for Tobias Vinke, and he easily spotted his bulky frame leaning against the boat's starboard gunwale.

The ferry was packed and everybody was standing bunched together for warmth with a cloud of steam rising off their bodies. He politely eased his way through as he wanted to get closer to Vinke. Partly so he could react faster should their target suddenly do something unexpected, but also because he wanted to get a look at him. To see with his own eyes the man they were hunting.

Pieter reached the side and casually moved alongside the large man, his face turned to look at the north shoreline but his every focus on Vinke, surreptitiously taking a quick peak at his features, his body feeling like a coiled spring.

Something about his face struck Pieter as odd, a red splotchy mark over his chin and neck, maybe a birthmark? He didn't want to stare too much and instead pretended to look down at the foaming water below, trying to appear like any other commuter.

Beside him, Vinke stirred and turned in his direction and Pieter felt himself tense. Slowly he moved his right hand nearer his service weapon in its shoulder holster.

His throat felt incredibly dry.

Tobias swung around. The man standing alongside him looked very pale, and the way he was leaning over the side made him wonder if he was about to puke up. Yet he dismissed this thought, for something had caught his eye over on the south side where the riverbank was quickly receding.

Something up on the roof of the train station was glinting, a piece of glass catching the light, and Tobias frowned in mild curiosity.

Looking through the telescopic sight Johan easily identified the distinctive features and dark clothes of the man standing and swaying amidst the other passengers on the ferry, the person he had come all this way to kill. Lotte had become almost obsessed with her plot to eradicate this interfering fool, who she claimed had caused her too many problems. She just wanted him gone. And here he was, falling perfectly into their trap just as she had predicted. Drawn out into the open.

Lining up the crosshairs on the person's head, Johan breathed slowly out and gently squeezed the trigger.

There was a quiet *pft* noise from the silencer, a split second later and the man's features exploded into a red vapour cloud, and a heartbeat after that the sonic boom of the round rumbled back from the far riverbank.

Pieter noticed Vinke shift, and then water-spray from the river flew into his face causing him to blink. He wiped it away, seeing but not immediately registering that his fingers were covered in red.

When he looked at Tobias Vinke again he saw the other man tottering and Pieter couldn't work out why, but then he realized that the top of the man's head was now a gaping hole and blood was spattering everywhere, all over the people around including himself.

Pieter watched dumbfounded as Vinke's body slumped to the deck.

Thunder or something rumbled quietly in the distance.

INTERLUDE

THE HUNT

Mark Hobson

A State of Sin

South Africa
12 Years Ago

"The secret to a successful hunt, Bart, is to drive your quarry out into the open. If they run to ground amongst the krantzes or in the bush or on the savannah, then it will prove very difficult, but if you can track them down and scare them into bolting, into leaving their hiding spot, then nine times out of ten you'll have them. And in that moment when they are caught in your sights or you have them cornered, you have to stay calm no matter how tired you are or how cold or hungry you might feel, no matter how much your heart is racing. But when you strike you have to strike fast, like a scorpion."

Johan Roost's hand whipped out lightning-fast, his fist clenched tight around the handle of the hunting knife, the blade stopping millimetres short of Bart's neck. Bart froze in fear, wondering if his uncle was going to slit his gizzard wide open. The silence stretched out, like the hot afternoon was holding its breath.

Then there came a burst of laughter from the others gathered on the verandah, and a slow lop-sided grin appeared on his uncle's sun-tanned features. Bart watched as he flipped the knife up, seeing it spin in mid-air, and then deftly caught it again and slipped it back into the sheaf on his waist belt. The big hand came up and patted him on the cheek and Bart gave a nervous little high-pitched laugh.

It was the eve of Bart's eighteenth birthday, and on the morrow, his uncle was taking him hunting in some silly rite of passage into manhood. The family had gathered on the front porch of Johan's lodge to enjoy dinner and drink beer and wine, to watch the sun go down below the peaks of the mountain range.

His mother and younger sister were with them. After their meal the two of them had set up a small folding table to play cards, while the men, Bart and his uncle, chatted about men's stuff, although truth be told Bart would rather be joining in with their game of blackjack.

Now Famke turned towards him and leaned forward, dipping her face so that it was level with his own and making him look at her.

"Tomorrow is a big occasion for you Bart. Not every young man like you gets to do something like this. Back home, we live in a big city where people go about their nice lives, driving around in their fancy cars or shopping for luxury goods. People forget their heritage, their roots, their beginnings. They grow soft and fat."

She poked playfully at his tubby stomach.

"But not us. Your Uncle very kindly invited us out here, to our mother country to reconnect with nature. It's a wonderful opportunity for you, a privilege indeed. So do you have something you want to say to your uncle? We talked about it on the plane remember?"

Bart gave a tiny nod and turned his gaze towards his Uncle Johan, who was sitting back in his chair and drinking his beer.

"Thank you," he mumbled shyly, "thank you, Uncle."

Johan Roost slapped him on the knee and then cuffed him gently on the chin with his fist.

"Don't mention it boy! Here, have a drink." He thrust a beer bottle into Bart's podgy hands and clinked his own bottle against it. "Cheers! It will be thirsty work tomorrow, so we men should have a few sun-downers first, what do you say?"

Bart gave a tiny smile, and drank from the bottle, but mostly just sipped at the froth.

Suddenly his sister dropped her hand of cards facedown onto the green baize of the card table, drawing their attention, and she looked around at them all with a sulky expression and a pet lip.

"It's not fair," said eleven year old Charlotte, crossing her arms over her chest. "I want to come too."

Johan and Famke exchanged a glance, and Bart caught his sister's eye and looked away.

"Now you know that's not possible, dear," her mother told her. "This is your brother's big day. A day for the men only."

"But why not?" Lotte insisted. "I can do things the same as Bart. Better even." She scowled at her brother.

"Your mother's right. The hunt will be no place for a young lady. It will be a long and tiring day, out in the sun and with the dust in our eyes, driving in the pickup with Dalton. They'll be blood and bad smells and all kinds of nasty things, plus it will be dangerous. One false move, one lapse of your concentration, and it could cost you a broken arm or leg, maybe worse. Isn't that right Bart?"

Bart nodded, but wishing he could swap places with Lotte and stay home tomorrow to help his mother.

Lotte turned her face away and stared angrily out at the farm, her eyes brimming with tears.

Johan sighed. He had no children of his own, and this visit by his sister with her family was a stark reminder of that. He liked the boy, cared for him dearly, and he was determined to try and bring him out of his shell and toughen him up because he was just too soft for his own good. But the girl. There was something about her that he found hard to resist. His niece could be a little madam at times, a real drama queen, but she had a side to her nature that, well, it melted his heart if truth be told. Which was silly! But she had a spark, a toughness to her that was severely lacking in her older brother. Johan, basically, doted on her.

"Listen," Johan said to her now, "you could come along with us tonight, if you like? If your mother says it's ok. What do you say?"

He glanced at Famke, who nodded and gave a shrug.

Lotte turned to him, a big smile lighting up her face.

The nearest large town was Mooi River, a sixty-minute drive away along unlit dirt tracks.

All three of them sat up front, with Lotte crammed in the middle. She and her uncle chatted away, both completely comfortable in each other's company, an easy rapport that they shared and enjoyed. Yet Bart barely joined in, their voices were just a faint murmur as his concentration was *elsewhere. He stared out of the window into the night, seeing the moths fly by in the truck's headlights but not really noticing them.*

A feeling of dread had been building up inside him all day long, leaving a solid knot of tension deep in his stomach, so much so that he felt queasy and nauseous. He suffered in silence. If the others knew, if they even suspected how he thought about tomorrow's hunt, then his Uncle Johan would admonish him severely, maybe even mete out a physical punishment. And his sister would laugh and ridicule him something rotten, the way she did whenever he cried or withdrew into his private little world. Lotte could be incredibly cruel like that. Her spitefulness, her name-calling, was horrid at times, even though deep down he knew she loved him. So Bart kept his thoughts to himself as they drove through the black night.

They reached the outskirts of town and drove by the white suburbs and gated-communities, the expensive homes with their swimming pools and barbeques and private security firms, and then drove along the narrow road that ran parallel to the main N3 Toll-road that bisected Mooi River. Passing a truck stop and then the tiny police station with its rifle range, they soon turned right and followed the road across the bridge over the modern motorway, and entered the poorer eastern section, where the blacks lived.

Sitting quietly in his seat Bart observed through wide eyes this sudden transition from wealth and comfort to poverty and hopelessness, from those that had a bright future and the security that their privilege brought, to the poor black community with no prospects, no hope, just a lifetime of struggle, beaten down over years of neglect. The change was stark and a shock to those unprepared for it, and it brought a lump to his throat and a tremble to his lips.

Bart glanced sideways out of the corner of his eye at his Uncle and sister. Uncle Johan was unfazed, he was humming to himself and his fingers were drumming along the top of the truck's steering wheel. Lotte's face was blank, totally devoid of expression, her small mean mouth just a tiny gash in her pretty face.

Bart turned away lest they see the pain on his face.

On the hillside here, a small township had sprung up over the years, a collection of shabby huts and dilapidated shacks, an area of poor lighting and high crime. They drove by a few people loitering at the kerbside – "fucking floppies" as Uncle Johan referred to them – and then turned off the road into a tiny parking area in front of a small building.

A State of Sin

The hand-written wooden sign above the door read: **DABULAMANZI'S TUCK SHOP.**

Looking out through the windscreen Bart saw it was a run-down liquor and food store that had obviously seen better days: the window was boarded over, the few advertising signs were either rusted brown or pockmarked with bullet holes from passing drivers, and the door was shut with a notice telling customers to ring the bell to gain entry. There were no other vehicles parked up, just a low wall with a couple of men sitting and drinking from a shared bottle. A single lamp buzzed and hummed with nocturnal insects.

Uncle Johan wound down his window and leaned his elbow on the sill.

"Hey!" he called across to the men.

One of them looked up. The other was too drunk or stoned to care.

"Come here my friend."

The man, a tall and lanky individual in his mid-twenties Bart guessed, came ambling across, a nervousness brought on by experience making him hang back as he approached their truck.

"You looking for work?" Uncle Johan asked gruffly.

"Yes sir," he responded, his voice little more than a whisper, his eyes downcast.

"Well I need some help on my farm for a few days. Odd jobs around the place. I'll pay you well, and it includes food and lodgings for a couple of nights. You interested?"

"Yes sir, thank you sir," the man said, but he glanced back at his friend.

"Just you," Johan told him. "Best get in the back, then."

Just like that, Bart thought to himself.

● ● ●

They rose at 5am the following morning, so as to avoid the worst of the mid-summer heat.

A low-lying early-morning mist hung in the valley bottoms and shrouded the rolling countryside around the farm, lending a chill to the air, but this would soon burn off once the sun climbed higher. It promised to be a scorching hot day.

The ideal time for hunting was before noon. Therefore they had brought the man out from the old stable block where he had spent the night tied and gagged, and bundled him into the back of the 4x4 Hilux pickup. At Johan's instructions, Dalton the gardener had briefly removed the gag to allow him to drink some water, and the man had used the opportunity to quietly plead for his life, his eyes looking at his captors beseechingly.

Ignoring him, Johan had told Dalton to stay in the back.

"If he gives you trouble, just kick him."

Then he and Bart had climbed into the front, and off they set.

Johan explained the rules to Bart as they drove along. They were simple, and fair. They would travel to a chosen starting point several miles from the farm buildings, deep into the hilly countryside and well away from any main roads and prying eyes. This was private land which had belonged to the family for generations, and so what went on here was nobody else's business, he explained.

Once at their destination they would set their quarry loose and give him a thirty-minute head-start, which was only right considering that he would be on foot and they, Johan, Bart and Dalton, would be riding in the pickup. If he made it as far as the outskirts of the tiny community of Elandkop at the foot of the mountain range – a distance of around about 12 miles as the crow flies – then he could go free. If they caught him before he reached safety, then sadly there could be only one outcome. The man, Johan told a terrified Bart, was young and fit, so it was by no means guaranteed that they would have a successful hunt. Some you win and some you lose, he had chuckled.

A short time later and they had arrived, and Bart climbed out on unsteady legs. The day was heating up and he felt a trickle of sweat roll down his fat neck and under his collar.

Uncle Johan thrust a hunting rifle at him, and then slung another over his own shoulder.

"Make sure the safety is off until we are in position," his uncle reminded him, even though they had spent the preceding few days shooting at tin cans for practice. "And when you do take the shot, remember to line up ahead of the target: he will probably be running fast, and this thing can kick like a mule. Plus, we want a head shot if possible, or into his heart. It's less messy that way. You ready boy?"

Bart nodded, wishing he could go to the toilet.

A State of Sin

"Right then Dalton, set him loose."

Dalton used a knife to cut through the ropes binding the man's ankles and wrists, untied the gag and pushed him out of the bed of the truck.

The poor wretch stood there, shaking like a leaf, his teeth chattering with fear.

"Well go on then, don't just stand there. Off you go!" He stepped forward into the man's face, who needed no second warning and turned and fled, his skinny body bolting across the rolling grassland, Johan's parting laugh crackling like a gunshot.

They watched him go, away from the sloping hillside where they were parked, making for a narrow stream at the bottom.

Johan tutted to himself and shook his head, his eyes narrowed as they followed the diminishing figure running for his life.

"They are always the fucking same. They always follow the bloody stream, thinking the shortest route is the best course to take. Big mistake that, Bart. What he should be doing is cutting out across country away from us, in that direction." He pointed off, to the north Bart thought. "Then he could lose us amongst the rocks at the base of that big hill there, the one with the flat top, and then swing around to pick up the line of the fence. Follow that for a mile or so, and then the land dips down into a series of gullies, and we'd never find him in there. After that, he would have a clear run all the way to the finish line. Bloody fool."

They sat in the shade of a large jackalberry tree to wait. Swarms of flies hovered in their faces and Bart watched a line of ants walking from the base of the trunk across the hard-packed earth, and he crushed one of them with his thumb, squishing it flat into the ground.

The half-hour went by too quickly, and when the time to set off arrived he dragged himself reluctantly to his feet and shuffled over to the pickup.

Johan told him they would drive to a spot several miles away where the dirt road bisected the stream. There they would wait for the fleeing man to come running right into their gunsights. To be on the safe side, Dalton was to take the truck over the stream and find a place to wait in the folds of land, and should their quarry make an attempt to head off away from them in that direction, he was to drive him back this way.

Bart and his uncle lay down side by side in the shelter of some rocks and boulders overlooking the narrow stream, and waited in silence. There was a stillness to the air. The sun beat down on them, flat and heavy. The mist had burned away, to be replaced by a cloudless blue sky, the intensity of the heat sapping Bart's strength. He found himself longing for the cold and ice of Amsterdam in the winter, and he wiped the sweat from his eyes.

After several minutes he felt his uncle tap him on the arm gently, and then nod his head down at the stream, and he followed the pointing finger.

At first he could see nothing. Then there was a sudden flurry as a pair of Sakabula birds took to the wing, and seconds later the fleeing man came into view, running and weaving as he followed the watercourse, glancing back over his shoulder.

"He's all your's boy," Uncle Johan whispered.

Bart brought his hunting rifle up and sighted along the barrel, which seemed to vibrate in his shaking hands.

"Breathe slowly. Try to relax."

Bart wished his uncle would just shut up. He wanted the whole thing to go away, he dearly hoped this was all just a bad dream and any moment now he would wake up in his bed back home, and everything would be as before. He hated it here in Africa, he hated his family for bringing him here, and most of all he hated himself!

His finger twitched, and the gun bucked in his hands, the loud report bringing a girlish scream from his lips, and in the heat haze caused by the firing rifle there was a bright scarlet eruption of blood from where the running man was passing below them. The figure stumbled and nearly fell – he'd hit him! – but then he regained his momentum and raced on and out of sight around a bend in the stream.

"Shit!" his uncle exclaimed under his breath.

Bart glanced across at him in confusion, and then he felt himself being dragged to his feet and pushed down the rocky slope towards the streambed. Together they trotted down to where the fleeing man had disappeared.

They found him a hundred yards or so further along. He was laying in the shallow water, twitching and breathing spasmodically and staring up at the sky.

As they approached he must have heard their feet splashing through the water, and in a sudden panic he tried to squirm away, gibbering to himself.

His Uncle Johan pushed him along, and then Bart was looking down at the man, who was coughing up blood, turning the stream red. Somewhere, they heard the engine of the pickup truck start up. Moments later, a car door slammed and Dalton joined them.

"A fucking gut shot," Uncle Johan told them. "Great!" He turned his eyes on Bart, who felt himself cringe away from their intensity.

Reaching for his belt, he withdrew the hunting knife from its sheaf and held it out towards Bart.

"You need to finish him off, put him out of his misery. A wound like that, it could take him hours, maybe days to bleed out."

Bart looked from the knife, to the wounded man lying gasping at his feet, and back to the knife again. He shook his head and stepped back, shivering and hugging himself even though the day was scorching hot.

A cold look crept into his uncle's eyes. It was like looking at two icy pits, right into his soul.

"Take the knife and do it, boy. If not, then so help me God I will tie you to that tree over there and leave you out here all night, so you can watch him slowly bleed to death. And in the morning, when the vultures and hyenas come for his body, stripping the flesh away, they'll come for you too. Those Strandwolves are a nasty breed, they won't be too choosy, especially when they see a fat boy like you. You'll be fucking carrion too. If the ants don't get you first."

He pushed the knife closer.

Bart looked around in panic. He glanced over towards Dalton, but he was looking down at the ground.

He wondered briefly if he could make a run for it. But where would he go? How far would he get, before he too found himself being hunted down?

Finally he turned his eyes back towards the man lying in the stream, slowly bleeding and moaning in agony.

Bart shouted, and his voice rolled across the countryside. He yelled again, a loud and guttural sound, like he was trying to expel something deep inside, and he was breathing hard, snorting down his nostrils, and he felt his features contort and twist.

Snatching the knife he ran headlong at the man and plunged the blade deep into his chest, who jerked in surprise. Bart stabbed again, their eyes locked together. He stabbed him over and over, in his neck, in his torso, in his face, in his stomach, he lost count of how many times he stabbed, so lost was he in his bloodlust.

Vaguely he heard his uncle whispering encouragement.

Mark Hobson

"That's right, boy, that's right."

•   •   •

They slung the carcass into the back of the truck and drove back to the farm. Sometime tomorrow they would shove the body into the cesspit behind the stables, but first Bart deserved a beer and a hearty meal, his uncle told him. He'd made the family proud.

Later that night, as he and Lotte lay in their beds side by side, he told her what had happened during the hunt, explaining the day's events in vivid detail. He felt a feeling of pride swell inside him, and he also sensed that something else had shifted within. Something that he couldn't explain or put into words. Just a notion that he had crossed an imaginary line, a boundary that up to now had been holding him back. He concluded that this was how it must feel to pass from childhood into manhood.

Things would never be the same for him again.

He heard the bedsprings on Lotte's bed squeak then he felt her take a hold of his hand, and draw him to his feet.

"There's something we have to do," she said to him in the dark, and she led him outside.

Everything was still except for the quiet lowing of the cattle in their pens and overhead the Milky Way and the Southern Cross lay serenely over the heavens.

Lotte guided him across the yard to where the pickup truck was parked, using a flashlight to light their way. The corpse lay in the back, covered over with a tarpaulin. With his help they pulled the sheet aside, Bart asking:
"What are we doing? If we get caught..."

"It's something that Dalton told me, something that they do in Africa. Something important. Here, hold this." She handed him the flashlight.

There was the glint of a sharp blade in his sister's hand.

"We need to... remove... some parts of the body."

"What?! Why?!"

"It's for what they call umuthi medicine. The Zulu inyanga, their witchdoctors, do it. It will make us very powerful Bart, and give us supernatural control over our enemies forever."

"We have enemies?"

"Of course, silly," Lotte told him, sounding much older than her eleven years. "It's me and you against the rest of the world."

Bart watched in fascination as she started to cut a strip of skin from the corpse's forehead, and then from one of its arms. "So that he cannot strike us even in death," she explained.

Next she carved deeply into the chest and cut and twisted until a piece of cartilage came loose from the bottom of the breastbone. "Our shield."

Then she turned the corpse over and removed tissue from the soles of its feet "To give us strength and speed."

When she was done Lotte tore off a strip of the man's shirt and wrapped the pieces inside.

Bart waited while she stepped back and looked at her handiwork, her eyes moving over the dead body, and then she turned to look directly at him and sighed.

"This next part you must do yourself."

She passed him the knife and he looked at her in confusion, not liking where this was going.

"You must open up the body, slash him from top to bottom. To release his spirit. If not, then he will haunt you for the rest of your life."

Doing as his sister said, Bart set to work.

Mark Hobson

PART 2

THE UNSHRIVEN

Mark Hobson

A State of Sin

Chapter 17
Marc Dutroux

The following morning, a Tuesday, Kaatje was taken for her surgery. Pieter was there when they wheeled her into the elevator and down to one of the theatres, and although he knew the prognosis for the outcome of the operation was poor, he nevertheless tried to maintain a positive attitude, for Kaatje's sake. She smiled back and even cracked a couple of jokes, but there was a tenseness there, a forced joviality.

There were a few comfy seats in the corridor just outside the surgical suite and Pieter chose one next to a coffee machine. It gurgled and rumbled away, and now and then it spat out brown dregs from one of the little spouts.

While he waited for news, he cast his mind back over yesterday's events, reliving the horrifying moment when their prime suspect, Tobias Vinke, had been shot in the head by a long-range sniper round.

Following the fatal shot, there had been a split-second of silence from the passengers on the ferry as they spun and watched him fall, a small fountain of blood pumping from the large hole at the top of his head. Then, when the realization of what had just happened sank in, there was complete pandemonium, with people screaming and pushing, shouting at each other as they wondered who amongst them had a gun, thinking the killer was on the boat with them.

Pieter had immediately known otherwise. In the build-up to the murder, there had been nothing to indicate what was about to happen, with no sound of the gunshot, telling him instantly that the round had been fired from some distance away. He had called out to those around him, pleading with them to stay calm; he was seriously concerned that the boat might capsize, or that somebody might get crushed or trampled, or even fall overboard, but it was only when he brought out his police warrant card and held it aloft – "I'm a police officer, please do not panic!" – that some kind of order was restored.

Then he had crouched over the recumbent form of Tobias Vinke and searched for signs of life, checking his breathing, his pulse, wondering if it was worth doing CPR or not, but when his eyes had looked more closely at the wound he quickly decided it was pointless. The whole of the top of his head was missing, with pieces of bone and brain splashed across the boat's wooden deck, and there was a smaller entry wound square in the centre of Vinke's face, right where the nose was. The bullet had struck him there and then ricocheted upwards, possibly off his jawbone, and out of the top of the cranium. It was an unsurvivable injury.

Standing up, Pieter looked around, his mind already trying to piece together just what had happened.

Where had the shot come from?

Ignoring the contagious fear amongst the passengers, who were now mostly silent with shock apart from one or two people who were crying quietly, he thought back to the exact moment that Vinke was hit.

Pieter had been standing at the rail and trying to blend in, but he clearly remembered sensing Tobias Vinke turn in his direction, as though he'd been rumbled – and then down he had gone.

His posture had been pointing south, towards the riverside. Therefore the round that hit him in the face must have come from that direction.

And if it was from a long-range rifle, then the shooter would need a good vantage point.

Pieter found his eyes going up to the roof of the large rail station.

Raising his walkie-talkie to his mouth, he'd called it in, quickly explaining to the other members of K Team what had happened.

"Check the station. Up on the roof."

A few moments later and the ferry arrived at the north riverside terminal, and as soon as the ramp lowered the passengers scattered. So much for getting any witness statements, Pieter thought to himself, but he let them go in any case.

Within ten minutes the area was swarming with emergency vehicles and medics, and Pieter had stood to one side on the riverbank to let them

A State of Sin

do their thing. Word came back that Centraal Station had been placed in lockdown: nobody was allowed in or out. The concourse and platforms, the shops and cafes, and all of the entrances were flooded with police officers, and several teams were sent straight up onto the station roof to look for the sniper.

Pieter waited anxiously, praying for a bit of good luck for once.

Nothing. There was nobody up on the roof, and nothing suspicious was found in the station itself.

Whoever he or she was, the shooter had somehow slipped through the net.

It quickly became clear what the repercussions of the killing of their prime suspect would be.

In one fell swoop, the whole game had changed, for he was sure the shooting of Vinke had been a deliberate act.

From being the search for a missing girl kidnapped and being held captive by some unknown assailant - a man who had brutally murdered her parents and whose sick motives for taking her were unclear - and rescuing her from his vile clutches, it was now a race against time to find wherever she had been locked up in some hidden location, possibly alone and with nobody to hear her cries for help, before she potentially died of starvation or thirst.

Sitting in the hospital waiting area, Pieter was reminded of the notorious child abduction case in Belgium some years ago.

In May and August 1986 two young girls aged twelve and fourteen were grabbed off the street and bundled into the back of a van. They were abducted three months apart but ended up in the same dungeon, tied to a bed with a chain around their necks, to be tortured and abused. Luckily for the two girls, an eyewitness to the second abduction was able to pass on details of the van's licence plate to the police, who swooped on a ramshackle, white-washed farmhouse on the outskirts of the town of Sars-la-Buissiere and arrested the home-owner, a thirty-nine year-old known sex criminal named Marc Dutroux. Initially, Dutroux refused to talk, but after several days of questioning he showed Belgium police the secret entrance to his dungeon of torture, and the pair of girls were rescued and reunited with their families.

As if this were not bad enough it soon became clear that Dutroux was also responsible for the abductions and murders the previous year, 1985, of four more girls and young women aged between eight and nineteen, as well as the death of an accomplice and local drug addict, Bernard Weinstein.

The saddest part of the whole tragedy was that police had missed an opportunity to rescue the first pair of missing girls, both just eight years old when they were taken. Having captured and locked them away in his farmhouse, Dutroux subjected them to the most terrible of ordeals for week after week. But then, a month or so later, Dutroux was arrested for an unconnected crime – he was caught stealing a car – and was sent to prison for three months. While locked away the psycho kept the whereabouts of the two young girls a secret, and imprisoned as they were back at his house, they slowly died of thirst and starvation. Even Dutroux's wife, who knew about her husband's sordid secret, did nothing to help them.

The case shocked not just the nation of Belgium but the whole world.

Now, going back over the events of the past few days and wondering if there were any clues that he and his colleagues may have missed, Pieter found himself struck with the terrifying possibility that history was about to repeat itself.

They had to find Nina Bakker as soon as they could before this case took on an even more frightful turn.

There was nothing to be gained by sitting here, he told himself.

Kaatje would be in the operating theatre for at least two or three hours. In the meantime, while he was at the hospital, there was something he wanted to check up on.

Pieter headed for the morgue, which was across the car park in a separate building but also connected by an underground passageway to allow the deceased to be moved there from the main wing without upsetting other patients and visitors. He went looking for Prisha Kapoor the Chief Pathologist, and he found her in her office at the end of the corridor, on the phone to her partner, Rowan.

They were in the middle of moving home, having finally had enough of Amsterdam and its noise and congestion and general madness. The horror of the Werewolf case in the spring had been the final straw for Prisha. The personal toll it had extracted had almost sent her spiralling over the edge, and so at Rowan's suggestion, she had decided to throw in the towel and

A State of Sin

take up the offer of a post as a lecturer at the University of Humanistic Studies in the city of Utrecht.

She was due to quit her current job in about a month to start her new career in the New Year. Pieter would miss working with her, for the wealth of knowledge and experience she had amassed in the time she'd held the position of the Amsterdam Police Chief Pathologist was second to none. Therefore, Prisha had told him that he was welcome to phone her at any time should he need advice or help with his caseload going forward.

At times like this, he envied her, wondering whether he should try and get out of the rat race himself. But he knew that was just a pipedream. Being a cop was all he understood, and the city – nasty and cruel as it was, a place that sucked the life from people like a leach draining someone's blood – well, Amsterdam, its streets and its people, defined who he was. There was a phrase for it that only Amsterdammers used: City Junkie. That's what he was. Hooked on the drug of this place.

He lingered outside the door to Prisha's office, hearing her soft voice.

"Probably another four or five should do, the ones with the blue plastic lids. We can take them down during the week," she was saying to Rowan. "Oh, and don't forget to pick up the spare set of keys. Yes, I'll try, we still have time on our lease. Bye-bye." She finished the call and noticed Pieter lingering outside in the passage. She waved him in.

The office was a mess, with files and papers covering every square inch of her desk as well as both chairs and the small camp bed that she kept in the corner for when she worked late – yet another reason for getting out, Pieter surmised. She wanted her life back.

"This looks a bit crazy. You busy destroying documents before your successor takes over?"

"Would be easier if I were. These are all old cases and reports, going back over the last twelve years. I'm trying to scan as many as possible and save them on my flash drive. Can you imagine, a whole career stored onto this?" She held up the tiny memory stick.

"Is there a metaphor there?"

"It's the story of the last few months for me." Prisha shook her head, looking at the mess around her. She reached for a pile of papers on the edge of the desk and dumped them onto the windowsill. "You can sit there," she told him, pointing to the tiny space she had cleared. "But don't touch anything on pain of death, OK?"

Pieter perched himself down, keeping his hands in his pockets.

"So how's your, erm, your colleague? Officer Groot?" She'd nearly said girlfriend, Pieter noted.

He shrugged. "We won't know for a while, probably a few days until they know for sure if the damage is permanent. But whatever the outcome, we'll make sure she gets all the help she can."

"We? Or you?" Prisha looked over the top of her glasses at him.

Pieter raised his eyebrows.

"Perhaps it's just office gossip, but the rumour is that you and she are..." She left the rest of the sentence unfinished.

"What? An item? It would be against policy to form a relationship with a fellow officer at the same station, you know that."

"Oh shut up! What rubbish."

"And a male senior officer and a young female rookie at that."

Pieter felt his face flush, but he was already thinking about Kaatje hopefully leaving the hospital soon. They had made arrangements for her to come and stay with him for a while, which wasn't ideal with his place being a four-story townhouse with lots of narrow connecting staircases. But he had reassured her that really, he spent most of his time in the living areas on the top two floors, and he would be there to help her find her feet and to deal with her – temporary, remember? he'd stressed to Kaatje – to help her cope with her temporary eyesight loss.

"You men," Prisha jabbed her finger at him playfully and shook her head, "you're all the same."

This brought him around to the real reason for his visit this morning.

Pieter asked her about the patients from the eye clinic, the ones he had shot and those that had subsequently been found later. The people with their eyes removed.

"We have ten dead ones so far, which include the three that you shot plus the one you ran over with your car. The others were found dead in various parts of the city, some by the police and some by members of the public. They had all frozen to death, which considering that they were dressed just in their flimsy nightclothes isn't surprising. Two of them were fished out of the frozen lake next to the clinic."

Prisha frowned and crossed her arms.

"Four have been found alive. Two males and two females. They were all in a terrible state by all accounts, wandering the streets, suffering from hyperthermia and of course unable to see anything. It's a miracle that they survived at all. But then, everything about this is surreal."

She moved away so that he couldn't see her face, and Pieter sensed her confusion and anxiety. Following on from events of several months ago this was the last thing she needed, another case that defied all logic. He was reluctant to press her on this, but he knew he had to have a few answers.

"What ages were they? The ones they found alive?"

"We don't know for sure. Nobody knows who they even are. They have been questioned by your colleagues, and also by psychiatrists, but without much success. They have very little recollection of events, in fact they have barely spoken to us at all. Mostly they've been communicating by drawing sketches as speaking seems difficult for some reason. Other than informing us that they went to sleep as patients in the clinic and then woke up hours or days later, walking around the city confused and scared, they have no memory of what happened to them, or even know what their own names are. A real mystery."

"But they are all adults I take it? Because when I was there, inside that place, there was a young child. A boy aged about six years old. I caught a quick look at his file, but there was no name, just a photo of him. Patient 27, that's how they referred to him. He was hurt during a fight, but not too badly, a bust nose. I just wondered if he has turned up."

Prisha was shaking her head, a sad frown marring her forehead.

"No. All the ones we have found, those who died and those we have who are alive, are all adults. No children. Are you sure there was a child?"

"Yes," Pieter replied quietly, then added under his breath: "he was in the ward, in one of the beds, and he attacked me. But when I escaped I lost track of him. I just wondered that's all."

He rubbed at his shoulder where the boy had bitten him, and he shut his mind to the memory.

Sighing, he stood and stretched, the tension cramping the muscles there.

"Somebody must know who they are. If they were patients in that place, there to have routine operations, then there must be some records, paperwork, that kind of thing."

He thought of Elena Vinke and the operation that had gone wrong.
And Kaatje.

They must all be connected, be a part of Julian Visser's crazy plan. Patients he picked at random on whom to carry out his sick experiments. But to what end? What was he hoping to achieve? Was he hoping to make some brilliant medical breakthrough, and these unwitting people were the unfortunate ones that had suffered from his failed operations? Or was it simply the work of an unbalanced, mad doctor? And how was it all connected to Lotte? Was he just another pawn in her game? A means to an end to orchestrate a scenario from which Tobias Vinke would exact revenge by kidnapping the child of the prominent doctor who he blamed for killing his own daughter? Was it even Christiaan Bakker who had carried out the operation on Elena, or his assistant, Julian Visser?

And ultimately, was all of this a part of Lotte's twisted plot of revenge against himself?

There were just too many questions and not enough answers.

One thing of which he was certain: Vinke had taken Nina Bakker. To replace his dead daughter.

To find where Nina was, he needed to find out more about Tobias Vinke.

He needed to go back to the beginning.

Chapter 18
Nature Versus Nurture – The Making of a Monster

Pieter drove from the hospital to Waterlooplein. The Christmas Market they held here was only open on Fridays and Saturdays, and when all of the stalls and wooden huts were packed away the flat, open concrete space was dreary and windswept. However, just around the corner on Sint Antoniesluis and across the road from Coffeeshop Reefer, and overlooking the wide canal, was the small Café No 1, which was always busy seven days a week even during a bleak mid-winter like this one.

It was squashed in between a second-hand record shop selling old vinyl 70's disco classics, and a sprawling bookstore popular with students from the nearby University, and so the café tended to attract a young, hip crowd who liked to lounge on the beanbags inside. Outside, on the pavement, a more sedate clientele preferred to sit under the large green awning, warmed by the overhead heaters.

He'd decided to pop over unannounced to see Vinke's ex-wife again, rather than phone ahead. He also thought that confronting her – if that was the right word – at work instead of in the safe environment of her own home might pay dividends. Sometimes it paid to catch people on the hop, to shake them out of their comfort zone. Not that she was a suspect or anything, it was just that this way could often have better results. It made people open up more.

That was the theory anyway.

He walked in through the main doors and instantly saw Saskia Vinke over near the counter loading up a tray with an order of Lattes and Café au Lait. She turned to walk across the wooden floor, and when she saw him she faltered slightly mid-stride. Quickly recovering, she gave him a weak smile, and then continued over to a corner table to deposit the drinks to her customers.

She came back over, the tray held at her side, the other hand in the front pouch of her small apron.

"Can we talk?"

She gave another of her non-committal little shrugs.

"In private would be best," he persisted.

"I'll ask my boss if I can take my break."

Her boss, a tiny man with a head full of hair cream, said something in Greek, and she led Pieter through a bead-curtain to a tiny backroom, where they sat at a small table. A pile of boxes containing plastic takeout cups blocked the fire exit.

"I saw it on the news about the shooting yesterday," Saskia said quickly, before he could begin.

"I was there."

"So it was definitely Tobias then? Who took the girl, Nina Bakker?"

"It looks that way. There is a small chance it was somebody else, but everything is pointing towards it's being him. His death seems to confirm it."

"Somebody wanted him dead, you mean?"

Pieter nodded.

"But doesn't that imply that he didn't do it alone? That he had an accomplice or something? That they had, I don't know, a disagreement perhaps?"

"It's a theory we're working on, sure."

"In which case maybe Tobias was having second thoughts about having abducted her. Perhaps he wanted to release her, or hand himself in, and the other person decided to prevent that."

Pieter could see where this was going, and he couldn't blame her for wanting to think the best of Vinke, even though they were separated. They had, after all, been through a lot together with their daughter's suicide.

"It's a complex case," he told her, hoping to skirt the issue. "There are lots of possible scenarios as to what happened yesterday. We are still trying to unravel the exact sequence of events." Which was only half-true, he reflected, thinking it wise not to mention the Charlotte Janssen connection, which as of yet had not been made public.

"But whatever the case, the death of your ex-husband does leave us with a problem."

"Yes."

Saskia went over to the tiny sink in the corner and poured herself a small glass of water. She lifted a lace curtain covering a grimy window and peered outside at the grey sky while she sipped.

"The address you gave us of his home in Warder, where you say he moved to after your separation, well we drew a blank there obviously. It seems he left some time in May. You wouldn't have any idea at all where he might have gone from there, would you? I think when we spoke on Sunday you mentioned something about how he was brought up as a child in that area of Holland? This was presumably at his family home with his parents? Do you know anything about that? Names of relatives who still live around there maybe, where he lived when he was growing up - locations?"

Saskia turned back to him, shaking her head. She looked tired, Pieter thought, pale and weary.

"I'm sorry. I never knew his family, never met them. Tobias had it tough as a child and he never really spoke much about that time. He carried that around for most of his life, his memories were a burden to him and so he closed that part of his life off from everyone - including me."

Pieter looked at her closely, but she was hard to read. Her expressionless face revealed nothing. It could have been the grief of course, but he sensed there was something very cold about her.

"There was one thing he told me though, about something that happened when he was just ten years old."

Pieter sat up.

"Tobias had too much to drink one night, about three or four years ago, and he became very tearful, very maudlin. He started to talk, telling me things that I think afterwards he wished he'd never spoken of - horrible things."

"Go on," Pieter urged.

"It was the incident on the fishing boat."

* * *

Tobias carefully climbed into the small motor-launch tied up at the end of the narrow, wooden jetty. It immediately began to rock from side to side, nearly unbalancing him, and so he quickly grabbed a hold of the sides. This made things even worse, and his heart skipped a beat: the water looked very cold and uninviting, even in the warm spring sunshine.

"*Keep still, you idiot!*" *his father's gruff voice growled.* "*You'll capsize the thing if you move about. Just sit down on the seat.*"

Tobias did as he was told, slowly lowering himself onto the wooden bench across the middle of the tiny fishing boat.

He was ten years old, and his father was taking him out over the water again, even though he hated it. Tobias couldn't swim, his parents deciding he was too young to learn, even though they lived by the sea, which even to his young mind seemed silly and dangerous. More likely they couldn't afford to pay for the lessons.

But his father insisted he come with him. He needed help to land the lobster pots that he'd placed two nights earlier. It was a two-man job: while he steadied the boat young Tobias would use the long fishing hook to snag the orange buoys marking their locations, and haul the pots up and over to the boat.

So his father had dragged him out of bed very early, when it was still dark outside, and after a quick breakfast of lukewarm porridge, had told him to put on his waterproof coat and gloves, and off they had set, walking down the narrow pebble beach to where the boat was waiting.

By the time his father clambered aboard and yanked the pull-cord to start the engine it was just growing light, and he aimed the prow of the motor-launch towards the purple clouds that shimmered above the eastern horizon.

A cold and harsh wind was blowing across the Ijsselmeer but Tobias turned to face into the stiff breeze, preferring the numbing cold to looking at his father's red and pock-marked features, the bloodshot eyes, the smell of whisky on his breath.

Vaguely he listened to the sound of the spluttering engine and his father whistling some old sea shanty: Blow The Man Down, *Tobias thought it was.* Drunken Sailor *would have been better, he thought to himself, which brought a tiny smile to his face.*

"*What you laughing at, you little kipper?*" *his father called out, the wind whipping away his words, and when Tobias turned towards him, his old man winked, which only made his face look even more grotesque. Nevertheless,*

Tobias felt himself relax a little. Perhaps, he hoped, his father would be in one of his rare good moods today.

"We make a good team, you and I son. What do you say? The two of us together, up and out nice and early while the rest of the world sleeps - doing men's work!"

Tobias nodded.

"It'll put muscles on you, like Popeye. I'm strong to the finish, 'cause I eats me spinach! I'm Popeye The Sailor Man!" He laughed heartily.

Fifteen minutes later, after they had travelled perhaps a couple of miles from the small harbour where they lived, they arrived at the first line of buoys bobbing in the water. In the distance, Tobias could make out the flat landscape of the far shoreline and the white finger of Urk Lighthouse caught in the morning sunshine. Overhead a few seagulls hovered in the wind.

While his father slowly manoeuvred the motor-launch from buoy to buoy, Tobias used the long pole to grab the nylon ropes. Then with his gloved hands pulling hard, he dragged each pot up from the seabed, and after lots of struggling and lifting, managed to bring them over the gunwale and onto the wooden bottom of the boat.

There were four pots in this batch and two of them contained a lobster each. Not a bad start, Tobias thought.

At his father's instructions he dropped the empty ones back over the side and on they went.

The next line of pots contained just one lobster, which his old man grumbled about, but there was nothing to be done but check the final bunch, the set which were furthest from shore.

A short time later and they arrived at the spot, and Tobias again set to work.

By now his arms and his back were aching, but he daren't complain otherwise he might get an earful of abuse, and so he pulled and lifted, using the hook and his hands.

As he was unfastening the rope on the final pot, which contained a pair of huge lobsters he saw, his gloved fingers slipped and the line unravelled and snaked out of his hands, and with a loud splash, the pot fell back into the water and floated away.

Tobias froze.

He hunkered down, knowing what was coming. But when his father's angry shout came it still scared the life out of him.

"What the hell have you done, you fucking retard?"

"I'm s-sorry d-d-dad," he stammered. "It was an a-accident."

Without warning, his father lunged out of his seat and hit him hard around the side of his head with his clenched hand.

Tobias yelped from shock and pain, which infuriated his father even more, who snarled and struck him again.

"Please dad, I didn't m-mean to do it."

"Little prick!" His father breathed heavily, fighting to regain his composure. "There were two in that one, and a fine size too. You useless idiot."

Tobias started to cry quietly.

"Stop snivelling. Wipe your nose and go and get it."

"But-"

"I – said – go – and –get –it," he repeated, saying each word slowly.

Tobias looked over the water to where the lobster pot was floating, just ten or twelve feet away.

"I can reach it with the hook. If we went a bit closer."

"Don't you answer back you whelp! Get yourself over the side into the water, and bring it back. Quickly, before it floats too far away. That way it will teach you a lesson not to be so clumsy next time."

"I can't swim dad, please."

His father glared back and then looked around the boat. Bending forward he reached for the mooring line coiled at his feet and threw it at Tobias.

"Tie this around your waist then. That way you won't sink down too deeply." He fastened the other end to a brass eyelet on the gunwale.

Tobias looped the rope around his middle and tied a knot, his whole body shaking, and when he looked again out over the water the thought of slipping over the side of the boat set his teeth chattering. Waves slapped at the hull, rocking the small fishing vessel.

"What are you waiting for?" With that, his father pushed him hard and Tobias toppled headfirst into the sea.

The water was freezing cold and he came up spluttering and gasping for air, and when his thin body started to sink below the surface once more he felt himself panic. He lashed out with his arms, which splashed water into the boat and over his father.

"Use your legs! Kick with your legs! You kept saying you wanted to learn how to swim, well now's your chance."

Tobias saw him lift the fishing pole and reach towards him with it, and for a fleeting moment he thought he was trying to help him back to the boat. Instead, he used the end of it to propel him even further away, out towards the lobster pot.

"Grab the damn thing then!"

Tobias somehow flung himself at the square pot and the orange buoy and he clung to them in relief, using them to keep himself afloat. On the boat, his father was laughing, enjoying the spectacle.

Tobias turned back. The small motor-launch seemed so far away, even though in reality it was only a few boat-lengths. Below him, he could sense the black depths of the water.

"Bring it back over. Push it in front of you and use your legs to swim. Get a move on now!"

Heaving the pot around, and also keeping a grip on the buoy, Tobias splashed and gasped his way back over, and when he was close enough his father grabbed a hold and lifted it on board, his eyes looking greedily at the pair of lobsters inside.

Tobias held out his hand. He was too weak to climb on board without help.

Meeting his gaze, Tobias' father slowly shook his head.

"Can't do that son. The boat has too shallow a draft. You'll tip us over if I pull you in."

"But dad... I need help...I'm sinking..." *he gasped.*

"Rubbish! Don't talk nonsense." *He cackled with more laughter.* "But don't worry, we'll get you back home. Maybe not in one piece if the crabs bite you, but we'll get you there somehow!"

Tobias watched as he spun away and tugged the pull-cord on the outboard motor and the engine roared to life, and he dipped the propeller into the sea and suddenly the rope tied to Tobias was yanked taut and away they went, his father steering them towards home and his son hauled violently through the sea on the end of the line.

The waves slapped him painfully on the stomach as he skimmed over the surface of the water and his face was pulled under so that seawater poured up his nostrils and into his eyes and mouth, and Tobias craned his neck sideways so that his face lifted clear. He coughed and spat out the water, choking and crying and pleading for his father to stop, but to no avail. Instead his old man gave him a cheery wave and increased their speed.

The nightmare went on seemingly forever with Tobias barely able to remain conscious. His gloves disappeared at some stage and within minutes his bare hands and face were covered in tiny lacerations from the continuous impact of the waves, and by the time they finally, mercifully reached the shore he could barely move as his limp body washed up onto the pebble beach.

From somewhere he dimly heard footsteps crunching their way towards him, and then a pair of huge hands were reaching down and lifting him up, and Tobias felt himself being slung over his father's shoulder. He was carried away from the boat, his father whistling another silly tune without a care in the world.

He kept drifting in and out of sleep so weak was he, but Tobias managed to open his eyes and was just able to register that they were heading down the dirt track, going past the three-barred gate leading to their yard. Instead, they were making for the old junkyard, the place where his father tinkered around with his old cars and boats, the place full of rusted scrap metal and engine parts.

Up the sloping, muddy grass they went, Tobias too tired to resist or even protest.

Just ahead was a flat river barge that had been hauled up out of the water. Father spent his spare time trying to fix it up and make it sea-worthy again, and sometimes he allowed Tobias to help out after school, to even use the welding gear if he asked nicely. But he sensed that today they were going there for a very different reason.

Up onto the deck, the sound of boots on the steel hull reverberating dully.

A loud scraping, then the noise of old hinges protesting loudly and Tobias watched as a heavy hatch was pulled open to reveal the dark and hollow interior of the barge's hold.

He felt himself pushed roughly through the opening, and only now when he realized what was happening did Tobias find the strength to struggle and fight back.

"No, please dad, I'm sorry."

His father ignored him and pushed him away, easily brushing off Tobias' hands.

There was more scraping of boots on metal, then the hatch was slammed shut with a ringing boom, and the pitch blackness closed over Tobias.

For a moment there was near-total silence except for his own tiny, shaky breathing.

Then he heard a sound. A quiet scuffling nearby, from somewhere in the total, all-consuming dark.

Sitting and hugging himself, shivering from cold and terror, Tobias listened as the rats crept closer.

Pieter needed some fresh air.

He thanked Saskia and hurried outside, where he stood on the pavement and sucked in several great lungfuls of air to clear his mind.

Jesus, he thought to himself.

Next, he drove back to the boatyard on Bickersgracht where Tobias Vinke worked.

Throughout the previous afternoon following the shooting, the site had been thoroughly searched by teams of officers, and police divers from the harbour unit had fished out the mobile phone from the canal. But when Pieter arrived after lunch on Tuesday he found the place quiet and the gates chained up and it took five minutes of shouting and rattling the padlock to get anyone's attention. Finally the portacabin door swung open and the owner, a fat man with more hair up his nostrils than he had on his head, came shambling across, scratching at his stomach where it poked out below his sweater. Pieter saw that he also had very few teeth, probably as a result of smoking too much weed or drinking too many sugary drinks.

He had to show his police warrant card to get him to open up, and even then he did so reluctantly, mumbling under his breath as he dragged one half of the gates open.

He led Pieter to the portacabin.

The mangy dog – who was called Otis – made a token gesture at snarling as Pieter walked by, but it was too old and tired to do much more and it slinked back into its kennel to chew on an old rubber bone.

The inside of the cabin was stifling hot. The small heater was turned up to max and all of the windows were shut. On the desk was a laptop playing a clip from a porn movie. The fat owner turned the screen away, but he didn't bother to hit the mute button, and so their conversation was conducted to the accompaniment of moaning and groaning.

Pieter got straight down to it, asking about Tobias Vinke and what the man knew about him.

"He was one of life's losers," he replied bluntly, nodding at his own analysis. "Yes, one of life's losers."

"How do you mean?"

"He just was. Some people are like that, they get what they deserve. They attract attention by simply being odd. They spend their whole lives being the butt of the joke, an easy target, and they do nothing to stand up for themselves."

"And that's how it was for Mr Vinke, was it?" Pieter tried to catch the other man's shifty eyes, but they moved about so much that it proved impossible. "You gave him a hard time did you?"

"Woah, not just me! Everybody did."

Like that made it alright, thought Pieter.

"What was he like as an employee?"

The fat man shrugged. He tapped at the keyboard on the laptop, his beady eyes like tiny gimlets as they now watched the movie clip.

"He was okay, I guess. He got on with his job. Give him a task to do and he'd do it all day without a murmur. I can't complain on that score, I admit. Can't complain."

"How long had he worked for you?"

He shrugged. "A couple of years maybe. Not too sure."

"Can you check your files for me? I need an address."

"Files?" He looked around the tiny cabin and laughed. "This isn't the kind of business that keeps files. I pay cash-in-hand for a few hours work here and there, whenever I need a hand."

"That kind of business eh?" Pieter remarked.

From the laptop came the sound of a braying donkey.

"If I ever needed Vinke I would just text him, and tell him to get his backside down here. And a couple of hours later he would show up."

A couple of hours? Pieter made a mental note.

"What about the other men who work here?"

"What of them?"

"How did they get on with Mr Vinke?"

A sly smile appeared on the man's podgy face and he gave a tiny shake of his head. "Nobody got on well with Vinke. Like I told you, he was odd. Mind you, after what they did to him once, I don't blame him for not being very pally. Don't blame him at all."

He chuckled quietly.

"I'm waiting."

Pieter thought he might be a little reticent about spilling the beans, especially if whatever had happened amounted to harassment, but to his surprise the owner of the boatyard seemed willing, even eager, to tell him.

"It was meant to be a joke. The boys just wanted a giggle that's all, to blow off a bit of steam. Anyway, they waited for Vinke to turn up for work one day, and when he came strolling through the gates - a couple of summers ago this was, before his daughter died before you have a go - well as soon as he arrived, the boys jumped him see, and they bundled him across to the quayside. He was screaming and hollering but it made no difference 'cause they dragged him over and shoved him into one of those oil drums you can see there."

Pieter turned to glance through one of the tiny windows, seeing a row of drums lined up alongside the canal.

"They pushed him inside and they screwed the lid on."

Pieter spun back. The other man was trying to stifle a laugh.

"What did you do?" he asked.

"Not much. It was just a joke, man," he repeated.

"So then what? They just left him in there for a bit?"

"Nah! Where's the fun in that? They tipped it over and rolled him around the place, backwards and forwards. He had a fair old ride around in that thing. The boys wanted to roll him right into the water but I put a stop to that, you'll be glad to hear."

"I bet you felt all warm and fuzzy inside afterwards."

He leaned his fat face across the desk top, making brief eye contact for the first time.

"Do you know what, officer? I damn well wished I'd let them. Knowing what a psycho he'd turn out to be it would have been for the best. For that poor little lassie he took, and for her folks. They'd all still be alive and well today. I've been torn up about it ever since."

The smirk on his face said otherwise.

"Hey, but the funniest part of all, when he was inside that old oil drum getting wheeled around the yard, he wasn't by himself in there. The boys, get this, the boys had put half a dozen rats in there first. Huge buggers they were. Huge!"

He rocked back and forth, laughing so much his stomach quivered.

"Some people have no sense of humour."

Chapter 19
A Winter's Night

On his way back to the hospital to catch up with Kaatje's progress he decided to swing by his house to pick up a few things for her.

He turned down the cobbled street alongside the canal, thinking back over the meetings with Saskia Vinke and Tobias Vinkes' boss and the events they had related to him. Horrible though they were, their recollections didn't provide any clues as to Nina Bakker's current whereabouts, and Pieter felt his frustration rising. Their investigation was in danger of grinding to a halt; it felt like they were constantly playing catch-up.

He drew up near the front door and climbed out of his car, and skipped up the steps. He was just turning the key in the lock when something made him stop, and he turned back around.

That hire car was still parked up opposite his house.

He'd first noticed it several days ago, and although he hadn't paid it too much attention since then, now that he thought back over the past few days he was fairly certain that it hadn't moved in the intervening time.

He nearly dismissed the quandary from his mind.

He was in a hurry, and so what if someone had hired a car for several days? Perhaps it was one of his neighbours, or maybe it had been stolen and abandoned here. Hardly a priority.

But something about it tugged at his mind, and so Pieter moved back down the steps and wandered over the street.

It had been parked on the canal-side of the road with two of its wheels up on the pavement, which was slightly odd as everybody else parked right outside their houses or, like in his case, in the garages.

The car had tinted windows and so he leaned close and cupped his hand to the glass and peered in through the front passenger window.

He couldn't make an awful lot out except what appeared to be a small, square aluminium case on the seat. Its lid was open but because it was angled away from his direct line-of-sight he couldn't see what was inside, so he moved around the car and looked through the driver's side.

Now he could see there was a laptop inside the case, hooked up to a gadget bristling with a number of tiny antennae, and coloured lights and numbers flickered across the screen lighting up the car's interior.

Pieter stood upright and stepped back from the window.

He knew instantly what it was, and this made him glance nervously up and down the quiet street in alarm.

An IMSI-catcher, used by criminals – and sometimes by the police – to eavesdrop in on people's mobile phone calls and read their text messages.

Pieter bent forward for a better look. It was a top-of-the-range model, not one of the cheap ones available online for a couple of hundred euros, and it must have some kind of remote function to allow it to be left here unmanned. Left here right outside his house.

He considered calling it in to HQ. Then he decided he was tired of doing things by the book.

Looking around, he bent over and scooped up a loose cobble from the roadway with his gloved hands. To lessen the noise he quickly took off his coat and wrapped the stone in it, hoping none of his neighbours would see him standing in the street, shoulder holster visible, breaking into someone's car.

He didn't strike at the glass. That would attract too much attention. Instead, and remembering a technique shown to him once by a lowlife car thief several years ago, he struck at the door's side panel near the hinges, just about where the internal window gear pivot should be. If done correctly it should loosen the pivot arm.

With a dull thud, the driver's window dropped down an inch or so. Tossing away the stone and putting his coat back on, Pieter shoved his gloved fingers through the narrow gap, and pulling and pushing, he forced the window down far enough to allow him to reach inside and pull the door catch and pop open the door, all without denting the bodywork.

Pieter lowered himself into the driver's seat and quietly closed the door and then reached over and picked up the aluminium case.

Quickly, he ran his eyes over the laptop's screen, noting the green lines flickering back and forth to show the signal strength of the phone-catcher. It was plugged into a portable USB hub, which in turn was powered by a large battery-pack, supplying enough juice to keep the thing running for days.

To confirm his suspicion that he himself was the target of the phone-catcher's surreptitious spying (what other explanation could there be?) Pieter took out his mobile phone and dialled his own work's telephone number, and sure enough within just a few seconds, his mobile number appeared on screen with the words **TARGET CAPTURED** flashing alongside.

He cut the call and sat for a moment, trying to think back to the first time he had noticed the hire car parked outside his home, and going over all of the phone calls and messages that would consequently have been intercepted.

His mood didn't improve.

He decided to try something else.

Raising his mobile once again, he switched over to his home Wi-Fi network – the signal was quite strong sitting just feet from his front door – and then did the same on the laptop, remembering to keep his gloves on while he used the mouse and keyboard.

Using his home Wi-Fi like this ensured that whoever was intercepting his calls would have no knowledge of what he was about to try. Hopefully.

With the laptop logged into his home Wi-Fi, he opened up its terminal dialogue box and typed in **IPCONFIG** to reveal two IP addresses. One for the laptop/phone-catcher combo sitting here on his knees, and another for a second laptop together with the word **SYNCED**.

The IP address of the remote user logging in to the intercepted calls and messages.

Back on his mobile, Pieter opened up a secure app called **FLASHFACE SCANNER 112** and entered his police password, and then ran this second IP address through the software.

Twenty seconds later and his phone chimed and he opened the file.

There, on the tiny screen of his smart-phone, was a postal address in central Amsterdam.

"Oops," Johan Roost said to himself.
Lotte looked over. He was on the laptop again, using the IMSI software.
"What?" she asked.
"It looks like somebody briefly switched us over to a Wi-Fi network, and then straight back again."
"So what does that mean?"
"It means we're about to get a visitor," he told her.

He drove straight over. He couldn't risk phoning HQ (for obvious reasons) and there was no time to head over to Elandsgracht for some backup as it wasn't on the way, and the clock was ticking on this one.

Besides, it was time to take matters into his own hands, to be proactive.

The Begijnhof was one of the oldest courtyards in the city. Dating back to the 1340's, it was built following The Miracle of the Host as a sanctuary for women to live lives of religious servitude, similar to a convent. It housed two churches, Pieter remembered from the few times he had visited, and consisted of a group of very old buildings clustered around a small green. There was a statue of Mary (or was it one of the Beguine nuns? – he couldn't remember) and in recent decades was used as a women's refuge.

There were two entrances, he recalled, and he chose the one leading off Spui Square.

By the time he pulled up the light was fading from the late-afternoon sky. Hopefully the place would be quiet, with the few tourists braving the snowy weather having drifted off back to their hotels.

Walking across the square towards the narrow arched entrance, which led down to a set of steps and into the enclosure, Pieter withdrew his service weapon and checked that the Walther P5 was loaded. The magazine contained eight rounds and he chambered the first bullet, the loud snap of the sliding barrel crisp and clear in the still air.

Moving to the side of the opening set in the high wall which surrounded the complex of buildings, Pieter edged nearer. He gripped the pistol's butt in his right hand while he supported his wrist with his left hand, for although the weapon was small it still had a decent kick.

Passing around the edge of the wall and holding the gun out to his front he stepped smoothly into the entrance. There was a short, stone passage with six or seven steps leading down, and then another archway. Beyond this, he could see the snow-covered lawn in the dim evening light and no movement other than drifting snowflakes.

It occurred to him then that this was an ideal place for Lotte to have holed up in all of these months. The women who stayed here in their separate apartments preferred to remain anonymous, very seldom giving their real identities, for most of them were here to escape abusive relationships. The charity that ran the refuge asked very few questions. So it was a perfect location for her to hide away while the police had searched everywhere for her.

She was right under their very noses - if she were indeed here.

Pieter moved down into the courtyard, breathing rapidly.

To his left was a short cobbled path leading to a set of steps and a doorway. The windows to either side of the door were in blackness, so for the time being he dismissed this direction and instead turned to check out the area near the lawn.

The statue at the centre was almost obscured with snow. Only her face was visible, and her stone features stared back at him, sending a shiver down his spine. On the far side of the patch of white grass was the large edifice of one of the churches, and running along the length of the building was a narrow passage flagged with gravestones, again leading nowhere.

He remembered now. The majority of the courtyard, with the houses and apartments where the women lived, were beyond the large bulk of the church and not visible from this side. The entranceway he'd used was really the smaller side entrance. He cursed himself for coming this way.

Pieter looked around, taking in the quiet setting. There was a hushed beauty to the scene, he admitted, with the soft snow settling on the ground muffling all sound except for the crunching of his boots. A few lights were on in some of the apartment windows, and the old lanterns gave the courtyard a Dickensian feel, a picture-postcard Christmas ambience.

But there was also a tension in the air, a tautness to the descending night, and he felt icy and bony fingers caress his spine like an illicit lover.

Somewhere a cat called out loudly, and the sound broke through his musings, and so he stepped forward around the square lawn towards the church building.

Just before he reached the brick corner, a movement caught his attention, and his step faltered. Not a sound, more of a shifting of the air, and a half-second later the explosive report of a gunshot shattered the silence.

The bullet struck the stonework barely two feet in front of his face, sending a chip of masonry flying over his head, and Pieter ducked down and scurried over to the side of the church. He cursed and thanked God in equal measures.

The shot had come from beyond the church, confirming his fears that whoever was shooting at him – and it had to be Lotte or whoever else was working with her – were hiding out in that section.

He risked a quick peek around the corner, which drew a second gunshot, this one not as well-aimed; the round hit the statue behind him and then ricocheted away, taking half of the figure's head with it.

Yet in that very brief moment, just before he whipped his face back out of sight again, he caught the bright muzzle-flash of the gun, coming from one of the windows near to the larger entrance tunnel on the opposite side of the small courtyard.

He noticed more lights coming on in several of the other apartments, their occupants no doubt drawn by the sudden noise, and he prayed they didn't venture outside to see what was going on.

Taking several deep breaths, he quickly swung his arms around the wall, took a quick aim towards the window where the shots had come from, and fired twice. The Walther P5 bucked in his hands, nearly spraining his wrists, and there was the sound of breaking glass.

Hoping his return fire would keep the apartments' occupants hunkered down, Pieter chose the moment to quickly backtrack across the cobbles and hurry down the narrow passageway leading down the side of the church, where the large building would shelter him from view and give him vital cover.

Reaching the end he slipped out and darted over to the far side of the lawn. There was a low wall surrounding the grass, as well as a set of steps running up to the front door of another apartment, and he crouched down low behind them. From here he had a direct view towards the shattered window but out of the line of fire. If he could quickly get around the steps he could use the shelter of the buildings to creep right up to the spot where the gunman was.

But even as he readied himself for this last rush forward the door next to the broken window suddenly flew open, and the silhouette of a tall man came rushing out. He had what looked like a large canvas bag in one hand, and in the other he held a small handgun, and he blazed away like some bank robber in an old western movie, his shots fanning out over the courtyard.

Pieter dropped onto his knees.

He stared in amazement as the man continued to fire shot after shot. Then he saw a second figure emerge from the doorway, sliding silently behind the first, using him as a shield. This one was smaller, lithe, moving with almost feline grace, and he caught a quick flash of long blonde hair, and Pieter knew in an instant that it was Lotte.

He watched as she raced for the opening to the short tunnel leading out of the courtyard, with the man hot on her heels, and in the next moment they were gone, their footsteps crunching loudly on the snow.

Pieter ran across the square, slipping through the deep snow, and was just in time to see them disappear through the far exit and he charged down the covered passage after them.

There was a crossroads of narrow alleyways at the end. The ones branching left and right were poorly lit, the tall buildings on either side leaning out like drunken old men, but there was just enough illumination for him to see these were empty. Just ahead was a third twisting little lane lined with bars and cafes, a short-cut that led through to the busy pedestrianised Kalverstraat, and he caught sight of the fleeing pair running flat-out by the bewildered patrons sitting at the tables drinking their beer.

He followed them, shouting and waving for people to take cover, but they just stared open-mouthed at him.

Halfway along and he saw the gunman up ahead turn and fire again, the bullet striking the ground and sending up a flurry of powdery snow, and now the people sitting watching the scene dived for cover beneath their tables, one old man taking his drink with him. Luckily nobody seemed to have been hit.

The running figures turned left and disappeared from view, and Pieter bolted down the lane.

Kalverstraat was the busiest shopping street in Amsterdam, lined with expensive boutiques, fashion stores, bakeries and fast-food joints, and was always jam-packed with people, and this evening was no exception. It was filled with Christmas shoppers hurrying through the snow to grab a few seasonal presents, and when Pieter burst out of the exit from the narrow lane he found himself hemmed in by the crowds, hoping that the man wielding the gun didn't open fire here.

For several seconds he thought he had lost them. He could not see them anywhere. Then he caught another glimpse of Lotte's hair, and he picked them both out amidst the bobbing heads, and Pieter pushed his way through the shoppers.

They must have seen him coming for a moment later he watched as they ducked down another alleyway.

Turning the corner, and relieved to leave the congested street, he ran after them.

At the far end, cars and trams flashed past. They were making for Rokin, the main road feeding traffic in and out of Dam Square, and beyond that was the rabbit-warren of the Red Light District.

Lotte and the man with her were halfway along when suddenly, from up ahead, trundling towards them came a motorcycle courier, with round helmet and goggles over his head and his eyes glued to his mobile phone.

Lotte's companion charged straight at him and swung the heavy canvas bag he was carrying straight at the unsuspecting rider.

The man didn't know what hit him. The bag struck him square in the chest, lifting him up and out of the saddle, and he pitched into the alley wall. The motorcycle spun to the ground with a grating of metal and Pieter watched in dismay as the man grabbed the handlebars and twisted the bike upright in one fluid movement, letting the revving engine propel it back onto its wheels. It was now pointed back the way it had come, towards the far end of the alleyway, and the man climbed into the saddle and swung the bag onto his back.

"Get on!" Pieter heard him shout, and seconds later Lotte was on the bike behind him, and with a roar, they sped off towards the stream of traffic up ahead.

Pieter raised his gun just as she glanced back over her shoulder at him, and their eyes briefly locked together, and then he pulled the trigger in a split-second snapshot.

There was a tiny fountain of blood on her upper arm where the bullet hit, and then they were riding out into the flow of traffic.

Chapter 20
Red Snow

With blood streaming from her arm Lotte clung to her uncle's back as they rode through the road tunnel beneath the River IJ. He weaved the motorcycle around the other cars and buses with confident ease, pushing the small bike hard, and rather than risk sliding off the saddle she clasped hold of the straps on the canvas gun bag, her cheek pressed against his shoulder.

Her arm stung where the bullet had hit her, and she'd lost quite a lot of blood, but thankfully she didn't think the injury was dangerously bad. Lucky for her the shot had only grazed her arm, slicing a groove through the flesh which would probably, she thought, leave her with a permanent scar, but it could have been worse she decided.

It hurt like hell, and would need some stitches, but she could put up with the pain.

Overhead the lights along the tunnel roof flashed by, and the headlights from the vehicles around them swept around the curved concrete walls, lending the place a strange otherworldly feel. Moments later and they emerged from the northern exit and the traffic spread out as the road fed into the faster motorway, and they quickly cut through the suburbs of North Amsterdam.

There was a set of rail tracks in the central reservation between the northbound and southbound lanes, and a long, red GVB train carrying commuters home kept pace with them, and Lotte vaguely noticed the curious stares they attracted from the passengers looking out of the windows as they cut a snaking path through the cars. She turned her face away and closed her eyes.

She kept thinking back to the craziness they had just left behind, the violence of the firefight and their narrow escape, and she couldn't rid her mind of her brief glimpse of Pieter Van Dijk as they had sped along the alleyway. The way their eyes had held each other's gaze for those few fleeting seconds.

Something had passed between them. She was sure it was a shared experience, a touching of their minds or something, and she was surprised at the emotional impact it was having on her now. It should not be affecting her this way, she admonished herself, and she shook her head in annoyance.

Nevertheless it was.

Under any other circumstances, she would have found the feeling touching, maybe poignant even. But this was the last thing she needed, allowing their past closeness to stir something deep inside her.

She needed to get a grip, she told herself.

To focus on her goal, to correct her mistakes in the spring.

To keep to her path of destruction and revenge.

Lotte rubbed hard at her face and her hand came away wet with unshed tears.

A short time later and they crossed the ring road, and then a few miles further on she spotted a Shell service station, and she tapped her uncle on the shoulder and pointed, and he steered the bike down the exit ramp.

There was a small Albert Heijn mini-market and a pharmacy next to the forecourt, and after setting the bike on its stand, her Uncle Johan led her over. He took her weight a little, and before they entered they turned up their collars.

The young man behind the counter was too busy watching Ajax on the TV screen to pay them much attention, and he barely said hello and goodbye when they bought a bunch of bandages, pain killers and antiseptic cream.

Back outside, Lotte carefully removed her jacket and peeled up the sleeve of her sweater.

The whole of her forearm was covered in blood, but the nasty wound just above her elbow looked to have stopped bleeding for now. The icy cold wind as they rode north had no doubt helped to numb the injury somewhat, but the sharp pain was still there, so he made her take three or four painkillers, and then tried his best to clean the wound and smear it with cream. Finally he wrapped a bandage tightly around her arm and then gingerly rolled her sleeve back down.

"It will do for now," he told her. "We can stitch it up later. Let me know if you start to feel faint, we don't want you falling off the back."

He tried to make light of the situation, giving her his winning smile, but she cast her eyes down.

"Is everything okay? You seem quiet."

"Yes, everything's fine," she snapped, and went back over to the motorcycle.

* * *

For several minutes Pieter stood looking down at the droplets of blood on the snow, ignoring the traffic and pedestrians at either end of the alleyway. The sound of approaching sirens came to him then, and he turned and hurriedly retraced his footsteps back through the sloughing snowstorm, along the busy shopping street, and then down the lane where the beer drinkers were just retaking their seats, and through the covered passageway into the Begijnhof courtyard.

He felt compelled to take a quick look inside Lotte's apartment before the armed response units arrived, who would then be followed by his colleagues from HQ, and then the forensic boffins. He didn't know why, just that instinct was telling him to go in first.

Crunching over the broken glass he stepped through the open door.

Just beyond the entrance there was a short hallway and a coat on a rack. Down one side ran a wall of undressed brickwork with a shelf set back into it, containing several peculiar wooden carvings, each one with a small plaque and a spotlight. He read a few of the inscriptions: A pair of gnarled hands clasping a pentangle was called **HOLD OF BAPHOMET**. A half-man/half-goat was **PAN THE GUARDIAN**. A voluptuous woman with parted legs was **SHIELA-Na-GIG**. **MEDUSA THE GORGON**. **THE RAVEN AND THE KEY**. **CADEUCUS OF MERCURY** with her angel wings and a black asp coiled around her naked form. **VENUS OF WILLENDORF**. Pieter moved away.

Further along, a doorway led into a modern study, with beautiful display cabinets holding more expensive ornaments, a brown couch and wooden chairs, a desk with a computer monitor, and a wooden floor covered in a square brown rug. It was spotlessly clean, Pieter thought as he stood there taking in the scene, beautiful and very plush. The window by the desk had shattered and spilled glass onto the wooden surface, and a draught gently blew snow through the opening. A lamp standing in one corner cast a gold haze over the room.

At the far end there was a huge glass wall and door leading to the bedroom, and beside them a set of steps leading up to the attic presumably. In the bedroom there was a large double bed, some potted plants and side-tables and furniture, as well as a bookcase, a cream carpet, and overhead a ceiling with wooden beams and more spotlights.

Pieter stepped over and passed through the glass doorway, and he stood looking at the bed.

He found his mind going back to the period during the spring when Lotte had stayed with him for several nights, having concocted some story about problems with her boss at work (a ruse as it turned out, for the person was in fact her older brother Bart). They had grown close for a time for his head was a mess back then, with pressures of work and the terrifying case that had gripped the city for several weeks taking their toll, and Lotte had breached through his defences to seduce him and visit him at night.

Thinking about it now he felt stupid, almost as though it hadn't happened, for reality had become mixed up with his feverish nightmares until he wasn't sure what was true and what wasn't. More than six months on and he still didn't fully understand everything.

Pieter mentally shrugged his shoulders and slipped back into the study.

The computer on the desk showed a screensaver of a woodland setting, but when he tapped a key at random the monitor came to life.

The IMSI-catcher programme was still running. He recognized his mobile number on the screen, and when he clicked on it a list of all the phone calls and text messages he had exchanged over the last few days appeared.

He recognized most of them, especially the ones between himself and Kaatje.

HEY, YOU FANCY TAKING A TRIP IN THE MORNING?

YES PLEASE 😊 WHERE ARE WE GOING BOSS?

IT'S A SURPRISE. I'LL PICK YOU UP AT YOUR PLACE. 8am SHARP.

He'd even tagged a smiley of his own on the end 😊

Huijbers had been right. He should never have involved Kaatje, a rookie cop fresh from passing out from the police academy at Eindhoven. Of course, at the time he had no inkling that Charlotte Janssen was behind the whole thing, otherwise he would never have brought her in on the case. But it was a decision that would have lifelong consequences for Kaatje.

Leaving the computer Pieter swung about to take a better look around when his foot caught the edge of the square rug covering the floor, nearly tripping him. Getting his balance, something caught his attention, a line scratched into the wood underneath where the corner of the rug had rolled back.

Pieter bent over and grabbed the thick mat, and a sense of deja-vu went through him as he recalled the foot-track spell left behind by the intruder in his attic room during the WEREWOLF case, but he grunted, tired of acting like a nervous old spinster, and he rolled it all the way back in an angry flourish.

Carved across the flooring in painstaking detail was an intricate design. A series of concentric circles and runic symbols, signs of the zodiac and crescent moons and ancient script with swirling letters and god knows what else. All beautifully worked into the polished wood floor.

Chapter 21
Visitation

Pieter waited until his colleagues arrived before heading back to his car. He briefly explained just what had happened, quickly telling them to put out an alert with a description of the motorcycle. He also showed the team leaders the various crime scenes: the apartment, the lane and the alleyway, and he pointed out the spent brass cartridge cases on the ground, and watched as a full search by the armed response unit took place, the armour-clad men moving from building to building, asking the residents to temporarily leave their homes while they made sure the place was safe and harbouring no more wanted fugitives. They even dragged the church caretaker out of his home on nearby Gedempte Sloot to open up the building to check inside. Satisfied that the whole place was clear, they next sealed the courtyard off and marked it out with little yellow flags and the forensic personnel began their work, moving through the scene dressed in white coveralls and looking like snowmen magically come to life.

Pieter went out by the smaller exit and walked across Spui Square, noticing that more police were checking out a second hire car parked nearby, which reminded him of the one outside his home with the IMSI-catcher. He went over to pass this information on to them and then drove back over to the hospital, his nerves still jittery. He couldn't stop thinking about the large symbol beneath the rug.

Arriving just outside Kaatje's room, he kicked himself. In all of the drama over the last hour or so he'd completely forgotten about bringing a few things over for her. However, on walking through the door, he was pleasantly surprised to find her sitting on the edge of her bed fully dressed and with her small overnight bag packed.

She turned her face on hearing him enter.

Pieter stood there confused, looking from her gauze-covered eyes to the bag.

"Hey, what's going on?"

Kaatje smiled when she heard his voice.

"They said I can come home. Well, not home home."

"Already? But I thought...?"

"The doctors told me there's no reason for me to stay here. Especially when I explained to them that I'd be staying with a friend. I think they probably need the bed, you know what hospitals are like these days? They ship you out as soon as they've patched you up. Besides, there's nothing to report yet on how the op has turned out."

She shrugged, looking all tiny and fragile, he thought.

He went over and sat on the bed next to her and gave her a big hug.

"That's great news," he said.

"Has something been going on while I've been in here?" she asked.

"What makes you say that?"

"Oh, it's just that when they brought me back up there was a lot of commotion going on just outside my room. I could hear the guard out there on his radio, and then some other people joined him, I think I recognized their voices from the station, and they were talking about a shoot-out or something. Is it connected to the case, Boss?"

Pieter laughed gently. He found her amazing.

"What are you laughing at?" She stuck her elbow into his ribs.

"Nothing. But don't you start worrying about work, you need to rest, put your feet up on the couch for a few days, let me wait on you hand and foot."

"Boring! I want to crack on with the case Boss, find the people who did this to me and get Nina back safe and sound. We're a team, remember?"

Kaatje hopped to the floor like a determined little pocket-rocket or something, ready to go. Then she wobbled and tottered to the side, and he grabbed her quickly as she sagged.

She let him support her, and this time her smile was a little weaker, and she leaned her head against his shoulder.

"Come on," he told her. "Let's get you out of here."

Pieter used the remote on his key fob to open the electronic garage doors, and turned the wheel to steer the car inside. Out in the street a tow truck was just winching the hire car away. The snow had stopped, the blizzard having temporarily moved on, and overhead the night sky twinkled with stars.

Punching in a six-digit code into the touch-screen display on the wall, he set the garage alarm, and then tapped in a different sequence of numbers to open the door leading from the garage to the house. The front door itself had its own alarm system, as did all of the windows, including the attic dormer beneath the bell gable. After his intruder earlier that year, who had somehow managed to get into his home - something he could still not explain - he was taking no chances.

Guiding Kaatje gently by the elbow he led her up the flights of narrow wooden stairs, explaining the rough layout of his home as they went. She asked a few questions but was mostly quiet, her pinched face and small mouth all serious and listening to his every word, which brought another laugh from him and another frown from her.

The main living area was on the third floor and Pieter paused on the landing by the window.

"Welcome to your new home," he said gently. "I'll take you to your room."

Kaatje took a hold of his hand and held him firmly, and then she pressed her tiny frame into his, seeking warmth and comfort he thought, but before he knew what was happening she kissed him on the lips, her mouth parting slightly. After a moment she pulled back, and he saw she was breathless, and he touched the bandages over her eyes tenderly.

"Make love to me," her whispered words came to him.

Afterwards, they lay on the bed holding tightly onto each other, their bodies bathed in sweat and their limbs still entwined. There was nothing to say to one another, for their shared fears had found an outlet and a temporary respite, and they sank into its soft welcoming void. To forget, if only for a short while.

They drifted off to sleep.

Just as oblivion took him, a thought pushed its way into Pieter's mind. Something he should have done. He struggled to remember what.

Something about the bed.

The salt. Yes, that's what it was. The circle of salt around the bed.

Sleep overcame him, and the thought melted away in the dark.

* * *

Nina had remained locked inside the small cage for over two full days now. Since her failed attempt to escape, she had seen nothing of Tobias, nor had she eaten or drank anything. Her empty stomach felt like a hollow pit and her lips and throat had become parched, her tongue all swollen up, leaving a bitter taste in her mouth.

Her entire universe had shrunk down to this tiny, square prison. She barely had room to sit up or to stretch her legs out, and after several hours her body had become painfully cramped, the muscles in her thighs and back feeling as hard as iron, all twisted and knotted together.

She was also frozen to the core. As punishment Tobias must have switched off the heating, and although there was a rolled-up blanket in the cage, dressed as she was in just leggings and a hoodie it was completely inadequate in keeping her warm.

There was also nothing to use as a toilet. She had held off needing to pee for the first night, but by the middle of the following morning her bladder felt like it was about to burst, and so with little choice she had hitched down her clothes and squatted in the far corner.

Throughout, she was petrified.

Petrified that Tobias would come stalking back down the stairs and kill her for what she'd done.

Then later and after several hours with no sign of him, she became petrified that he had just upped and left, having decided to abandon her here to a horrible fate, to die slowly of hunger.

But the following morning she had heard the faint sound of the van revving and driving away as he'd set off for work, just like on the other days. Which had led Nina to believe that everything might still be ok after all. Her ordeal would go on, and her situation was a whole lot worse than before, but at least she was alive, and hopefully not alone.

The thought of Tobias coming down to see her didn't seem so bad anymore.

Anything was preferable to the silence and the loneliness.

The hours stretched on and on. Down here there was no real way of knowing the time, but over the last few days the daily routine of waking, eating her meals, reading, watching a DVD, had at least given some kind of structure to her days, and this allowed her to judge the approximate time of day, or at least work out if it was day or night. But trapped in the cage, with no distractions or break in the monotony, she soon became lost in her own thoughts. And when she had eventually drifted off to sleep towards the end of the second day, and then awoken later feeling refreshed and with a clear mind, she knew it was the following morning and Tobias had still not returned, he had not been down to see her or to bring her food and something to drink as he always did, then it had dawned on her that her worst fears were realized. Tobias had indeed left her for good.

Nina had never felt so low. Even when she had first been snatched from home and bundled into the oblong metal box in the back of the van, driven away through the night and then carried down here, she had never felt such hopelessness as she did now.

The thought of spending her final days in this cage, growing weaker and weaker as she slowly died, wondering if anybody would ever find her body and know of her fate... it was enough to break her completely and Nina had wept openly, crying out for her parents who she knew were dead also. These feelings of utter wretchedness pressed down on her and crushed any last lingering shred of hope.

But later, much later, having cried herself to the point of exhaustion, a sound reached her. Very faint at first, so quiet that she wondered if her frightened mind had imagined it.

Then it grew louder, a steady drone that increased in volume, coming closer.

Something in the yard outside.

Sitting up, Nina listened carefully, and after another minute she recognized the sound.

A motorcycle. Yes, that's what it was. Somebody was outside on a motorcycle.

The engine cut out and she held her breath, straining her hearing.

She heard a door opening. Footsteps across the room above her.

* * *

Lotte stood in the parlour and looked around at the dust and old furniture, the mouldy, musty smell making her nose wrinkle.

So this was the place? she thought to herself. Tobias Vinke's home, and where he'd brought the girl. Miles from anywhere, way off the beaten track, a spot where nobody would think to look. Just as he'd told her. At least his part in the plot had mostly gone according to plan, until the final few days when he'd started to get cold feet. But her Uncle Johan had taken care of that.

And now here they were, come to babysit the kid she thought in annoyance.

Not quite how things should have turned out.

But no matter. It wouldn't be for long.

She heard her uncle enter the room behind her and watched as he dumped the carryall containing the sniper rifle onto an old armchair. From the back of his waist belt he removed his small handgun.

"I'm going outside to check on our security. Then we'll take another look at that arm of yours."

"Look in on the girl first. She should be down in the basement."

"If you say so."

He pushed open the door into the kitchen.

"It's a fucking mess in here!"

Lotte ignored him. She was still perturbed by her mixed-up emotions, triggered by the earlier crossing of paths with Pieter Van Dijk, brief though it had been.

The distraction was becoming a hindrance, coming at a time when clear heads and calm restraint were required. But pushing thoughts of him to the back of her mind was proving difficult, which irritated her even more. And now that the immediate danger had passed, and they had made it out of the city more or less in one piece and reached the temporary safety of Tobias' hideout, she found herself struggling to let these feelings go.

Try as she might to ignore this unwanted intrusion, Pieter was dead-centre in her thoughts. And for the first time in many months, she felt her resolve weaken.

Lotte paced back and forth across the old, threadbare carpet, her gaze no longer looking at her surroundings but instead with her thoughts turned inwards.

Damn it! Why was this happening now?

Yes, the two of them had a bond, but built on a lie. The friendship, which became very intense, was really nothing more than a sham. She had drawn him into her intricate web over many months, helped by her mother Famke, who likewise had befriended Pieter's father, the old drunk on the houseboat. But inevitably their relationship, both platonic and later sexual, was bound to have left behind some residual emotions for both of them.

She stopped beside the window and briefly lifted the curtain to peer out at the night, but all she could see was her own pale reflection staring back.

She was human, she concluded. Not as strong as people presumed.

But she needed to put this to bed quickly.

Lotte was in her astral form once more, moving through the night, with the city far below her.

She travelled with ease, and some inner sense alerted her to her destination, the house she was looking for, and she swooped down and glided smoothly through the outer walls and into the bedroom.

Floating above the bed, invisible in the real realm, she looked down at the sleeping figures embraced together.

Pieter... and the girl! The girl at the clinic!

A wave of anger passed through Lotte's astral incarnation, and for the briefest of moments she appeared as a ghostly shape, rippling and surging with energy, like a shimmering cloud flashing with lightening...

...while back in the parlour, tears appeared in the eyes of the reflection cast in the window...

In a fury, the apparition opened its mouth wide in a silent scream, but Pieter and the girl blissfully slept on.

A white miasma floated out from between its lips, like a cloud of condensation, and it twisted and snaked through the air, across the bedroom, and then slipped silently into the girl's mouth.

Kaatje breathed in the ectoplasm, drawing it into her core.

* * *

A shifting of the bed woke him and Pieter lay there for several moments looking up at the dark ceiling, his groggy mind slowly coming alert.

All was quiet around the house. There was a draught coming from somewhere, raising goosebumps on his bare arms, and he wondered if he had left a window open? Unlikely at this time of the year.

Rolling over, he reached for Kaatje, seeking her warm body. But when his arm touched the empty mattress alongside him he raised himself on one elbow, and twisted around to flick on the bedside lamp.

Blinking his eyes and scratching the stubble on his chin, he threw back the covers and came to his feet, wondering where on earth she was. The bedroom door was wide open, hence the chilly draught. She must have gone to the bathroom, he guessed, but she should have woken him. She shouldn't be stumbling around in a strange house, not until she had a better sense of the layout.

"Kaatje!" he called, still half asleep, and he shuffled tiredly out through the door in his shorts and t-shirt.

The bathroom was next door, at the end of the passage and thankfully away from the top of the stairs, and he gently pushed open the door, softly calling her name. Pulling the light cord, he saw the tiny room was empty, and so he turned and headed along the landing. He walked by the doorway to the kitchen and around the wooden pommel at the head of the flight of steps, thinking she must be in the lounge: perhaps she couldn't sleep and had decided to pour herself a drink.

He heard a faint noise then, a tiny scraping of bare feet on the carpeted floor behind him, and he was just about to turn back when there came a terrible screeching that made him jump out of his skin. His heart missed a beat, giving him a sickening feeling like the floor had just opened up beneath him, and he twisted just in time to see Kaatje launch herself at him from the kitchen doorway.

Her features were almost unrecognizable, all twisted with anger and her lips peeled back, and the bandage over her face was hanging loose so that he could see her stitched-up and watery eyes. She flew through the air towards him, and something in her hand caught the light from the kitchen and flashed brightly, and Pieter stumbled back and threw up a protective arm as he realized she was holding a knife.

She slashed down and the blade cut into his forearm, drawing a thin line of blood in the skin. Pieter twisted to the side as her feet landed on the floor, and he used his arm to swing her away from him, using her weight and momentum so that she tottered sideways.

It gave him enough time to duck as she swung the knife back towards the top of his head and the sharp blade embedded itself in the doorframe. Kaatje tried to tug it free but it was stuck fast, and Pieter hunched his shoulder beneath her slender frame and lifted her up. She lost her grip on the knife, and she screamed in frustration as he hefted her into the landing wall and pushed her down to the floor, his weight bearing down on her.

"Kaatje! God damn it! Stop!"

For half a second he wondered if she was sleepwalking.

"Wake up, please!"

Again her face twisted in hatred, and she spat and hissed at him.

Somehow she managed to lift her leg and plant her bare foot on his chest and he felt her push with superhuman strength, and then he was being propelled backwards, and he yelled in fright.

His back struck something hard and he realized it was the railing around the top of the staircase, the only thing that had prevented him from plummeting down to the floor below.

Badly winded, and still stunned from the suddenness of her attack, and wondering how the heck she could even see where he was, just like the patients at the clinic he thought, Pieter looked up.

Once again Kaatje was coming through the air towards him, her nightdress billowing around her.

Pieter rolled sideways and Kaatje landed with a grunt onto the landing floor. Quickly recovering, he slammed his elbow into her back to pin her there, and then he wheeled himself back over and lay across her body, using his arms to hold her shoulders and head down, the blood from his wound soon smearing her white nightdress red.

Kaatje kicked and twisted beneath him, bucking sideways to try and throw him off, but Pieter sprawled himself widely over her thrashing body, refusing to let her slip out from under him. He held on, hoping she would tire, for he didn't want to have to hit her: the mere idea gave him a feeling of revulsion.

Leaning his face down towards the back of her head he whispered into her ear.

"Kaatje, stop now. Calm down. Wake up and stop struggling."

Slowly her struggles grew weaker. Perhaps it was his soothing voice that had penetrated through to her, perhaps it was exhaustion, or maybe she just snapped out of whatever freaked-out spell she was under. Whatever it was, Pieter felt her thrashings and kickings gradually subside, become more and more feeble, and he gently shushed her, coaxing a calmness back into her thoughts.

Finally, her movements ceased, to be replaced by quiet sobbing.

"Pieter?" she implored. "Pieter, please help."

Lying there and trying to regain his breath from the violent struggle, he was vaguely aware of his mobile phone ringing insistently from the bedroom.

* * *

Having checked on the girl in the basement and then done a quick circuit outside to make sure everything was secure, Johan strode back into the lounge, shivering and dusting the snow from his coat and looking forward to getting the log fire going.

He stopped dead at the sight which confronted him.

His niece was lying on the floor, twisting and thrashing, grunting like some beast, having some kind of fit he thought in alarm. But when she turned over onto her back and he saw her eyes, which were rolled back into her head so they bulged out of her face like white marbles, Johan faltered and drew in his breath.

He looked at her in dismay, wondering if he should help.

Yet when he saw a strange white mist coming out of her mouth, a little bit like smoke but all shiny and sticky-looking and flecked with black, and he smelt a pungent stench like rotten food or corrupted flesh, then, slowly, he drew away and quietly backed back out of the room, his fingers all shaky and sweaty as he pulled the door gently shut.

Chapter 22
Waterland

Pieter looked down at Kaatje's sleeping form on the large bed.

Exhausted and mentally drained, confused and scared and tearful, she had fallen asleep in his arms on the landing, and he had carried her back to the bedroom.

He was still breathing hard but more from shock than anything. His arm throbbed painfully and the tips of his fingers felt numb, but thankfully the blade of the knife had not slashed his arm too deeply. The injury seemed to only be superficial. He'd washed it underneath the bathroom taps to stem the bleeding and wrapped it in a towel.

God, what the hell was going on? his confused mind demanded.

None of this made any sense, this whirlwind of bizarre events and incidents.

He heard his phone start to ring again and, glad for the distraction, he walked around the bed and picked it up, glancing at the *CALLER ID*.

Floris de Kok. He was one of the civilian desk-jockeys at HQ, a good man who had offered invaluable help during the Werewolf case, and who specialized in organising the files department as well as working in the surveillance unit.

It was shortly after one in the morning, so whatever he was calling for it must be something important.

* * *

Prisha Kapoor and her partner Rowan, who hailed from Dublin, currently still lived at their place in Amsterdam, a neat little corner-apartment overlooking Erasmus Park. Most evenings and weekends were spent shifting their belongings over to their new place in Utrecht, but their lease here still had a month or so to run, and so luckily for Pieter they were in town when he rang in the early hours of the morning.

Surprisingly they were still up – watching old repeats of The X-Files, Prisha told him. When he explained his situation and stressed the urgency of it, he heard Rowan call out, "what's he waiting for? Tell the eejit to get his arse round here. To be sure to be sure," she added for his benefit.

Twenty minutes later and Pieter pulled up on the quiet street just outside the building's glass door, and helped Kaatje out of the car. She was half asleep, dressed in his thick winter coat over her jeans and shoes, mumbling to herself, with the bandages back over her eyes. She seemed very docile and subdued now, as though all of her strength had evaporated away, and this left Pieter more concerned than relieved.

But he didn't have time to think about it right now. Later, in the cold light of day, he could assess the events from earlier and try to make sense of them, but for now he needed somewhere Kaatje could stay, with somebody who he could trust.

Prisha buzzed him in.

She was waiting in the doorway to their apartment, and she ushered them inside.

The TV was off. In the background, some calming meditation music was playing, which sounded like whale noises to Pieter. On the wall was a framed print of MC Escher's impossible staircase. Rowan was in to all this wacky stuff, he remembered.

"What happened to you?" Prisha asked upon seeing the long strip of fabric dressing on his forearm.

"I'll tell you later," he told her, and she didn't press him on it.

Rowan led Kaatje away and sat her down on an armchair close to the fireplace, tutting and fussing over her.

"Look, I appreciate this. I'm very sorry for springing this on you both like this, at this time of night, but I didn't have-"

"Say no more," she interrupted him. "It sounds like something serious is happening. Is it connected to the Nina Bakker case?"

Pieter swallowed and nodded.

"You'd best get going then. We'll take care of Kaatje."

Back out on the street Pieter took out his mobile and rang Floris de Kok back.

"Talk to me," he said as he climbed into the car.

"Boss. Something important came in about an hour ago, and I thought you should know. We've had a hit on the ViCASnl system which looks very promising."

Floris was referring to the national crime-linkage database. Pieter had put in a request for any suspects or vehicles that matched their own to be flagged up and referred over to them, for cross-checking.

"Go on."

"Well as a matter of fact it was the people over at NCSC, the security camera nerve-centre at Bos en Lommerplein, who spotted it."

"They sent us something the other day, which turned out to be useless," Pieter pointed out, remembering the CCTV footage outside the Bakker's house.

"Yeah I know. But I did a little checking of my own this time, just to see if this had anything going for it, which it does. Enough for me to ring you and wake you up anyway."

Pieter tried not to let his irritation show; sometimes de Kok was slow at getting to the point.

"Give me a few more details will you?"

"Right. Several nights ago there was a hit-and-run fatal road accident out at Ransdorp. A guy riding his bicycle was found dead at the side of the road early in the morning. Hit by a vehicle a few nights before it seems. The dead chap has been identified and his family have confirmed he'd popped out on an errand and not come home, so they reported him as missing, and the spot where his body was found points to the fact that he was on his way back when he was hit. He was lying in a ditch, which had frozen over, hence the reason he wasn't spotted for a while."

"Okay. But hit-and-runs happen all of the time."

"True. More often than people realize. If you are driving along late at night, say for example out in the sticks like in this case, where it might be dark and with no street-lighting, and suddenly a pedestrian or another car or a cyclist appears from nowhere and, boom, you have no time to react, before you know it you've hit them. Now, most people would stop to help, phone for an ambulance, or give them first aid or whatever. Do the right thing. Sadly, however, not everybody. Some people panic and drive straight on, shitting themselves but making a snap decision not to stop, to head straight home in the hope that maybe they just hit a cat or something. And even if they know that isn't the case, that they've just in fact run over another person, they don't always think rationally. They don't want to ruin the rest of their lives and go to jail all because of a few seconds of inattention. Especially if a child is involved. So they go home and spend days, weeks and sometimes years having to live with what they've done, and unless there are witnesses, they get away with it. As you said, it happens all of the time."

Pieter, sitting in his car outside Prisha's apartment, sighed loudly.

"Look, I already know all of this stuff Floris. But what does this have to do with our case? Why has it been matched up?"

"Because the local police don't think that this was simply a hit-and-run. They think it was intentional."

Pieter switched his mobile to speakerphone and clipped it to the holder on the dashboard.

"They spent a whole day at the scene studying the tyre marks on the road, and they've come to the conclusion that the driver turned his vehicle around, and then swerved straight into the guy on his bike. They say the skid marks prove this. They are also fairly sure that the body was moved. It was found about fifteen feet back from the edge of the road, and the position it was in – laid straight out nice and neatly beneath the ice – makes them think the corpse was rolled into the ditch. Plus the bike was in there with him too.

Okay, so they decided to check around, gathering any footage from nearby CCTV cameras. Anyway, they came back with something interesting. An image, of a man wearing overalls and driving a dark van. He was snapped driving through the village itself, very near the accident scene, and the time display on the image matches up roughly with the time the victim's family say he was away from home on his errand."

Pieter heard his mobile chime quietly.

"I've just sent the pic over."

Pieter snatched hold of his phone and tapped on the MMS text. He leaned forward in his seat, his eyes screwed up as he studied the tiny image. It showed a profile view of a man in the driver's seat of a black van. Although the shot was grainy, it was in colour, and must have been snapped just as the van was driving by a streetlight in Ransdorp so that it was easy to see the brown overalls he was wearing. And even more promising, he had a baseball cap on his head, exactly as Mr Clegg, the resident at the nursing home on Vondelstraat, had described.

"The police out there decided to put the details into ViCASnl to see if anything came up at their end, and hey presto, the people at NCSC struck lucky. Not bad for a bunch of hick cops, eh?"

Pieter said nothing back initially.

"What do you think Boss? Is he our guy? What are you going to do with this?"

"I think I need to go out there and see for myself, Floris. I also think you should do more checking. Get in touch with Bos en Lommerplein and have them do a trawl of all the cameras around that general area. Also tell them to start from the Amsterdam ring road and work northwards, as far as Ransdorp and then beyond, to see if they can pick up this van and find out where he was setting off from and where he was headed to."

"They're not going to like it, being told to get out of their beds at this time, on a cold night. You know what they are like, that lot? Most of them are just seeing their days out to retirement, a nice and easy number."

"Floris, I really don't care what they think." Then he added: "But well done on this."

The skies over Holland always have a washed-out quality to them, like the colour has been rinsed away. The flatness of the land seems to suck out any warmth or vitality, even in the middle of a hot summer. At this time of the year, in the middle of a freezing winter, as the sun reluctantly wakes from its slumber, creaking and groaning like an old man, the clouds overhead seem to settle over the countryside like a shroud over a corpse.

This area of the country to the north of Amsterdam was known as Waterland. Driving towards the village of Ransdorp, Pieter could see why it was christened thus. With the lightening of the sky the flat expanse stretching off to the horizon seemed to sparkle with ribbons of silvery ice as far as the eye could see, the thousands of frozen canals and ponds and lakes and marshes creating the illusion that he was driving along a narrow causeway straight out into the North Sea.

He enjoyed getting away from the smothering claustrophobia of the city, if it were only for a few hours like this morning's little trip. Whenever he did, it always gave him a feeling of lightness, like he was walking on the balls of his feet and bouncing along, light as a feather, which was wonderful, until it came time to return. Then he would feel his mood darken, his body would draw into itself like a boxer flinching and waiting for a punch, and his mind would switch back, from day-tripper back to city cop.

Ransdorp itself was tiny, a hamlet rather than a village if truth be told, with beautifully painted houses and neat gardens behind white-picket fences. It was little more than just a one-street kind of place, with a small Brown Café pub and a guest house, a hardware store, a few shops selling postcards and fridge magnets during the summer season, and not much else.

It was too tiny to warrant its very own police station: instead, the three police officers assigned to this part of the Waterland region worked from out of the town hall, just across from the church.

Pieter had arranged to meet the most senior officer in the car park, and when he pulled across the gravel he immediately spotted Geert Blom waiting for him. He couldn't really miss him because he was grossly overweight, the buttons on his uniform threatening to burst free and become lethal projectiles.

He was sitting at the top of a very high set of steps that led to the town hall's front entrance, looking down on the village like he was expecting a flood at any second. He had a shock of blond curly hair on the top of his head, and a pleasant face with a full smile.

Geert came down the steps to greet him, lumbering across to the car as Pieter climbed out.

He held out his hand, and Pieter shook the sweaty palm.

"Good morning. I'm Geert Blom, but you can call me Barry if you like."

Pieter raised his eyebrows.

"After Barry Foster, the actor? He played Van der Valk in the TV series? Some people say I look like him."

Pieter nodded and smiled.

"You've come to see the crime scene, you say?"

"If it was a crime and not just a road accident."

"Oh, it was definitely deliberate, my friend. We're sure of that. Come along, we'll take my car. It's not far, but I wouldn't want you getting yourself lost and in a dizz."

He led Pieter to a small police patrol car parked alongside the church. Pieter climbed into the front passenger side, and when Geert dropped his bulky frame behind the steering wheel the car on that side dipped right down and Pieter's head nearly hit the roof.

They drove down the narrow lane past the church and turned left at the end, passing over a swing-bridge. Geert drove surprisingly fast in spite of the covering of snow, almost racing down Ransdorp's main street, flashing by the guest house and yet more colourful houses, their red-tiled roofs shining brightly in the morning sunlight. Pieter had the impression that he was doing it for his benefit. If he could get away with it, he'd probably like to switch on the light and siren as well.

Five minutes later and they were away from the village and driving through the countryside, the road here narrow and straight, with a frozen ditch running parallel with it. Then Geert was pulling over and he pointed past Pieter through the passenger window.

"That's where he was found, just there. You can see where we had to smash the ice to get him out."

Pieter climbed out just as a snow flurry threw itself at him, and the icy wind took his breath away.

Geert sensibly decided to stay in the car, so their conversation was conducted through the open door.

"Who was he?"

"A chap called Eric Fischer, a house painter. Forty-eight years old, married with twin boys."

"Was he local? Did you know him?"

"Oh yes, he'd lived around these parts all of his life. One of the good ones he was, and his missus, but his lads can be a pair of cheeky monkeys, I tell you. They go around the place spraying graffiti everywhere, thinking they are ghetto kids - out here?" He shook his head with a rueful look on his jowly face.

"So he would have known the area well then, even late at night? Enough to find his way around in the pitch dark?"

"Oh, you can bank on that, Officer Van Dijk. He had eyes like a wily old fox did Eric."

"What was he wearing at the time? It's Inspector Van Dijk by the way."

"Oh yes, sorry. What was he wearing? A coat and scarf, I think."

"Was it a dark coat? Did he have any reflective armbands on, or those running shoes that light up? Was the light on his bicycle switched on at the time?"

When there was no response, Pieter turned back from gazing at the icy ditch and glanced back into the car. Geert Blom just looked at him and shrugged.

"Well, you need to find out. Perhaps it was an accident, and the driver failed to see him if he was dressed in dark clothing."

"But I've already told you it wasn't an accident," Geert responded defensively. He pointed ahead through the windscreen, and Pieter followed where the stubby finger indicated. "You see that lay-by up ahead? That's where we saw the tyre marks where the van driver swung around to face back the way he'd just come, back towards Eric on his bike. And you're standing where the skid marks were as he swerved across the road to deliberately hit him."

Pieter stepped backwards and looked down, but he could see nothing because of the covering of snow.

He climbed back in and dusted the snow off his hair.

"Do you want to see the body? We still have it if you do - although it's not a pretty sight."

"No need. We can head back now."

Back in his own car outside the town hall Pieter checked his phone and saw he had an email.

Some initial data had been retrieved from Tobias Vinke's mobile phone, which they had fished out of the canal by the boatyard.

Tracking a mobile phone was relatively easy, if it were turned on. Changing the SIM card after every call would negate this to a certain extent, but not completely. Some criminals used cheap phones, known as burners, and after using them once they would ditch them somewhere, dropping them in a litter bin or throwing them over a wall.

Once police had a suspect's number they could zone in and locate the general areas that it was used in.

Having found Vinke's phone in the canal, they soon established a number of sites of interest.

According to the email, most of these spots were in central Amsterdam itself, which didn't really help them an awful lot. But on several occasions over the past week, the signal from his phone had pinged off two masts outside the city. One in the town of Edam, which was about fifteen kilometres further north of Ransdorp, and the other at Hoorn, which was around twenty kilometres north of Edam. Both towns were strung on the main coastal road out of Amsterdam, the N247, which suggested that Vinke had his phone turned on whilst driving into this part of North Holland. The death of the cyclist here in Ransdorp, if it were indeed the work of their prime suspect, seemed to back up this theory. And if they took this hypothesis forward, and continued Vinke's probable route along the coastal road, it suggested that he had holed up with Nina Bakker not at his previous home in Warder, which they had raided without success on Sunday, but somewhere closer to Hoorn.

It was still a large area, but the digital forensic cyber-cops who specialized in the field of mobile phone data extraction were trying to shrink this area still further by checking as many phone masts as possible in the vicinity.

The net was starting to close.

Vinke may have been dead, but Pieter felt sure they were very near to finding the spot where Nina Bakker was being held captive.

He was also convinced this would lead them to Lotte and her accomplice, the sniper.

* * *

On his way back to Amsterdam Pieter made a quick call to Prisha Kapoor to check up on the situation with Kaatje.

It was still quite early, and the road south was growing busy with morning commuters heading for work. Prisha told him that Kaatje was fine. She had taken a sleeping pill at her suggestion and was still sleeping soundly.

"I'm going to work from home today, and Rowan is taking some more things down to Utrecht soon, but she'll be back just after lunch. So there's going to be someone with Kaatje all day. It's best to let her sleep. You get on with the case. Everything is good here."

Pieter thanked her and ended the call, and followed the flow of traffic south to the city.

Chapter 23
Mission Briefing

Pieter sensed the tense atmosphere as soon as he arrived at the main Police HQ on Elandsgracht. There was a strange hush throughout the large building, which he recognized from the few previous occasions he'd experienced it. It was the nervous anticipation when a major breakthrough on a big case was in the offing.

As he climbed the stairs to the squad room a junior clerk intercepted him and directed him to the conference room on the second floor, next door to the media suite. He was just in time, the man told him. Something was definitely going on.

The large room was filled with people. Pieter stood in the doorway momentarily and glanced around.

A set of tables and chairs had been arranged in a large horseshoe-shaped cluster in the centre of the carpeted floor. At the open end, most of the wall was taken up with a large Smart projector screen, which was used either for briefings before a big operation or for video conferencing calls. Above the screen was a camera, and to either side a pair of speakers. At the moment the projector screen was blank.

There was room for about twenty people around the tables, and each place was equipped with a laptop and a Wi-Fi hub, plus a small microphone. More chairs had been arranged around the walls, while in one corner there was a desk for serving tea and coffee and pastries.

It looked like they had been busy while he was gone.

Most of the seats were already occupied, but looking around he noticed somebody waving him over to a vacant spot. It was Floris de Kok, and Pieter moved across and sat down next to him.

"What the hell's going on?" he asked under his breath. It was strange to see Floris here in the main building: he spent most of his time down in the basement, filing away his beloved paperwork. The fact that he was here at the centre of things, like a troglodyte blinking in the daylight, filled him with apprehension.

Floris couldn't stop grinning, enjoying himself immensely.

"I think we might have found them, Boss. I did as you said and told the people over at Surveillance Command at Bos en Lommerplein to go through all the cameras en route from Amsterdam to Ransdorp, with instructions to track the van they picked up in relation to the hit-and-run. They weren't too happy with the sudden workload, especially as it meant they had to put in an early shift, but it looks like they came up trumps."

Pieter saw the door open and Commissaris Huijbers come through, hunched over and rolling his shoulders in an attempt to look all menacing and streetwise, mealy-mouthed and frowning, his baseball hat pulled down. Two members of his personal security team came with him, though why he thought he needed them in here escaped Pieter, and they trailed after the police chief as he made for the chair at the head of the table, two or three places along from Pieter. He lowered himself into his seat and clasped his big, meaty hands together on the tabletop. His bodyguards stepped back.

Huijbers gave a nod of his head and the lights in the room slowly dimmed and the projector screen flickered to life.

The familiar figure of Dyatlov appeared from the shadows, the ex-Spetsnaz commando and head of the Armed Response Division sporting his usual buzz-cut, and his short, squat and muscular frame drew the room's whole attention and the general chatter ebbed away.

Behind him, the screen was now divided into six smaller squares, each segment showing either a still photograph or moving video footage taken from various CCTV cameras. Pieter saw the familiar-looking black van from the photo-still that Floris had sent him several hours earlier, and each frame was time-stamped with a slightly different time, but all dated from the night of the hit and run at Ransdorp.

"Right ladies and gentlemen," Dyatlov began in his thick Russian accent. "Time is short so let's commence the mission briefing. This is a very time-sensitive situation."

He strolled over to the screen and turned sideways on, looking at the flickering images. In his hand, he held a tiny remote control.

"Our colleagues at NCSC have come up with some excellent work at very short notice. This was their target." He indicated the black van in one of the video clips. "This first image was taken at the passenger ferry terminal at Buiksloterweg, on the north side of the river. It's dated Friday evening, at a little after 6pm. It shows our suspect – and we are fairly sure the driver is Tobias Vinke – leaving the car park next to the old Toll House building. We then pick up the same vehicle at various points as he drives through the suburbs towards the ring road. As he leaves the city the camera network switches over from city district to the motorway network, but we can still follow his progress northwards for several miles."

The set of images flickered and then disappeared, to be replaced by six more, each one following the black van, and each one showing a change of the time in sequence from shortly after six in the evening.

"However, at some stage after crossing the main ring road, Vinke branches away to the north-east, using minor roads as he hits the more rural areas beyond the city limits. We lose him for a short time until we pick him up again here."

Dyatlov pointed to a picture in the top left corner of the screen, and Pieter recognized it as the same image that Floris had sent him, showing Vinke driving through Ransdorp shortly before the hit-and-run.

Dyatlov continued.

"We follow him at various points along his journey. Here re-joining the N247, here driving around Edam, and again at Oosthuizen. If you would like to switch on your laptops, I have provided each of you with an interactive map plotting his route."

There was a flurry of movement and clicks as each person seated around the desks powered up their laptops and scrutinized the screens, their eyes panning back and forth from the maps to the projector screen.

"He travels around Hoorn on the N307 as far as the town of Enkhuizen right at the very tip of the Ijsselmeer Peninsular. After that, this camera here," and all eyes were fixed on the big projector screen, "shows his driving up onto the road along the Houtribdijk, the 30km-long dam across the

Ijsselmeer stretching to the shore at Lelystaad way across the water to the southeast."

Dyatlov paused for dramatic effect, his eyes taking in each face in the dimly-lit room, his gaze lingering slightly on Pieter's and giving him a nod.

"We have checked the cameras at the other end of the dam. They show nothing. No sign of the van whatsoever. So, people, he drove up onto the road across the water here, but did not exit from the far side. Which means, when this footage was taken, he stopped overnight somewhere in between the western ramp onto the dam road and the eastern exit ramp. He holed up on the dam itself."

The split-screen CCTV images disappeared from the big screen, to be replaced by a single satellite image of the Houtribdijk Dam. Pieter leaned forward in his seat to study the large photo. The atmosphere in the room was stretched taut.

The Houtribdijk Dam. Built between 1963 and 1975 to hold back the North Sea from flooding Amsterdam, it was one of the biggest building projects in the world, and is still a marvellous feat of engineering to this day. Seen from above like this, it resembled a thin crooked brown line anchored on the two towns at either end, with the huge expanse of grey water, part of the North Sea to all intents and purposes, all around. The sea had frozen in places where the water ran up to the edge of the broad road that ran along the top of the embankment, creating a silvery sheen to the image, and Pieter realized they were actually looking at a real-time live satellite feed. They'd spared no expense in setting this operation up, and in double-quick time.

Dyatlov went on, his own eyes now fixed on the screen, his features etched with concentration.

"There is actually only one point on the dam where he could have been staying. One place where he could have been holding Nina Bakker. One location where the woman Janssen and the shooter could now be. And that is here, right at the very centre of the dam."

He operated a button on the remote control and the picture zoomed in, focusing down to a small shape alongside the roadway. It showed a pair of concrete jetties, and a number of tiny buildings, either houses or sheds. Vehicles on the road nearby continued to move east and west.

"This is Trintelhaven. A former dock where small fishing vessels and cargo ships would stop off at one time, years ago, to either refuel or unload their cargoes. There used to be a windsurfing place there once, and a roadside café, and a junkyard, but now the place is rundown and empty – or so we thought. There are a few buildings there, but from what we've learned today there is only one site that is habitable."

Dyatlov looked across the room.

"Floris de Kok. Would you care to tell everybody what you have learned?"

Pieter spun in his seat, open-mouthed and looking at his companion in surprise.

Floris glanced at him out of the corner of his eye, and then nervously cleared his throat as he pulled his microphone towards his mouth. His arm was shaking slightly, either from nerves, or perhaps from his long-term medical condition.

"Erm, yes," he began, and then remembered to press the button. There was a high-pitched whine of feedback, and then he started again. "Sorry. Yes, I decided to check through the records, going all the way back to the mid-seventies when the dam was completed. I wanted to see who owned the land there, as I believe the small boatyard was a private business back then."

Everybody was looking at Floris, and when Pieter saw him lick his lips nervously he gave him an encouraging smile and a nod.

"In more recent times, actually up to about two years ago, as Mr Dyatlov said, there was a small diner there, but this has since closed down. The same with the watersports club that held meetings at Trintelhaven. So I decided to go further back.

In 1976, a year after the dam and the road crossing opened, the land was first rented and later purchased by a family, a Mr and Mrs Huisman. They later had a child, a boy, and they lived there for quite a few years, from where the husband ran several small businesses.

Then, when the child was about eleven years old, the family was involved in a road accident in Belgium. They had gone on a small holiday, travelling around in a camper van, when they were hit by a truck near Brugge. Mr Huisman, it later turned out, had a bad drink problem and this was thought to be the cause of the crash. Anyway, both the parents were killed and their son was badly hurt with a serious head injury, a blow to his frontal lobe. He survived, after spending a month in hospital, but the injury seemed to have a long-term effect on him. His personality changed, he suffered from violent mood swings, was expelled from various schools and finished up in a care home for a period of time. Up until his early teens, when he was adopted by a couple who were unable to have children of their own, and he went to live with them."

Floris glanced around at the sea of faces looking his way, and he averted his gaze to look down at the tabletop.

"His new family's surname was Vinke. So the boy became Tobias Vinke."

The room suddenly erupted in conversation, the loud buzz giving the place a charged atmosphere. Dyatlov's voice called out over the hubbub.

"Let him finish please."

When the last of the murmurs died away, Floris went on.

"It seems that after the death of his natural parents, the land and house at Trintelhaven passed on to Tobias Vinke, although the place remained empty for many years. Apart from allowing the diner to open and the watersports club, he doesn't seem to have done an awful lot with it, until a few months ago, in fact. Following the suicide of his daughter Elena Vinke and the breakdown of his marriage, Tobias Vinke must at some stage have moved back to his old family home, where he lived and, we assume, readied the building in preparation for his kidnapping of Nina Bakker. That must be where she was being held, and where Tobias Vinke was heading to after the hit-and-run at Ransdorp last week, and where he was going on Monday, before he was shot dead."

Floris sat back in his chair.

"So yes, that's the place. I'm certain of it."

"Thank you, de Kok," Dyatlov said in his crisp and clear voice, and Pieter gave Floris a gentle pat on his shaking arm.

Dyatlov resumed with his mission briefing.

"So folks - Trintelhaven is our primary target. It's highly likely that Nina Bakker is in that house, although this doesn't guarantee that she will still be alive when we get there. Sadly she could have been dead from day one after her kidnapping, but we can't waste too much time pondering on that. We need to hit the place soon and hit it hard and catch the bad guys hiding out there."

He paced back and forth across the front of the projector screen, his shadow rippling across the satellite image.

"We need to coordinate perfectly on this. It is essential that we move in simultaneously from both ends of the dam, and also have our air-assets overhead to be our eyes and ears. Obviously, it will mean closing the road to traffic to avoid any civvies getting hurt, but if we do that too soon we risk giving the game away and the whole operation falling apart. Therefore, timing is crucial. I'd also prefer it for everybody present in this room to fully acquaint themselves with the exact layout of the area. You and your men, and me and my men, are the ones who will be going in. We can't afford any cock-ups or wrong turns once we get there. So, I have arranged a little something for you."

Dyatlov used the remote control once again and Pieter and everybody else in the conference room watched as the satellite image disappeared from the projector screen, to be replaced by a dull grey wavy picture.

At first, Pieter couldn't make sense of what he was seeing. Yet as he watched, a little confused, he suddenly realized what was on the screen - the strange waves moving across the image gave it away.

They were looking at an overhead shot of the grey sea, the rippling effect caused by the swell and rolling of the water. It was taken from a camera on a drone, flying above the Ijsselmeer, and broadcasting live footage back to Police HQ.

The camera angle shifted as the drone slowly revolved in a hovering position and suddenly the long, snaking Houtribdijk Dam came into view in the near distance, the shoreline alongside the wide concrete embankment frozen with ice, and cars and lorries trundling on the road along the top.

The drone moved forward. There was no sound to the live video, but the sense of speed was dizzying, and within a minute or so the dam seemed very close, although the camera may have been at maximum zoom. The drone operator would be under instructions not to get too near.

Once again the drone altered direction. Now it was flying parallel with the dam, the picture focusing on the traffic. Up ahead, the now-familiar Trintelhaven dock came nearer and nearer, and then in the next instant the drone was rising up into the sky and hovering in place above their target, the concrete jetties and buildings below looking like a child's model. The camera panned and zoomed back and forth, showing the buildings, the junkyard, the pebble beach alongside Vinke's family home. And there, near to the front door of the house itself, Pieter saw the motorbike from last night.

He sat there shaking his head in amazement. After all this time, they finally had them, trapped and with nowhere to go.

The screen went dark and the lights slowly came back up.

"Let's rock and roll people!" Dyatlov told them.

*   *   *

On his way out Pieter caught sight of Commissaris Huijbers conferring with a group of senior officers near the door. It looked like he was giving them their final instructions, Pieter thought, or at least that was the impression he wanted to give: the man in charge, controlling things from HQ while the cavalry went to the rescue. But then he noticed Huijbers was wearing a flak jacket, and Pieter pulled up in surprise.

The small cluster of men broke up and he dashed across to catch the police chief.

"You're coming with us, sir?"

"Of course I'm coming with you Van Dijk. I just need to make a couple of phone calls, and then we move out. Did you think I'd want to miss out on the fun or something?" Huijbers snarled.

"No, but..."

"Besides, I intend to slap the handcuffs on that Charlotte Janssen myself."

Then Huijbers breezed past and was gone.

Chapter 24
Clawhammer

They set out in two separate convoys.

One would snake east past the docklands district and leave the city on the A1 motorway, and then branch off to race north on the A6 as far as the town of Lelystad, where the eastern ramp on and off Houtribdijk Dam was. This half of the Armed Response Division had the shortest distance to travel, so once in position, they would wait until their colleagues 30 kilometres away across the Ijsselmeer Sea were ready to go at their end.

The second convoy, whose personnel included Pieter, Dyatlov and Commissaris Huijbers, would go charging through the IJ road tunnel and then head directly north along the same road that he had taken that morning, but continue onwards to Hoorn and then finally the town of Enkhuizen, where the western end of the dam was anchored.

Once both groups were poised to strike they would be given the signal and the assault would be launched in a pincer movement, the two convoys closing in on the small dock at the centre of the dam.

As they travelled north, the roads ahead were cleared of other vehicles and all the traffic lights were locked-off, closing all the side lanes, and flashing a continuous green to allow the police vehicles to plough straight through each junction and intersection without slowing down. But as instructed, the dam remained open until the last possible minute.

Pieter was in the point vehicle of his convoy, as was Dyatlov. They travelled in a Lenco BearCat 4x4 Armoured Truck, a huge monster of a vehicle painted a dark grey colour. He sat in a bucket seat just behind the driver, facing towards the rear exit doors. Down either side ran a pair of plastic benches, where ten members of the assault squad sat, talking and laughing and checking their weapons.

Pieter wore a dark blue flak jacket and a helmet, but he was otherwise dressed in his usual clothes, and was armed only with his Walther P5 for his personal protection, having refused the offer of an assault rifle. This was Dyatlov's bread and butter, and he had no intention of interfering with the operation by being at the head of the police raid.

Every few minutes he twisted in his seat to glance out of the front windscreen to check on their progress. He couldn't see an awful lot for the vehicle had an anti-riot wire cage across the front, and the small slit-windows of bulletproof-glass restricted his view still further. But he did look down at the speedometer on the futuristic-looking dashboard and saw they were travelling at 140km/h, the vehicle's maximum speed.

From overhead, he heard a deep *thrum-thrum* noise that seemed to make the air wobble. He looked up. In the roof were a pair of hatches. These were pulled down, but he could see through their glass apertures, and he caught a quick glimpse of a helicopter as it flashed across the sky. One of the pair of Police AW139's, painted with their blue livery, there to lend air-support.

Pieter knew that just behind the lead vehicle came four huge Spartan APCs, two armoured ambulances, and finally a long Command and Video Observation truck, the mobile command centre, with Huijbers onboard.

As the road veered through the outskirts of Hoorn and curved east, making towards the tip of the Ijsselmeer Peninsular, Dyatlov, who was sitting up front next to the driver, turned and called out.

"Minus five! Weapons check!"

In the back, the assault squad snapped on ammo magazines and cocked and readied their weapons, and slowly the general chatter and banter fell away as the members of the team put on their game faces.

Pieter shared their sudden tension. His chest felt tight and his heart seemed like a slow and sluggish lump of flesh, and when he tried to swallow his spit he found his mouth to be too dry.

Another quick glance through the front windows and he saw the large blue control tower marking the ramp up onto the dam just ahead, and a long line of wind turbines stretched away to the south across the water.

"Operation Clawhammer! Blowtorch!" Dyatlov said into his communication gear. This was the signal to launch the assault.

Pieter felt the BearCat thunder up onto the ramp, its huge tyres singing on the frozen surface of the road, and he desperately held on to his seat as the cabin vibrated violently from side to side.

If the road across had now been cleared of all other traffic, and if they maintained their current speed, then by Pieter's quick estimation it would take both teams around seven or eight minutes to converge and join at the centre of the dam.

But just as he was thinking this, the driver suddenly swerved hard to the left and swore loudly, drawing Pieter's attention to the front once more.

"How the fuck did they get here?" Dyatlov shouted, pointing ahead at something beyond the windscreen.

Pieter craned his neck to see what the problem was and then saw to his dismay the pair of TV news crews parked up alongside the road's outer rail, and the realization of what this meant struck him like a blow to the solar plexus.

The media had been alerted to the raid, which meant all element of surprise was gone.

He knew in an instant who had made the call, who wanted the whole world to witness his moment of glory as he personally made the arrest of Europe's most wanted criminal.

"Huijbers, that dumb fuck!" Dyatlov snarled, as he too reached the same conclusion.

He struck the dashboard in fury.

"Go around, go around!" he ordered the driver. "Push them off the fucking dam if you have to!"

They veered around the obstacle and then lurched back to the centre of the roadway without hardly dropping their speed, and the driver straightened his course. Snapping a quick look out of the rear windows Pieter saw the vehicles behind form up two-abreast so that the convoy of police vehicles were now in a wedge-shaped formation, the BearCat at the front. With their lights flashing, and the helicopters keeping pace above them, it must have made an awesome sight as they charged over the dam.

They passed underneath a footbridge that spanned the dam, and then the road divided in two for a short stretch with a barrier down the middle, and the convoy of vehicles smoothly separated before merging back together again. The top of the dam flattened out and was much broader from this part onwards, with a sandy beach running alongside on the left and a series of sand dunes on the right. Beyond was the frozen water.

Pieter looked at his wristwatch and found himself counting down the minutes to when they would reach Trintelhaven. There was nothing much for the occupants to say to each other, as each of the passengers knew their precise role and had trained hard for just such situations. Instead, they listened to the low rumble of the engine and the occasional messages coming over the radio. Pieter tried to listen in, but the military-style jargon soon became too confusing to follow. But from what he could hear, the second strike-team was making good progress on the far side. The people holed up at the centre-point of the dam may well be aware that the police were coming, but it was too late to turn back now.

Several minutes later and Dyatlov called back over his shoulder: "Vries, check the top-side."

Pieter watched as one of the heavily-armoured men jumped to his feet. Reaching up, he grabbed hold of a short ladder that was folded up beneath the truck's roof and pulled it down, locking the bottom into place in two holes in the floor. Going up two rungs, he flipped open one of the hatches. A blast of cold air blew in and the roaring sound of the engine assaulted Pieter's ears, and the smell of diesel filled the interior. The heavy-set cop climbed the rest of the way up the ladder and poked his head and shoulders through the opening.

A moment later and he called down: "All clear. Coming up to the turning on the left."

His words, nearly lost in the maelstrom of sound, were relayed forward by one of his colleagues.

"What do you see ahead? Talk to me!" Dyatlov shouted.

"I have eyes on the other strike-team! Approx. one kilometre and approaching fast!" Vries replied.

On some unspoken signal, every man in the back of the truck suddenly seemed to stiffen with even more apprehension. Weapons were grasped ever tighter, helmets were straightened, and those wearing infra-red goggles lowered them into position - still turned off but poised to be flicked into life once needed. Someone could be heard whispering a quiet litany.

Vries remained upright in the roof hatch. Pieter could just about see him with his hand on the controls of the truck's smoke-grenade launcher, waiting for the instructions to start lobbing the small tin can-shaped canisters to spread a blanket of thick, cloying smoke all around.

Then he felt the truck swerve hard to the left as they left the main roadway, and the men on the benches tilted sideways in unison.

Now they were bumping over the hard, frozen ruts of a small dirt track leading down towards the small dock at Trintelhaven, and Pieter felt the vibration rattle his teeth. He looked through the windscreen in time to see them whip by the branches of several fir trees, then they made a hard right and he watched open-mouthed as they crashed straight through a three-barred gate and slid to a halt in a gravel yard.

There was a series of explosive popping sounds as the smoke grenades were fired, then a hydraulic hum as the truck's rear hatch glided down, and the men piled out, roaring and screaming at the top of their lungs.

Pieter followed them without thinking, his thoughts all scrambled and confused, his head ringing like a punch-drunk boxer's, but once outside someone grabbed his shoulder and hauled him back, and then he heard Dyatlov screaming in his ear: "Wait here Van Dijk! I'll tell you when it's safe!"

Then he was gone, disappearing through the smoke with his men.

Pieter moved to one side as more vehicles roared into the yard, and then back-up squads of armed personnel poured into the house. There was a cacophony of loud shudders, and through the curtained windows he saw the bright stuttering light of flash-bang grenades going off inside. There was more shouting, doors being kicked in, and in his mind, he could visualize the men moving from room to room and detaining the occupants. But no gunshots nor signs of resistance. Which was good.

Movement caught his eye just then and he turned to see a line of armed police snaking across the concrete jetties. This would be the other strike-team securing the perimeter.

Then he heard the loud engine of the mobile command centre and saw as the long vehicle slid to a halt just beyond the wrecked gateway, and moments later Huijbers appeared, flanked by his bodyguards as he stomped into the yard, baseball hat on his head and a huge grin on his face.

"Bloody awesome Van Dijk," he shouted, his body all energized and bursting to the seams with adrenaline. "What a sight to behold. Coming across the dam, and then seeing the men go in, I tell you I had tears in my eyes."

A State of Sin

Pieter stared back at him. He thought about asking who had tipped off the media, just to see what he said, but just then Dyatlov emerged from the house and waved them across. The assault was over.

Huijbers set off at a jog, his wide girth making the ground shake, and he pushed straight past Dyatlov. "Where the hell is that woman?" he called as he disappeared through the doorway.

Dyatlov caught Pieter's eye, and the Russian gave a tiny shake of his head, and Pieter felt his stomach give a peculiar backflip. *Oh God*, he thought to himself. *Nina? Had they...? Please, not now, right at the end.* He went inside, feeling the blood drain from his face.

He found himself standing in a small and dusty room filled with old furniture, the upholstery on the chairs all faded, a musty smell of age and decay in the air. The door was hanging off its hinges, as was the one leading into what looked like a kitchen. There was lots of activity in there, people moving about, and he stepped over to join them. From somewhere above he heard more footsteps.

The kitchen was a wreck, possibly from the assault. Smashed furniture and broken crockery and shelves and curtains and broken glass lay everywhere. A path had been cleared through the mess towards another doorway, and Pieter glimpsed a set of steps beyond, leading downwards.

Moving over, he squeezed by members of the assault team and went down.

Huijbers was already at the bottom, standing in the centre of the basement and looking around, hands on his hips and shaking his head.

Pieter saw in a moment that the place was empty, just like the house at Warder, but whereas then he had felt frustration, now he felt relieved. Relieved that he wasn't looking at the body of twelve year old Nina Bakker.

"Fucking bastards have gone," Huijbers said needlessly. "Taken the girl with them. They must have been holding her in there by the looks of it, but they fled just before we arrived."

Pieter said nothing, he just turned to look at where the police chief was pointing, seeing the small cage in the corner underneath the stairs, and a chill went through him. The front was open, the cage door swinging back on its hinges. Inside he saw a thin blanket, all crumpled up. There was a sharp smell of urine.

He turned a full circle, his gaze taking in the small room, seeing the bed, the small table and couch, the shelf of books and DVDs, the television in the corner. There was even a bathroom with a shower and toilet.

Huijbers stalked back up the staircase, mumbling and cursing under his breath, and after one final glance around Pieter went after him.

Pieter followed him back outside. Up on the roadway, one of the blue helicopters was just touching down, its rotors buffeting the air. The back of his throat feeling tight from the hazy smoke drifting around the yard.

He found Huijbers standing near the gate.

"Where the hell is Dyatlov?" He was livid, his face all red and blotchy. "This is impossible. They've got away twice now, first at the other house and now here. Between the two of you, Van Dijk, you've royally screwed this up."

"Now just a minute-" Pieter began, unable to bite his tongue any longer, but then one of the other men was shouting and gesticulating at something out across the water beyond the small pebble beach.

"Sir, look sir!"

Pieter and Huijbers both looked across the slate-grey expanse in unison.

"It's a boat sir!"

Pieter spotted it after a moment, a small motor launch bobbing about and nearly lost in the waves. It was about half a kilometre offshore and increasing the gap with every second, but even at this distance he could make out the three people onboard, two adults and a shorter person. A child, without a doubt a child. All three of their faces were looking back towards the house.

Huijbers headed onto the beach, his boots crunching over the pebbles, and Pieter was racing alongside him when he caught a strange flash coming from the boat followed by a very faint sound, a bit like a zipper on a coat being pulled up. He frowned in puzzlement, and at the same time saw the surprised expression that appeared on Huijbers face, and the man's mouth opened like he was going to whistle. A red dot appeared on his forehead, a tiny hole, and then his baseball hat was flying back through the air like a strong gust of wind had caught it. In the next instant, he was walking forward on legs that seemed all rubbery, he was cutting a strange diagonal course over the beach, his arms were at his sides and his feet were twitching away like he was auditioning to be in Riverdance.

A State of Sin

Pieter stood transfixed as Commissaris Dirk Huijbers fell onto his knees and then toppled face-first into the pebbles.

Chapter 25
Ijsselmeer Sea

Carefully, Pieter laid Huijbers' head back onto the ground and his hands came away all sticky and bloody. He remained kneeling there for several moments, looking at his fingers, his mind numb with shock. Then he wiped the gore onto his trouser leg and came unsteadily to his feet.

Several of the men had gathered around the Police Chief's body, their mouths agape and their faces white, not knowing what to do.

Pieter recognized Vries amongst them and he grabbed his sleeve and drew him to one side.

"Get Dyatlov on the radio," he instructed him in quiet tones. "Tell him what's happened and inform him that the suspects are making a break for it across the water and that it looks like they are heading for the eastern shore. He needs to order the other strike-team to return to that side and try and cut them off. Tell him that they have Nina with them"

Even as he was saying this he knew it was a futile gesture. The boat could be making for any point on the far shoreline, there were dozens of spots where they could come ashore. All they needed to do was run the motor launch up onto the sand dunes, and they could be away in minutes. But they had to do something as in the space of just a few short moments the whole operation was turning into a shambles.

"What about you? What will you be doing?" Vries asked in his no-nonsense voice.

Pieter looked past the man's shoulders, his eyes drawn up towards the roadway, and the helicopter parked there.

"I'm going out there after them."

Pieter set off at a jog along the pathway that led around the small harbour, making for the concrete jetty on the far side.

Running with all his gear on, the flak-jacket and waist holster and helmet, was not easy. He felt clumsy and cumbersome. Plus the ground underfoot was icy and treacherous, and he had to skirt around numerous frozen puddles. By the time he reached the other side he was badly winded, and he had a severe stitch.

On the way over he'd noticed a pathway winding from the jetty up the flank of the dam incline. It led to the roadway running along the top. He made towards it. Thankfully there was a handrail, which he used to haul himself upwards.

At the top he paused briefly to get his breath and then slipped through the gate that led out onto the roadway and ran over towards the blue helicopter.

The pilots had kept the twin engines running at low power, enough for the rotors to keep turning slowly, and when they saw him coming over one of them gave him a thumbs-up through the cockpit window and somebody in the main passenger compartment slid open the side door.

Pieter clambered into the back. There were several armed men strapped into their seats, their faces set with grim determination. He moved by them and poked his head between the pair of pilots' seats.

"Get us in the air fast." He jabbed his forefinger towards the motor launch out at sea, which was now nothing but a tiny speck in the grey expanse. "Can you catch them?"

"You watch this baby move," one of the two pilots replied, and they both reached for the controls.

Pieter found a spare seat and fastened himself in. He left the sliding door in the open position, and when the helicopter lifted off a minute later, he watched as the roadway seemed to drop away, and then slide beneath them in a grey blur, and he had to take a deep breath to fight against the sudden nauseous feeling in his stomach.

The road surface soon gave way to the white frozen shoreline alongside the dam, and then they were skimming low across the choppy waves of the Ijsselmeer.

The noise of the engines slapped his eardrums painfully, making him grimace, so someone handed him a pair of ear protectors. Pieter removed his helmet and slipped them over his head.

He heard a tinny voice come through the headset.

"Looks like they are altering course."

Pieter leaned out through the doorway to get a better view of the motor launch up ahead, the cold wind sucking the air from his lungs. He could just make the boat out, which now seemed to be heading in a southerly direction, towards the dam. It passed out of view below the helicopter as it moved further to the right, and so he leaned forward in his seat, straining against the safety harness, to look out of the cockpit window.

He still couldn't see because of the instrument panel, and he shouted in frustration.

"Where are they? I can't see them!"

One of the pilots tapped the side of his aviation helmet, indicating he couldn't hear Pieter clearly. "Use your mike, Inspector," came his voice in Pieter's ear.

Pieter found the tiny microphone attachment on the front of his headset and he twisted it up towards his mouth.

"Where the hell are they?" he repeated. "What are they doing? Are they making for the dam?"

The pilot craned forward to look downwards through the cockpit window, and then he gave a shake of his head.

"They went inshore to one of the small fishing jetties sticking out from the dam. It looks like they dropped someone off, but now the boat's heading back out across the water again."

"Who did they drop off? Dammit, speak to me!"

"I can't tell from this distance, sir. What should we do? Stay with the boat, or follow whoever just got off?"

Pieter gritted his teeth, wondering what the hell Lotte and her accomplice were playing at. They were trying to confuse them, to draw them away, that's what they were doing. Were Lotte and the girl still in the boat? Had they taken her ashore? Where was the sniper? Still onboard, or making a run for it on land?

"Sir, what do you want us to do?"

"Shit!" Pieter shouted loudly, and then came to a decision, praying he'd chosen the correct one. "Stay with the boat!"

They swooped even lower, the undercarriage of the chopper seeming to be perilously close to the white-topped waves. They were travelling very fast now, the pilots working in perfect sync as they adjusted and manipulated the throttle and collective controls to thrust them forward, their feet gently pressing the pedals to control the main rotors and tail rotors to alter their direction.

Within a few minutes Pieter caught sight of the motor launch once more. It was much closer now, but whoever was using the outboard motor was hunched forward, making it impossible to see their features, and the spray flying up in the boat's wake as it kept changing direction obliterated his view further so that he couldn't even be sure how many people were onboard.

Up ahead he saw the distant shoreline, the land flat and barren, with the white-painted Urk Lighthouse standing out against the backdrop of dark clouds.

He turned to one of the crewmen in the back of the chopper.

"Do we have a winch?" he shouted, not sure if he was miked up or not

"No sir. We're not a search and rescue helicopter."

"Pilot, get us right over the boat, as low as you can."

"I can't risk going much nearer. We don't have skids, just retractable wheels. If the swell gets us, we're in trouble. And this wind is a bitch."

"Okay, okay, just get us as close as possible."

They closed the gap still further, chasing after the frothy wake thrown up by the small vessel, and Pieter thought he caught a glimpse of blonde hair streaming in the wind.

Closer still, until they were right above the boat and keeping pace with it.

"Take us down!" Pieter shouted.

"Christ!" the pilot bellowed back angrily, but he did as he was told, grimacing as he adjusted their altitude.

Now they were barely a dozen feet above the speeding boat, the chopper swaying and bucking, and Pieter could feel spray from the sea dashing against his face.

He could see clearly that the boat had only one occupant, and even before the person turned their face to look upwards at the helicopter flying right overhead he knew it was Lotte, because of the slim and petite form.

In a repeat of the previous night, during the shootout at the Begijnhof, his eyes locked onto hers, and unbelievably she was smiling and laughing with her head thrown back.

The chopper dropped within six feet of the speeding vessel.

Charlotte Janssen screamed with exhilaration.

The thrill of the moment was exquisite, with the boat speeding over the choppy waters and the wind and spray blowing into her face. She felt so alive that every nerve in her body seemed to send electric vibrations through her being, and when she turned again to look up at the helicopter flying just feet above her head, seeing Pieter seated in the open doorway, she could not stop herself from laughing.

She wasn't sure if it were an outburst of joy or the rapture of madness, the ecstasy of uncontrollable delight, or the white-hot burn of insanity. Whatever it was, it felt intoxicating.

As soon as it became clear the police were coming, her Uncle Johan had insisted they grab the girl from the basement and make a bolt for it. It was all over the internet, with news crews on the spot streaming live footage of the convoy of vehicles coming racing across the dam from both directions.

He'd run down the basement steps. In the few moments he was gone, she had made a quick phone call – "Mr Trinh, I require your services once more" - and then her uncle reappeared with the girl, dragging her by her wrist through the kitchen and into the parlour. She was screaming and crying, her stupid little face wet with tears, and so Lotte had stepped over and slapped her once, the stinging blow leaving a red mark on her cheek, instantly cutting off her bawling. After that, she had remained silent, her body rigid with shock, and so getting her down the beach and into the small boat had proved easy, and off they had set just moments before the first police trucks arrived.

Part way over the water Johan had removed the sniper's rifle from the canvas carryall, and Lotte had watched as he had effortlessly fired one single round back towards the house, the rocking and bouncing boat no impediment to his marksmanship.

Then he had shouted across to her, telling her to steer towards the dam, towards a small wooden jetty. He would take the girl and draw the police away, while she tried to make it as far as the opposite shoreline.

Dropping them off, Lotte had once more set a course eastwards, but only moments later she'd heard the familiar thrumming sound of a helicopter approaching fast.

Now she was looking directly at Pieter, and she smiled.

Without giving himself time to think of the risks, and hoping he had judged it right, Pieter snapped open his seat's safety harness and pulled off his headset and then jumped straight out of the door.

His leap lasted maybe a second, no more, but it was the most terrifying single second of his life.

He just had time to register the look of total surprise on Lotte's face before he landed on top of her. He heard her muffled scream, followed by a howl of pain which he realized came from his own lips as his jaw hit the wooden side of the boat. Momentarily stunned, he shook his head to clear his senses and then turned to grab her.

Lotte was pushing and shoving, her legs trying to find a purchase on the seat. She'd let go of the rudder stick on the boat's engine, and now she grabbed at Pieter's hair, then clawed his face and eyes, and he had to swipe her arm away. Her face was pushed close to his own and he saw her brown eyes now blazed with insanity.

Quickly using his greater strength he rolled her over and forced both of her arms behind her back, giving them an upward twist which made her scream, and then he reached for the cuffs hanging on his belt and he snapped them over her slender wrists.

She was panting and he was panting, but the brief fight was over.

Pieter sat back in the boat and looked at her as she twisted and glanced back over her shoulder at him, smiling that insane smile once more.

The roar of the helicopter just feet above them and the waves crashing over the sides of the motor launch drowned out all further thought, so he came to his feet in the rocking boat and hauled her up. Turning around he saw the chopper was now at head height, and the crewman was leaning down with his arm outstretched.

Together they managed to manhandle Lotte through the doorway. Pieter clambered in after her, his foot catching the outboard motor on the way up, sending the empty boat into a crazy spin so that it turned in quick circles, creating a whirlpool like a miniature version of the Lofoten Maelstrom.

Pausing in the hatchway, he gave her a hard shove into one of the seats. Immediately three or four guns were levelled at her.

Sliding the door shut – the sudden drop in engine noise and the violent downdraft from the rotors was wonderful – Pieter stood with his legs braced for balance, one hand grasping a metal stanchion. Without once taking his eyes off her he reached for his discarded headset and spoke into the small microphone.

"Take us down onto the dam."

Pieter could taste blood in his mouth and he guessed he had lost a couple of teeth from the whack he'd taken. He was also soaking wet and freezing cold and physically spent. But there was still a job to do. They'd got Charlotte Janssen into custody, but Nina Bakker was still somewhere down there, still a captive and frightened little girl.

The pilots spun and pitched the helicopter downwards and they quickly slid sideways towards the dam below, and moments later they touched down on the centre of the road.

Pieter opened the door again and pulled Lotte out of her seat and pushed her outside onto the tarmac. He kept a firm hold on her arm as he jumped down behind her.

He pointed at two of the armed men in the back of the helicopter.

"You two, come here. Pilot, get your bird back into the air and start searching for the man and the girl. Switch back over to the police radio frequency and guide me in when you spot them."

He tossed his headset back through the doorway, and he, Lotte and the two policemen stood back and watched them lift back up into the sky.

Walking Lotte across the road he quickly unfastened one half of the handcuffs and then closed it over the metal guardrail along the roadside overlooking the frozen shore below. He locked it again, but stayed crouched alongside her, his eyes looking into hers.

"Why?" he asked quietly in the sudden calm. "Why did you take her? Why did you kill her parents? If it was me you wanted, why not just come and kill me?"

Lotte laughed gently, but she had tears in her eyes.

"You fool. I don't want to kill you. That would be too easy. I want to destroy you, Pieter. To take the silly girl, kill her while the whole world is watching, and see you suffer forever."

Pieter gave a tiny shake of his head and he reached up and gently rubbed away the dampness on her cheek with his thumb.

"I don't think you want that at all."

Lotte twisted her face away to dislodge his hand, her chin trembling, and then gazed off into the middle distance with her watery eyes, seeing but not seeing the real world.

A double cracking sound brought Pieter to his feet, and at the same time one of the policemen shouted a warning: "Gunshots sir! From the beach!"

Pieter instinctively ducked, braced for the rounds to hit one of them, but when nothing happened he realized they were not the sniper's target.

"Oh God!" came the cry.

Above them, the helicopter was turning, twisting around in mid-air, and as it pointed back towards them they could clearly see the two small bullet holes in the front of the cockpit canopy and one of the pilots slumped over his controls.

His colleague was desperately wrestling with the joystick, and he had a look of sheer terror on his face as the machine continued to spin around and lose altitude fast.

Those on the ground could do nothing but watch helplessly as the helicopter now shot upwards, pointing straight at the sky, but their brief flickerings of hope lasted just seconds as now it pitched all the way over and came skidding and shaking through the air towards the dam. At the last second, it spun sideways, and then hit the roadway about two hundred yards away, the fuel tank exploding in a bright orange fireball. The ground shook and flaming debris scattered outwards, while the main rotor blades came free and cartwheeled over the sea beyond the far side of the dam.

Pieter and the two policemen cringed back from the blast of heat that rolled over them, and they shielded their faces as a second explosion rippled outwards, shaking icicles loose from the guardrail.

The helicopter, and the men onboard, were no more. All that marked their existence was a fiery grave and a column of ink-black smoke rising into the sky.

Pieter looked across at Lotte, still handcuffed to the railings, but her face was blank. She wasn't even looking towards the burning wreckage - she showed not a flicker of concern or alarm.

In contrast, the two policemen couldn't tear their eyes away. They had mates on that helicopter, he realized, buddies they had trained with.

He strode over and drew them away.

"Clear your heads, boys. Now's not the time to go under."

They both nodded silently.

"Stay here and watch her. I need to get out there after that lunatic. If she moves a muscle, shoot her."

Chapter 26
Frozen Shore

Leaving the small group of people, Pieter hurried down the road and approached the burning wreckage. The top of the dam was quite narrow at this point, with just two lanes running east and west. But the helicopter had come down near the edge, the pieces of twisted metal scattered over the asphalt and guardrail, leaving a gap just big enough for him to get through. Yet even as he approached he could feel the intense heat from the flames. Raising one arm and using the flap of his open coat to protect his face, Pieter dashed through quickly, and emerged on the other side coughing but unsinged.

Without the helicopter to guide him, he had no way of knowing where Nina and the sniper were. He could use his walkie-talkie to call for the second chopper, but it could be miles away and he didn't have time to wait. So he went over to the guardrail and looked northwards out over the Ijsselmeer, his eyes scanning for movement.

The strip of land on the other side was quite narrow here, consisting of just sandy grass. Other than the short fishing jetty where they had come ashore there was nothing: no running figures and nowhere to hide. So he turned and dashed across the roadway and looked south.

Slanting away from the railings at this point was a concrete incline leading downwards in a shallow angle towards a line of large boulders. Beyond these, there was a flat and wide beach sheltered by a long spit of land, a surf break consisting of a thin pebbly headland curving out into the water. The headland was still under construction by the looks of it, Pieter saw, for towards the end were several huge cranes and some lifting machinery. The beach and water had frozen along this section, but on the far side of the spit of land the sea looked tempestuous and wild, the strong gusty wind whipping up white-capped waves. Unless they had another boat to escape on there was no way they could cross the sea.

Pieter scanned the beach again, but he could see no sign of them. Which only left the surf break and the cluster of machines.

He withdrew his firearm and checked to make sure it was loaded, and then flicked off the safety. Lifting one leg over the railings, he started to slide himself across, but a sudden gunshot sent him tumbling back onto the road, the metal guardrail ringing where the round had struck, just inches from him.

So that settled it then, Pieter thought. The sniper was definitely out there somewhere.

What was he thinking, just standing there along the top of the dam and silhouetted against the sky, and making a tempting target?

He hunkered down behind the barrier, wishing he hadn't left his helmet behind in the helicopter.

He quickly risked another peek over the top, looking left and right, and was rewarded with the briefest glimpse of someone hiding in the line of boulders below the incline. Someone wearing a grey hooded coat.

Okay, so there he was.

What about Nina? Was she with him too?

She had to be, he surmised.

The sniper was using her as insurance, a human shield no doubt to aid his escape.

But then Lotte's words from just moments before came back to haunt him. Her threat to kill Nina in front of the world's media, broadcast live across the globe.

Was that his plan?

The final act of brutality a means to avenge Lotte?

To prevent that he somehow had to separate the two. To get Nina away from him, or at least to try to distract him long enough to deal with him one-to-one. Perhaps take him by surprise.

Then he had an idea.

Keeping his head down he scurried along at ground level, moving away from the beach and the gunman's hiding spot, heading eastwards along the road. After a minute or so he took another look to get his bearings. He was now opposite the spit of land, and about a hundred yards, give or take a few, from his previous position. Ducking back down once more he went even further along.

Once he felt he was far enough away, Pieter very quickly slipped over the guardrail and slid on his backside down the concrete incline to the shoreline at the bottom. The spit of land was only a few feet high but it was enough to hide him from the gunman's line-of-sight on the far side, the simple flanking manoeuvre straight from the textbook.

Now he could approach on this side unobserved.

He was right at the water's edge here, and the narrow rocky shore was frozen over so that his boots broke through the thin ice, and within seconds his feet were soaking wet and cold.

He cut towards the line of large boulders running back towards the gunman's hiding spot and dropped in behind them, breathing a sigh of relief.

Clinging to the seaweed-covered slab he carefully peered around the edge.

He was rewarded with the satisfying sight of the hooded figure still in his hiding spot, his back to Pieter, and unaware of the policeman just yards from him.

And Nina Bakker, the little girl he had spent so long looking for, she was there too. After all this time, after all the lows and the disappointments, the fruitless searching, finally he had found her. Here she was, almost within touching distance, her wrists tied together with a length of nylon rope, her clothes wet and torn, her hair clotted with dirty sand, but seemingly unharmed.

All he had to do was raise his gun and fire at the gunman's back and finish him off, and her long and terrifying ordeal would be over.

But just as he started to bring his weapon up the movement must have caught her eye for she turned just then and saw him, this strange man with his dishevelled appearance and bloodied mouth and soaking wet clothes and his haggard-looking eyes, rising up from the rocks like some frightful sea creature, and she gave a small involuntary gasp.

The man beside her spun and saw Pieter crouched nearby, and he grabbed Nina and threw his arm around her neck and pulled her over, wedging her frail and shaking body against his own, and he pointed the barrel of his rifle straight up beneath her chin and pushed it hard against her throat.

"Come on, you bloody bastard cop!" he snarled in a thick South African accent. "I dare you!"

Pieter leaned over the boulder with his firearm pointing at the man, but Nina was in between them, stopping any chance of a clear shot. Her small face crumpled and he watched her mouth open as she started to gasp for air.

"Is that what you want? Then do it!"

The gunman's face was pitted and weather-beaten and suntanned, and his steady gaze was that of a cold and ruthless killer and Pieter had very little doubt that he wouldn't hesitate to pull the trigger. He swore to himself and lowered his weapon and stepped back, hands raised.

It was all the opening the gunman needed. He dropped the barrel of his rifle, levelled it towards Pieter and fired one-handed from the hip, and the round struck the boulder, zinging off the stone into the sky. Pieter fell away and went down into a rock pool. There was a scream, and when he pulled himself back to his feet he saw the gunman was running out along the spit of land, pulling Nina along with him.

Pieter clambered out from behind the boulder and stepped awkwardly from stone to stone with his arms stretched out to either side to keep his balance. Jumping down onto the dirt track that connected the narrow headland to the dam, he raced forward onto the pebbles, his feet slipping and sliding on the uneven surface.

The gunman was already about halfway along the spit of land and approaching the cluster of machinery, one hand still maintaining a hard grip on Nina's upper arm. Pieter could see her struggling, and her screams and begs for mercy was heartrending to hear. He watched as the man gave her a shake to quieten her, and Pieter felt his fury reach a peak, making him push on with even more vigour.

It occurred to him that he should call for some support. He had their man trapped, and there was nowhere for him to go, but he needed help.

He reached for his walkie-talkie on his belt, but when his hand failed to find it he looked down in alarm. Damn, he must have lost it somewhere. Probably when he fell into the rock pool.

He could use his mobile, but it was standard practice during an operation for phones to be turned off lest their signal interfered with police communications. In all likelihood, Dyatlov and the other operatives wouldn't have turned theirs back on yet.

Up ahead he saw the man slide to a halt and turn back and bring his rifle to his shoulder, and Pieter ducked low as the gunman loosed another shot in his direction. Then the man was running again, and seconds later Pieter watched as the gunman and Nina disappeared amid the jumble of cranes and dumper trucks near the end of the headland. Pieter jumped to his feet and gave chase.

He could feel his lungs labouring and the muscles in his thighs screamed with agony from running over the uneven pebbles underfoot, and blood pumped through his temples painfully, but a minute later he reached the relatively solid ground of the deserted construction site where the tracked vehicles had compacted the land flat.

Moving beyond a huge yellow excavator he paused beneath the archway of its long mechanical arm and looked around, hoping to catch sight of them amidst the abandoned construction equipment and pickup trucks and prefab huts.

Everything was still, and the only sound was that of the waves on the far side, their booming and crashing heightening the sense of isolation in the desolate spot.

Pieter trod quietly, moving carefully around the site with his firearm aimed forward. He hardly dared to breathe in fear of giving himself away.

He stepped from spot to spot, using the machinery as cover, peering around each corner, checking below the huge tracked vehicles, glancing through windows.

All the while he could sense eyes watching him.

Rounding one of the mini diggers, Pieter drew to a halt.

There they were. At the edge of the pebble surf break, overlooking the frozen water on the sheltered side. The gunman was standing several feet away from Nina, he had his rifle raised and aimed straight at her. It seemed like he was waiting for Pieter.

He was grinning, which seemed like an unnatural expression for his hard face. It was more of an insane smirk.

The man shouted, his words nearly lost in the strong wind.

"Come any closer and I'll kill her!"

This time when Pieter raised his gun he kept it pointed straight at the man's head, his aim steady. He gave the tiniest shake of his head.

"It's over pal. This ends here. There's nowhere else to run. Just let her go."

"Fuck you!" the man bellowed back.

"Do you really want to be remembered as a child killer?"

"I – said – fuck – you! Idiot, you don't get it, do you? I'd do anything for that woman, she's my blood, my kin. Damn you all," he finished through gritted teeth, "and damn the kid."

His finger flexed and pulled the trigger.

Handcuffed to the guardrail up on the roadway, Lotte closed her eyes and slipped easily into her meditative state. She reached out with her mind, brushing through the dark folds of consciousness separating her from the three souls out on the headland, searching for them with the eye of the raven, gliding above the sea.

She sensed the emotion in her uncle and she homed in on his psyche, drawn downwards as though through a narrow tunnel.

Her lips moved, whispering silently.

No.

The voice popped into his head, the whispered command staying his hand just as he was squeezing the trigger, and his finger relaxed. Johan snapped his head around, wondering who had spoken into his ear in their hushed tones, panic and fear making his whole body shiver, as if a woman's soft fingers were caressing his spine.

Push her.

The words came again, more insistently, and this time he recognized the voice. But he hesitated, unsure.

Push her, now.

Blinking away his confusion, knowing he had no choice but to obey the command, Johan swung the rifle around and grasped the barrel, and then struck the girl in her midriff with the rifle butt, sending her rolling down the pebble embankment towards the frozen water below. He watched as she landed at the bottom and slithered out across the ice, the momentum carrying her away from the shore, out towards where the ice was thin and weak, and her weight slowly crumpled and cracked the frozen water, the tiny fissures spreading quickly like a spider's frosty web, and in slow motion Nina Bakker disappeared through the surface.

Pieter watched in horror as Nina slipped beneath the ice. He raced over to the edge, no longer concerned with the gunman, who raced away through the construction site.

"No!" he shouted, and sprinted down the incline, falling in his haste and tumbling the rest of the way.

He rolled over and struck the hard surface of the frozen water with his back, the impact cracking it wide open, and he plunged beneath the glacial surface, the shocking cold making him gasp. Water filled his mouth and he came up coughing and choking, his heart aching in his chest. He felt the sandy bottom beneath his feet and steadied himself for a few seconds in the waist-high water, and then he started to wade further out, his arms sweeping away the floating pieces of ice, pushing himself through the water towards the spot where Nina had disappeared.

The frozen surface broke open before him like crazy paving, and then he plunged his arms and upper body back below the surface, searching for Nina's small body at the bottom.

He couldn't find her. Had she floated further away? Was she trapped, unable to get back to the surface because of the ice above her?

Pieter came back up for air. Somewhere behind him, he heard the roar of an engine and he turned in the hope that help had finally arrived. Then he saw one of the white pick-up trucks from the construction site racing back along the spit of land towards the dam and realized that the gunman was getting away. He watched as the vehicle went over the connecting dirt track and smashed straight through the guardrail, and then spun to the right and raced away down the roadway along the top of the dam.

Pieter had no time to think about their quarry breaking free. He went back down into the water, grasping and moving his arms left and right until finally they bumped into something soft, and he grabbed a firm hold and lifted it clear.

Nina came up in his arms. She was unconscious, and a quick look at her face revealed a deathly-white countenance and blue lips. Her head lolled backwards. Was he too late? Was the poor girl dead?

Pieter staggered back towards the pebble incline and clambered out of the water, and as he did so, she gave a tiny cough and a wheeze, and then she jerked herself awake, and she began to cry pitifully, clinging to him.

He sank down onto the ground and held the crying girl tightly to his body.

He heard car doors slam and when he glanced up he saw a line of police vehicles and trucks above lined up at the side of the dam road, their lights flashing brightly in the late-afternoon gloom. More were squeezing past the burning wreckage of the helicopter. Then figures were coming down the concrete incline, calling out and waving as they hurried towards them.

Chapter 27
Safe Haven

Once he'd seen Nina safely into the back of an ambulance, with the paramedics fussing over her, treating her for hyperthermia and wrapping an emergency foil blanket around her quivering shoulders, Pieter instructed an armed guard to keep watch and never to let her out of his sight.

Stepping down from the vehicle he saw Dyatlov come bounding over.

"I thought I told you to keep out of trouble, Van Dijk," he barked gruffly, but the big smile that appeared on his slavic face suggested that he was mightily glad to see Pieter still alive and in one piece. His big hand reached out and slapped him on the shoulder, and then he shrugged off his heavy coat and offered it to him, and Pieter slipped it on, grateful for its warmth.

"What a shit-show. You know, she's starting to seriously piss me off," the former Russian Spetnaz commando said, glancing over to where Lotte was still handcuffed to the guardrail. "But at least we got her this time my friend. From now on, I promise you we will throw a ring of steel around her wherever she goes."

Dyatlov was clearly pumped, even though he had lost lots of good men. Pieter wished he could feel the same way.

"We might have caught her, but the other guy, the sniper, he got away," he pointed out.

Dyatlov pulled a face and sucked in air between his teeth, but then he shrugged as though he was determined not to let this mar what was ultimately a good result: Nina was safe and well, at least physically if not emotionally, and their No 1 suspect and the most wanted person in Europe was under arrest and destined to spend the rest of her life behind bars.

"It all came at a big cost," Pieter continued. "There'll be hell to pay."

"Huijbers was an asshole. A vain, fat prick who wanted all the acclaim for himself. Well, he got his big moment all right, in front of the world's press. Good riddance, if you ask me."

On the road behind him, somebody had thought to use one of the bulldozers from the construction site to push the still-burning wreckage of the helicopter out of the way, making room for the ambulance holding Nina to move past. More sirens could be heard in the distance, probably fire-crews coming to douse the flames, and overhead three or four choppers buzzed around in the sky like irritating gnats, some belonging to TV news crews.

Dyatlov moved away to re-join his men, so Pieter went back along the roadway to where Lotte was sitting and leaning with her back against the rails.

She looked up as he approached.

She smiled at him, and her brown eyes seemed to reach out to him, as though trying to convey they shared some common bond, some secret unbreakable alliance only they knew about. Once again an invisible spark flitted briefly, a connection, and Pieter quickly averted his gaze to break it.

He'd had enough of her games.

Unfastening her from the guardrail and then cuffing her wrists back together once more, he marched her towards the nearest police vehicle.

* * *

Harderhaven was a tiny fishing community east of Amsterdam built on land reclaimed from the sea. It was early evening by the time Johan Roost arrived in the beat-up pickup truck. After slipping through the net closing in around him, he had driven hell-for-leather through the large town of Lelystad. Then he had cut further east, trying to put as much distance between himself and the chaos on the dam, hoping to lie low for a few days while he worked out his next move.

A State of Sin

Lotte had told him about this place. She owned a small bungalow out here, in this backwoods part of Holland so-to-speak. It was a bolt-hole, a safe place to come should things go bad for them. Considering what had gone down today, the bloody mayhem followed by his last-ditch escape (aided somehow by Lotte, and he tried not to think too much about *that*) then he thought this certainly qualified. So he found himself driving out here to wait things out.

Following the quiet coastal road through the small cluster of homes and holiday lets he cut the headlights and slowed down to a crawl, looking into the darkness for the turning.

He saw it just beyond an empty industrial estate and found himself moving along a narrow lane with a small yachting marina on one side. Further on it swerved left past a line of whitewashed stones on the grass verge, and then he was driving slowly along a narrow strip of land close to the water's edge.

There was hardly any lighting here, just a couple of small security lamps casting out a feeble glow, and the track was slippery and covered in snow, making his path even more treacherous.

A row of overturned rowing boats ran parallel with the track. Johan counted them, and when he reached the seventh one he drew the pickup truck up alongside, cut the engine, took a flashlight from the glovebox and stepped out.

Crunching quietly through the snow he grabbed a hold of the wooden boat and tried to flip it over. It was much heavier than it looked, so he lay the flashlight on the ground and bent and gripped the wooden side with both hands and, grunting and cursing, he rolled it over.

On the ground beneath was a flat piece of corrugated plastic weighed down with stones. He kicked these away and slid the plastic to one side, revealing a shallow pit dug out beneath. Taking the flashlight again, he shone the strong white beam of light into the hole.

At the bottom lay three green metal boxes with black numbers and letters stencilled on the side. One box was longer than the others, and this one he knew contained a variety of different firearms, all military-grade weapons such as C10 and C15 assault rifles, RPK light machine-guns and Uzis, CZ Scorpion machine pistols and K-100 handguns. The other two boxes contained hundreds of rounds of ammunition as well as blasting caps and plastic explosives.

This was one of three similar arms caches in the local area and he would be visiting the others over the coming days to retrieve even more firepower, but for now this would do. The weapons had all been smuggled into the country from Slovakia over a year ago, and much of the same stock had been used during the gunfights at The Weeping Tower and The Waag during Lotte's ambitious but ultimately doomed plot several months ago. These arms dumps out here contained the leftover guns, and they should be more than adequate for his task.

Heaving the heavy boxes out of the hole one by one, he dragged them across to the pickup truck and lifted them into the back, working as quickly and quietly as possible. Then he covered the hole over again and flipped the rowing boat back into position to hide the spot.

Climbing behind the wheel of the truck, Johan started the engine and slowly navigated his way along the trackway as it followed the icy watercourse out across the swampy and frozen marsh.

Five minutes later and it came out by the bungalow. The place was barren and desolate, and there was a smell of seaweed on the gusty breeze. Outside were a tiny and dilapidated wooden landing and a small boat, which was half-submerged beneath the frozen water.

He'd phoned ahead, using one of his burner phones, to check if the place was occupied. He'd been slightly surprised when somebody did actually answer, impressed that any of the survivors from the clinic had made it this far, blind and hardly dressed for the conditions as they were. But then again, he reminded himself, these weren't normal people anymore.

He'd told them to leave a light on, not for their benefit but as a beacon to mark the spot for him, and he was gratified to see an orange glow shining through a single window.

Parking up outside, Johan switched off the engine and sat looking through the windscreen and checking his mirrors, trying to see into the shadowy undergrowth around the house. When he was sure that all was clear he slipped out and hurried along the pathway, up onto the porch, and pushed open the door and stepped into the main living area.

There were four of them, sitting on chairs and huddled around a log fire, two men, a woman and a very young child, a boy of five or six.

They had changed into proper clothes, he saw, having switched their pyjamas for thick woolly jumpers and trousers.

A State of Sin

In the background, he heard a radio playing quietly, tuned to a news station.
Feeling suddenly apprehensive, Johan hesitated briefly and then strode further into the room, and he coughed gently to get their attention.
"I need a hand outside. We have some gear to bring in. Charlotte is in trouble and she needs our help."
In perfect unison, the three adults and child came to their feet and turned to face him, and he vaguely noticed the boy's nose was all crooked as though it had recently been broken. Across his throat was a large white plaster, right where his voice box once used to be.
The child's mouth opened, emitting a peculiar mewling sound that made Johan's skin crawl.
Then his gaze flicked up over the boy's face, expecting to see the strange eyeless gaze staring blindly back at him, the way Lotte had described.
Instead, a pair of new eyes watched him, and they made him squirm with revulsion. They were huge, and bulbous, and looked like they had burst out through the skin, and were pure white, with tiny jet-black pupils at their centre that seemed to bore right through to his soul.
God, what the hell kind of unholy mess had Lotte left him with now?

* * *

Pieter stayed until the police truck holding Lotte pulled away with a pair of Spartan APCs acting as escort.
He needed to call Prisha Kapoor and speak with Kaatje, to hear her voice. It would ground him back in reality. But when he pulled out his phone he saw it was damaged beyond repair from his tumble down the embankment followed by his icy swim. So he made his way back along the roadway, skirting the wreckage of the downed chopper. The fire was out, but the heat of the inferno had melted the snow for a hundred yards around. The road's surface was now covered in fire-retardant foam. He retrod his route back down the winding pathway to the small dock and Tobias Vinke's old home. It was fully dark by now so he had to pick his way carefully.
The mobile command centre was still parked near the ruins of the three-barred gate and he wearily climbed up the two steps and pushed open the

rear doors, and asked one of the communications operatives if he could use a phone line to place a quick call.

Prisha was in the kitchen, making three mugs of hot chocolate and listening as Rowan and Kaatje talked quietly in the other room, when the doorbell rang.

Since Pieter had dropped her off in the early hours of that morning, Kaatje had slept through most of the day. The sleeping pill, as well as the strain of the past few days, seemed to have totally knocked her out. So she and Rowan had left her snoozing on the couch, tip-toeing around her but keeping a close watch. In the middle of the afternoon, the young police officer had stirred and rolled over and then sat up. They had then eaten a light meal – salad sandwiches – and then chatted and waited for any updates from Pieter Van Dijk.

So, when Prisha heard the doorbell ring she naturally assumed that he was back, and so she hurried across the living room and swung the door wide.

She stopped dead and then stepped back one pace when she saw the diminutive little man standing in the hallway in a long grey trench coat with a black trilby hat on his head and glasses perched on the end of his nose. He carried a small leather bag in one hand, looking a little like a doctor on call she thought.

"Oh, hello," she said. "Can I help you?"

The man gave a tiny smile and a curt nod of his head, and he looked up at Prisha with steely eyes that flitted back and forth.

"I've come for Miss Groot. Kaatje Groot."

Somewhere behind her the phone began to buzz.

Pieter heard the line ring and ring, and just when he was about to give up and try Kaatje's mobile number, someone finally picked up.

There was a long drawn-out silence, and then a rustling noise and a loud bump.

"Hello, is that you Prisha?" he asked. "It's Pieter. I'm calling to see how Kaatje's doing. Can you put her on for a moment?"

Another pause, and then a voice he didn't recognize.

"Hehehehehe."

Mark Hobson

Author's Note

This is of course a work of fiction, but as with the first book in the series - WOLF ANGEL - some parts are based on actual events and real-life crimes.

For a brief period during the 1970s and 1980s, Amsterdam became the world's most favoured location for high-profile kidnappings. With the influx of drugs and the arrival of underworld figures from Eastern Europe, abductions came to be seen as the route to easy riches for crime kingpins. The most famous case involved the kidnapping of Freddy Heineken, one of the world's richest men and CEO of the famous brewery company.

In 1983 he and his chauffeur were snatched off the street outside the main Heineken Headquarters in Amsterdam, bundled into the back of a van, and driven away. Their kidnappers, a group of failed bank-robbers, kept them prisoner in an old, disused boatyard in the docklands area of the city for three weeks, demanding a ransom of 35 million Dutch guilders. The money was paid, and the two men were later released unharmed. The kidnappers were eventually caught and served prison terms, however one of the men escaped to Paraguay and another, after finishing his sentence, went on to become one of the most notorious 'mafia-style' crime bosses in The Netherlands. He was assassinated in 2003.

The year before, in 1982, Toos van der Valk, wife of the hotel magnate Gerrit van der Valk, was kidnapped and held prisoner for several weeks and likewise released, this time after the payment of 13 million guilders.

Although the abduction of twelve year old Nina Bakker in this novel was not carried out by organized crime kingpins, or for monetary gain, I have drawn parallels from these two famous cases and the subsequent bungled police investigations. Our kidnapper, Tobias Vinke, may have been a dangerous psychopath but he did carefully plan and execute his crime and held his victim in a spot eerily similar to the Freddy Heineken case. Sometimes true crime is just as fascinating as any fictional book!

Once again, all of the locations that I have used throughout the story are real places, and many are worth a visit:

The Vrije Geer Nature Park at Osdorp, where I have based the eye clinic visited by Inspector Pieter Van Dijk and Officer Kaatje Groot, is a beautiful location and perfect to sit on a bench for a couple of hours to read a book or to watch the wildlife. It is a little away from the city centre but due to Amsterdam's excellent public transport system, getting there is easy. Amsterdam can get a bit crazy, so if you are staying for several days and fancy escaping the noise and the crowds, then hop on a tram and ride out here.

Café Zoku, where Kaatje goes after her dressing-down from Commissaris Dirk Huijbers, is about a ten-minute walk from the central hub of Dam Square. Between the two is the 9 Streets area which many locals regard as one of the most beautiful parts of the city (it's certainly one of the most photographed by tourists). Also on the way is Anne Frank's House, and Westerkerk. The café itself serves excellent lunches, and the window seats upstairs offer lovely views of the canal and trees just outside.

Hollandche Manege is the prestigious riding school on Vondelstraat attended by Nina Bakker and the place where her friend Elena Vinke has her tragic accident. It dates back to 1744 and was modelled on the famous Spanish Riding School in Vienna. Members of the public are welcome, either to ride the horses or to take a cappuccino on the balcony café. Over the road is the wonderful Vondel Park and on sunny days horses are taken there to ride and exercise. The park is home to a small flock of parakeets, and they make for a somewhat bizarre sight flying around at the heart of the bustling city.

The Western Islands, where Tobias works intermittently at the NV Damen Boat Yard for his fat slob of a boss and where his work 'mates' rolled him around in a barrel full of rats, is a great place to just wander and look at the old wharves and swing bridges. Many of the warehouses have been converted into luxury apartments or art galleries, attracting a young and ambitious class of residents, but if you explore the smaller nooks and crannies it is still possible to discover the remnants of the area's maritime past. Most tourists don't even know of the place even though it is just a stone's throw from Centraal Station.

Bickersgracht is a cobbled and narrow lane, poorly lit at night and with the overgrown allotments where Pieter hides encroaching across the fence, creating a creepy atmosphere of shadows and danger. It is not unusual to see the odd rat go scuttling across your path, on its way to and from the nearby canal and boatyard. However, during the daytime, the area is safe to explore... mostly.

The passenger ferries across the river IJ are a great way to get to North Amsterdam, and they are completely free and operate 24hrs per day. Just follow the pedestrians through the tunnel below Centraal Station to the embarkation point; you can't miss the small blue boats! The journey time across to the A'Dam Lookout tower (and the amazing film museum next door) takes just 5 minutes and you can enjoy superb views back towards the city centre just like Tobias. Alternatively, if you take the boat to the NDSM Pier further upriver the crossing takes 20 minutes, and once again it is free.

The Begijnhof is one of Amsterdam's oldest historical sites and best-known almshouses, home to the Beguine Sisters since the fourteenth century. The peaceful little enclave has been a women's refuge ever since the Protestant Takeover of 1578, when the city came under Calvinist rule. It lies at medieval street level and at one time was completely surrounded by water on all sides. One of the oldest wooden houses in Amsterdam can be found here, very close to Lotte's apartment. I based her home on that of a friend who allowed me to stay for a number of days in 2019, however the pentagram on the floor and the strange wooden carvings are added for the purposes of the story.

Moving away from Amsterdam we venture north into the flat and watery landscape of Waterland, a place of beauty and calm during the summer, but a bitterly cold and frozen world of ice in the winter.

The huge Houtribdijk Dam is one of the most spectacular feats of human engineering, a 30km long dijk connecting the western and eastern shores of the Ijsselmeer and constructed to hold back the North Sea from flooding Amsterdam and huge swathes of northern Holland. At the centre are the tiny docks of Trintelhaven, Tobias Vinke's lair and the place where he holds Nina captive. His bungalow is there, as is the scrapyard and motor launch on the pebble beach. However, this is private property so ask permission before having a look around.

Finally, if you did enjoy *A State of Sin*, it is always helpful as an author to receive short reviews on Amazon or Goodreads. Your words are as important to an author as an author's words are to you.

You can keep up-to-date on *The Amsterdam Occult Series* as well as other upcoming projects and novels on my website: www.occultseries.co.uk

And please check out my Facebook page *Amsterdam Occult Series and Other Titles.*

Pieter and Lotte will be back soon.

Mark Hobson
October 2020 – April 2021

Real-Life Terror in Amsterdam

During the writing of the first two books in the series, I visited Amsterdam on many occasions to conduct research, wishing to explore the city and find some great locations, and to try and better understand what makes the people of the place tick. I thought to myself that there is only so much you can learn by using the internet from the comfort of my own home and that I needed to get there for myself.

In 2018 and 2019 I spent nearly three weeks in Amsterdam. For the purposes of writing the novels and settling on good plots, I quickly learned that I needed to get away from all of the usual tourist sites and explore the darker side of the city, to wander down the creepiest alleyways, call in for a drink at the most notorious of cut-throat pubs, to go to the places that all of the travel guides tell people to avoid. After all, this is a horror story, isn't it? I needed locations that felt suitably frightening. I wasn't there to look at tulips.

So that is what I did, and I kept telling myself: what could possibly go wrong?

I had my mobile phone with me, in case I found myself in difficulties.

I had a set of excellent maps, in case I got lost.

I even learned how to scream for help in Dutch (well, not really).

Big mistake.

On two consecutive evenings, I faced my own real-life frightening episodes. Not of the supernatural kind – which would have been quite fun for a horror writer – but of the more human, down-to-earth and quite nasty, but still unsettling, variety.

One evening, quite late on and when the tourist crowds had sensibly gone back to their hotels for the night, I decided somewhat foolishly to have a walk down the narrow and unlit Blood Street. I was searching for creepy places to set a particular scene in WOLF ANGEL involving a gang of killers racing away through the night after dispatching their latest victim.

So there I was, aimlessly walking up and down the alleyway, poking my nose into places I shouldn't be, camera slung over my shoulder and looking every inch like the stupid, naïve, British tourist. Suddenly, from out of the shadows, stepped a gang of youths. Quickly surrounding me, they grabbed my arms and pinned them to my sides and pushed me up against the wall, and commenced to go through my pockets and rob me.

Luckily I only had on me my camera and phone (which, oddly, they didn't seem interested in) and a small amount of cash (which they wanted), and as soon as they had the money they were gone in a flash, leaving me standing there, breathless and shaken but thankfully unharmed.

Lesson learnt, I went back to my digs.

The following night, having realized how stupid I had been, I decided simply to pop out to have a beer, have a little walk around Dam Square and the busy Leidseplein with its pavement cafes and nightclubs, and do nothing or go anywhere that was in the slightest bit dangerous.

But on the way back, ready to hit the sack and get some shut-eye, I was approached by a man of unsavoury appearance. He was a drug dealer. A very pushy and aggressive drug dealer, who was determined that I should purchase some of his 'skunk' despite my insistence that I had no wish to. Once he realized I wasn't going to part with my cash, he decided that he would just part me from my cash anyway.

Pissed off at his cockiness, and still somewhat upset about the previous night's street robbery, I told him where to go (like all Dutch people, he spoke perfect English, and so my fruity language was not lost on him).

Obviously, I hadn't really learnt my lesson after all, because he took exception to my refusing to hand over my money. In the blink of an eye, there was a flash of cold steel in the moonlight (I like to add lots of tension whenever I tell this true little tale) and out came a small knife which he pointed at my belly.

What should I do?

Meekly hand over my cash? (this would have been the sensible option).

Stand and fight? (anybody who knows me would laugh at the very idea!).

Or turn and run? (yes).

Now, when I was younger I was fit and agile and a very fast sprinter. I could outrun my PE teacher (much to his embarrassment). However, now I was in my forties, I had barely moved faster than a sloth for many years, and I was running over slippery cobbles. But I can tell you, when I fled with him tearing down the street after me with a knife in his hand, screaming and laughing like he was an escaped lunatic, I shifted faster than Usain Bolt with the tourist trots. I could feel the rain dashing against my face, the wind breezing over my bald head, my legs were pumping away and adrenaline was coursing through my system.

The guy chased me for about a mile, through the twisting streets, over busy lanes of traffic, across bridges. He only gave up the pursuit when I finally crashed through the door of my digs, panting and badly wanting to take a pee.

It was a terrifying experience, probably the most frightening thing that has ever happened to me. I was glad to be flying home to the UK the following day.

But it did inspire me to include a couple of scenes in my books, having experienced the real thing up-close-and-personal so to speak. So my trips to Amsterdam weren't a complete disaster or a waste of time. Perhaps I should return to the city soon. It's a good way to beat writer's block.

My own moment of real-life terror in Amsterdam.

Mark.

ABOUT THE AUTHOR

Mark Hobson is a writer and historian. His works span numerous genres from military history to thrillers and horror, both fiction and non-fiction.

He lives at home in Yorkshire with his 3 cats.

Mark Hobson

Books by Mark Hobson

Now May Men Weep – Isandlwana: A Story From The Zulu War
Ntombe 1879 (non-fiction)
Isandlwana – A Military Enigma (non-fiction)
The Curse of Modern Britain
Grey Stones (coming in 2021)
Hanslope Green (coming in 2022)

The Amsterdam Occult Series
Book One – Wolf Angel
Book Two – A State of Sin

WOLF ANGEL
AMSTERDAM OCCULT SERIES
BOOK ONE

The City of Amsterdam is gripped with fear.

A series of brutal murders have left homicide detectives baffled. With no motive or clues to work with, they find themselves probing blindly through the city's dark and violent underworld.

But Inspector Pieter Van Dijk is not convinced this is the work of one lone psychopath.

Drawn deeper and deeper into the shadowy heart of the case, he unearths a terrifying history of family madness and occult conspiracy echoing across the decades.

Brilliant... gripping...a well thought out and well-written book

A dark story with lots of action

This isn't Jackanory

Available from Amazon

ISBN: 9798696036946

Mark Hobson

A State of Sin

Printed in Great Britain
by Amazon